GERONIMO
REX

GERONIMO REX

Barry Hannah

GROVE PRESS
NEW YORK

Originally published by The Viking Press
Published simultaneously in Canada
Printed in the United States of America

FIRST GROVE PRESS EDITION

Library of Congress Cataloging-in-Publication Data

Hannah, Barry.
Geronimo Rex / Barry Hannah.
p.   cm.
ISBN 0-8021-3569-2
1. Young men—Southern States—Fiction. I. Title.
PS3558.A476G47   1998
813'.54—dc21   97-51147

Grove Press
841 Broadway
New York, NY 10003

98 99 00 01 10 9 8 7 6 5 4 3 2 1

This one's for Meridith
and our friends Horace,
Wyatt, and Brown.

GERONIMO
REX

BOOK ONE

1 / Blue Spades

In 1950 I'm eight years old and gravely beholding, from my vantage slot under the bleachers, the Dream of Pines Colored High School band. This group blew and marched so well they were scary.

The white band in town was nothing, compared—drab lines of orange wheeled about by the pleading of an old bald-headed pussy with ulcers who was more interested in his real estate than in his music. But the spade band was led by a fanatic man named Jones who risked everything to have the magnificent corps of student musicians he had. Jones was joked about and sworn at by educators, black and white, all over the parish.

Everyone voted on a special bond of fifteen thousand dollars to renovate the gray plank barn sitting in a basin of clay and pine stumps north of town. This was the colored high school. The bond was approved and they dumped it all on Jones, the principal, to administrate. It was well known that he was not a drunkard, lived with his wife, and was struggling to do something with the school. But the reason they voted him the money was that his school building was uglier than anybody could bear—I mean even too ugly for a casual dove-hunter to drive by and see. It looked like an old chalkboard eraser floating in a pool of beer. They awarded Jones the money at a ceremony where the white parish trustees whetted each other to death explaining what unprecedented heroes they were—most of the bond, of course, coming from white taxes.

Well yes Jones was struggling to do something for the school. He happened to be combination principal *and* band director of Dream of Pines Colored. His band was made up of squirrely, breathless boys and girls who wanted to avoid the physical education class. They whittled their own tonettes out of bamboo and otherwise got by on gift instru-

11

ments from World War II; had lard-can lids for cymbal and a tuba full of flak holes and so on. Jones was good and sick of this. He was fed up getting the Best for Homemade ribbon at the state band contest every year, and having his band chuckled about by his colleagues, who said here comes Scream of Pines again. Here comes perennial dilapidation on the forced march again.

Jones was a marching band fool. He did take the fifteen thousand, used a thousand of it to repaint the exterior of the school building, and sunk the rest of it in new instruments and uniforms for the band. Then he drafted a hundred and twenty students into the band, which was the entire student body of Dream of Pines Colored, except for sixteen weaklings he left to the varsity football team—these boys were real mewling sluggards—because the school had to at least field a team to give the band an excuse for marching at half-time. The football team went out the fall after the bond money was awarded and got cut up in games to the tune of 70–0. But the score didn't tell the whole story —these boys were out of breath and puking from just having run out of the locker room.

All the burly and staunch were in the band, with their new blue Napoleonic tunics and shakos, overridden with stripes and scrolled lightning filigree, and they were playing tubas, trombones, French horns, trumpets, and euphoniums, or bombing the hides of fresh, brilliant drums. And didn't Jones and company have a band. In two months during vacation he rehearsed the hundred and twenty boys and girls. He met with them in a pine-needle clearing above the high school, right in the out of doors, and drilled them by section—now trumpets, now clarinets, now saxophones, etc. —eight hours a day, many of them standing up with their new, unfamiliar instruments, and the girls sitting on Coke cases, until the kids were ashamed to come back next day without their parts down perfect. It must've been like the mouth of an oven there in the clearing; the sun over Dream of Pines is so bad you begin thinking it's an eye looking at you alone. It gums up your days; I can vouch for that. Of course it came down through the usual rank clouds from the Dream of Pines paper mills—and settled on you, dragging down to your body the wet junk of the air.

Jones told them they wouldn't get to wear the new uniforms, wouldn't deserve to wear them, until they came in one morning playing faultlessly. In two months, he had them all considering serious life careers in music. Jones was that good. The tone-deaf dummy on cymbals quit smoking so he could conserve his wind, and looked forward to studying at a conservatory after graduation. Three girls quit doing what they used to because of loss of energy on the clarinet. And Harley Butte, the mulatto fellow who tied up with me eventually in a sorrowful way, was fifteen then, and practiced marching and playing the French horn in the privacy of his own home. Harley told me later that the school bus which carried the band to out-of-town games and other parade events became like a church inside, that year. Jones rode in the seat near the driver; there were a hundred and twenty Negroes paralyzed against one another in the seats and aisles. And no more, the smoking; no more, the liquor out of the wallet-sized pepper bottles; no more, the wet finger with agreeing girls, or even any kissing, much—none of the universal acts of high school band trips. They knew they were too good, and had too much at stake. No one wanted to lose a dram of power on his horn. The instruments followed in a trailer truck that Jones rented right out of his own pocket money.

First time they hit the field at an early September football game, it was celestial—a blue marching orchestra dropped out of the blue stars. The spectators just couldn't imagine this big and fine a noise. They were so good the football teams hesitated to follow them; the players trickled out late to the second half, not believing they were good enough to step on the same turf that the Dream of Pines band had stepped on. The whites living on the border of the mills heard it, and it was so spectacular to the ear, emanating from near the colored high school, they thought it must be evil. I mean this was a band that played Sousa marches and made the sky bang together. The whites in town put a spy onto them the next Friday night. He found out Jones was billing the group as "The Fifteen-Thousand-Dollar Band" over the public address microphone. This was a slight lie, one thousand of the fifteen having been spent on paint for the unsightly barn. But aside from that, Jones's band was easily the best marching band, white or colored, in Louisiana. That's all Harley Butte knew at the time; he didn't have much privilege of scope to broaden his judgment at the time. He'd only been with the band to the state

13

contest from 1947 to '50, and he knew they beat everybody down there. Then he sat in an end zone down at Baton Rouge and saw and heard the Bossier City band, which was supposed to be the best white band in the state, and he knew Dream of Pines was better. While the fact probably was, by what I saw and heard that afternoon hiding under the bleachers at the colored football field, Dream of Pines was the best high school band in at least the world.

The way it was affecting me, I guess I was already a musician at the time and didn't know it. This band was the best music I'd ever heard, bar none. They made you want to pick up a rifle and just get killed somewhere. What drums, and what a wide brassy volume; and the woodwinds were playing tempestuously shrill. The trombones and tubas went deeper than what before my heart ever had room for. And I just didn't know what to think.

Then Jones, who was standing on the bleacher above me and making it creak viciously, called them to a halt with this "No, no, no!" "My ass," he said under his breath.

He'd been waving his arms and yelling at separate people in the band. Now I could detect that one or two people were out of step. They were rehearsing in uniforms on a bright day when any kind of nonconformity could be seen, like the dirt spots in the grass of the field. But when the band put their horns to their lips, I had no doubts about them, the way Jones did, jumping up and down and scolding them during the music. I understood by Jones that some poor trumpet man was going to be canned if he didn't make his part, but I heard nothing wrong. The band to me was like a river tearing down a dam when they played, and you just don't hang around finding out what's imperfect when that happens.

That Jones must've had some ear, and some kind of wrath to overcome that music the way he did. They stopped and listened to him. He went on, cracking the bleachers over me for emphasis. This was the kind of wrath you didn't mess with. I got the notion he'd kill me if he found me hidden down there to peek on his band in what he thought was its imperfect state; it was scary, all the way around—the great music out there, and Jones above. And of course, the waves of brown faces on the field, though I was never taught to fear Negroes generally. In those Napoleonic shakos, with their faces dead serious and hearkening

14

to Jones, though, they were a weird forest that sent dread right down to my bones.

"Tighten it up!" Jones bellowed.

The band was so thrilling that musicos from five parishes, mainly colored band directors, met on a bluff an eighth of a mile from the football field to scrutinize Jones's band with the intention of revamping their own band shows in the coming weekends so they wouldn't be embarrassed off the field. Others came to prove to themselves they shouldn't even show their bands against Jones's, and went off the bluff to their cars planning for everybody to have the flu on a certain weekend. Jones marched his band in incredibly difficult and subtle military drills, by the way, so that horn ranks were split all over a hundred-yard field but still sounded like the best thing they ever got up in Vienna.

The wildest success of the band was in 1950, the year I watched them. They did a pre-game show that dismayed the waiting football players from Alexandria so much, that the Dream of Pines weaklings were able to rally for a safety against them and, well, lick them—2–0. It was the only win for them the decade Jones was there.

Jones made his band rehearse in uniform toward the last of the week. This is the way the uniforms went seedy in five years, and were a disappointment to Butte when he saw the band march at Eisenhower's inauguration later, during his stay in the army.

When I saw them, the band was still regal, and Jones had just added three majorettes up front. They weren't the chorus-girl types who did a lewd fandango to novelty numbers, either. They looked like muscular, brown eternal virgins who strutted properly in a vehement gait; they wore the Napoleonic uniform briefed up to the knees, with black boots that put you in mind of discipline. The band seemed half a mile deep and long to me. And there was this astounding rigor that the first signal from the percussion put into them; everybody snapped straight, his hat plume shuddering.

"Sloppy, sloppy," I heard Jones mutter. I knew this man was crazy. What could he be talking about? I never saw his face, not ever.

Harley Butte was out there with them playing his French horn, I guess. It was his senior year and the third year of "The Fifteen-Thousand-Dollar Band." Tooting his heart out

15

somewhere in that weird island of blue, was old Harley, in the middle of a ball field just outside niggertown, where everything else was ugly as old cooked oatmeal with a few snarls of green in it—the yearling pines.

Harley was ten years older than me. He was born in 1932, the year John Philip Sousa died. This always meant a great deal to him. Sousa was his god, like World War II was mine.

2 / Green Netherlands

There are these rolling lumps of turf, with the forest looking deep and sappy, and real shade on the road and big rocks lying mossy off the roadbank, all of which at one time belonged to the Sink brothers, who were the paper mill barons of Dream of Pines. They called it Pierre Hills, and put two mansions out there on this premium property. The sign saying Pierre Hills on a turnoff from the highway would make you think it was a subdivision under development, or something like that. But it isn't. There were only the two Sink mansions—which were simply big and New Orleans style in a fat way—nestling in all that luscious gloom of oaks and hickories. And none of the other hundreds of acres of Pierre Hills was for sale. Eat your heart out. The Sink boys had it for their own park, after tearing down every pine tree of beauty back in Dream of Pines for lumber and paper pulp. Dream of Pines was a smelly heap a mile east of Pierre Hills. By the time my old man moved us into our house between the Sink mansions, however, the Sink brothers and the rest of their friends managing the mills had stoked up such a glut of wood in the mill production that Pierre Hills itself breathed a slight fart of the industrialized woodlands.

So when we got into it, Pierre Hills was not the exclusive rolling green it used to be. Still, it was a great privilege for the old man to get to buy in and put a house out there. He always thought the Sinks had been kind to him. He paid so much for the land that my mother left him for a month in protest and stayed with her mother in Vicksburg, Mississippi. I mean apparently he shot about nearly everything from two good years at the mattress factory he owned. He was third richest man in town, after the Sinks. When my mother came back, he had the house he meant to build just starting. He and she fell down in the truck ruts and made love the afternoon she came back. It's shadowed enough to do that in Pierre Hills. My mother is a fading egg-white brunette I can understand a man could miss after a month. And at heart, she's wild for any kind of project—any kind of definitely plotted adventure. So I suppose it happened—luggage from Vicksburg being kicked everywhere. I can see the beauty. They were in between their big old shingled house in Dream of Pines and the huge country home of square gray stone we finally had in Pierre Hills. I always thought of it as the bottom half of a small English fort. My mother had a miscarriage, her last baby, when we were two months into the place. I remember everybody saying—I was six—that it was an awfully late and dangerous time to lose a baby. The Sink boys never sent condolences or anything. This came up. My aunt was sitting in the kitchen and mentioning this, while my mother was at the hospital. My old man didn't really allow anything to be said against the Sink brothers. He always had a blind admiration for anybody holding monstrous wealth; he thought it took an unearthly talent to become rich beyond rich. He loved the city of New York because it was so incomprehensibly rich. He loved paying homage to it, and I guess that's why we took all the New York magazines and newspapers. They filled up the house, and nobody read anything in them beyond the gaudiest headlines. I think he *enjoyed* paying out the ear for the land his house is on. And, by the way he acted, I got the idea we were owning this land in Pierre Hills on probation. No misbehaving or loose talk, or we were off.

The old man had a Buick. He liked to wheel it up our brick drive, which was bordered by a dense cane patch. He was one of these magazine handsomes who was turning gray in the hair at forty-five; the gray strands were flames from a hot and ancient mental life, or so he thought. His mental life was always the great fake of the household. He had three years at L.S.U., makes sixty thousand a year, has the name of a bayou poet—Ode Elann Monroe—and has read a book or two over above what he was assigned as a sophomore. So he's a snob, and goes about faking an abundant mental life. He always had this special kind of bewrenched and evaporated tiredness when he came home from the factory. "Show me a bed, Donna, [my mother] the old head's been working overtime today," he sighs—and he's demanding Quiet Hours outside his study after supper. His study, where, if my guess is right, he sits scrutinizing his latest hangnail and writing his own name over and over in different scripts until he bores himself into a coma. About midnight, he charges out of the study, ignoring Mother and me watching the national anthem on the television, every insipid show of which (TV was brand-new to us then) he adored better than breath, but denied himself for the mental life, and he is banging into the walls of the hall making toward his bed and sleep, so frightened by the mediocrity of his own thoughts that it's truly sad. He always thought a college man such as he was entitled to life on a higher plane, and always endured the horror of knowing that his thoughts in the study were no different than the ones he had during the day when he added a random sum on the to-the-good book. I found his name, written in different, sometimes perversely ornate, scripts on the top of variously sized and colored note pads, on the desk of his study in the mornings. Perhaps he wanted to do an essay, or a poem, or an epitaph. I don't know what he wanted to write on the blank lines. I remember once he was intending to write a letter to the editor of a New York paper, but never finished a copy he thought presentable enough. God knows, I'm on his side in this hustle about the mental life. I've *inherited* a major bit of the farce from him, by what I can tell. And both of us jump into sleep like it was a magic absolver. Both of us, I would imagine, yearn too much for the hollows of a woman, knowing from the first touch of sex to sex, it's all a black dream leading into sleep.

I'm second-grader Harriman Monroe. My mind is full of little else but notes on the atrocities of World War II. I saw them all in photographs in a book compiled by a national magazine. It was on some playmate's daddy's shelf. Then I'm eight, third grade, and have in part understood what I saw. I'm not clever enough to be horrified yet.

The Sink brothers had two peafowl that came trespassing in our cane patch alongside the driveway. It did my old man no end of good to see the birds prissing around on his land. He wanted to be such neighborly chums with the Sink brothers. North of us was Sid, and south of us, Ollie. The peafowl also had two quaint names which I refuse to remember. The female was a whore, and the male lived on her, and was jealous as hell. They went into the deeps of the cane and loved it up, and in between time, laid an inch-high carpet of green droppings back in the romantic, cavey places, and the cock ran me out when I tried to get in there to play, not knowing all the swell places were already floored with dung. A peacock, by the way, will drill your ass if he knows the odds are anything near equal. He got me a couple of times I won't forget.

Then one day I got in the cane when they were gone, went back to the deeps, where the Jap snipers should've ideally been sitting in the high crotches and just ready to be potted by my air rifle. I hit a dip and slid off into that peafowl dung I didn't know was there. It was all in my hair and up the barrel of my gun, and my lever had this unmentionable stalactite of green hanging on it. I looked around and saw there wouldn't be any decent playing in here until maybe I was twenty.

I wasn't thinking about the birds or the cane this other day, walking out for the papers at the end of the drive, when the peacock all of a sudden beats out of the deeps and starts hammering at my thigh. I ran and finally shook him off. Now I was afraid of him, but I wasn't about to detour around the cane walking back on account of any bird. I picked up a piece of stick I'd thrown at the mailbox a week ago, pretending the stick was a grenade and the mailbox was a German's mouth; it was a healthy length of hickory, never a very feasible grenade. I walked back on the cane edge of the drive, and got to where the cock ambushed me coming out. The old boy was roosting about four feet off the ground this time and jumped on me at head level, making a loud racket in the cane as he launched himself. This terrified me, but I stood still and swung on the peacock with both arms. I caught him on the head, and his beak swerved like plastic. He dropped on the bricks like a club, his fantail all folded in. I toed him. He was dead, with an eye wiped away.

The old man sails into the drive in his Buick. He's over-due home from the factory, and thinks everybody is thrilled by his making the turn so perfectly into the narrow brick drive. He rams to a halt, seeing me and the dead peacock. Up beside me faster than the shadow of a passing airplane. "It's not dead, is it, son?" He leans over and peers at the cock's head. "Pray to God. He *is* dead. Why would you kill a lovely bird like . . . You know who he belongs to, don't you?"

"He came at me. Twice."

"This small, beautiful bird came at you. You better tell the truth, buddy. What do you think we're going to do about this?"

"Put some lime on that sucker, he'll melt into the ground without a stink in three-four days." The old man's jaw dropped.

"Who taught you about *lime?*"

"Aw, the Nazis used it on bodies in concentration camps."

"Oh yeah? You're really getting an education, aren't you?"

"Yessir. You want me to handle it?" The old man was looking away at some hopeless horizon.

"I want *what?*" he said.

"You want me to handle this peacock. I'll drag him up in that cane. You get me a little lime, and nobody'll know nothing." Now the old man's roasting me with a hard look.

"You get your little ass up to the bathroom and get your pants down. I'm going to handle *you.*"

But he snuck and got the lime, and lied to Ollie Sink when he called a few days later wanting to know if we'd seen Bayard. By then Bayard—God help me, I did remem-ber the sucker's name—was a crust back in the deeps.

No more than a week later the old man and I are stand-ing at the bay window looking out at the leaves dropping from the trees and running north over the yard in an early cool autumn wind, while the old men is trying to explain the concept of a yard chore and what it had to do with Duty. He wants me to *rake* the yard, he means, every Sat-urday for the next ten years. He says a man gets to know the earth like that, but such simple acts as touching a yard rake to a decomposing nut. Quite incidentally, too, I'd haul away uncountable yellow tons of leaves in a wheelbarrow before I even got my growth. I personally always was of the school of let them lay and rot, and just imagining all the moldering beauty underneath they must be causing; I couldn't bear to think of moving artificial rake against them. Meanwhile, I could learn about all this unspoiled earth grit by watching our female terrier, Maggie, go wild up against our screen door when she was in heat. And her suitors—bird dogs, a spaniel, a Doberman, and two beagles looking gruesomely depressed by their own desire—standing politely on the porch for two days and then, fed up, mauling each other with high croaks, were the daily theater. Finally, only the Doberman was left, and he and Maggie would stare balefully through the screen at one another. He was a grand black thing, with somebody's chain around his throat. Nobody went out the front door while he was still there. He saved me immediate Duty on the leaves; no child could've been expected to go out in the front yard with him there. The old man took it hard that the Dobe was doing a mountain range of turds round the front step. What if one of the Sink boys accidentally dropped by to see how our household was progressing? Even though neither one of them ever even sent a Christmas card?

But the old man couldn't do anything about the Doberman, either. It was the gentleness of his that my mother always bragged on him about. I didn't see this side of him, or wasn't ready to see it, until a couple of days later, when it was too sad to miss.

Toward the last pales of Maggie's heat spell, there was a day when the Doberman was gone from the porch, and we thought it was all over. But the morning after, there was a new suitor-dog outside. He wasn't on the porch. He was out in the edge of the cane. He was a sick, scabby, and practically hairless combination of Spitz and setter. From way over in the cane, he watched Maggie at the screen with wheat-colored rheumy eyes. You could see he was trying to respond more than he was; he just lay there nodding and raising his ears, then falling asleep unwillingly, it seemed. There was a mule with him. The mule was emaciated and showed burned, hairless marks where an old harness had been. His nosy face looked older than stone, and he crumbled around the knee knobs with tremens. This mule stood in the shadowed bend of the cane behind the dog. Apparently the mule and dog were friends, joined up to see the

21

last of it together. They were both clearly terminal. A big mule like he was, by the way, is a sensational sight to behold when you get up early and just look for the usual cane and St. Augustine grass. He seemed to be looming back and sponsoring some last romantic wish of the Spitz-setter in front. I think the dog had brought them as far as they could go.

The old man and I saw them together at the bay window. Both of us were looking for the leaves, and then, surprise!

"All right, Daddy, I'll go be getting the lime in the garage while you get the shotgun. Better put in some double-aught shells."

"Just hold it . . ."

". . . put both those scarecrows out of their misery in a minute, you get a good shot to the brain on 'em. I can tell they ain't gonna run." I was thinking, "Big Game. See something *big* collapse, at last."

"You better quit running your mouth that direction, Harry. I don't want to hear that kind of . . . We're just going to leave those poor fellas alone. They look like they're on the move." My mother had come up, in her robe.

"That's the strangest thing I ever saw in my life. Did you ever see a mule and a dog go along together?"

"I believe they may have hydrophobia, Donna. Now what we're going to do is just ease out to the car, me and Harry, and see if we can't just not disturb them driving out. And they'll go on away. But Honey, you don't go outside till they do."

"You want me to call the sheriff?"

The old man faked three paragraphs of thought.

"I don't think so. We don't know anything for sure yet. They look like they're on the move. Don't they? You ever seen a mule and a dog hang around together more than . . ." He chuckled, and kissed her. He took me to school in the car.

The animals didn't leave. They were still out there four days later. The old man's sense of beauty was hurt. The mule looked like an upright hewed-out cowchip, the dog just a mangy rubble. We had a lovely yard, ordinarily. He sent me out to scare them off, but there was a massive odor coming off them when I got near; I quit waving; they'd ignored me anyway. Another day he sent me back in my room for my air rifle. He wanted me to pop them. I was

22

groping away at the lever in an unworldly bliss and breaking out the screen door, when he called.

"Wait!" he said. "Don't do that. No use to hurt them if they just *can't* move." The old man's as gentle as a nerve, I find out. It got him into tight moments later. When he gave me money, and other prizes; when he raised up Harley Butte, a mulatto, to a foreman over white workers at the mattress factory. There were certain bawling natural demands he couldn't deny. He thought Harley wanted the foreman position to a suicidal degree; he thought the mule and the dog had seen enough trouble.

"There's an organization I've heard of that handles these types of animals," he said. The dog and mule outside were getting sicker. The mule lay down. The dog attempted something drastic toward Maggie. It brought him out to the middle of the yard, and the mule wallowed loyally out in the grass too, ten feet behind him.

There was no SPCA around, burrow the phone book as the old man did. He would not call the sheriff, or any kind of exterminating veterinarian. Everybody knew that the Dream of Pines vet was an incompetent softy who always advised death for the least bruise on dog or cat, such a hater of animal pain he was.

I was spying in the cane one afternoon and caught him, the old man, out in the yard right by the dog; he was whispering something to the creature, and smiled. The dog lifted up, grunted pitifully, and moved a couple of feet over, then collapsed. I moved in to the old man's thigh, not caring about any secrecy then. Where the dog had lain in the grass, hair remained, and hundreds of maggots.

The old man winced, and groaned, "Harry. This is the first time in my life I ever knew God let things like this happen." The old man was born on a farm, but he was the spoiled child, with his mother practically holding her hands over his eyes until they moved to a thirties village called Town, Louisiana, twenty miles east of Dream of Pines. "Don't let's tell Mother about this now."

He looked over at the mule.

"I guess you're getting worked on too. Old fella."

He scanned his yard beyond the mule, with his eyes full of tears.

"I've read books about it," he said flatly. "But somebody has been keeping the real information from me. When

23

things die, they get eaten by worms. They really do." He milked the cleft of his chin with a hand.

He hadn't wanted the sheriff to come over and finish the animals with a quick .32 slug. He didn't want the sheriff's checkerboard demarcated car in his driveway. The old man, as a snob, thought he was too well reputed for that. He knew that a number of people in Dream of Pines worshiped him as the boss of the only clean and decent factory in town, and stood in line to apply for work under him, quitting the paper mills because of toxic dirt in their skin, and the old man gave a 10¢ better wage per hour. Because of gentleness, modicum gentleness on his part: he thought no one should work for 85¢ an hour, be he a wino goof-off, even. He was not a hero of tender feelings; this gentle portion of himself mixed up his mind quite a bit, and landed him in protracted confusion, when some simple act was called for. In his study, thinking about a case like the dog and the mule in the yard, he'd get a box of matches and strike them one after another just to see them burn. Like me, he'd have to *dream* an answer before he knew it was right. He'd wake up and know what he ought to do, having just seen some righteous version of himself in his dream. Either that, or my mother told him in a simple sentence what she thought he ought to do, and he'd do it immediately, the old man thinking, like me, that the voice of a female was God's direct edict. The old man and I always tended to trust every girl we ever knew, and little else but our own dreams in sleep. Eh, old man?

Mother didn't say a word this time. The animals stayed two weeks in the yard. The old man came in to breakfast beat out and his mouth curled around a Camel. His eyes were dull and bloody. He drank coffee like there was bourbon whiskey in it. Who knows what he thought on in the office, a little acoustically insulated glass cell on the mezzanine of the factory.

Then on a Saturday night he woke me up sometime way into the sleeping hours. He wore these dull flannel pajamas with duplicated scenes of the Hawaiian islands on them. My mother was up; I heard her rustling around the old man's study, and calling out softly to him asking where the cigarettes were. A cigarette was a rare experience with Mother, like fireworks once a year every July Fourth at the country club. I knew something extraordinary had happened. He'd

24

dreamed something, or the old lady had risen up in the night and commanded something in short, simple English. She was babyishly nasal like Elizabeth Taylor in the shadows, and had to be listened to.

He said he wanted me to be up at six to go out in the yard with him. There was a fellow he'd phoned a while ago who owned a tractor and would be waiting to drag the animals off with a special sort of chain harness. He left me feeling drab and alarmed on the borders of sleep. I wanted to personally shoot the big mule sucker and see him cave in; and wanted to go to sleep at the same time. Mother came in and sat on the end of my bed.

"You do know why Daddy's waited so long to kill them, don't you, Harry?"

"No, mam."

"He thinks he can shoot them in a kinder way than what the sheriff would." She caressed my foot under the covers.

"A bullet to the brain is just a bullet to the brain, though, isn't it, Mama? You can't die quick in different ways."

"I don't like to hear you talk like that, Harry. Little boys aren't supposed to be thinking about bullets to the brain."

"But Daddy's waited wrong this time. They ought to've been put out of their misery a couple weeks ago."

"Oh, Harry. Daddy has to think it out. You don't have to do that." She'd smoked her annual cigarette and was looking around my room for somewhere to put the butt. I was the last child, and had a married brother and sister living out in far parts of the South. Mother always looked at me like I was not quite real, having come as late to her as I did —when she was thirty-eight—and I was an experiment, bizarre in the natural order of things. These children, children of the thirties, must have been appearing to her mind when she looked at me. I was born in 1942, and was as strange as World War II. She always treated me as if I were an interesting waif. I was at the house as an only child from the time my brother married, when I was seven.

"You know, you were a happy surprise to us. Daddy and I want you to turn out especially good," she said. I slept on that.

The animals weren't on the lawn as the old man and I came out at six. They'd gotten in the cane and smashed it up, wallowing. The mule was lying dead among some broken stalks. The dog lifted up his head in the foot-high pin-plants on the edge of the cane. He smiled when the old man shot him with the twelve-gauge.

The man with the tractor was late. We just hung out between the cane and the porch and had ample time to study the corpses. A dead mule was such a big thing my mind couldn't really gather it in. I had to think about him in pieces, like the dead feet, the dead eyes, the dead backbone. The wet pink scab of the dog, with the red shotgun dots on his skull.

The sun came up and we heard noises from the Sink mansions. At last, the man with the tractor came up the drive. His name was Swell Melton; he regularly was manager of the Self*Wash Laundromat in Dream of Pines, but that didn't take all his time. All he did, as a matter of fact, was keep replacing the adhesive tape on the sign over the washers saying "Please Do Not Die In The Machines As It Colors Your Next Man's Wash." He was a lean, jaded fellow who got along with everybody, even the old man when he called him about the tractor at midnight. He wore the gray cotton pants and shirt which made you get the idea he was hovering about in a semiofficial position.

He didn't hesitate a second about the dead animals. He backed up in the cane shallows, jumped off, and tied a chain around the mule's rear feet, then strapped the dog's corpse to the chain with a rope. Then he cranked up and towed them off. The dog hung off the load in a grotesque way as the tractor dragged him and the mule, scraping, out the drive and to the Pierre Hills road.

The old man and I were hypnotized by the sight. He held on to his shotgun by the barrel, and we both wandered out behind the tractor to the road. Ode, the old man, looked like a moronic recruit in the marines.

We were standing out in the road beholding the tractor disappear at five miles an hour as Ollie Sink crept up to our backs in his black Chrysler. He wanted by, and we were blocking his way. The old man turned around and did an inane thing: he tried to hide the gun against his side. Ollie, a big red face above white shirt collars and a black coat, glowered at the old man like, yes, he now knew how his peacock Bayard had disappeared, with this early morning gunner Monroe running around the hills. Ollie's eyes were fixed, burning through his windshield, at the corpse-heap dragging behind the tractor ahead; then he observed the old man's shotgun, and the old man's guilty face, and ripped off in his car. The old man was trying to get up a neighborly sentence to shout to Ollie. But a dead mule *and* dog, seeming to be secretly spirited away in the early hours like this —he couldn't say anything about the scene that Ollie was seeing.

I think he gave up trying to be a perfect neighbor to the Sink boys that morning. I don't know what the deal was when the old man got us into Pierre Hills; what clause in the deed said if he was to buy from those land-scathing bastards, he had to like them reverently too. But he quit it that morning, and all I heard the rest of my years in the house was how depraved and ugly and destructive of the woodland the Sink brothers were. My mother flew into them, after the old man let out the plug, beginning with how tacky their big houses were and how stupid their wives were, at the bridge dinner and other social events at the country club.

"That peacock Bayard needed killing," said the old man, taking another cup of coffee with his Camel. "Don't tell anybody else, Harry, but I was proud of you when you bashed him. I'm not for causing hurt to animals—you know that." He let out a stream of smoke and closed his eyes so it made him look confident and handsome as Bogart. I could see Donna's love for him in her eyes. After all, he was Ode Elann Monroe: slayer of the Spitz-setter. Puller of the trigger when the chips were down.

3 / Yellow Butte

Harley went in the army two years as a bandsman. He was such a success he enlisted for two more, and two more again. He was a sergeant of music when he got out. He was company director sometime during his tour of duty, maybe at Fort Sill, Oklahoma, which Harley thought was way up North, until he was stationed at D.C. He marched in a

27

group playing "Hail to the Chief" for Eisenhower's inauguration. Then he waited at the parade's end and got to see his old high school band, Dream of Pines Colored. Even the people who voted the bond for Jones's school were proud that the band had gotten this invitation from the Inaugural parade committee. The old man and others thought it was very classy for Dream of Pines to be represented by Jones's band in D.C. Even though they hadn't voted for Ike. Even though the one coat of paint on the main building of the high school had weathered off and the place was too ugly to forget, again, and Jones was pushing band out there so feverishly that there really wasn't anything to the school but the band and those sixteen bad-luck sluggards on the football team. Jones didn't make the trip to D.C. with the band. He was in jail for floating a bad check at a Shreveport store in payment for two new sousaphones he thought his band had to have to play in style for Ike's parade. The sousaphones made it up; he didn't. Harley Butte, waiting on the band in formal army parade uniform, was tragically disappointed not to see his old director and spirit-father Jones with the band. He knew none of the kids playing in it now.

I do believe that Butte thought Jones was a black son of Sousa. Apparently there's no overstressing how much Jones emphasized the music of that man John Philip Sousa, composer of such monumental marches as "Stars and Stripes Forever," "Washington Post," and scads of others. Novelist. Jones put the two novels by Sousa in the outhut they called the library at Dream of Pines Colored. Harley read them, the only two books he ever finished in his life, not counting a few theory and composition manuals he polished off as an undergraduate at Grell A. & M. later. I always thought Harley was lying to me about Sousa having written any novels, and I had to look in the encyclopedia to find out it was true. Well, it's weakening it to say the fire of Sousa traveled from Jones to Harley Butte. Harley knew he was Sousa's grandson, and liked to remark incidentally in a mystic way that he was born the year Sousa died. In D.C., there must've been a bleak absence in his heart when he found out Jones wasn't along with the band. He was standing there, say, by a tree on Pennsylvania Avenue waiting to link up with the father of the whole thrust of his life, Jones, and to maybe have a few words with him, casually, and ex-

28

plain to Jones that *this* pupil of his was going somewhere, from those sessions that July in the pine clearing down in Louisiana. Harley was a mite proud of his army band uniform, and of the number of horns he had mastered during his tour in the service, and of having led that company band back at Fort Sill. He was playing cornet at this time.

But Dream of Pines came by him playing a novelty number, "Happy Days Are Here Again," and there was no Jones in his simple white uniform with black shoes marching at the head rank a foot or two to the side and crying instructions, like there should have been. There was this hepcat Negro he didn't know, some apostate sub for Jones who had taken over the band for the D.C. trip and rehearsed them in roadside parks on the way up, when the buses stopped in Tennessee and Virginia. He had tried to make them over in two days to a wailing hepcat band with tricky steps and freed rhythm. They'd all turned at Eisenhower's stand and done a dance-bow to him, still playing, then all jumping back to the march with a sudden lope. The sub director thought the old Sousan military legend of the band ought to have something done to it. It was not eyeful enough; it needed some flashes. Their blue uniforms were getting drab and didn't hold attention like they used to; they didn't look like the scary celestial horde of old. But Butte disapproved of the acrobatic drum major, and of the addition of several more prissy majorettes, and of the complex mambo rebellion the drums were laying down. He thought Dream of Pines Colored looked like some group dragged out of a tonk.

It would've all been disaster for Butte if he hadn't seen the movie he had the night before and still had the martial symphonia of it rushing in his head. He'd gone into a movie house on Pennsylvania and seen the premiere of *Stars and Stripes Forever,* the *life story* of John Philip Sousa, with Clifton Webb. Webb wore a German artist's beard, and a pith helmet, and played many instruments, as Butte knew he had to, to be able to compose the works he had. Butte saw Sousa lead a band of deluxedly white-uniformed men down a street in Pennsylvania, and the movie house where he saw it was on a street named Pennsylvania, and, well, GOD, looking like Clifton Webb and Sousa together, got into his very blood all over again. Harley saw the movie just three times, being habitually a moderate man when it came

29

to entertaining himself. Sousa was leading the band down the streets of somewhere like Haiti when Butte's mind blanked out in pure joy.

Harley had had a bad moment as tentative director of the company band in North Carolina, and he remembered this in Washington. When he was with the band in Washington, it was indeed a disgrace for him to be merely in the ranks as only another cornetist. This novelty music had done it to him. He'd gotten busted out of his director's position for having an uncouth band at Review Day in North Carolina. This was just after all his glory as sergeant director at Fort Sill. Butte re-enlisted because he thought he was famous as an army musician; he'd written a couple of numbers after the manner of Sousa, dedicating both marches to the old boy himself; then they shipped him to North Carolina, where he got this band that was predominantly Negro. They were all kids who hadn't been at their instruments over a year, and they thought it was all a joke. They got out of drill because Harley told the CO the band needed rehearsal by section. Harley told the kids it wasn't a joke. But these cats didn't dig a Sousa march. Eight of them got together secretly in the band hall with this one cat who played on the broken-up piano that was there for no clear reason—maybe officers' dances years ago. They did boogie-woogie on the sly. Harley walked in one day and caught them red-handed doing that. Trumpet, tuba, drums rigged into what the guilty fellow called a *trap set*, with pennies taped loosely to the cymbal to make it friz, and a high, yearning Negro on clarinet who just wouldn't be denied. Harley despised boogie-woogie as frivolous, and he didn't know what Dixieland *was*. That's what the fellow on clarinet claimed to be doing, when he wasn't playing this melancholy murk called blues. Harley told him to stop that. He feared the clarinetist was insane, and he knew the man could destroy a march, by himself; so wild a screech the man could lift in the air if he got the spirit. Harley was right. When he got the band out to play in place at Review Day, they were less than best—everybody going his own way on the tunes, and the clarinetist wailing an alien part to the trio of "Washington Post" like he was playing solo on the moon. He hit blues notes at the top range of the horn, and loud. All this, with the besodden khaki troops marching by to strict drill. The CO didn't like that stuff either; his

30

boys were out there in dress uniform drilling it as seriously as they could, and the moment required serious music. Harley was demoted and shipped as a cornetist to another company band at D.C.

Harley hated and feared this novelty stuff. He called it all *juking* and *trash bop*.

Then rock-and-roll broke out.

He was at Fort Shelby, Mississippi, back down South, for the last three months of his service life. Nothing had gone right for him since back at Fort Sill, except he didn't have to go to Korea. Now it was 1956. They had him playing tuba, a concert tuba with a strap on it for marching. That big rascal was no fun to carry, either. It was scalding green summer in the southern Mississippi pines. He knew this scene. Looking at a hot pine tree long enough made him nauseated.

On the day of his twenty-fourth birthday, he was sitting on a cot in a hot barracks. His colored buddy who played euphonium in the company band switched on the radio between their cots. A certain Negro rock-and-roll screamer from Georgia named Little Richard came on howling something about somebody that saw his uncle coming and jumped back in the alley. This was followed by panther sounds.

Butte sat up, closed his eyes, and nodded incredulously.

"Don't that make you proud now? Shhh— Sounds like somethin' from Africa," he said to his buddy.

Next day, playing in place with the band for the last formal military review he ever saw, the strap on his tuba broke, and he almost fainted from heat exhaustion trying to keep it on his knee. He fingered the huge valves and tried to be resonant on his instrument, as usual, while the besweated plungers slipped off his fingertips and crushed his knuckles springing up, and the bathtub weight of the horn dragged down his arms and cut his thighs where it rested. Harley was only a thin, middle-height mulatto. The sun worked on him, and he found himself having to stare at a stand of six-foot pines across from the parade ground.

This time it was different, looking at those pines. He didn't get sick, but his waking sense left him. The rows of pines began moving like people, corridors of them, in step. Then they had instruments, and were a limitless horde of bandsmen in green uniforms, but made no sound. They

31

were dreadful and glorious in silence, though there was all the pumping and stepping and setting to, and awesome flashes of brass, silver woodwind keys, and white drum hide. So then Butte thought he could hold on in this sun and not faint. What a secret, roaring sight he'd seen.

After the review was over, he found himself restored and happy. He knew what he would do when he got out. He'd go to Grell A. & M. and get a degree in music, which ought to be easy, with what he knew already. He'd hold down a job somewhere and maybe do it in odd hours, but he'd do it. Then he'd look around the states, choose the high school band he thought had the most potential, and offer to direct it. Naturally he'd get the job; wasn't any other colored cat knew as much about march as he did. They'd love him: some *big* dead-serious band. He'd write a few pieces for them during concert season. He'd have them crowded around him like an orchestra on the stage of some city auditorium. He'd come down with the baton, and the breathable air in the place would just quit. The spectators would faint for a minute because the band was using all the air of the place to hit that first, oceanic note; then they'd revive, getting used to the thin oxygen of the place, and hear the band going big, high, low, but never thin, on something like "The Liberty Bell"—his band as ponderous, frightening at ebb and storm tides, as the Atlantic Ocean, which Butte had seen, once. Then talk about march season. He'd be dressed in a neat, simple tunic, and maybe be wearing a German artist's beard, and flick his baton in the gridiron lights, and genuinely bring those mothers in green uniforms out of the surrounding pine trees, playing. It would be a surprise assault on the musical world the first fall he showed them.

So Butte went to work at my old man's mattress factory last of the summer. Something he didn't count on was getting married, but he did, to this moderately good-looking mulatto girl who was a native of Dream of Pines. The girl got pregnant immediately, and Butte never conceived of anything but that she'd go in the hospital at retail rate. If he'd taken her in at the charity price, he might have been able to start at Grell night school right away. As was, Butte concerned himself with saving a hundred and fifty dollars out of what the old man gave him during that period of fall semester at Grell. It wasn't completely disheartening to him. He knew he'd start to Grell in January and make a name there. He didn't despise the frame-making position the old man gave him at the factory. Matter of fact, he was lucky as loaded dice to get it. He could have gone to the mills.

However, one day in September Butte got low. It was after work, and he got to feeling blue about not being in Grell now when it was starting, and about being married and expectant with his wife so quick, and not having that old unboundaried feeling he had during free time in the army, and being in the rotten mill air of Dream of Pines again, living in a house on the outer edge of niggertown, where the clouds from the mills were sometimes just too heavy and juicy to float and fell on an individual homesite with an acidic fog that would peel the paint off the floor. Harley had drunk a little beer in the army. He was sure Sousa had done it at one time or another, because Harley found out he could write grand marches under the influence of a few beers. So he got home, told his wife something, and walked down the road to the bottom of a hollow where the Black Cat joint was.

He sat on a stool and treated himself to a few Regals, which were going for 20¢ in those days. He was the only drinker there as it turned night. By the third beer, he was really enjoying his newlywed melancholy, feeling hopeless and yet sure something would turn up.

"As far as I'm concerned, you don't have to play that moaning on the machine," he said to the barman and owner.

"That's Fats Domino," said the barman.

"I said I don't want to hear it. I'm your only customer here."

The barman went to the juke and turned down the voice to nothing.

"Fats Domino's from New Orleans," the barman said.

"You mean that fucking stuff has gotten over here, too?"

"Was you in the service?" The barman chuckled, opening another Regal for Butte.

I was riding down the gravel of the Black Cat road a minute before this. I owned a black Chevy station wagon with a big console speaker for bringing in such cats as Elvis, Mickey and Sylvia, Little Richard, and Fats Domino, fixed in a pecan frame behind the second seat. My radio,

33

with this speaker, brought in these singers like they were alive and struggling in the back of the car. You could hear the grace note of one of those cat's sighs. My wagon had 350 horsepower, moon hubcaps on the wheels, and was called a Snatch-Wagon by all the envious pubes round my high school. I guess it was sort of a sad affair, since I could drive it in, sure enough, and be the prince of the Dairy Dip for fifteen or twenty minutes, but had never touched the flesh of a girl; no girl's backend had ever warmed the seat beside me. I listened to Elvis and Fats, and was assured by all their groaning around in unsuccessful love, that I *had* touched lots of girls, and had a special *Love* who always put me down, didn't phone, had some guy newer and richer. I was fourteen, and this Chevy wagon was supposed to be my mother's car, but I usurped it from her. The old man took a taxi to work and let her have the Buick. By this time, he was running scared of me. I'd broken out with a pepperish acne and lugged back and forth in the hall as if I was inventing ways to destroy myself; it was as if somebody had caught me in the hall and blasted off a shotgun loaded with BB's at my face, two or three BB's making it into my brain and festering there for years to make me crazy. I don't deny I was a case in the teen years. I didn't always know what I was up to.

I had this box of M-80 Salutes on the seat beside me. An M-80 is a brand of firecracker that explodes about like an eighth of a stick of dynamite. It'll take the bottom out of a new zinc garbage can, and goes off under water. They're illegal everywhere now, though you might pick up some out at a combination service station and grocery way in the sticks. Throw them anywhere, nothing defeats the use on these babies. I had a few left over from July Fourth which I'd been saving for a purpose of indefinite evil. Actually, I wanted to lodge one up the skirt of the school librarian and watch her rave off in pain and smoke. She'd called my unsatisfactory personality to attention a couple of times. Also, I had a few keen visions from television movies working on my mind: such feats as the GI lucking a grenade into the slit of a pillbox and smiling as fire washes the Japs off the hill.

I lit an M-80 off a cigarette and tossed it down the gulley onto the porch of the Black Cat, then floored the Chevy away, showering gravel. I don't know, the Black Cat was lit so dull and looked like such a lovely place to toss in one. It was a wooden joint which might really fall over with the blast, with great shrapnel tearing out because of the rusty tin signs around the door. I was feeling wonderful at the moment when I heard the terrific charge go off behind me. I winked to myself. "You're supposed to be at the football game, Harriman," I laughed out loud. It was such fun I vowed to do it again, and turned the Chevy around when I got to the highway pavement.

"That Fats Domino mess has gotten too loud again," Harley was saying to the barman.

"Man, you got some ears I can't eem hear it."

Gah Dimmmmmmmmmmmmmmmm! went the little item on the porch. Smoke rushed in through the screen door. The barman fell with a beer in front of the jukebox. Then they heard a car zinging away.

"I thought I uhs dead," said the barman. "What was it?"

Butte went to the window.

"A car racing off. Somebody is throwing firecrackers."

"I tell you what. . ." said the barman. He walked over to the bar and lifted up a short shotgun. "That was too much firecracker."

"What you goin' to do?"

"See if he does it again." Then he put the gun back.

"Come here with it. I believe he's turned around and coming back. Give me the gun," pleaded Butte.

"Really, man. I don't want you to shoot nobody . . . be some trouble for me, now."

Butte snatched the gun. "I don't like anybody scaring me like that," he said. "Look out! He's pitchin' one down!"

"Watch it! God d. . . ."

Gah Dimmmmmmmmmmmmmmmmm!

"Got damn! You come back here, man!"

Gurraw Dimmmmmmmmmmmmmm! went the shotgun in Butte's hands. He fired from the porch. Then he went back in.

"I didn't kill anybody, honcho." He smiled sickly and laid the gun on the bar. "I got a rear light and lots of the backend of a station wagon, though."

"It was a white man, wasn't it?" said the barman.

"It was a white child."

"Chile? . . ."

"Yes sir. I do believe it was my boss's son, little Harry."

35

"You in for it, man."

"I think I can handle it."

Butte and the old man got along. The mulatto really had
nothing against making mattress frames. Where he worked
was a wide concrete shop with twenty men spread into four
job groups. Harley liked to hear the music of the hammers
and springs, and he liked to see the mattresses take shape
through the glass where the women were working with sewing machines alongside his area. See them get stuffed and
stacked up on the dock behind the tremendous doors, and
the automotive lorries taking them out twelve high. Butte
got along well with his innerspring squad, too. Two of them
were Negro, and two white, and all they did while they
framed was make jokes. It got to where the jokes went
round to every man in a regular circuit, and you got booed
if you came in some day without a good joke or only had a
half-ass joke. Butte had plenty of stories from the army he
didn't even know he'd remembered. He and the on-and-off
wino white fellow competed for laugh king. His squad
knew he was clever and fast on the frames. He turned in
more tickets than anybody at five o'clock, and the old man
paid them by the piece after a certain number. He was always ready for overtime. He liked the way his wife treated
him when he got home late and tired in the arms. She respected that he was weary, and helped herself to him in
gentle ways. The old man saw how Butte was succeeding
with his squad in the shop. Harley came into his office one
day and told the old man he'd like to buy one of those in-
nersprings for his own bed, and he was wondering if the
price of it couldn't just be taken out of his check this time.
It seemed easier that way.

"You made a lot of money this month, didn't you, Harley?" the old man said.

"I think I've got in enough for a little more than three
forty this time."

"Good for you. You look like a man who's going somewhere, to me. Don't think I don't like that."

"Mucha blige," said Harley.

In December he asked the old man couldn't it be arranged for him to take some college work in the afternoons
over at Grell starting mid-January. It would mean he could

still work till two o'clock. The old man fell into his study for about two weeks of fake mental hernia, at home, and hollered at anybody who disturbed him, thinking we were out to spoil his mental life; but sneaking in the den behind the couch and standing breathlessly still, the old man watched Jack Paar late at night. He thought, as regards the intellectual life, Paar was the last word. Then at the factory he finally called in Harley and told him that Grell arrangement would be all right. He could keep his job. The old man told Harley he wanted to see him make A's. Winkadoo.

My old man looked something like Paar, and nourished the hell out of that fact.

Harley went to Grell. The college amounted to an exploded quad of three-story ocher buildings. The band room was in a mossy basement of one of them. He was a smash his first semester, what with all that overwhelming cognizance about instruments and Sousan music. By next fall, he took over the unofficial leadership of the thirty-piece band, the old director perfectly willing to let Butte drill and play them, and take the football trips in the yellow bus with them. At Grell, it so happened that football was inmidst of its first golden age since the school was founded. Butte took what he got.

He wore pith helmet, whistle, and sunglasses in the late afternoons. As director, he was a hard man. In a month he was marching perhaps the best twenty-piece band in the nation. And at the end of football season, there were fourteen of them left—hard-bitten Sousa-lovers every one.

Butte would take trombone, flute, trumpet, or sousaphone along and fill in what absent parts he could, when they sat in the bleachers. Once, at a game between Grell and Alcorn A. & M., he played a trumpet with one hand, beat the bass drum with the other, and directed the group by use of an elbow.

This was one of the weekend nights when his wife, who was not a member of the Grell student body, sat with the band, one baby on an upright mobile board beside her and another one active in her womb, while she played bell lyre, and pretty decent bell lyre. Her stomach was too big for her to hold the instrument in her lap, so she perched it on a bleacher and sat sideways, tapping the tone bars, with one eye on the director, her husband. Butte would see her wrapped in her old woolen coat, a Scotch plaid scarf tied under her chin, and see his son asleep on the padded board beside her, and his wife's eye on his conducting, and the weather was nipping cold. But the Disciples-size band would be playing, say, "Washington Post" especially well, and the air around his ears would be warm. He'd look on the wife he'd trained to bell lyre, and the kind of love that leaves no room for anything else in the soul and body would take hold of him.

It goes without saying that Butte never told the old man just how interested he was in band. Ode Elann Monroe thought Harley was grooming his life around being a foreman of the innerspring shop. You don't tell an employer who's giving you a raise every month that your real mental existence is somewhere else entirely. Harley did eventually make foreman, over a horde of protests—two illiterate letters from Dream of Pines racists which the old man read to us in an ironic redneck voice one morning at breakfast. And the old man felt a wee bit ill-used when Butte quit him two months after he got his Bachelor of Music degree at Grell and moved his wife and four boys over to Mississippi, where he'd happened to land on a vacant directorship of one of the biggest Negro high school bands in six states, counting Texas.

He didn't tell *me* quite all of this poop about himself, either. But he told me most of it. When things got to where Harley and I could talk—behind the factory or leaning on the fence of that neat yard of his on the edge of niggertown (Harley's yard was as neat as any yard that grew nothing but Johnson grass as I've seen, and he had the lattice fence, which was an absolutely revolutionary improvement out that way), or even in my own room out at Pierre Hills that he came to as a detour off mattress business with the old man—I and Harley knew that we were in for at least forty-five minutes of talk, peripherally of music and mostly about his life. Harley had a fine middle-range voice. He never emphasized any of his troubles to me, and went over the facts of his life like they were just that, facts; no whining. This man knew his dream was taking him somewhere.

But Butte always had some problem he felt required a 9:00 P.M. interview with the old man at our house. I don't know but what he felt guilty about succeeding at the facto-
38

ry and with the Grell band at the same time and wanted to talk it out with the old man, though he'd kill himself before he told all about his progress out Grell way. He told *that* part of it to me.

4 / Ubi Sunt

The halls of my high school were wooden and olden. The maids used uncountable tins of wax and bottles of furniture oil on the halls and rooms every weekend. I enjoyed the waning smell of cleansers and polishers Monday to Friday. You could count the days by what your nose told you. By Friday, the school was filthy all over again. In sunlight, you could see a ragged trench down the middle of the wax on Thursday, but the channels underneath the lockers were always bright as newly buffed 1920 oak.

We had open lockers. Nobody stole, except now and then a sad case who'd swipe your compass for geometry and then sit right by you and use it in class—so screwed-up he didn't think of hiding things he'd stolen. Twice a crazy boy from out in the sticks brought a loaded pistol into class, but they caught him both times. All he wanted to do was show and tell. Then they caught him exposing himself in the back row of civics class and shipped him. Then there was a scandal in the library over this bunch of greasers who were tearing the brassiere advertisements out of the magazines and taking them home. I also remember another boy who sewed a tiny square picture of a Kotex box on the front of his tee shirt. He'd walk down the hall, get in front of some lovely and popular girl coming the other way, then throw open his jacket and flex his chest, a broken grin on his face as she saw and shrieked. Then there were the football guys, half of them mill boys and rednecks, the other half boys from middle-class subdivisions stuck around town. If they were sure of the slightest secrecy in the halls, they'd cram you in a locker, or hold you by the throat and twist out your tee shirt so you were left with embarrassing female protrusions where your paps were supposed to be, or maybe they'd just come up behind you and swat the back of your head with a flat hand. All this was just pure bliss for them. It wasn't malevolence or bullying. They did it to each other. They'd cold-cock some buddy, then wink and grin slyly, and say, "Uh oh!" like a hand had come out of the blue and done it and they didn't have anything to do with it. One day when I was a freshman I was writing a Latin test as a big hand curled around the crook of my desk and I commenced being dragged along in my desk sideways through the aisle. I looked over and saw one of those football scoundrels pulling me beside him with one arm, his face beaming with pleasure. The teacher had gone out of the room. When he had my desk top crammed against his, he fell to cheating off my paper with an open, completely guileless face. A moment later, he shot me scooting back to my rightful row with a terrific push from his left leg. It was a beautiful feat of strength, and I don't think his main point was to cheat. Real depravity at Dream of Pines was rare. And the principal tried to run a pretty tight ship. You could get busted for smoking a cigarette in the basement head; for profanity or insubordination; for setting fire to a wastebasket.

We were all crazy about beauty and power. Some of us fell in love with our own voices and joined the glee club or the forensic club, and some the band, some football; some went in for automobiles; some for clothes, driving to Shreveport and Dallas to buy them; some of us just lent money and looked at the beautiful girls; the guys went around adoring their own erections and body hair; the girls, their expanding breasts—everybody having at it with his aboriginal ego, for beauty and power. Even those mill boys in my home room who were in bad health and held startling contests at breaking wind while devotional was being read by a member of the Bible Club over the P.A. system —they were having at it in their way: Beauty and Power.

The room fans on second level brought in the smell of that oily peanut butter off Monday's sandwiches, or that heated tunafish odor from salads the cafeteria maids were scooping. It was Federal Aid lunch, and cost a quarter.

We had one teacher Harvard-trained by way of postal correspondence and another who had half a master's degree. And there were twenty others actively, passively, strangely, cryptically, feverishly incoherent, each in his special style.

I had the head football coach for biology. Here was a fellow whose ambition it was to impress us with the nightmare of a soldier burning alive in a shell-struck tank— something he'd witnessed in World War II—and also with the unknown but true prevalence of tapeworm among the kids of the South. He could make you uncomfortable with his rugged poetry on these subjects, but he seemed to have nothing else to say. It was known that he also felt deeply about masturbation, but he didn't care to broach this in mixed classes. At three o'clock he ran off to coach the varsity in his Marine Corps shorts. He was positive the trouble with his *team* was either tapeworm or masturbation, and out there he made himself vocal about it, yelling out at this boy or other that he must be sleeping with his hands under the covers, or needed a physical examination. This always got a big laugh from the line coach, a flaccid baboon who taught factory arts and made a point out of being hilariously obsequious to the head coach. He wore sleeveless jerseys and had marvelously huge, sopping armpits.

My sophomore year I went out for football, but caught a cold and quit. I was just about good enough at it to make first team out at Dream of Pines Colored, which by then must've been featuring tuberculosis victims on its varsity. I heard their band when I was out on the field, though. They were about half a mile away and still sounded like a heavenly orchestra to my ears. It seemed silly to be out there at practice in my clouted, filthy pads when I heard them.

I was the sort that tended to bear grudges. I didn't like anybody correcting me on anything for any reason. I was down and out. I was not proud. The old pubic pox was still scattered on my face, and yet I yearned for everything beautiful in life. I was ready to be abused and picked on. I got into a fight in the locker room at the gym over a yachtsman's cap the old man had brought back to me as a souvenir from Miami when he went to a convention of mattress people there. And I won that fight, against a fat kid one grade under me, using depraved tactics like sitting on his chest and hitting him in the face, and using, really, everything I had in me. I admit I hit him as often as I could with

41

the knuckle wearing the Trojan-head ring—a gift from Mother.

The spinster librarian got on me one day for not smiling in the hall. She said she knew my folks would be disappointed in the hard personality I was showing. Then I broke down—not to her, not in front of that bitch, but in my mind: Aw sweet Jesus, don't you know when you're as ugly as a shotgunned butt of pork, and you love everything and hate everything at the same time, when you haven't got a face decent enough to look at the girls you want to look at, and when you haven't got a talent to show, being neither introvert nor extrovert, because you don't have the talent to go either way, and you start loving the rain because you might be seen with more shadow on you than usual, and hating the sun because it exposes all the corners you want to creep into, and you avoid mirrors and beautiful objects, like your old glass agate marbles, the rock garden in the country club foyer, and the color photographs in *National Geographic,* because you're afraid of these beautiful things looking back and folding up into cinders from your ugly stare—don't you know, Librarian, that you can't go around giving everybody a smile like your ass was made of candy? Much less you, with that ecclesiastical look of sour menopause on your spinster face, would I smile at, Miss Dedder. You stand there telling me about my smile. And you Miss Dedder, owed some poor man your sex sometime back in the thirties, and ignored him; you might could've made some poor man sane with it, way back then in Louisiana, with Huey Long and his crowd rearing up, but you didn't, did you? And you telling me about my lack of smile. You sit behind that desk six hours a day surveilling around the tables to make sure none of us write filthy slurs against the status quo in the margins of your precious books, or that the rednecks aren't tearing the brassiere advertisements out of the magazines. I looked away from her and went my way down the hall.

In chemistry we were led by a chubby, angelic mamma who asked the class what atomic piles were. We were discussing isotopes or rather being lectured to about them by a guest from the waterways experiment station. Our teacher was embarrassed that none of us knew what atomic piles were. I finally yelled out that I guess they were the worst disease imaginable, and there was fragmentary laughter around the class. Such was my early wit.

In the same class, sitting directly behind me, was a freckled bottle blonde who would go it to the extent of a finger. I wasn't in her clique, but I liked talking to her. She'd read the novel *Peyton Place* several times and told me it was the best novel, going away, for all time. She would knock herself out in class by taking ten deep breaths and then blowing on her thumb. She actually fainted back in her seat, with a smile, for a minute or so. Her name was Winona. She spoke with some authority, implying that she knew quite a bit for her age—and I knew positively of a few colleagues who'd couped her digitally. She was always telling me what I needed. You need a beer, she'd say. I liked to be mothered that way.

At Dream of Pines High we had teachers quitting all the time for reasons of pregnancy, higher pay in the insurance field, or personal despair.

In the eleventh grade I drank my first beer, and my facial condition evaporated. I looked in the mirror and couldn't believe what a finished piece of young manhood I was. This one old fossil teacher in history was always yelling about how time flew and how hateful it was. But I loved time, for getting me older and good-looking. I still had a few scratches around the cheekbones from the disappeared pox, but it would take a really finicky critic to say I wasn't handsome—though maybe a little guarded and unholy-seeming, like a sheik. I'm told I looked like an Indian long-distance runner. I was five foot ten and yearning toward six feet. My grip on the veneered scroll on the top of the stair rail felt good to me. I could bend a beer can into a crimped wad with my right hand. I still have this Asian cut of face which no one in my family can account for. The Monroes were French-Irishmen with memories of the Middle Ages, according to the lineage-tracing my old man once did with a bonus research offering from whatever encyclopedia we have in the house.

In English lit I ran into a teacher that was deep. Her eyes twinkled with arty secrets, and it didn't hurt anything that she was lovely of face and had the figure of a schoolgirl. She read poems with a nice, calm movement of mouth. I don't know why she was at Dream of Pines, which was known as a tough school. She was the only good teacher there. I can still feel the dull, light rhythms way in the back of my head from the poems we read in her class. We had Sir Thomas Wyatt, who composed a poem about his old girlfriends and the girl who said "Dear heart, how like you this?" as she put her arms long and small around him, and I can't forget old cobwebby Sir Thomas and those girls stalking with naked feet in his chamber. We had "The Love-song of J. Alfred Prufrock," with timid Alfred who wouldn't even eat a peach, but was fond of women's fore-arm hair as seen by lamplight. The peach and the arm hair related to each other, the teacher told us. I asked this brilliant fellow with crewcut and bifocals how that was, and he sent me an unfriendly note, not wanting to talk in class: "The peach and the arm are both fuzzy and fleshy. Don't ask me any more questions." I was pleased to find that out, and later I showed up that bifocals prick by handing in a poem of my own composition which the teacher raved about. She read it in class. It was about a deep-sea diver talking to the ocean and had a line

There within you, fin and sinew . . .

which she claimed was superb poetry by anybody's stand-ards. See the bifocals jackass, who made an unadulterated A in everything, fall apart at the jaw when she read out my name at the end of the poem. Of course, nobody else in the class gave a damn, and I personally was embarrassed by some of the extreme gentleness of the poem when she read it. I'd written it in a gust of all the culture I had in me. Our teacher had the knack of convincing you that you had to possess a museum full of culture before you deserved any-thing at all. You had to know all about the castles of Eng-land. You had to know about T. S. Eliot. You had to know about war-weary France.

She taught French too, and I got into it after a week in her literature class. She played the records of a French singer whose name was Edith Piaf. Her husband had brought the records back from occupied Germany. This Piaf woman sang like a petite untrained whore whose bed had been bombed out from under her; she trembled, with her voice from the bomb-metal soil to the bomb-dust sky. Oh, she could tell some stories, though I didn't understand any of them. I remember "Non, je ne regrette rien" with those beautiful Paris *r*'s. I linked her exclusively with World War II. It was what the teacher said about the records coming from occupied Germany. And I could just imagine this little Piaf woman huddling down behind some statue as gunfire streaked up and down the *rues* and *avenues*. Our teacher had been to Paris and held forth on it unboundedly. The French tongue weighed heavy on my mind, and I feel it like a sinner that I never learned it very well. Even in college, I never understood but about half of Molière. But the Piaf woman made me sentimental about war all over again. With the help of the two movies in Dream of Pines, which showed almost nothing else but war romances.

I grew sentimental about the casualties of the Korean War from Dream of Pines. I asked around about them until I must've been a great bore. We lost six boys from the town, as a matter of fact. The noblest casualty was the son of Ollie Sink, the mill baron. His boy was shot to death on Pork Chop Hill, but only after he'd rendered heroic duty as a corpsman. Ollie had a daughter remaining. Two colored boys from niggertown families I never knew were cut down. One of them was Harley Butte's cousin, a boy who'd played baritone horn with Butte in Jones's first-year band. Then one GI had returned safe from the war, but went insane for speed with his Mercury convertible when he got back and got killed at a driveway coming out of a joint into the highway. It was one of those crashes everybody in town claimed to have heard. Then I talked with a fellow who ran a sort of half-ass sporting goods store with his father. He was awfully bitter that nobody seemed to've cared about what had happened in Korea. He'd been in the conflict. He unbuttoned his shirt and showed me the worst purple stitched wounds I've ever seen. They looked like *new* wounds, in fact. The gooks had overrun a station where he was working the telephone and thrown in a grenade. He told me about the gooks throwing a woman naked down a hill and then sending down a man dressed in colonel's uniform to drag her half-living, screaming body up the hill by the hair, just so one GI would peep up enough that they could get a shot at him. This old boy claimed to have risen up and shot down the peasant dressed in colonel's uniform, in spite of the threat. He claimed that the stone he was behind disappeared in shot from the gooks when he stood up,

45

and that his survival was miraculous. Marveling about why he was still alive took up all his time. He held up a dusty mitt and spoke right into the pocket of it.

But in 1958 the girls in my class were hearing breathy, forlorn Elvis Presley over the big horn speakers at the parish fair. Royal American Shows furnished the main attractions there. It was October and chilly, with one rain a week. There were the animal exhibitions, the home arts tents, the rides, the concession booths, the freak shows, and two female variety acts, inside long tents with bleachers and a raised stage. One was "Rock" Brook's show—white girls— and the other was "Harlem in Havana"—interblended girls all tending to a brown mustard color. Both of them had bands in rickety white plyboard bandstands. I attended the fair three nights in a row, and saw all the girls I knew turn away from their dates and seek as near a decorous spot as they could near the speakers carrying Elvis's voice. Then their dates would have to sit by them and buy the cerealish hotdogs from the concessions and try to get their girlfriends to eat it while they were hearing Elvis finish his tune. I saw six or seven guys living through the agony of an Elvis song and a hotdog getting lukewarm. The girls would get into this state where their eyes wouldn't focus and they would open their legs primly to make way for the moisture Elvis caused them. Of course I didn't know that then. I just watched their dates gripping them and trying to resurge as lovers to them after the tune was over and they were on their way to the home arts tent.

I personally hoped that Elvis, that Hollywood redneck, would drown in his own spit. I hoped that he would knock up some nigger girl and have to marry her and that his career would crash into rust. My opinion of him had changed. I hated him for all the women he detracted from me and the rest of those pathetic amateurs taking girls over to the home arts tent. Now understand that I never had a date, not until senior year and the prom, when you had to be a headline toad not to have a date. I never had the guts to try, before then. But I felt for the guys who were trying.

I was with another guy, walking past the false "You Must Be Eighteen" barrier to see the creamy mustard Negresses shake in their jeweled brassieres at "Harlem in Havana." On Friday night at the dollar-fifty show this one gal came on five minutes before midnight and got down to it so

46

you saw her totally nude and even her moss about five seconds before the strobe light went out. I couldn't accept it; to my mind she became a life-size puppet toward the last. The guy I was with came out talking shrilly about how we'd seen a nude woman. But then the lights came on, and I saw the whole hurriedly screwed-together planks of the bleachers, the stage, and the bandstand, and I couldn't believe I'd seen an actual nude woman in this sordid tent affair. But she'd been very pretty, with the three dark spots of nipple, nipple, and V'ed hair.

Back in the late fifties, with a couple of classmates standing the first time outside the "Harlem in Havana" tent pavilion and seeing the light-colored Negresses parade out to the outer stage to entice us inside with a few subdued but promising jerks to the band, the girls cloaked in sheeny robes and brassy wedge sandals, I first got the idea that playing hot music on a trumpet might be an exciting thing to do all one's life. I looked away from the viciously weary faces of the girls to the bandstand balcony above them, where the "Harlem in Havana" banner draped. Up there was a Cuban-seeming fellow with a horn who wasn't weary. He stood up playing the hell out of a trumpet. He could make that sucker scream, and the drummer was laying down something thick and Latin behind him, and the ferris-wheel lights were shooting out off the brass of his horn so it looked like and sounded like he was holding a wondrous rainbow bird with a golden throat in his hands.

There wasn't any forgetting that.

5 / Horning In—A.

Tonnie Ray was passionately busy all her days at Dream of Pines High. In junior high she was one of those neutral-looking skinnies very much concerned with the concept *personality*, because she didn't think she had any, and she was right. So she got together with small groups of like

47

spirits and went around telling, keeping, and betraying incredibly inconsequential secrets, and that was about it, for Tonnie Ray Reese. She changed skirts every day, and was generally clean, and could be counted on to be scandalized by a shady joke or bad word. When "John was home" the first time, that is, when she had her first menstrual period, she missed a day of school. A girl actually asked about her when she came back. So she missed school every first day of her period for a while. She liked to create that mystery, and liked to reply in coy ways to anybody that asked about her absence—like she would say "I was with John," which was sort of romantic too. She and her group were the giggling poultry of the recess yard, huddling here and there with their little egg-secrets. But in high school she was very busy; she had gotten desperate. The only boy who'd ever asked her out was an absolute grub. Tonnie Ray wanted to get into a good crowd so badly; she wanted in with the popular crowd. And now she'd quit her old crowd and was really of no crowd. All she thought of was emulating the popular set and it kept her busy and extremely nervous. She would sit by the popular cuties in the cafeteria and listen to all the recent anecdotes on parties and dates, and then laugh along knowledgeably at them. There were several girls like Tonnie Ray at Dream of Pines. They were all equally frantic. Frantic to please, if you were the right person. We called them roaches, mainly, I guess, because they were as addled as maimed insects, and sucked up to such social crumbs as were offered.

I and the couple of guys I ran with paid a bitter kind of attention to Tonnie Ray and her type. We'd watch her collar some cheerleader, or class officer, or football player and start chattering away with them, making out to have crucial deals going with the honchos of the school. The guys and I winked at each other as her nervous voice rose in cries when she spotted somebody important in the hall. I don't know why Tonnie Ray and all the roaches rubbed us so raw. But we despised them from a special place of hatred in our hearts. We hated them so much that we'd skip lunch and loiter out in the hall in hopes of seeing one of them in the act.

"Look at Tonnie Ray leach up to that cheerleader babe," I said to a guy.

48

"I know. Wouldn't you love to put a shotgun down her throat and let it off coupla times?"

"It wouldn't be enough."

I confess that the guys and I, who weren't really hoodlums at all, talked theoretically on and off of assassinating Tonnie Ray. We had a prolonged deliberation over this idea throughout the rest of high school, but never could imagine anything quite excruciating enough for her. And we beheld with agony the fact that Tonnie Ray *was* making friends, she *was* getting in with the popular set; she became stylish and finally, to our horror, was one of the "Personalities of the Week" in the student newspaper.

"I say once a roach, always a roach," one guy said.

"Damn right." We were a bereaved consensus of three.

"Wouldn't you like to pick up a pair of ice tongs and just . . ."

"Not good enough."

We had the mill girls at Dream of Pines, too. These were the daughters of anybody who held a position below master foreman at one of the paper mills. Some of these gals were twenty-one and had given birth. *These* girls didn't roach or advertise themselves. They even seemed to resent being spoken to by students above their class. Of course you noticed them right off; their clothes were not terribly sharp and they tended to be a bit bruised around the legs. They swarmed in at lunch from another building where vocational arts were taught. They'd look at you straightforwardly with either lust or disdain, and you could pick up on unknown swear words by just hanging back in a locker and listening to them crowd into the cafeteria line. We liked them. We looked studiously at their bosoms and hips and had nothing to say when they disappeared.

I fell hard for one of them, under the influence of a dream I had of her. In the dream she was completely charming, said nothing, and was lusciously red-haired, and just before I awoke, she coyly threw her wrap aside and was milk naked. It was one of those dreams that mesmerizes your waking life. I waited in torture to see her again. When she came in with them, I tried to get her attention but couldn't. Her name was Ann. She had fine orangish hair and passable skin. Her hair was actually her best feature, but she peroxided her bangs so her hair went into

49

toasted yellow around her face. Ann never wore a dress to school—always pants, with a raincoat like dirty beach sand thrown over her and a tee shirt underneath. The raincoat had a habit of draping on one nipple to one side and exposing the other slightly, the way it dropped. Ann dear, with that unamused face of an operatic slut, gave the impression that she wouldn't have cared if she had a burning sparkler on both nipples.

I already knew she worked at the old man's mattress factory in the afternoons. Her father worked there too, in another shop. He was a legendary wino who'd probably vomited or slept on every square foot of the pavement in Dream of Pines at one time or another. But he could cure himself for periods reaching to a year. Her mother was some species of obese dwarf who wore a swath of garbage for a dress and black high-top tennis shoes. I'd seen the mother before on the porch of a two-room plank house hard by the biggest Sink mill. Ann's old man used to work at the mill until he lucked into a place with the mattress factory. The mother waited for them sitting on the porch and just being a slum unto herself. God knows what she fixed them to eat. I often thought about that. I could see Ann, who by the family standard was Helen of Troy, being slowly destroyed by some monotonous supper of grease and cornmeal wads.

Three days a week she skipped lunch because, I guess, she didn't want to pay the quarter. She'd sit in the Film Room, right outside the cafeteria, and wait for her friends. While as for me, I always had a bunch of dollar bills in my wallet. She needed me; I knew she did. In my dream she'd been so happy to please, and the body which she had let me see I loved and pitied too for its helplessness. My feeling for her threw me. It got me in soft places I didn't know I had. I was a fool over some rare idea like taking her out to my house and giving her a shower and letting her sit on the edge of my bed in a towel and holding her face in my hands.

There was a story about Ann. Back in the tenth grade she was rumored to have given birth to a dead child. She was known to be a follower of the Dream of Pines basketball team, and some boy on the varsity was supposed to be the father. I saw her on the front row at the gym several times, sitting in her raincoat, alone, smiling out at the court as if enchanted by the game in a calm way. She didn't clap, or cheer, and was otherwise placid—not strictly a fan—except for the fixed smile. I used to think she was an idiot or a gypsy. She looked a little like the woman on a package of Muriel cigars. She smoked in the gym while she sat there. This was not allowed; there were signs up all over the place, and I saw her get called down for it several times. She never hid her cigarettes and in a minute she'd have another one going strong and have to be spoken to again by somebody officious like the scorekeeper, who was also a Baptist preacher. Well, about the third time he walked over to her, I thought she was just clearly insane. But she finally quit smoking when he told her she'd have to leave the gym if she didn't. And she remained transfixed to the game with the smile getting dimmer and dimmer as the game neared a close. Nowadays she never smiled, that I knew of. She ran with a crowd of girls that looked like hicks, lady wrestlers and carnival women. I wondered if it was true about her baby. Maybe having it had hurt her, and maybe she was pregnant again, and maybe eating made her sick. No wonder she looked right through me when I said hello and called her name in the hall.

Dear Ann you need me, need me, I beckoned to her mentally. My good looks, my sympathy, my $800 checking account. What do I care if you're in trouble again? You haven't ever met anybody like me before. I don't run. I know what life's about. I believe in my dream about you. I'll watch you give birth, even in Mexico if that's what it takes. I know life, honey. The ins and outs: no sweat. I'll watch the baby *come out*, dearest, and kiss your lips when it's over. I know it'll hurt and you've been hurt so much already. And about other matters that might come up: I won't expect marital privileges with you. I mean not until a whole lot of soft talking between you and me. I imagined us together in a modest cottage overlooking the Pacific Ocean at Malibu, California, by this time. I would be a fisherman and bring back natural things to eat from the hills. *National Geographic* illuminations of blue, green, and wheaten shades, with rocks, surf, and coves as private as the planet Mars, took over my head and carried me sleepily down all the roads of color-photograph geography. I did feel sleepy throughout all this thinking about Ann and me. I'm the sort of fellow, anyway, who isn't inclined to ever

51

bring himself fully awake. I have a tremendous respect for people who *do* meet life with eyes wide-awake—like Ann, for example—but I've always been a coward that way; I think that if I ever did wake up completely, life would be too harsh and would lead me to suicide. Whereas, at the borders of sleep, I've usually adored life and could take down every breakfast bowl of thorns that came along.

Where my passionately imaginative kindness for Ann came from must have been the dream. I'd never been this way before. I wasn't ordinarily even courteous to folks I didn't know. For two weeks I was miserable over her. Aw, that she ignored me, that she maybe wasn't even conscious enough of me to be doing even that. I tried hard to dream about her again and get her to give me some message in the dream, but I couldn't. The memory of her in the dream was waning, and I got in a desperate funk. I made a fool out of myself when she came by one day. I started singing a song, "I've got the money, honey, if you've got the time," loud, putting myself directly in front of her face and doing a little hazardous bop stop. Ann looked at me worriedly, she did notice me, and then drew in her lip while glancing around it her crowd and deciding it was only her I was trying to entertain. Oh yeah, it was embarrassing as hell for me to have to do this. I was probably red in the face and silly as a sheik in drag, but I thought music might get her. She looked back at me once as she went on to the cafeteria. I was sure I had something moving now.

But no. I decided she was extremely shy. I couldn't wait any longer, though. Next day I found her sitting in the Film Room by herself. I stepped up to the wall and printed out a note, went in and put it on the desk she was sitting on, then fled. The note read: "I dreamed about you and I like you very much. If you're in trouble I want to help out. Do you know, want to know what I dreamed about you (us)? Even though you might of thought it was stupid of me singing in the hall yesterday I meant it, *I Have The Money Honey* as in the song I was singing. I know I don't have a very good voice. You know who my father is don't you. I have $1000 in my bank account. Please call me at 212–5037 at Pierre Hills soon. You know that song 'You Send Me'? I listen to it on the radio and think, You Send Me. Cares, Harry Monroe."

She never called. I went out to the mattress factory in the

52

afternoons and watched her from my old man's glass office. It wrecked him with curiosity that I came down and watched the work. Ann worked behind a sewing machine in the shop just below us. She knew I was watching her. Then one day I noticed with a shock that she was violating the smoking ordinance. A great careless cloud boiled out of her mouth and floated up in the rafters. The old man chose this moment to rise out of his chair behind the desk and walk over to the shop window beside me, meaning, I think, to put his arm around my shoulder in a father-chum gesture. I knew he'd see Ann smoking. I could think of nothing very smart to distract him, but moved wildly, looking for some trick. There were several piles of job tickets on a table near me, and so I just dashed my hand through them and knocked them all over the floor. Sure enough, the old man stopped. He bent down and picked up a couple of handfuls, then rose up and stared at me.

"It was an accident. Let me help you," I said.

"I worked on those tickets all morning," the old man spoke, very dry. "It looked like you just . . . *knocked* them, son."

"Something nervous happened to me."

"That was *crazy*." His face meant something deeper than this. I felt sorry for him; he started hopping from ticket to ticket on the floor.

"Let me help."

"You *can't* help. You go on home and . . . get well, boy. Sometimes you scare us. You know that? Donna says you close up your room in the afternoons and lie on the bed listening to the phonograph in the dark. What does that mean?"

The only answer to that was I liked to do it. Hell—kick a guy because he favors salt in his beer, peanuts in his soft drink, dark with his music: he happens to be a guy who likes to grip the sheets and close his eyes until greenish movies featuring him as the hero appear, changing scenes and milieux with the changing climes of music—Harry happy, Harry sad, Harry bitter or melancholic, Harry truculent, but always Harry marvelous, Harry celebrated by the high-class babes of Paris, Berlin, London, Rome, New York, Baton Rouge, New Orleans, and of such shady places as Vicksburg, Natchez, Biloxi, Mobile, Savannah, and

Charleston, twentieth-century holdouts of the romantic Southland, where it would be all magnolias, swamps and bayous, Spanish moss, cigarillos, piers, catfish, subtly brewed Bourbon drinks, and extravagantly well-dressed, complex, historic vagina, for Harry suave. Caving in a pier by his sheer presence. And lately, dreams of Malibu, California, in the simple cottage with Ann. Kick in a fellow's head for wanting the dark, and the evocative phonograph. Very well.

I suffered in behalf of Ann and in behalf of, really, myself, the way I happened to be. I had enough pride to be proud of it, though. Times were when I felt like God's special friend, I was suffering so much. Like the Jews. We were reading about the unspeakable persecution of the Jews under Hitler in history about that time. Of course I had dug into all that lore years ago. The old teacher was married to a Jewish woman from Chicago. He held forth on the sins against the Jews as if he suffered a chronic nightmare one week a year about it. The atrocity photographs he showed were the only attraction of the year's history class. He'd bring them out of an old cardboard folder and just sigh pitifully as he passed around the pictures. Guys would take his class for reason of the photographs alone. The pictures they were really awesome and sordid, showing open mouths and exposed pubes. The year I was under the old boy, a girl in my class threw up, and the principal came in the next day to say he couldn't show those pictures around any more. So right in front of us the old boy got his folder together, put on his overcoat, caught up his briefcase, and quit the school, giving us some kind of hopeless salute. So what? everybody says. The only thing he was good at was telling about the Jews and about how time flies—tempus fugit, and all that, with a few other Latin phrases that seemed to grip him personally but never affected any of us. The principal read to us out of the textbook the rest of the year. And let me take this opportunity to say that this man, the principal, had an acute breath problem; air like from a cavern full of dead men came out of his mouth, and I caught it all, being on the front row, attempting as a sort of last ditch effort to create a scholarly air around myself by sitting there. I was doing so mediocrely at Dreams of Pines, and my parents wanted me to get in such a mighty college. They had the money. They wanted me at Harvard, or Princeton, or better

54

yet, Columbia, in New York City. As I said, my old man was partial to New York because it had all that unimaginable money.

Another time I came to the factory to see Ann. I had managed to force myself into another dream about her. This time she was a kind of puppet that said, "I love you. I need you. I love you. I need you." She'd taken off her clothes again and revealed a painted-doll type of nudity, showing two red dots and a black V that seemed varnished and inaccessible. The old man happened to be out of the office. I waved at her vigorously at the office window. She was talking to a stumpy fellow in gray coveralls and smoking a cigarette. When the fellow saw me, he hiked off instantly to another shop. Ann kept her eyes on me. Then she lifted up her hand and gave me the finger. I couldn't believe it. But the familiarity of the old signal somehow gave me some hope.

I followed her home. She was in some smoky car of the women's car pool and I was in the black station wagon of old. They let her out at her slum-pocket and she walked rapidly over her lawn toward the house. I say lawn, but what it was was a soil flat that looked beaten out by a goon whose duty it was to let no sprig grow. I drove up with her and began calling her name. She seemed to be ignoring me and was almost running into her house, thinking to be rid of me in there. What a dump to run to for safety. I saw her doing this, and I could not believe the story about her having a baby. This was a furiously shy girl I was dealing with.

I lay down on the car horn. I had quite a horn. It was loud, and by some accident at General Motors, played a whole harmonic chord, like C against E and G. It sounded like a band tuning up. It pierced, was rather regal, and could not be ignored except by the deaf. All right. Ann gave up and walked back to my car and got in, leaving her door open. She was the first girl I'd had in the car.

"Ann. Why aren't I good enough for you?" I said right off. I knew good and well that wasn't the issue. All the signs were that I was too good for *her* and was bending down to her heroically.

"You do *talk*, don't you?" I asked her further.

"I know a guy that would kill both of us if he knew we were together," she said. God, she'd spoken to me. She

55

looked beautiful in the sunset at five-thirty—that was when I was talking to her. Her raincoat came apart.

"You don't wear a brassiere, do you, Ann?"

"Don't you talk like that." Her voice was steady. It had a low harsh music in it. That pleased me.

"I'm sorry, Ann."

"Don't write me notes. Don't follow me around. You're not big enough or old enough. You wouldn't want me if you knew you might get killed for wanting me."

"I heard you had a baby. Did you?"

"That's for me to know and you to find out."

"You did, didn't you? I don't care. I had a dream about us. You liked me and took off your clothes . . ." I stuttered this out.

"Oh yeah?" she took it up. "What'd you do in this dream?"

"I just stared. Looked at you."

"You see. You're not ready to do anything yet, you see." She looked away from me toward the sunset, and then all around at the scraggly pines growing outside her lawn; she seemed to be inspecting the whole globe. It was just a minute before night, and very red in the sky. "You know I'm the best piece of ass at Dream of Pines that has ever been, don't you, Harry?"

"No, mam," I got out. No, I didn't know she was anything as deluxe as that. Ann laughed.

"They say I am. I am the girl whose butt don't often hit the mattress, they say. Some guy was looking in a window and observed that when I didn't know it."

While she was saying that she was taking me all in, probably for the first time. I was exhausted by all I'd found out about her. I'd always thought of her as my private discovery.

"You come back around when you grow up some," Ann said. "I haven't got anything against you." She got out of the car.

"What do you think of Malibu, California? I've got love for you. I've got *money!*" I yelled when she seemed to be leaving the car. She came back and put her red-haired head in the window.

"Don't think I ain't dreamed of all that money with you . . . Harry . . . Everybody knows *love* is the loveliest word there is, also. Don't throw it around like you do."

She went in. By God, I wanted her more than ever. She had a little intelligence, which surprised the daylights out of me. You bet I'd wait around and grow until I was man enough for her. I'd grow hair all over. I'd seen what a woman she was when I talked to her. All set. Ann and I would wait on each other. An enormously profitable way to spend your spare time, waiting, growing, for Ann.

Two weeks later I drove the car up in the garage and there was the old man. It was twilight. He was sitting on the hood of his Buick. I knew by his weak smile that he was after me.

"That's the way to park that old caroobie," he yelled. I knew something was on his mind, like a ton of bricks. The old man gets friendlier than a faggot Japanese when he approaches me on bad trouble. He wants to establish that all is normal except one tiny thing, and that thing is the business at hand.

"Guess what Mr. Mick told me the other day?" he says. No relation to anything. I am alarmed. Mr. Mick is Ann's wino father. Her name is Ann Mick.

"He said the reason he gave up wine the last time was that the air from the paper mills in Dream of Pines was so bad it cut into his wine and ruined it the minute he pulled the cap off. It was like mixing wine with raccoon dung, he said." Big laughing in the garage. I'm struggling toward the house but the old man has got a great humorous cuff on me.

"It's a shame about Mr. Mick," I say. Let me go, old man.

"His daughter goes to your high school," says my father. His voice has the crisp delight of profundity in it. What am I supposed to do? Deny that she attends the school? "She works for me on the sewing machines. She's the worst worker I have. She smokes in the shop. Somebody told me she does something worse than that with somebody else back of the stacks at coffee break. I'm thinking of letting her go."

"You know I have a crush on her," I admit.

"I'll say a crush. With dreams about her, and singing songs to her." He lifted out of his vest pocket the very note I gave her in the Film Room. It was the blue-lined notebook paper with ripped ringer holes, and then it was very crumpled and folded and almost yellow. "You don't want me to read it, do you?"

I snatched it out of the old man's fingers.

"You put our phone number in there," he mused.

"Did Ann give this to you?" I asked.

"No. It's been through several people before it got to me. You'll be happy to know that. First, she gave it to her father, and he thought it was such a precious joke that he handed it over to Harley Butte, his foreman. Then Harley kept it a week, thinking about it, and finally decided I ought to see it. He gave it to me. He said he thought I wouldn't think it was very funny, and he was right. I don't think this note's very funny. With all the fine girls you could be interested in . . ."

He had me down. He began accusing me of trying to embarrass him. He said he didn't need that, and that my mother Donna, who was a very fine lady, didn't need that. He said it was a slander to her name that Ann Mick was the first girl I chose to show any interest in, because (he whispered) Ann Mick was a little "harlot" that everybody knew about. He finally got so upset, saying we wouldn't mention any of this to Mother, and that this matter was "Closed. Closed, you hear?" I couldn't understand him. I'd agreed to everything he said long ago, out of sheer fright and humiliation. But he was forcing himself into a nervous panic, still holding onto my arm, and looking out into the dark back yard as if there was some specter there which yet threatened his life and family. I do believe he was holding to me protectively and not just to keep me from running in the house. I'd seen the old man nervous and full of clamor before, but never like this.

The old man was a converted Presbyterian and was occasionally flooded by the idea of being morally circumspect. He'd quit smoking and use up a bottle of Listerine in one week trying to expunge every hint of the weed within and without his body. He'd begin drinking worlds of milk and throw out the one bottle of sherry in the house, which he and my mother touched only about twice a year anyway. He'd walk to work and back, a distance over all of five miles, with his hair combed neat and slick and a modest pin-on bow tie at his throat—other days he despised bow ties as menial-looking—and he would have some book in his hands: a dictionary, or a book of poems by a Presbyterian missionary to China, what did it matter. He never cracked it, but made sure to have his name signed gloriously on the flyleaf, and all he wanted out of it was the sober sanction that a piece of literature in the hands gives one. He'd get home drunk on sunshine, goodness, and his own sweat. He would be concerned about his family name, which meant that he was concerned about me. He called me into the kitchen, where he'd have two glasses waiting. There he began, "Well. Tell me what you've been doing," and engaged me in a sort of contest at milk-drinking while we waited for the answers to come out. It all ended with our drinking so much milk we were ready to puke; the old man churning himself into a dull butter of meditation about my life. Not one understandable sentence having passed between us.

So I thought after I left him in the garage that he was only being a Presbyterian again, with all this business about the family name and so on, but that was not it. Or that was only partly it. I think I saw into this matter later.

I went to his office again one afternoon to look at Ann. He did not see me come in. The old man was sitting on a stool near the shop window and peering down at someone very concentratedly. I walked over—I suppose quietly— and looked past his shoulder. There was Ann bent down at her machine. I know he wasn't looking at the middle-aged women around her.

"You didn't fire her, did you?"

He jerked around coming out of a very soulful smile. Then he seemed to become concerned over what he was doing. He squirmed around right-face on the stool. He bit his lips, closed his eyes, and failed once at crossing his arms.

"Who?" he said weakly.

Oh, Daddy, oh, Ode Elann Dupont. You've been in love with her too, haven't you? Or at least you like to look at her very much, don't you? I do not think I was wrong about it. The fishiest grin I've ever seen popped out on his mouth. I looked past his shoulder down to Ann on the floor, and seeing her, blooming heavily forward, unbrassiered, under her tee shirt as I'd never seen her before, her legs crossed, her hairstrands falling over into her eyes like wispy copper as she bent to the machine doing her little bit, I knew she was too much woman for me, for one thing,

59

and for another, no man could look on her without becoming a slobbering kind of rutting boar; she did not enchant you: she put you in heat. You thought of a pig-run alley full of hoofmarks running between you and her—lots of hoofmarks, dried deep in the clay—for after all, she was known to have mated with others. She was at the edge of a water hole, bending down for a drink with her feminine parts up in the air. I thought of the old man looking at her.

He seemed depraved and perverse, this old boy who should've been out of the running years ago. I didn't like him. I suspected him of really having tried something with Ann, of maybe keeping her in some kind of wagebondage lust. I thought of the old boy naked, using her like a trampoline. I'm sure he never did anything but look, like me, but uncertainty in me has always bred a phantasmagoric imagination.

Well, to the credit of his honesty, the old man instantly gave up the sham and said, "She's quite a slut, isn't she?"

We broke out laughing when he said that. The old man and I are both amused by the concept of a whore. The idea of women being gored for lucre by some poor man has always been a joke to bring down the house between us. We heard it called the oldest profession, and then thought of a cavewoman doing it for a glowing coal, a piece of fire from his cracking wealthy bonfire; an Egyptian woman doing it for a leek; a Hebrew woman doing it for water; a Roman woman doing it for an acre of German tundra; a World War II woman doing it for a radio. The only contact the old man and I had for years was whispering whore jokes to each other. We started giggling when the word *whore* was first mentioned. The worst of them all was told by me during a terrible period of my college life. It was about a seventy-year-old whore thrusting a bag into a dark closet where her lover was hidden; he thought they were potato chips, but they were actually the scabs off her own body. The old man closed his eyes and edged away after I told that one, not knowing his own flesh and blood son all over again. I really hadn't wanted to tell it, but it had gone around for bowelish laughs among the terribly unhappy crowd I ran with at college. My resources were low; in my crowd, whatever gagged a maggot passed for humor. After I'd told the old man that joke, the whore jokes between us stopped completely, and there was, as a matter of fact, no

60

further communication between us. I did us in as father and son when I told that last rotten one.

However, now we laughed together. I forgot all the vile imaginings about the old man. I forgot everything and laughed with him till I cried. I do believe it was all because of the pleasure of finally forgetting Ann. He'd called her a slut, and I at last believed him. She was a comic whore. I told her goodbye. You'll be waiting a long time for me to grow up enough for you, Ann, I thought. The old man and I got out our handkerchiefs and wiped the tears off our cheeks. He reached over and held my shoulder. Too bad for you, Ann, I thought, looking at her still, past him. She looked up and saw us in the office and her mouth fell open with some surprise. That's the most I ever evoked from her. Too bad you don't get to go to that cottage in Malibu with me, Ann. What kind of gimp did you think I was? You whore. How dare you?

What a farce! I had come to the office with my suitcase packed and in the bed of my station wagon. I was intending to draw out the $800 in my account that afternoon. I had come to the factory for no other reason than picking up Ann, persuading her, and driving straight to Malibu with her. I thought I'd drop in and see her through the glass window again, and see the old man too, for sentimental reasons. I was laughing over the ruins of my first dream. The facts were of course that Ann was not strictly a whore. She never took money, that I had heard of. She did it with mature athletes because she liked it. I knew that. But it was somehow less humbling to the old ego to think of her as a whore than as a woman of pleasure. There were too many muscles involved in that.

And sometimes things are so monstrous you can't do anything else but laugh. The old man liked to have her around him; he liked to look at her and think of her putting out; he liked to think of that tee shirt rolled up to her chin and of that red hair writhing and of her yellow teeth biting her underlip and of her shut eyes and smile when she was getting her paroxysms. Great God, he was the same as me, and that was what was monstrous. He could not bear to be picturing the same woman that his son was. He thought it was depraved. All that he knew of Presbyterian decorum was brought into question. That's why he got so upwrought at me in the garage.

61

There was a light rap on the office door, and then the door opened and in stepped that devil Harley Butte. Don't think I hadn't been thinking of this man for a couple of weeks. I'd never heard of such an officious nigger. I just couldn't figure him, the man who handed my note to Ann to my old man. Mainly what I couldn't figure was what the old man had said about Harley *thinking* for a week before he decided to hand the note over. I didn't know anything about a thinking nigger at the time. I knew of wild niggers, romantic niggers, lazy niggers, comic niggers, fishing niggers, foxy niggers, even rich niggers, but I knew nothing about yellow thinking niggers.

Harley was colored more toward white than I'd imagined him. He was my size and handsome, with points of brown at the brows and eyes, and stiff hair; he had an orange pretty face. His eyes closed every other breath he drew. He was a baby bursting forth with dark points of maturity and had on his face a sort of amazement that all this growth had come to him so suddenly. He looked toward me, immediately shut his eyes, and talked only to the old man.

"I'm afraid they've scheduled another game on Friday afternoon. I'll have to have Friday off again, Mr. Monroe. I can't help it. I'm the director of the band, and there isn't any way I can get out of it."

The old man looked to me.

"Have you met Mister Butte, Harry?" The *Mister* threw me. Especially as used toward a man whose parents you wondered about first thing when you saw him. Yellow man. I made a point out of despising him as a mixed breed. I became an authority and a prophet about his certain doom. I gave him no more chances than the chances a child begat of human sperm and sheep egg had. I knew there were special laws against doing it with sheep, because something would produce—something unspeakable. I thought, Butte, you'll probably die at thirty at the latest, of simple natural causes. Go ahead and be a foreman for the old man, be the band director out at Grell, hand in notes I wrote, kick around a few more years, then you'll be *gone,* buddy. You look too strange to make it, my friend. It satisfied me to think such thoughts.

"I don't think you're going to get much out of him. Your boy doesn't like me," said Harley. He and the old man laughed.

"But now, Harry and I know each other from way back. I and he were introduced one evening he was throwing firecrackers. He was having lots of fun."

The old man bent his brows impishly. I couldn't tell whether he knew what Butte was talking about. It's among the old man's habits of snobbery to make out like nothing is unknown to him. I began feeling watched, or worse, spied upon, and went home.

Butte is a spy in the old man's hire, I thought. I was outraged. What else has the yellow son of a bitch seen? How long has he been watching? Then I imagined that unlikely scene with the old man and Ann again, such things as his saying, "Come here, my pet, and sit on my lap," with him sitting in nothing but an underwear shirt, and Harley Butte smiling cynically at the window, every now and then lifting up binoculars to spy out for me. It all a depraved inside joke on me.

Put some shotgun holes in that yellow son of a bitch, then he can sigh and play his intestines like a flute, I thought. Then I regretted dismally that the old man had been able to make me give up Ann so easily. Something filthy had been going on against me.

I went to bed and lay there. I had the phonograph way up loud on an old record of marimba music. *Looble Loo Loo Loooble Boooble Looooo Loo Pi Pi Looble!* "Catch a falling star and put it in your pocket . . .!" was the tune. Ordinarily I detested this record, but now it evoked bereft, dispossessed emotions in me. I imagined that it was the musical version of the cliffs and seascape of Malibu, California, where I had wanted to take Ann. I saw the *National Geographic* picture flood out of its frame in thick gorgeous colors of blue, wheat, and green, and I saw the cottage sag into rivulets of white. It was dripping away, all gone: *Loo Looble!* And I was left floating on this bed somewhere between Dream of Pines and Malibu, alone, Harry tragic. The suitcase was still in the car, the silver ballpoint which would have signed for the release of my money was in my hands.

Ann, I whispered. Ann, Ann, Ann. You were going to be so sweet at Malibu. You were going to have a clean white tee shirt and be always just coming out of the bath. You and I were going to wait until your red bangs grew out and there wasn't any more of that yellow peroxide in your hair.

63

We would have gone swimming and one day I would give you a mild kiss on the foot and love would grow gradually from there. Maybe one day you would come in with your tee shirt rolled up coy so I could see your navel. Another day I might come in mistakenly and see your bare breasts. I know they look like crushed ice with rubies on top. Another day I would accidentally get in the shower when you were already in there and you would say, "Oh, you silly thing," and then we would have love, with you moaning against the shower wall and water droplets on our faces. We could not help it, all the forces said "Love." But you had been my legal wife for all this time and I had held back like a shy hero. Ann. I loved you.

But I did not love her any more. She was a whore in the comic strips. She probably took money from beasts who smelled of the locker room and the paper mills.

Thank the old man for reminding me of that. I hated him. I saw him in his undershirt having his way. Vomit fumes came up in my throat. And I thought I could taste in my mouth the body of a yellow nigger; he was standing, pressing spread-eagled against my esophagus walls; his eyeballs boiled out a rancid muck which dripped down to my lungs. He had the rubbery smile of a minstrel entertainer from the old days.

I didn't know I was taking the flu that night. At around five in the morning, one eye seeped out a tear, and then the other began raining down my cheek. I thought it must be sadness over Ann, so I just let go and let the disease of my world have me.

6 / Horning In—B.

It turned out that at the last football game of the season I was too dejected to be held back any longer. I was sitting high up in the bleachers beside the band with the same buddies, and we were making up original profanity about how bad the band was while we took the Coke cups into our jackets and sneaked a dip of Dom Pedro muscatel into them when the other team made a touchdown and everybody stood up to despair over it. I don't know of another evening when defeat was so totally evident in the air. You could smell it. The rain was coming down in a frigid mist, our team was being swept away by an old rival team from Alexandria that seemed to achieve some advantage of grip on the mud, the drums of the band sounded like clubs against sodden paper, and Dom Pedro with Coke made the worst toddy perhaps in the history of alcoholic mixtures. The other two guys had hung beneath the bleachers to throw up once already, but I was more stubborn. I had my eye on a small trumpet-player in the band and kept down all the booze in me I could to prepare for what I was going to do at half-time.

The band went out dutifully at the half and fell apart in some unrecognizable formations and music as the home crowd drizzled out of the bleachers to leave for their homes and fires, until only about twenty folks were left. The band came back, the members wiped off their horns and put them in their cases; the old bald-headed man who led them told them he wanted them back in ten minutes. They swarmed off toward the masonite blockhouse where the concessions and restrooms were. I noted with pleasure that the boy I was watching took his horn with him. I dropped below the bleachers and followed his legs through the tiers to the blockhouse.

He only wanted to pee, and there was a tremendous line outside the restroom door. He waited a minute, then swerved off, looking all around him, and walked up the clay bank behind toward the woods on the edge of the stadium. He got in the shadows of the pine scrubs and then darted into them resolutely. I followed him. Ten feet into the woods, he had his striped uniform pants down and was making water. In one hand was his golden trumpet, with its march music stuck on a little wire clamp protruding from it.

"What you think you doing, boy?" I sounded like a deputy sheriff. "Just hold it right there, band boy."

The little man—he must've been twelve or a small thirteen—jumped when he heard me and went into a spasm trying to hustle his pants up. I knew his name; it was Lloyd

65

Reese, Tonnie Ray's little brother. He was the brother of a roach. I didn't think he knew me, though.

"Harry. I thought it was somebody . . . You're Harry Monroe, aren't you?" Lloyd said when he finally buttoned up and turned to see me.

"Give me the horn, you little fart." I grabbed the trumpet but Lloyd held on, unexpectedly, with his skinny crablike hands. I hit him in the mouth. His march music flew everywhere and he crumpled back ino a huge weedplant. Lloyd howled like a wounded cat. I grew panicky thinking he might be heard down in the stadium and charged into the weedplant thinking to calm him down with a few blows. I hit at his face a couple of times, and sure enough, he got quiet. But he began whimpering and I felt pretty sorry about that. His tiny pointed kneecaps showed under his pants; his uniform was covered with wet grass crud.

"Now look, Lloyd. All I wanted you to do was give me a lesson on this old horn. I'm interested in playing it. Lloyd? You hear?"

"You hurt my embouchure," Lloyd whimpered, putting his hand to his lips. I didn't know what *embouchure* was, but guessed of course that it was a diseased condition of Lloyd's and got very afraid of him dying on me.

"You're all right, Lloyd," I pleaded. "Give us a tune, buddy." I gave him back the horn and Lloyd played an airy little version of "Lady of Spain" with no hesitation, sitting down, rather pitiful in his rumpled orange uniform and with his brown hair jagged on his forehead.

"That's fine, Lloyd. You really get in there with it, buddy." Actually it had been rotten playing, but I appreciated the fact he thought I would kill him if he didn't play something.

"My embouchure is ruined," said Lloyd.

"Nawww! Now look. I want you to teach me the keys. I'll blow on it and you make the notes for me." I eased the horn out of his hands.

"That's silly," little Lloyd said.

I looked down at him from my height and he didn't think it was silly any more. I sat by him and pursed my lips on the mouthpiece as I'd seen him do. I blew and a rugged whiff came out. He reached over and began fingering the scale for me. I was surprised to see there were only three

66

valves. I'd always thought there were more—I mean, for all the different sounds.

"No valves down for C," Lloyd said. "First and third down for D. First and second down for E; only first down for F." I felt the tones go up in a grand ascension. "Don't blow so loud!" said Lloyd.

In ten minutes I could play a few bars of "The Marines' Hymn." I played it over a couple of times and then began to give it a little finesse and surge, delaying the notes jazz-style and bellowing on the tones when I finally hit them. Wild *Jesus!* I knew I had been made for this horn, or that it had been made for me—whichever! Look how I was coming along in ten minutes.

"Say, Lloyd. Aren't I doing pretty good?" I said. I really enjoyed the taste of metal on my lips.

"My band has started to play. I'm supposed to be with them, you know."

So they were. It must've been the fourth quarter by then. The frosty rain was drilling down on Lloyd and me up here in the weeds. A giant oak stood right behind us. Its big leaves were clattering under the rain; it might have been sleet. The band, however, was cutting right through it with a brassy grunt.

"Look, Lloyd. Wouldn't you agree that I was exceptional as a beginner?"

"I'm going to be in big trouble now," Lloyd said. He had a spindly crooked nose that seemed to seek a less troublesome life.

I gave him back the horn and he collected his wet sheets of music in the weeds and left for the stadium. I yelled to him when he went down the hill that I thanked him very much. Then I drove home, ignoring my buddies, and got in the bed. I needed no phonograph music. The sound of myself on trumpet was good enough. I loved that trumpet. I wanted one of my own.

As my luck would have it, that little Lloyd Reese turned out to be a genius. He is studying anthropology at Cambridge in England as of this date; this will be his second Ph.D. and I think the small fart even has two or three books out by now. How could I know who I was messing with?

He got back to the bleachers in an unbelievably disheveled state and with no horn. He had tears running down his

67

cheeks and there was something pronouncedly wrong about the way his fly was buttoned. The little snake stood in front of the band and declaimed about how I had beaten him, stolen his horn, and further, how I had threatened him until he had to agree that I could *molest* him. He shouted this out so a few townsmen nearby and some of the sub football team could hear him. Then he fainted, and there was a big scene where his sister Tonnie Ray ran out of the stands and supported him in her arms. What a hell of an actor Lloyd was. He knew what crowd to speak to. The townspeople who remained in the rain were the violently loyal to Dream of Pines; the football subs would kill out of pure mean frustration.

Things were not rosy for me in Dreams of Pines for a few months. Half of the high school thought I was a violent homosexual and the other half didn't know for sure. I was the first even suspected case at Dream of Pines. There was suspicion at home the Saturday morning after I'd first played the trumpet. I remember the phone ringing early in the morning, but I didn't know what was happening when the old man replied into it with sleepy surprise. To the lasting credit of the Reese family, it was not Mr. Reese calling the old man at this hour. The Reeses probably knew what a smart fraud Lloyd was and had found out the truth some time during the night. But they were, on the other hand, a gutless family for never denying Lloyd's accusations against me. They were a family in one of the subdivisions and I have no doubt they were trying to be as quiet as possible about Lloyd, who was not yet so known for his aberrant lying as he was later.

It was broadcast throughout Dream of Pines that I was a desperate queer.

The old man woke me up at eleven with a sad look on his face. I've never seen him so miserable. My mother was standing at my door, already preparing to intercede on any brute thing her husband might say to me.

"I am always here to give you anything," the old man announced. "I always have been." He was crazy with nervous confusion. I didn't know what this was all about, but he approached me at a time when I was voraciously greedy.

"I want a trumpet," I began. His eyes widened. I know now that, according to what he knew by the phone call, all the evidence as to my being homosexual was in.

"Don't you already have a trumpet in this room?" he asked.

"No. Are you *nuts?* I found out just last night that I wanted a trumpet." The old man blushed. I swear it.

"I want a trumpet. I want the title papers for the Chevy wagon. I want a hundred dollars. I want a private tutor to teach me trumpet. And I want . . . a pistol." I threw that in because it was the only thing I could think of on the moment that was shiny and expensive.

"You can have all that," my mother said. My father looked back at her mournfully.

To this day, the old man doesn't know but that the sordid story about me he heard over the telephone is partially true. Who could have, would have, called him? I keep asking myself. I think it was Ollie Sink or his wife. They were there during the rain at the game, and lately they had become members of the Baptist church, in a deep vengeful sort of way. Ollie had mailed some tracts about the end of the world to the old man. Without postage, that is. I saw Ollie putting the envelope into our mailbox while I was reminiscing around the cane one afternoon.

I got the pistol first. I'm sure the old man thought it was the most manly thing to give me. It was a miniature snub Italian-made automatic; it was heavy, a .22, and was a smooth brute that shot with a loud sound. Next he told me informally that the Chevy was mine for keeps. Next he told me I had another hundred dollars in my savings account. This was toward college, he made me understand. Next he gave me a piece of property in southeastern Texas that I have not to this day seen. He assured me it was a nice wooded bluff from ten acres he had bought and would make a splendid site for a house in the event I got a wife in the next ten years. How he did emphasize my getting a wife. Last came the trumpet, which not he but my mother brought into my room one evening. It was a brass and silver plated beauty lying in an alligator case of blue velvet fur. Mother had picked it up on a secret trip to a music store in Shreveport. The horn was a Reynolds Contempora model exquisite by even professional standards. I didn't know that and only said, "Thank you very much," to my mother. Bless her heart, she had gotten me on purpose the finest horn in Louisiana.

It was well known in Dream of Pines how miraculous

Harry Monroe became, in such short time, on trumpet. I had a private tutor all right, but that doesn't explain it. My mother got me a weird old fellow who had played for years in a Shriner's band. He was retired from the automobile trade and never went anywhere without a can of beer, but I don't want to take anything away from him; he played trumpet terribly well for a guy his age. He'd had lots of practice playing fast circus music, and he could still cut away with a solo of high-ranged brassy spunk. His name was Ralph Medford; I think he had been in the First World War; he called the trumpet the long horn, as opposed to the shorter cornet. And as a teacher, after he got through wandering around and admiring the pieces in our house, he was competent: stiff on my learning the scales, stiff on my never playing over phrases and tunes I had already mastered; when I learned something, I got no praise—Mr. Medford just lost interest in the exercise altogether, and gave me to know I ought to do the same. He had eyes that reminded me of broken grapes and a handsome tanned scalp where he'd grown bald. His car was one of those old Hudsons that looked like a zeppelin somehow incapacitated and made to creep along the earth; it made a sucking sound coming in the driveway and going out it, to wherever he lived in Dream of Pines.

But—not to stampede away the idea of grand old Mr. Medford—I was amazingly talented on this horn, and was past any help he could give me in about six months. I played the Arban book all the way through and then won the state solo contest down at Shreveport, or thought I had. I learned later that several trumpeters won first-place ribbons in that contest and none of us was necessarily the best. It was not a contest to establish the state's best trumpeter. Mr. Medford thought I had won best-in-the-state too; he drove me down there and played the piano for the little virtuoso piece by Raphael Mendez that I did, and maybe was in love with his own piano-playing, which was, by the way, rotten. The judges were from schools in New York and Chicago. There was also a judge from Eastman Conservatory who looked at me peculiarly—had his tongue out through a horseshoe beard. I went free-lance, attached to no high school, and that was a rarity.

Medford went into my old man's study very honorably one day and told him that he had taught me everything he could and that I was better than he was now and he thought he ought to step out. He said also that he suspected there was some practical joke being played on him, because I had learned trumpet just too rapidly really for him to believe that I had been only a beginner. The old man probably looked at him in some flat way and wrote him out his check. I never knew how proud the old man was of me. I don't know but what he was embarrassed by my musical progress. In one way, of course, every good thing I did in music proved me a little more of a pervert—if you accepted Lloyd Reese's story about how I had *molested* him and stolen his trumpet.

Once I heard the rumor about myself in full from one of my buddies who'd stayed for the game and witnessed all of Lloyd's testimony. My buddy knew it was false, and he and I went out in the bushes on that hill of the stadium and kicked around trying to find Lloyd's horn. I don't know what the little snake did with it; as I've said, he was a genius. After the night I was alleged to have molested him, he quit band and went secretly into his great discipline of anthropology, a course that wasn't even offered at Dream of Pines.

I put the Italian pistol under the seat of my car and drove around pretending I was going to nail Lloyd. I discovered how much I detested this place, with its rancid paper mill air and its rumor-hungry dead Baptist subdivisions. I couldn't drink coffee any more because the taste reminded me of the atmosphere. I saw those rain-gray stacks of pulpwood down by the tracks again, and right above them, a steely little airplane creeping across the hot tops of the pines and my stomach wanted to throw up everything in it. I'd seen Dream of Pines too much. I drove by Ann's house with only a gassy, diarrhetic feeling in me. And then I sat in my car in the garage for two hours one night thinking about Dream of Pines until I decided I wanted to see everything in it burn—the subdivisions, and Pierre Hills, and especially those houses on the track like Ann's house, and Ann tangled up with her current lover in the back seat of a car parked in her front yard, Ann on fire like a building, with her ribs broiling in an X-ray view, and the guy she was with screeching as his crotch turned to embers and flames took his head. And you bet I wanted Harley Butte's house on fire: Harley lying in bed with his musical instru-

71

ments having been made into molten brass by the fire before he wakes up, and then he wakes up to be scorched to death, howling, by the molten pool. I also wondered what my old man would do if he woke up with walls of fire in all corners of his room. I had a box of wooden matches with me and struck them one by one in the car, studying each one from the initial ragged burst of yellow to the cool blue wavering blade at the last. I wanted Dream of Pines High School to burn too; to turn into the coal skeleton like the matches did.

It's hard to tell whether my trumpet-playing profited by all this fire I was dreaming up. I did stay at the old trumpet every afternoon after school. I would play long after my lips had given out, even after they would begin tasting bloody, to prove something or other. The bruises on my lips finally calcified until they were tough enough to play high and low for long periods without giving out. I went around with a strange, purple mouth.

I was directly accosted as regards the Lloyd rumor only once. In May, I was at a spaghetti supper sponsored by the Lions Club. I went alone, because I liked spaghetti, or the brand of it mixed up for the Lions Club by the only Italian lady in town. "Music's golden tongue," she said as I went by with my tray. I did not expect the smile of genuine approval I saw on her face. It was pure sunshine from Naples. God be kind to her. I ate my spaghetti, roll and salad, and thought of Italy, the beauty of it and its immense distance from Dream of Pines.

I went out by the storeroom door and down the greasy steps to the parking lot. This group standing by a Ford noticed me, and a fellow on the second-string football team, a small halfback type, started yelling to me that I was a queer, a queer, a queer. He wouldn't quit. I sized him up, and noticed that Tonnie Ray Reese was leaning beside him, maybe as the date who had put him up to it. And I'm sure the guy had been drinking. I ran over to him, grabbed him by the shirt, and hit him in the face. The poor bastard didn't know anything to do but try to body-block me; he destroyed himself missing me over and over and crashing on the blacktop. Then I dragged him up against the car window and hit him around the mouth, using the Trojan ring with a raised knuckle again. He commenced sobbing and finally fell down cold-cocked. I myself had the sick

72

heaves. I felt all that Lions Club Italian sauce climbing up in me. My fists hung down throbbing and there were tears in my eyes. I don't think I was meant to be a fighter.

"Prick," Tonnie Ray Reese whispered to me. "Bully." Tonnie Ray had beer or wine on her breath.

I didn't have strength enough left to contradict her. I only looked at her face and saw the glum mouth and the lusterless wax-paper sort of skin and a broken curl of hair at the eyebrow. We used to think of killing you, I thought. I used to think of ironing you to death, Tonnie Ray. The Roach. Made it this far, that you go out with a halfback and get socked away on two beers, have you? Were intending a little scrimmage with him later, were you? Were going to show him a whole view of one of your crabshell kneecaps, were you, or even shuck off the sneakers from your claws during a moment of gay abandon? To be written up about slyly in "Who and Who" of the school newspaper: "*Cute* Tonnie is not ignoring a certain suave tailback. In fact, as W&W has it . . ." meaning they are mutually masturbating each other to death. I was getting back my wind. I introduced myself to her in as literate a fashion as I was able, sweeping my hand out a little.

"Prick. Bully. But not a queer. Your little brother lied about me."

From then on to the end of high school, Tonnie Ray had a crush on *me*. And, by way of her tremendous mouth, my reputation around Dream of Pines improved.

7 / Horning In–C.

In June I left for New York.

The old man finally took me seriously as a musician when I got a letter from Dr. Perrino inviting me to take part in what he called a "brass clinic" at N.Y.U. Perrino was the man with the horseshoe beard from Eastman who'd heard me down at Shreveport. I told the old man I wanted to go.

"I wanted you to go. But I want you to promise me one thing. That you'll go over to Columbia University and talk to the dean."

"What about?"

"About you *going* to Columbia."

"Listen," I said. This was hard to put. "I don't think I want to beg *any*-body to let me into his college. Don't ask me to do that."

"Not *beg*. Tell about yourself. Tell about your music," says the old man. "Use your style. You have a style. You're my son, aren't you?" He grins, and blushes.

I suppose he meant I would woo that dean at Columbia as if I were Jack Paar of New York and the dean were a horny old maid. I didn't have that kind of confidence. It surprised me that the old man had this much trust in any "style" I had. I'd never heard anything about this. Could the old man be thinking of me as a seventeen-year-old version of himself, making a smash in New York on his first visit? Yes.

What a shame it was he never got closer than a Gray Line tour to the city. He saw it, all right, a couple of years back, gorged his eyes on the skyline—all those frightening gray clusters of turrets, banked against one another like fingernails growing from the hands of corpses—and on the harbor, and on the brick caverns everywhere. It hurt him in his soul to be seeing the city only as a tourist, though; he felt awfully left out and inadequate and went into a six-month gloom back in Dream of Pines. When I was in college, my mother sent me letters about her trying to coax him out of it. He would have loved to be *invited* to New York, like me. I'm sure he thought New York was calling me to its marble palaces of Art. I lied and told him I'd drop by on the dean of Columbia.

New York. Perrino taught us trumpet men in a basement room overlooking Washington Square. There was a huge green lawn out back with a wide brick walkway running down it. There were adult people walking by barefooted out there, and lots of beards and pipes, books, but most memorable, queer lovely girls with heavy eye make-up, jeans and tee shirts, and pagan-seeming sandals. No fool could deny New York its women. I'm the type that can pick out obscure graces in a crippled hag, but I know the kind of beauty that burns your eyes, too. First night I was in New York, I bought myself some tennis shoes and wore them without socks, like I'd seem some of the milder beatniks do, and walked around the fountain at Washington Square thinking to pick up some romance. And I did.

This group of four girls came up to the edge of the fountain where I was sitting all tired out with trying to attract a lover, which is hard to do when you're too shy to make the first move. I merely said hello, and they got very friendly. They wanted to know where I was from. Eventually they invited me over to their place for a Wine Party. They giggled and implied that this was an event that was going to tear the rafters out of the house.

"Sounds good. Am I going to have a girlfriend?" I said.

"Oh. We're all engaged to be *married*," says the brunette.

But the red-haired girl in the back that I hadn't noticed much came up and slipped her arm in mine coyly.

"I'll be your girlfriend tonight," she lisped in a voice of antic falsity, playing that game of pretend-lover that certain kinds of girls like to play with unthreatening men. I didn't much like this, but I was taking anything New York would give me, and so we paraded over to their place. She put her pale hand in mine.

On the walk we ran into a crowd having a hassle with a big cop. The trouble was he was running two colored musician beggars off the square and the crowd didn't like it. But someone in one of the brownstone houses had complained of the noise. I looked over at the musicians, expecting to see a trombone or something like that around somewhere, but what I saw was an utterly destroyed little man who seemed made out of brown wires slumping beside the cop with a scratched bass ukulele in his hand; the ukulele had the back completely out of it; he had his hand full of small change. His partner was on the other side of the cop, looking sullen and paying no mind to any of us. He held a comb covered with wet tissue paper. On his head was a sea cap of dirty white with crossed captain's anchors insignia above the bill.

"Officer, who are they hurting? We had to get up close to even *hear* them!" pleaded an older bohemian sort of woman who had a pigtail plait which whipped back and forth. Everybody in the crowd looked anguished. "They were lift-

ing the spirits of this fucking slumpy swamp!" cried a
bald-headed fellow in an army jacket. I looked around at
the terrain of the square, which was very green and solid. I
really expected the cop to come out with his billy club
soon, with the crowd pressing in and shrieking at him.
There must've been a dozen of them. He was huge and
thick, in his double-breasted blue, and he bit his lip reflec-
tively as if deciding who to bash first. "Don't be a *tool!*"
somebody yelled. "Why don't you arrest the goddam square
that complained?!" "I'm not *arresting* anybody," the cop
says finally. "You go around telling people to get off of free
turf, though, man." ". . . by what philosophy was these
two a crime?" moaned this one guy shaking his head and
spreading his hands; I think this was the first real Brooklyn
voice I ever heard.

The cop answered him, *"This* is your philosophy: you
want New York to turn into a town wit' streets full of beggars, like D.C.? You want to get hustled for a quarter every
time you put your foot in the street? We're cleaning up the
beggars."

"What you mean is you're sending these men back to
Harlem. I'll bet you'll give a free ride back, courtesy of the
Police Department, huh?"

"Everybody shut their goddam mouth!" said the man in
the army jacket. "Let these men do their number and you
see if they're not earning their money. O.K.? All right, everybody step back and let's hear them." The cop frowned
but dropped back a couple of feet from the musicians. The
crowd eased back too, falling in like a jury gallery around
the girls and me. The bald-headed fellow stayed in front
and got up on his toes with raised hands like a conductor.
He thrashed downward. "Hit it, cats, like never before!"
The Negroes didn't stir immediately. But they did play,
with the little morose man stomping on the ground and
strumming and fingering the bass uke for all he was worth,
while the taller fellow in the sea cap waved back and forth
with the comb and tissue paper. I couldn't hear a damned
thing. I attempted to get in closer, stretching the arm of the
redhead, who didn't want to move but held my hand. I
heard some low thrumming, a foot hitting the ground, and
an occasional buzz off the comb. No song, exactly, got
through to where I was, only a scratching beat and a low
hum. It was like hearing rock-and-roll from somewhere far,

far away. Even so, I got caught up in it, danced around a little, and attempted to draw up the redhead in an embrace. My mind lifted and I became rather careless hearing this scratchy music coming off the pavement. The girl didn't find it agreeable. "Stop it, stop it," she whispered. "There isn't anything to dance to." "I'll kiss you. I'll try to do other things. Right now we've *got* to dance!" I found myself saying. God, I felt torn-away and reckless off this scratchy music. I never even looked to see how she was taking it. My feet and hips went out every way. The musicians quit.

"Well, I believe that settles it," says the cop. "Nobody'd call *that* music."

"*I'd* call it music, you deaf shit!" yells the man in the army jacket, who was still dancing solitary. "These men *earn* their way. I think *that* settles it!" cries the Brooklynite, who had been bumping and snapping fingers while they played. "Let's pay these men for the entertainment." He thrusts down in the pocket of his big gray pants, and everybody in the crowd is opening purses and going down in pants for change. The cop steps between the musicians again to prohibit talk any further. His hands are up. But behind him the subtle darkie on uke has his backless instrument turned over, and wiggles it, inviting donations. Silver flies past the cop and strikes the wood, sometimes getting and sometimes glancing off into the grass or on the pavement. A *binging* music of falling coins sets up around the musicians and the cop. The cop holds up the billy club at last, and this grim stick is standing on his hand about nine feet in the air. I myself have a handful of quarters, dimes, and nickels ready to loft over him to the musicians and am just waiting for a decent chance. I see the man who played the comb sprawling on the pavement behind the cop; his sea cap is off, he is grabbing everywhere for coins. Somebody's legs spread and I get a view of this, and also the gun and bullet belt of the cop moving toward us more. "Come on, honey!" says the redhead. She pulls on me and tells me there's going to be some trouble if we don't get away. I see her light face is drawn thin in terror, and her mouth is all pretty and wet. I get an instant lust pang; her face is parallel to the ground while she tugs at me; the other girls are retreating, and I notice an incidental panty under a flaring dress. But I raise my fist filled with coins.

The cop has come up three feet from the crowd and is

77

grabbing hands of people who are still trying to get coins to the musicians. Fellows around me start throwing the coins hard; the crowd starts *stoning* the cop with quarters and nickels. People keep back the dimes because they don't carry well. The cop begins to get stung; some of these lowbred bastards around me are throwing at his face, and pink slices appear on his cheeks as he tries to hold down the hands. A huge fifty-cent piece sails against his brow and blood falls down through his lashes almost instantaneously. The action pauses. Then everybody falls back a little and starts throwing even harder. The coins sail in coveys toward the cop. I suddenly realize that the idea is to throw your coins *through* the cop to reach the musicians. But what a cop! I think. He's still standing with outspread arms, club in one hand, blood streaming off his forehead into his eye, and a look of placid *boredom* on his wide face, while the coins pelt him. I got the feeling he considered all this child's play, with him as the resigned papa. Behind him the Negro man is spread-eagled on the sidewalk with hands reaching and heels scraping, trying to drag in the falling money. The knees show through the holes in his trousers. The poor bastard was trying to make a net out of himself. This does it; I throw my coins softly toward the walk, but a couple of them drop on the cop's knee. Mine was the last bunch. Everybody else had run out of coins. The cop sees me and comes alive. "Oh. A smart-ass, huh?" He wades into the crowd and they split, turning back their faces toward me. I'm too shocked to move, and feel the girl's hand rip out of mine. Without hesitation, as I turn away from him, he whales me across the back with the billy. My body leaves the ground and I come down crumbled in pain and running amuck, shouting "God damn!" The cop's shoes thunder behind me. "All right, Mister Filth-mouth! Go talk that one over!" he roars. Then he crunches me a farewell one across the back of my thigh with that piece of lumber again. It was a nasty, scalding hurt, but I stayed on my feet out of sheer panic and found myself running low on the sidewalk, legs and shoes flying by my face. I stopped by the fountain and looked back. Why? Why? I'm wondering. Why did he hit me? What's wrong with this place? I felt spooky all of a sudden in this city. Those concrete rungs around the square pool seemed unnaturally gray and morbid to me. The brownstone apartments were stuck together

78

with the spit of old, crazy men. The ache of my backbone and thigh taught me there was no happiness in this place.

The bald-headed man in the army jacket is holding the sleeve of the cop's uniform and berating the cop with obscenities. The cop is shaking his head. The beggars are slinking off, sea cap and neck of ukulele high. The Brooklynite is facing my way giving a shrug I can make out from fifty yards. "Who . . . ?!" I can't help hollering out at all of them. "Who am I to get done like that? . . . What kind of country do you think this is? . . . This place has got some goddamn rules, hasn't it?"

"No sir. You poor bayah-bee," comes this voice from beside me.

I haven't been deserted by my girls. They are all four standing beside me, the redhead foremost; I notice that each girl is wearing differently colored pastel tennis shoes of the same type—there's blue, orange, yellow, and violet. The redhead reminds me of everything Ann Mick could have been if she'd taken care of herself. Her name is Sylvia; her mouth is constantly red and wet, and she's used some chalk over her eyes to make the upper half of her face glow dull green and sultry. The others are not beauties, but they all have a little style. I mean they poise around on their calves giving the impression they have the universe by the tail, being engaged to be married and having run through all the preliminaries of romance. I can pass them by without any grief, but as for the redhead who's offered to play at love tonight with me—even the hint of red in a woman's hair makes me gimp around like a pogo stick; puts me up in the air like a pole-vaulter hung up over the bar and dreaming about his shocking soft fall into the sawdust.

"He hit you, didn't he?" remarks the brunette.

"Poor bayah-bee! I was trying to tell you about this crazy place and get you away from that policeman," says the red-haired girl. She put her arm around me so far her fingers met my navel. "Now you're hurt. Listen: we were in Central Park one afternoon and this *Negro* man jumped out of the bushes and started hitting this woman and she just *laughed. Laifed.*"

"Oh, Sylvie. It was *apparent* that they *knew* each other very well," says another girl, whose face was like that of a cat without any hair.

"It was a *white* lady," Sylvia explained.

79

"Oh, Sylvia," the others sighed, exasperated.

"You sound like you're from the South," I said.

It turned out they all were from the South. They were coeds from the University of North Carolina doing a summer session at N.Y.U., principally for the reason of living in New York for eight weeks. Their stay was drawing to a close. They had had to study to make their grades, and nothing of particular excitement had happened to them, until me. They thought my getting beat up by the cop was exquisite. "I'll bet that hurt," says the humid-eye girl with a blotched yellow face. I never could figure out whether it was a peeling suntan or a disease. "You were really uncontrollable dancing and throwing those coins at the cop. You were really an item. How old are you?" I lied. I told them I was from Tulane up here in New York to learn jazz and told them other false halves of stories proving that New Orleans, my birthplace and ancient lover, was holding its breath waiting for my return to one of the premium night clubs on Bourbon Street. I had a lot of Italian and French names at my disposal, and managed to lapse imperceptibly into a Cajun dialect that had them all groping to understand me. I recited straight through a brief history of the Acadians (I *did* learn something in Louisiana history!), which really put them on the marvel. Except for Sylvia, the girls were tepid academic sorts. I caught on that they resented Sylvia's betraying they were all from the South. And as for their speech, I couldn't understand much, with them trying so hard to lose their accents and bend their mouths around some weary idea of New Yorker dialect. A lot of sputtering and pronouncing of *Ayie* for *I*. The thicker they came on with the New York, the thicker I came on with the Cajun.

We walked past places like the Gaslight Cafe and several clothing and music shops on MacDougal Street and went off into an alley where the door of their apartment was. Sylvia kept her arm around me and mentioned the fact that I must be still hurting and made other soft, nurselike sounds in my ear that the others couldn't hear. She was truly one of the *sweet* girls of the South. She never used bad language, a cigarette was a tremendous experience to her, she was extravagantly *interested* in me, she had popping, lashy gray eyes, and the innocence of a World War One

80

bandage-mistress. She kept her skirt over her knees and sat sideways.

The Wine Party amounted to one bottle of champagne in the house and me as the only visitor from the other sex. The furniture was benches, scattered cushions, and books with notebook paper leaking out. The girls drank half a glass of champagne and started complaining immediately of being sleepy and drunk. That left me half of the magnum to myself, and I was feeling no pain by the second glass. One of them got up and played a Maynard Ferguson record on a dinky portable phonograph, for my benefit, I guess. Ferg depressed me, as usual, sailing about three registers above his band where there weren't even any notes, as far as I knew. I told them—sour grapes—that Ferg was quite all right as a "novelty" trumpet man. It got them excited that I was able to cut a pure genius like Maynard. *"Technically,* he's competent," I threw in, implying there was something lacking about him that certainly no one in this room except me could possibly understand. Then I became the intellectual idol of the crowd.

"I never thought about it, but there *is* something wrong . . . something is missing . . . something *bothers* me about modern jazz," said the owner of the phonograph, the brunette, and I did not hasten to point out that Beethoven would sound like a tin dish thrown down the alley on that music box of hers.

"Anyway, let's *dance!*" I said, getting up. Ferg and crowd were into a hard bop number now, and I couldn't keep still. Apparently these gals weren't used to dancing and thought it was a bit gauche and goofy to do, but I had them all up imitating me in a little number called the beaubitch back home, which requires a lot of shrugging in time with hands on the ribs. All five of us were out on the floor, kicking paper around and jarring the phonograph. Ten minutes of this, and we'd passed high tide in the party.

"My God, what a night!" the girl with the dehaired cat's face sighed. She and the other two thought they'd turn in. God knows what passed for fun among this crowd—probably a flat tire on the bus back to North Carolina. I noticed the apartment was strange in that each girl went to a separate sleeping room, tiny rooms; each room had a thin plywood door, and the girls closed each one resolutely.

Then I heard *breathing* in back of the doors, and a bump of wood somewhere.

"You know what those girls are doing, don't you? "whispered Sylvia. We were sitting on the longest wooden bench. I didn't know what she was talking about. "They're all listening to us. They're leaning against the doors holding their breath."

"Why?"

"They know I'm engaged. They want to hear what you and I are going to do. They know I like you."

"Really? Thank you. I like you, Sylvia. What can they hear?"

"Almost everything. They can hear in here just about what we can hear in there." I listened and did in fact hear one girl who seemed to have her lungs pressed against the door. "Let's just talk a while. We can turn up the record player."

She talked a long while, beginning on an excursus about her roommates and ending with her boyfriend. It seems all four of the girls had gotten so scared of New York by their second week that they had each written letters to the boys back home saying Yes, darling, she would marry him. Sealed With A Kiss. Dumped into the envelope almost an ounce of an intriguing perfume she had bought in a weird shop in Greenwich Village. Caused the faithful weather cocks to spin around deliriously on the roof down at Charlotte, or Ashville, Winston-Salem, or Rayford, once the boy received the letter.

As for Sylvia Wyche, the girl from Durham, N. C., she was affianced to a sad cat who couldn't even make his C's at Chapel Hill. He was from Rayford and drove fast cars which his old man, an old bard as concerns gasburning engines, rigged up for him. Sylvia said this boy was good-looking and she had never figured out any way of forgetting him. She said this boy, in his one semester at Chapel Hill, was the best-dressed boy on campus. He wore seven different suits, rotating them every week, and her heart went out to him and his family because she knew his folks couldn't afford to dress him like that and he wasn't even *comfortable* in those Ivy League suits, but wanted to make himself proud so badly as a college man. He attended all his classes and received D's and F's. Sylvia liked him also because he knew when to call it quits. "Here, I'm going to make a B at

N.Y.U. in History of American Indians, but I'm still just so *unhappy*," she sighed. But her lover-boy went back to Rayford and getting speeding tickets and having his driver's license suspended and working at the fiberglass plant.

She almost never stopped talking about him, and sung out his name, *Charles! Charles!* so it went echoing in agony down the hall of doors.

"Are you really everything you say you are, Harriman? Are you really a trumpet player from Tulane that plays on Bourbon Street in the night clubs? Are you as sweet as you seem, even so, when you know that you really ought to be swell-headed and have nothing to do with a nothing like me?" Sylvia had finished a second glass of champagne and was flinging around doing her limbs everywhere. I swore to her that I had always tried to be sweet when I saw somebody like her, who deserved it. She put her hand on the neck of this striped shirt I was wearing and dragged it down so it peeled off my shoulders.

I had been shyly cupping her breast in my hand since we'd slid off the bench and eased to the floor (hard as a bone, ugly tiles of brown), but I was so high from champagne it was like my hand was working separate from me. I didn't expect that Sylvia would be this serious so soon, and my body was still lax, my head still thinking about poor Charles in the fiberglass plant down at Rayford.

"Let's get these out of the way," Sylvia said. She reached up in her skirt and dragged out her panties, which were yellow. She got them over her blue tennis shoes with a little effort and kept them clutched in her hand. I had my arms under hers and was not daring to look. The phonograph was going high. Sylvia stared at me for several moments, giving me her face. She was tense and desperate, and the long hairs along her forehead were lying stiff in an upside-down crown of red, and I could see tears of sweat bursting out of her pores; her eyes were green and watery.

"*Please* don't think this is stupid, but—Do you know what a girl's hymen is? That's what makes a girl a virgin. I don't want you to go through that. That's for Charles. I know I have some space before you get to that, and I want . . . Please, now."

I was kneeling between her legs studying the white, unfreckled thighs, the shocking red hair with roots of brown. She was lifting the purple wound below it so very

83

high. Her tennis shoes came back to rest under her thighs. What a sight! There are some I've talked to who have no trouble comprehending the beauty and slavish, passive cunt of a woman, with its thorny, rather prohibitive hair. But me! I'm so sensitive toward these way-out foreign shores, it's like I'm a blubbering near-corpse washed up in Rangoon harbor, with crabs ganged around me and pinching me out of the water, and I stand on the beach seeing a temple of jewels in a flying architecture. So I go in.

"Not too far!" she begs of me. My first woman is telling me that. "Don't, don't, don't, don't. Please, please, please. No, No, No!" These are the words I got from Sylvia, who labors with brown shirt and pearl buttons and pale blue skirt lying around her stomach. Her tennis shoes flap on the floor. Sylvia looks down astonished. She looks up at me, with some kind of cautious love on her face.

"I love you," she huffs. "Again! I don't çare."

I got out of there. The phonograph had stopped sometime about three-quarters way through our act. I could hear the silence and all our sighing. The hall doors were bowing in, cracking at the joints of the plywood; the girls had listened to enough and were *lying* on their doors to hear more. Sylvia had been loud. "A-a-a-a-a-a-ahhhhhhhhhhhhhh-wrrrrrr!" she'd yelled and had kept it up almost all the way.

One thing about New York: you really *can* tell somebody goodbye. You aren't going to see them again. Not in the bus station, not in the train station, not at the airport, and even if you do see one another (like I saw Sylvia at the airport with her friends, running back and forth along the seats, so nervous about her life that she couldn't stand to take anything as slow as a bus back to North Carolina, and her friends were raising their eyes and seeing her off), even if you *do* see one another, this is Idlewild Airport, and there are ten people between you and whoever you don't want to see.

I left the apartment with Sylvia hanging on my jaws thrusting her tongue back in my throat with French kissing. *Pop!* I'm free. Out in the alley walking toward MacDougal Street, breathing the warm midnight of the hottest June New York has had in a while—says the radio back at the hotel. I mount the stairs of my hotel and lie down to sleep on a bed between a trumpet-player from Oklahoma and another one from Oregon, high school prodigies like me. I think our hotel had a name like The Bibi. Anyway, it was in walking distance of N.Y.U.

Perrino, still sporting his horseshoe beard and instructing trumpets, was odd. Eastman had given him license. He came to us wailing; he had his hands over his head, and you could see written back in his eyes that he had obtained some ruinous Ph.D. from somewhere. His tie knot waggled down on his open collar, and his clothes were like bandages coming apart over a horrid wound to his chest and soul. He wore sandals over black socks, which seemed to represent the same anguish at his feet. He was slightly chubby, with bags under his eyes like rotting bananas, and behaved as if he were the last gasp of Italianism in America. We rehearsed a Shostakovich brass chorale under him. He was never satisfied. He shrieked and kicked over the stand, bellowing that we were all out of tune.

Toward the last of the clinic session he caught several of us watching the girls through the window of the basement while we were playing. He charged over and raked down the Venetian blinds.

"You watch *me*," he screamed. "What you think I'm doing with this stick—picking my nose with it?" He ran the baton in and out of his fist and closed his eyes, then opened them hugely. Then he grew cold and bit both his lips. "I hear all these original *styles* going round this room. All you little green-asses want to have some *style*, don't you? You want to be big jazz men. Huh?" He collapsed, hands to knees.

"What?!!" Nobody had said anything. "Listen here, shitties, don't try to distinguish yourself with an original tone when you're just beginners. You play all the notes set in front of you for a while, and you'll develop some style out of *that*. Music. You have to know enough of it. Music will *teach* you your tone and your style. Trust it. Do the notes," he pleaded. He ran toward the back of our ensemble. "Don't look, but I'm getting out my thing and laying it on the shoulder of one of you boys. Nobody knows whose shoulder I've got my thing on." We heard a sound like a belt buckle hitting the floor. Nobody looked back. "You must play this chorale *as a team*, nobody having any style, or I'll come around and lay it on *your* shoulder. The man who has the most individual style has a thing laying on his shoulder!" He counted us to start, and we played the cho-

85

rale in a perfect, soft harmony, nobody wanting to stand out.

"That's more like what Shostakovich wanted!" Perrino exclaimed. He jumped up and down to the front of the ensemble. "Only it was too timid. What's the matter? Is anybody afraid of getting an old thing *in his mouth?* Do you take me for a *fairy?"* He started limp-wristing and lisping around in a great imitation of the Prince of Queers. "You silly gooses!" he hissed to us.

Oh, Perrino was odd. But his lesson stuck. Forever after that I hesitated to play with any volume or any particular style for fear some dago wild man would be sneaking up behind me to lay his prod on my shoulder. Perrino had a great bit to do with destroying me as a jazz man. Our last night we did a free brass concert on the mall in Central Park. The public loved us, and Perrino wore a sharp blue suit and intimated over the microphone that he had taken us bunch of yokels and whipped us into style in about two nights. Perrino was a monstrous bastard from the word go.

My last night in New York, I went out by myself again and sat on the Washington Square fountain. Everybody was having a good time. The pool was thick with people sloshing about. It turned dusk. I saw the bald-headed fellow in the army jacket again. He was having a water fight with the side of the pool. Then a big Negro waded up to me. It was about dusk then. "Y'know, man. I know I lead an essentially nonexistent existence," he says. He brought up his hands, and they dripped water all over my pants. Then he lay down in the pool and seemed worlds away from me. I couldn't answer him; I didn't know what he meant. But I liked his calling me *man.* I did like that. Everybody at home was so fond of calling me son and Harry, in condescending tones of voice. "Y'know, man . . ." echoed through me. It was as if he'd known I'd had my first woman. "Y'know, man . . . Y'know, man." New York and Washington Square weren't so bad. All those adult types out in the pool having such a good time. And at least one man who took me seriously. *Two* men! I thought. That cop wouldn't have come after any juvenile like he came after me. This was a week after the cop incident, and I was all ready to settle down and see what became of me in New York. Then the airplane took me out, with this boy staring

86

down at the lights and not holding back a tear when it came.

"You saw the dean at Columbia."

"Yes, yes, yes. Nothing doing. Columbia is all filled up already with its quota for five years."

"He liked you, didn't he?"

"He said he wanted me to go there. If there was any way . . ."

This was the old man and me. Something had happened to me. I had seen a little of the world and was able to lie freely. I have no idea what Columbia University looks like to this day. I saw nothing but Coney Island and Greenwich Village. I gave the old man a phony description of Wall Street and Madison Avenue, which he fed on. The Museum of Modern Art for my mother. "It's just too much to fathom, Mother." Mother wanted to know about New York generally. "The city didn't do much for me. It's just concrete blocks with people trying to live under them and between them." My mother was delighted. She knew there wasn't any place more imposing then Memphis. She copied what I said down in this diary that she kept about once every five years; she kept notes on important events of her lifetime in that book.

8 / Where's Your Daddy?

I always wanted to ask Harley Butte, "Where is your daddy?" "Who is he?" "What does he think of *you?*" His mother was black. She lived in town, not too far from Harley's own house, up a hill full of dandelions and wild clover, in a house with a huge rectangular porch in front; the house had a sunken first story or basement, and the porch was on the second level and had steep wooden steps running up to it. These steps had no rails; they were about a yard wide— just a slight improvement over a ladder. The porch itself was a sloping platform on which four decrepit rocking chairs sat; there was a banister running across it, but only about a third of the original support sticks were left. Some of the other sticks were lying on the ground under the porch. This house was a ruined summer home that some white family had lived in seventy-five years ago. A forest of tremendous oaks and beeches used to stand here; Spanish moss and shade hung around it. Just below it was a lake wider than a mile. Now, the bed of that lake held all of niggertown. Driving across the tracks at the mill, you really *decline* into niggertown. Once I heard about this lake that used to be there, I thought of being underwater when I passed Ann Mick's house and went on down into the spade community. I'd see colored people down in these brown hills and think about them as fish, dark fish breathing something different from what I did, some thick gas in brown water with the gases of the paper mills boiling on the top of it. Harley's mother's house was without paint, and the timbers stood forth in a dark, grainy brown like a limb you'd pull out of an ancient lake. She was the only one there. Harley himself lived in a neat cottage with a white fence on a rise on the other side of niggertown. His mother called herself Mrs. Butte, and must've been about sixty-five.

Butte was her only son. He was cream-colored. Yellow. Almost orange. Who was his father, and where was he? That's about the only thing I never asked Harley.

He started coming to the house at night in June. He was worried and upset. "Where's yoah daddy?" he'd ask.

My old man had treated him very square, and Harley was concerned Ode Elann might think he had been stringing him along these years making him think he was interested in staying on at the mattress factory all his life. He liked his job as foreman, and it was a very responsible job, and maybe he had given the impression that he had sworn his life to the Monroe Mattress Factory. He'd gotten excited about his job at odd times.

But he was in the process of finishing his degree at Grell A. & M. and already had the offer to direct the Gladiator Band at that high school in Mississippi. One hundred and forty Negro musicians were waiting on him in south Mississippi. They were hidden in the pine trees holding their breaths until he got there, gave the signal, and they would prance out gloriously in their green uniforms. Harley checked on this. The band where he was going wore *green*

88

uniforms, with white filigree and legstripes. His head was turning around on its stem in anticipation.

He told me this, but I know he never got it across fully to the old man until the very last time he came to our house, in August.

First time he appeared, it was nine at night and the old man wasn't in the house yet. He was still at Kiwanis meeting. Harley drove in the garage in his new Plymouth and I let him in the door. We had nothing to say to each other. Harley wore a light suit of tan, a blue shirt with a zag-striped tie and Marine shoes battered to gray with scuffs. It was what the scholar-studs down at Tulane were wearing. Harley had taken to wearing black horn rims, too, and had the beginning of that little scruffy musician's beard the old man groaned about all summer. Butte was putting up some brave vibrations, all right.

I told him he could wait in the den. I told him cautiously that he looked very . . . jazzy tonight. He pulled out a pipe and said something I didn't catch.

"Huh?"

"I said jazz doesn't have anything to do'th the way I'm dressed. Jazz is going to hell in a boat made out of a Negro's asshole."

I know my face hung out and I was even slightly embarrassed. Then Butte laughed. His voice was always hoarse from yelling at the student musicians out at Grell. His eyes boiled mirthfully over the match he put to the pipe. Butte was still rather pretty, in his yellow way, even at thirty. And always shocking, like a baby jerked up abruptly to adult size.

"You like classical music, then. You're a musician, aren't you?"

It turned out he liked the march from *Lohengrin*, the march from *Aida*, the marches of Purcell, assorted British and French marches, most recent march music in general, but above *all* that, John Philip Sousa. Oh, there had been times when he'd felt low and sorry and didn't think he liked Sousa any more, for months. Then he would climb up out of his gloom, he would wade out of that prune-syrup swamp of misery; something would lift him up, like hearing a march over his car radio when they were giving college football scores, or just waking up one morning feeling good and *reasonable* for a change. And he would rediscover

89

Sousa. Sousa would have changed a little. Sousa would be a little wilder, Sousa would be more playful with the horns, Sousa would be less cautious, Sousa would be tending a little more toward chaos, toying with the very structure, the magnificently ritualized harmonic of the March form itself. Harley saw as he picked up a score-sheet of some well-known Sousa march and went down the parts with his finger, saw for the first time, the titanic *laughter* of the giant musician. Like in the Finale of "Stars and Stripes Forever" where the silly piccolo whistles out an obligato over the melody and the whole band. Sounds like a god striding the earth, tongue in cheek, whistling a mischievous tune to himself. It would be Sousa again. Sousa bolder, Sousa better, Sousa even more uncanny. He read all the old scores again and heard all the new voices in the formulas of his wizard John Philip. And then he and John Philip were ready to sail together again.

"Since I was fifteen I spent most of my time liking Sousa," Butte chuckled. Butte was the proudest slave I ever laid eyes on. He became a scholarly lunatic, an absolute pedant, when he talked about Sousa. It was hard to shut him off. My mother called him from the kitchen. She was putting back the globe on the ceiling light after changing the light bulbs and asked him to help her. It didn't bother him, apparently, that he had been in the house less than thirty minutes and was already the houseboy at beck and call. He put his pipe in the ashtray, took off his coat, and backed toward the kitchen still jabbering away at me. I'd just asked him if march music was the *only* kind of music he liked; didn't he get bored with it after a while?

"I've asked myself that . . . am I a one-way fool? No, I've heard every kind of music and liked bits and pieces of some. But I got a reason and an answer I'll tell you . . ."

"Harley, I'm *holding* this thing up! . . ." my mother called again.

"Yes mam . . . Wait a minute, man, I'll tell you."

He rushed into the kitchen apologizing and I sat there on the couch having forgot for a moment how queer Harley was because again somebody—another colored fellow—had drawn me into his confidence by calling me "man." Maybe only in casual lingo, but "man" again. Back to Washington Square in New York and the fellow at the fountain disclosing to me, "You know, man . . ." and God knows what

90

followed about the secret of his person—a little experience has told me he was most certainly high on some drug and was being the tourist's quintessential beatnik but I don't care. "Man" was an agreeable way to start a conversation. You flatter the other guy by acknowledging that he's made a few scenes too. It's nigger jazz talk, I guess, and I've believed it for many a year now.

But you know Harley wouldn't have cared for this sort of talk. To him, hearing the blues was like having some smegma-covered old uncle wrap around you and slobber in your ear.

There was a terrible bump and crash on the kitchen floor. My mother squealed. I ran in and saw Harley getting up out of a mass of glass fragments. The stool was lying over in the corner. Harley had come down with the light globe in his hands after the stool skidded out from under him.

Dark blood was streaming in a web over one of his hands. He put his arm in the sink and turned on the water. Mother saw him gripping his wrist and said she'd get some bandages. Butte grunted and I heard a piece of glass plink in the sink.

"How is it?" I asked him.

"Well, it's almost like cutting yourself." He stared at the wound and sneered slightly. He noticed me looking at the blood and lowered his arm out of sight in the sink.

The healthy maroon blood flowing out of Butte's cut got to me. I felt tremendously sorry for him. He stood there bleeding like any normal person, accepting it, not too surprised that there really was blood in his body, holding the wound out of simple duty to himself, and trying not to make much mess. And *hiding* his wound, a bit hangdog and ashamed, trying to get it out of my sight. It's how we all act when we get hurt, but at that moment the whole thing struck me as unbearably pathetic—the glass all over the floor, the knocked-over stool, Butte's utter helplessness when he fell. In the next room a minute ago Butte was a clown. Now he was a full-blooded man, and it was almost more than I could take. When I meet a man head-on as a man and not as an item, I always have to double back. My first impulse is to become chaotically polite; a hospitable ninny. I reached down to get my shirt tails out and rip my shirt off to make a bandage for him, when the old man

91

comes in the door and meets my mother with her arms full of bath rags and white gauze.

Tonight the old man has digressed wildly from his normal dressing habits. Perhaps he has seen Jack Paar with something similar on, or maybe he is trying to prove that age is only making him more of a sport. He wears a blazer of light blue, that is, the blazer is *draped* over his shoulders and the arms are dangling while his real arms are pressed against his stomach; his shirt is open at the throat and there a kerchief, an *Ascot* of navy and red splotches, hangs around his neck. On his feet are glistening brown RAF boots. A new cigarette, most likely lit right outside the door, burns neglected in one hand, fine celebrity style. He's coming on stronger than I ever dared to, and he's around fifty. There's *my* daddy, Butte. I loved the old man at that instant. What guts it took to wear that outfit to Kiwanis meeing. To be president of Kiwanis that year, and show up in his Jack Paar gear; wrap the gavel, standing up with the movie-tone Ascot bursting out of his shirt. They would say he was absurd; the men with the clip-on black ties, they would think he was being struck by an indecent youth-panic in his mellowing years; he would be *embarrassing* them, those of them that were sure by now if they were sure of anything that ninety per cent of the good life lay in taking age mildly. Or maybe not. Maybe they patted him on the back for his courage and were good envious joes. God knows the crowd my old man ran with at Kiwanis. I never did. But anyway, how many hours had Ode Elann spent in his study worrying about wearing the duds he bought? Uncountable. To him, it must've been like coming out in leotards and cape with golden signet letter of his initial on his chest. (I heard later from my mother that this particular night at Kiwanis it was the old man's duty to introduce and make social with a female journalist speaking to the Kiwanians as guest lecturer. He doted on the photograph she'd sent from her office in Chicago, because she looked hard, passionate, and beautiful. But that picture had been taken in the 1940's and by the time she got to the Dream of Pines Kiwanis Club, she was a rueful gray hag who quoted the prose of John Dos Passos and did nothing else but drink an amazing amount of coffee and say "Pardon?" to anything anybody asked her. Terrible disappointment for the old man, in his Ascot, and I pity and love him even

92

more for dressing to please that tough big-city gal in the 1940's photograph.)

So the old man has entréed into the kitchen and is hunting for that assurance from Mother and me that his clothes are all right, anyway, and dashing; that we will take him back into the house even as the crazy Riviera cosmopolitan free-liver that he sometimes is. And he sees my mother with an armload of bandages that could just as well be for the personal wounds he has suffered showing up in this outfit for that Chicago journalist woman who so badly failed her photograph.

Then he sees Harley at the sink and notices all the glass mess in the kitchen. Harley is wearing his striped tie and blue shirt, and for a moment there is a question of who is more the wardrobe stud between them. The old man advances his RAF boots a little, and they seem to win hands-down over Harley's scuffed Marine shoes. Perhaps the old man has never seen Harley in even this much a real suit before, and what a bracing striped necktie Butte is wearing. The old man recedes a little. The edge of his effect has been taken off somewhat by Harley. Resentment and concern cross his face. But what is this? The high-yellow man has his arms in the sink. Harley turns around fully toward the old man, and my father winces at the sight of Butte's young beard. He doesn't like it. It doesn't quite do for a foreman at the mattress factory. It looks like, or makes you think of, some kind of bull nigger who would stick a knife into you for nothing or possess a woman and then break her spine to let her know he was through with her.

Either that, or a completely harmless and ascetic musician, and the old man doesn't know anything about that. The old man didn't know that there is no such thing as a physically violent musician; I mean a musician really convinced of his own music.

"What's going on?" he cries at last, like somebody was setting fire to his house.

"I wasn't watching what I was doing and got myself cut," says Harley. I feel that Harley knows his presence, and mainly his beard, is not wanted around here and he is trying to leave the house, in a business-like way as possible. Whatever he wants to tell the old man has been spoiled.

My mother wants Harley to get to the doctor and I offer to drive him. She has wrapped his left arm in a huge, beehive-like glob of gauze and no blood is showing. Harley tells me to drive his car. The new electro-rubber smell is still in it. We whip out.

"Not to the doctor. I ran cold water on it and it's closed up. I ain't bleeding any more," said Harley.

I told him I was worried about infection and he told me not to worry about that; he knew our house and everything in it was clean. He said he knew Betty Perry, our colored maid, who cleaned our house. She was an ex-nurse from a hospital in Dallas; that I didn't know. Betty had never said anything about being a nurse.

"Same old story," chuckled Harley. "She fell in love and followed a man to this town. Turn on the radio. I want to get back to what we were talking about."

I did, and we got some patter from a Shreveport disk jockey; he was raving about the *sound* about to come up. It happened to be Mose Allison, a white fellow from Tippo, Mississippi, who sings more like a Negro than any non-Negro on the planet: "Gonna find me some kinna worldly companion, eben if she dum, deafm, cripple, and blind!" Mose ended it. I thought Mose was extremely fine. I wanted to *be* Mose, as a matter of fact.

"Cut it off," Harley ordered. "You see, here's some nigguh that just wants and wants, and *yearns*. He thinks it's something special to sit on his butt and just yearn after things. Okay, *give* him . . . give him . . . (this was a mild crisis for him, since for all he knew I was still a firecracker-throwing thug) give him Marelynn Monroe and, he's *still* gonna find time to plug in his electrocuting guitar and make up gripings about how it's not so fortunate as he thought— *yearning* again."

"But that's the *nature* of the blues, Harley. Anyway, that song we heard was sung by a *white* man making out to be colored. His name is Mose Allison."

Butte couldn't get over this. Some white man making out to be colored. Some man granted the same racial strain and cultural heritage as John Philip Sousa, and then . . . Butte sighed and told me he thought that made it twice as dismal. I had heard of the supposed snobbery of this high-yellow brand of fellow toward the regular blacks. I couldn't tell if this snobbery worked in Butte or that he'd come by this love of Sousa independent and honest.

"A good march doesn't leave you yearning like that. Say

94

Sousa. He starts out at some place and takes you to another place and sets you down. You ain't yearning after anything when a Sousa march is over. You're *there* and you're happy to be there. Then the punch-note on the climax—sometimes, not all the time—like 'Amen!', like putting a roof over the place you're at."

I heard a band hitting the punch-note and understood what Harley meant. There *was* great safety in the end of a march, I remembered.

"Do you think about this sort of stuff when you're at the mattress factory?" I wanted to know. Harley turned toward me and I could feel him staring as I drove. We were barreling down one of those avenues with silvery streetlight arms and twelve-foot pines in the front yards. Everyone had his yard trimmed beyond reproach—green carpets, shaggy needles, the lukewarm wind flying by. I had no idea where we were heading.

"You mean do I think about my music when I'm working? Do you have to ask *that*? I'm a musician, aren't I? You bet I do, every minute of the day," Butte said. I turned and saw him looking at me like I was crazy. "You're a musician, ain't ya? You play the trumpet. Don't *you* think about your music all the time?"

I certainly didn't, and suddenly, in Harley's presence, I felt very lazy and feckless. No, I didn't think about my music very constantly. There were even times when I'd walk in my room, see my horn on the bed, and be surprised that it was there, that it was mine, and that I was supposed to be able to play it.

"But I guess you're thinking about girls now, aren't you?" Harley answered for me. He hissed and seemed rather disappointed in me.

"Look. I feel sorta like a fool driving us around in your car. Where are we going?"

"I thought we would talk. I have to tell you something that I want to tell your daddy but can't make myself do it. I don't want you to tell him either."

"Well hell, what is it?"

"I'm quitting him in August. I'm getting through with school and I have another job I have signed papers for."

"Why can't you tell the old man that?"

"He's giving me a lot of money nowdays for being a foreman. He's paid me for hours I wasn't there and was out at Grell taking classes. And . . . and I don't think he knows I was studying to be a band director. He'll be mad and he'll think I'm outa my mind to do it. I'm taking a big cutback in salary to take up this band. He'll ask me about the money I'm making."

"Where are you going?"

"Mississippi."

"I'd think," I began, sniffing the air now that we were right up next to the mills and going over the tracks and down to niggertown, and becoming awfully wise off that old smell, "you can't get out of Dream of Pines without being cleaner than when you were in it."

We drove aimlessly around the gravel and the pavement for a while and then I took myself home. Harley vented himself freely. He wanted to tell me what brought him to the mattress factory and how lucky he had been to land into it just after he'd gotten married. He'd had a busy four years, from the factory to Grell A. & M. to home, and wake up again. But at least, he said, it hadn't ever really been hard knocks. He mentioned the fact that he had quite a bit of cash in his pocket at this very moment. He may have been the biggest mark in Dream of Pines at this moment, in fact. Harley considers it a miracle. He pats the dash and confides, "I don't owe as much on this car as you'd expect, either." I begin driving the car rather daintily. His face is crossed by the angelhair glow of some streetlight, and brush shadows from a pine tree make their way across it. He is the color of the inside of a carrot. His head is high and alert, and his mouth seems to give him pleasure, moving, telling, laying it all out. He tells me about the army. He is going to make it back to that place of honor when he was briefly director of the company band at Fort Sill, Oklahoma. There aren't going to be any woodpeckers who want to play jazz standing in his way. He would know how to handle that situation if it rose again. He knew so many more horns now; he could compose and arrange an original march given two free nights.

"I've been *over* a lot of people now. Not only at Grell in the band but at the factory too. I have been given charge. In three days, no, in *one* day, I can tell you the people who come to do business and the ones who come in for a escape from somewhere else."

Harley was inclined to grow sort of tipsy off something

he'd just said, if he thought it was particularly wise or correct or charming, and burst out with something else to go himself one better. This was what kept him talking constantly, open-endedly, once he got your ear. Not to say he was never wise or all the rest. But like then, he followed up on the idea of what a personality judge he was, and remarked, "If I meet a new married couple, at the end of five minutes I can tell you if they're gointa stick with each other or not. I can tell you in one minute whether a certain person is instructable or not."

"Oh yeah? I guess that makes life fairly easy for you, doesn't it."

"Look here, Harry. I've put in my *hours*. I *have done my homework* in this university of life. I have did my time in Ups and Downs College."

Was it some scene I had seen in the movies, or was it something I had read? The man carrying a wad of money on him, new car, being very expert and gabby, while just around the corner . . . I didn't want to think of that with Harley here. I liked him, and it was terribly pleasant to be sitting here in his car on our driveway and listening to Harley on Harley, even though he made me ashamed. I think now it was the bastard's *function* to make me ashamed: I had had it so lazy and soft and didn't even care much for what I had, while all the time Butte was attacking away under the name of some idea or other. Only it was this *bad* idea that was coming into the car with my not wanting it, resenting it when it came, but trapped by it. I looked at Harley's confident face—the thickish lips opening and shutting like small weiners making coos—and I thought of bad luck and broken dreams. His queer ocher skin, was it, or was it the bandage on his wrist, his Tulane sports outfit, and all of it, the fat wallet, the new car, the drunk hope in his voice. My brother in the insurance field once told me that his company avoided selling life insurance to Negroes. The percentages for the company just didn't pay off. Of all things, I thought about that fact just then. His company was an astute and studious firm that did huge volume all over the States. I thought of that. Either the Negroes did not pay the premiums or they died too soon, and maybe too often by violent accidents, which meant double indemnity. The facts rolled *chock, chock* in my head. What a nasty, morbid way to think; nothing had ever come to me like this before.

Then this horrible, filthy scheme of romance came into my mind. I began noticing Harley's skull, seeing it as an item, a tender ball, a *noun,* to lay a tire-tool against, to whap. His skull invited me, *me,* to knock him out. And it wanted this bad luck, begged for it. And the wallet, and the new Plymouth. Take them. Easy business. Fly. Out of Dream of Pines, toward Malibu or green, rocky Canada. Hell, the insurance companies knew what Butte's chances were anyway. Course of nigger Nature. Then get that one moment of fame you always wanted to come by casually some day. Be seen in the great spotlight of the cops, be fired upon, but yet escape, and have maybe fifteen minutes of local TV devoted to you. ". . . described as brooding but mild by his shocked father. Was a promising musician. But was at times rowdy, says his admitted girlfriend Miss Tonnie Ray Reese. She was 'not wholeheartedly surprised,' said Miss Reese." Wouldn't I stop *thinking* on this scheme? Finally, it was shut out for me by the flat thought that I was too much of a bore to even borrow his car without permission. And only then did I return to the only fact there should have been: I was too humane to hurt Butte; I cared for him; I'd protect him from as much as an insult.

What this runaway thought-scheme had to do with Harley or me, I had no idea. Bad, bad news had appeared in the car with us; I had an itchy, criminal feeling.

He thought I was observing him because of being avid to hear more of his life story. He speaks as he unwraps the gauze on his arm to discover just what his cut is like. I become overly polite again, wanting to make up for the horrors that were in my mind, wanting to ease him, aid him. He is going on about my old man again, raising Ode Elann into some unknown idol that he's ashamed to cross or show the triflingest intimation of ingratitude toward. So I jump in to help him out.

"Now come on, Harley. He's only human, and most of the time he's downright silly. . . . Did you notice what the old man was *wearing* tonight?" I giggled familiarly; I thought it would change Butte's point of view. "When the time comes, why don't you just tell him to go to hell, and leave?! You don't owe him your future."

Harley lit into me, I mean a full-blown scold. He wasn't

98

even very courteous about it, and I began to feel the grill, and squirm. Did I know how many people looked up to my daddy, did I? he wished to know. Did I know whose beautiful house I was living in? Did I know what man in Dream of Pines paid above the Minimum Wage years before he *had* to pay it by law? Did I know who air-conditioned first, who stayed out of the workers' way and off their backs and *didn't* hang up a lot of Don't Do This signs around the factory? Who paid for more than one wino to dry out at the parish hospital? Who was phoned and stood in more times than once as collateral promisee for even a *relative* of a worker trying to be admitted to the medical clinic?

"You better think about putting your daddy down, boy. Wouldn't this Dream of Pines mess be some hell without him."

I've said it. The bastard's *function* was to shame me. Brood on the thankless jackassism of my life for short periods. I'd never known quite all these tales about the old man. Or more: how they apparently *seemed* to Harley. I got out of the car wrung every which way.

The old man was by himself in the den watching the last bit of the Paar show. Still wearing his playboy cosmopolite rags and boots, worshiping Paar. I did love him all over again, but I can't say loving him then made my life any surer, or even better. I was still sitting on the dry rim of a cornucopia, my back to this feeling of huge, socked-in, unliberated plenitude. Along my back charges of danger and joy ran worrisomely.

9 / Bully and Prince

Who's to say exactly what I was senior year at Dream of Pines? I continued practicing the trumpet, but the introverted privacy of the musician bored me, and I stepped out to do things like act the second lead in the senior play. I did a solo in auditorium assembly one day, playing variations off "Down by the Riverside" with good old Mr. Medford chording me—the last thing he did before he died—delightedly on the piano. Mr. Medford discovered how much fun jazz was, and then he died the next week. I attended his funeral, and was seen by the class president, whose uncle Medford was, and my stature as a loyal fellow was increased around the high school. God forbid, but I profited by the death of this honorable old trumpeter from the Shriners' band.

Tonnie Ray Reese went after me the whole length of the year. I walked down the hall and she was in front of me, winking with both eyes. She was still plain as a stick, but she'd had something marvelous done to her hair. It was all over her ears in upshot curls, and she had been down to Shreveport for some advice on cosmetizing her face, and came back with two bubbling coals for eyes and a wide pink swipe for her mouth. Also, her breasts got somehow hoisted to where she was making the impression of coffee cups under her sweater. Her legs could not be cured: they were poor as warped rice. She also had some odd heaviness around the stomach and hips. Tonnie Ray was not exactly a flower, but her hair and face were making toward it. I still hung with the group that ridiculed her above all others. She tried too hard. She was a roach dipped in paint, trying to make it as a famous class chum. But to her credit, she was so much in love with me that she was never mentioned once that year in the school newspaper. Bob and Earl teased me about her, and I felt compelled to suggest one halfhearted way of doing away with her.

"Set her still, ram a hook in her gums, and take off with a Corvette that's got a line running from its bumper to the hook. Make sure it's a gravel road."

"Yank her brains out the top of her head," continued Earl, dully.

But what did senior year come down to? It came down to senior prom, when you had to be a total failure not to have a date, and the only girl I knew that was even likely was Tonnie Ray Reese. The roach. The spittoon made out of the shell of a creepy insect. I phoned her three days before the weekend. Her brother Lloyd answered.

"Is Tonnie Ray there?"

"She's here. She's sitting on the commode, crying," said Lloyd. A shriek came out of the back of the house. I heard it making toward the phone in frantic blurbs.

"This is Harriman Monroe," I stated, for politeness.

Lloyd dropped the phone immediately. Then I heard a whining rancor on the other end. This was Tonnie Ray. She said "I don't know" about five times, and finally gasped, "*Yes,* Harry. I can get away from this other boy who asked me two weeks ago, I think."

Earl and Bob had some really grotesque dates from an unknown junior high school two parishes away, and were in no position to ridicule me at the dance. It was held in the top loft of Dream of Pines' only hotel. Earl and Bob both got there drunk, and thought I was lining up Tonnie Ray in order to kill her. I met them in the men's room.

"You gon drive your car off a cliff and jump out it the last moment, innuh?" Earl asked me. He was near ready to pass out. His date was fourteen and all broken out with specks of acne.

Give Tonnie Ray the honor that she showed up in a manageable gown. It was white, with my corsage pinned on her side under her breasts. She could move in it to the beat of the band (five Negroes with expensive electric amplifiers who weren't anything special, combined with a tenor singer who *was* good, especially on the blues and Memphis-sounding stuff) without causing any strangeness, like the other girls in their evening gown wads, crinoline petticoats; they were all like iron-lung victims trying to kick around. But not my girl. She got hot and sweaty, and before long wanted to kiss when we hit the floor for slow dances. Tonnie Ray's gown was all silk and hung straight, like pants made into a gown. I'm telling you, putting my face back to the base of her neck and smelling her hair, odorized by a spray of peppery violets, I could almost forget she was a roach. My hand came off her waist full of sweat; I noticed the silk around her waist was wet.

"Let's kick away," I whispered. "We'll drive in a roundabout way to the house party."

There was a house party we were invited to, in a house built over a big lake, a modern house of open-face brick and cedar rafters owned by the father of one of the classmates. The mother was an alcoholic, and it was rather sad, when we got there, to see her coddling the school drunk beside the fireplace and sympathizing with how sick he felt, while she reached for her own bottomless glass on the hearth and stroked the young drunk's head in her lap. I looked away before things got too intimate and they began throwing up on each other.

Some college bucks were in the house, two old grads from Dream of Pines and a couple of others from L.S.U. and Tulane, all of them sold on themselves, looking at the ceiling or the baseboards and wearing those little titty-pins with chains on their sweaters as fraternity men are wont to do. Their penny loafers and their cultivated slouches; hair raked aside violently into a part; little fingers curled around the little fingers of their girls, college men enjoying their own smirks of careless possession. Their dates were girls who had not gone unnoticed by me during the last few years. They were girls who had been pretty so long they looked tired of it. Ah, the perfect medium-sized bosoms, the thin necks, the burning hair (they were wearing it short, then), the graceful legs, which demanded your hands around them and the long caress, from knee to ankle, like milking a cow. They weren't for this boy—not yet. Rock-and-roll was pounding out of a speaker by the hearth—Ray Charles on "What'd I Say" and "Sticks and Stones"—a speaker as big as a giant Negro's mouth. Couples slogged on the rug, with arms going up in the dim hearthlight. Over to the right, in a lighted dining room, the drabs and roaches were sitting in foursomes at tables playing bridge; this was the gang not too much on looks but high on spark, talent, or personality. This house party wasn't for every senior at Dream of Pines. I understood it was for people who had become conspicuous in any conceivable way: homecoming queen to second-place winner in the state hundred-yard dash. I suppose there were forty of us there. Earl and Bob, my buddies, didn't make it. Tonnie Ray Reese, of course, did. She looked around bug-eyed at all the celebrities under this single roof.

We'd just driven over thirty miles on gravel roads and had knocked off a pint of vodka with Seven-Up and smoked as many cigarettes as we could get in our mouths. (I myself was carrying three different brands in my coat at the time.) Also, we'd gone to work against each other's mouths for about an hour, and I had a rosy-tasting tobacco and alcohol spit rolling around in my throat. Tonnie Ray went off to change into suitable party wear. I made my way casually toward the head, and passed Ollie Sink's niece in the hall. She noticed me, stopped, and gave me a smile of withering sweetness. This girl, whose nickname was Lala, had tiny bones and a sort of emaciated prettiness that grabbed you only if you thought on it a while. The big brown eyes were there, all right, along with the small lips, which always seemed to have a glint of juice on them. She stepped like a baby stork, and wore girlish-ritzy clothes. Her family was rich, and yet she was shy and always seemed to be apologizing to you with those big eyes. I imagined that her hard little brassiere was stuffed with hundred-dollar bills. She was dressed in a pants and sweater outfit of creamy pink. I was high enough at the moment to think I loved her and had always loved her, only her. But I couldn't think of anything to say. So I just ran back and blocked her and looked at her sincerely.

"Oh, Harriman," she said timidly, looking down with closed eyes. "Tonnie Ray looks so *nice* tonight!"

Those days I was wearing an affected serious-musician's hairdo, with long lanks and a part almost in the middle. I thought this would really sink Lala, and was slaughtered by what she said. Yeah, Tonnie Ray. Lala passed by and didn't feel my hand as I reached to her back in agony and swept my fingers down the soft fuzz of her sweater. I thought of Tonnie Ray and went to take a leak.

I was thinking wistfully of Lala Sink and having that minor orgasm of urination, when I felt somebody's breath on my bare backside.

I turned and saw one of the college honchos standing behind me. He held a blown-out match in one hand and was sucking a cigarette.

"Hey! Watch where your breath goes," I complained.

"Sorry, buddy. This is a crowded head."

I recognized him as the Tulane romeo I'd seen playing little fingers with this magnificent natural-blond gal from Dream of Pines. They were standing against the sliding glass door, on which the hearth fire and mantle were reflecting, and they did indeed look like an ideal couple in a ski-lodge plate from *National Geographic*. He had a dark, slightly skeptical handsome face and the girl was like pale butter molded lovely, and the way she was lounging toward him, his slouching power in his fern-green windbreaker, the chain of his fraternity pin lobbing back and forth brilliantly, you imagined he was the one who had molded her. I hated him with a hate that came deep, out of my dreams. And I had been drinking, of course. But I pulled it off rather well, I think.

"You're a lucky dog, brother."

"Why . . . what . . . wh . . . ?" he wanted to know.

"Come on. You know what I mean. Your girlfriend. Blond. Personality. She's simply tremendous. You couldn't do any better if you tried."

"Thanks. Thank you very much."

"Listen. *I know*. And Earl and Bob. We've *all* gotten it from Sherry, and I mean, she can put it to you. She can really throw the junk at you. Man! She'll grind you out of the backseat of a car. (I whistled and wagged my head dazedly.) Uuuummph!"

He collapsed as much as a man can and still stand up. His face broke and fell into a saggy frown, as he watched me zip up—an action I made a lot of to-do about, realizing that it gave a sort of authenticity to everything I'd told him. At this point I was a dramatic genius, having acted in the senior play, etc. I left the head; the Tulane romeo was by the commode shredding like a cigar butt you might see in a toilet.

Tonnie Ray was in one of the bedrooms chattering away with another roach. She was still in her evening gown. The fact was that she was prettier in that gown than she'd ever been before, and maybe knew she'd never be that pretty again and was hesitant to get out of it. I called to her and said let's go out to the pool. She said wait a minute, and I said come on, *now*. Tee hee, I was such a brute, she giggled to the other roach, also still vainly wearing her evening gown. This other girl had on one of those huge, stiff bell-like contraptions and looked like a pumpkin seed stuck up in a bowl of sugar. I made off with the intention of deserting Tonnie Ray and her sickening friend. Tonnie Ray swept out in the hall, however, and clamped on my arm with her swimming suit in hand. She managed to do a lot of winks and poses to the society we passed in the kitchen. The old man parent of the house was trying, with the help of two boys in dinner jackets, to cram a horrid, bloody pig corpse into the rotisserie of his electric range. Everybody had to eat a slab burned to char outside and completely raw inside that morning at the house party breakfast.

The pool was in the back yard. It was late May and still cool, but there were a few body-conscious football players thrashing in the water yelling for their dates to jump in. I dragged Tonnie Ray into the bathhouse, a building made of two separated rooms with V-shape roofs and curtains inside hanging from a rod which went across the middle of the V. The view from inside gave you a triangle of glass above curtains at two ends, three tables in a concrete room like a teepee, and a brownish single light bulb hanging on a frayed old-timey wire of pleated yellow and black. We were alone.

"This is the girl's room, stupid!" Tonnie Ray laughed. Her voice was as thin as an ill-poached egg thrown against the treble strings of a harp, like I did once. Besides that, it had a little wavering crackle in it. Tonnie Ray was slightly drunk.

I was very sad that night, especially after seeing Lala Sink and wishing for her. Almost sorrowfully, I was resigned to getting from Tonnie Ray whatever I could get. Oh, I thought of taking Tonnie Ray out to the pool and drowning her in her evening gown. I felt some betrayal to Earl and Bob for not killing her in an inventive way. But I went on. Said what I had to say.

"I know where we are. Let's change together." My curiosity mounted, with a little conscious effort from me.

"Ohhhhh. Naughty!" she rebuked me coyly. But she sat up on one of the tables and started working her panties down. Her evening gown fell back to her knees, and her feet became coiled in a mess of garters, stockings, and shoes. When I saw her open her knees a little to make room for everything, I leaned over, grasped down her thigh, and put my middle finger up to her prize, felt her slippery flaccid sex, and plunged in. My finger was attacked by salty, numbing chemicals. It seemed to float. Solid to muscle to jelly to gas. I was trying very clinically to understand it. She reared up her face. It looked like an old servant in a horror movie, only . . . there was a wide swipe of red

105

smile on it. Her feet turned together in her white high heels. She was uniquely unalluring. Then her head went down and she started working, seriously. I saw a woman, how a woman does, in the act, without her man. This was a sight. I looked on like a doctor.

"Harry, Har*ry!*" she began spewing. "You are a serious musician, and I am your date to the senior party, and ooooooh! . . . Oh, Dream of Pines High! What fun it's been . . . oh, I was such a . . . success! Yes. Success, success, success, suc, suc, success! The parties—I had *dates,* real *dates.* I didn't miss a *thing!*"

Her dress thrashed and scrunched around her hips, wide white silk sliding everywhere. Felt to me as if I had my arm down in a bin of popcorn. Tonnie Ray had her moment. She froze, lifted up, and moaned like an emergency stroke victim. Then a big expulsion of shark's breath blew out of the lifted dress. It was hard to forgive her that. I was really outraged. I pinched her with my thumb on top.

"Wow! Golleeeeee! Yes! Do it again! Oh, you have been to New York to study music . . ."

What do you mean "Yes?" I thought. Oh, ugly, ugly, nauseous ugly . . . When would you ever stop? *You're* a roach. You have been some serious roach . . . have been away to some foul garbage lair in the basement of the filthiest most monstrous city dump in the country to study being a serious roach. Her feet turned together in the wad of stockings and panties. Ugh. The crabshells of her knees rattled together.

". . . and now it's all over, Harry. Can you believe it? Our best days are over?" God save me, then. "The parties and the friends and the good times," she went on, still lying flat. I leaned over to check out her face. All the beauty parlor glow had sweated off of it, and the original pasty shell with nose-holes expanding showed, the chin clopping away. "Oh, Harry! I think I'm sick. I'm going to . . ."

"No, Tonnie Ray, don't, please. Sit up. We were going to change together, remember?" I helped her up.

Then I saw a pair of girl's horn-rimmed glasses lying by a bundle of clothes on a table. I grabbed them and *wore* them; they were extremely thick. I saw a haze of brown and gray, and Tonnie Ray hovering four feet off the ground in it.

"Oh, Harry, silly . . . Uuuuuuuuurrrrrppp!" Curdled Seven-Up broke out of her. A speck hit my spectacles. I jumped in the air and my pants knees got really washed.

"Aaaah!" I screamed in horror. "Stop!" But she wouldn't. The sheeny mound of white fell off the bench. Then it moved off low. This was Tonnie Ray, saying, "I feel better."

I commenced ripping off my clothes. It was unbearable that I had Tonnie Ray's muck on me. But it was so beautiful not to be seeing Tonnie Ray clearly. And the world of these thick glasses was rather delightful. Everything waved by me. I didn't really know where I was. The vodka was working on me too. I got down to my shorts and tee shirt.

"Yoo hoo! I am naked!" sang Tonnie Ray's voice off to a corner, near the board shield of the girls' bathroom. I made out the exit door through the edge of the spectacles and rushed that way with hands out, fearing slightly that I would bang a shin on something metal, but keeping on. I felt on a table some girl's slip and grabbed it.

I dipped down with it to swab off the vomit that had globbed onto me through my pants. Successful at that, I brought the slip up to get the speck off my left spectacle, which was glowing yellow and carrying a small but rancid stench—right from Tonnie Ray's abdomen—over the rim and into my eye, which was watering. I also had my other hand out still trying to get to the door. I made it, opened it, and a refrigerator-size bright light from the walkway with the boys' door on the other side burst on me.

But there were persons on the walkway. There were human voices, almost in my face. I never dared to take off the spectacles to see who it was, but there were boys and girls.

"He's in his underwear in the girls' dressing room."

"He is wearing girl's glasses! He is slobbering on a . . . girl's slip. Sssst. He is slobbering on a girl's slip!"

"A-ummmm!" clucked a girl's voice.

"It's Monroe."

"He was with Tonnie Ray Reese," called an athlete's voice. "Check her *out!* He had done something *to* her!"

Some bodies knocked me out of the way and coursed past into the dressing room. Immediately they came out, bumping me violently *into* the walkway. My borrowed spectacles fell off and shattered on the concrete. I was looking at Lala Sink, standing there in her pink pants outfit and holding her neat swimming bundle at her stomach. One boy held my arm from behind.

"Tonnie Ray is sick. She looks . . . wounded . . . in some way. She is lying on the floor . . . (he gulped and whispered) . . . without no clothes on."

"You girls go on in there and help her."

"You better come with us, Monroe."

I looked back and saw the very same halfback who had had a date with Tonnie Ray that night after the spaghetti supper, the same guy who had called me a queer, the same one-hundred-sixty-pounder I'd beaten until he whimpered. Seeing him, I became a little more canny about the situation. I eased into the door of the boys' room.

"Just a minute," I said.

I went in and found a swimming suit hanging on a hook, shucked off my underwear, and got into it. I flexed around a second or two and breathed out hard to get the cigarette trash out of me, then waded out to the walkway scene. Others from the swimming pool had come in to congest the area.

I had a hard time getting the halfback fellow off to myself. The crowd wanted to just cram the area until they understood every particle of the horror alleged against me. And the two boys wanted to hold me until somebody could get the law. I jumped free, however. Then the girls and boys backed up and gave us an area.

"All right, son of a bitch. Marquess of Queensberry rules!" I spoke to my halfback friend—his name was Everett. He saw me squaring off in my bathing suit and scamping up and down in front of him. He didn't know what the hell I was getting at. He thought he was getting into some kind of strange, *unholy* fight; something even beyond no holds barred, or razor fighting. Fright took hold of his face. He put his hands on the lapels of his dinner jacket, but hesitated to take it off. I hit him one solid on the cheek.

Everett's technique hadn't improved much since our fight a year ago. He charged at me with a body block and cracked the boards of the dressing room missing me; then he got up to do the same thing again and I couldn't help stomping him a scornful one in the ribs—it was like I owed him one for being so stupid.

108

He howled in pain.

Then the big guy with him who had been holding me, a first-string end, moved in on me, and when he wrapped around me, it occurred to me for the first time that they were not intending a fair fight. "You ain't going to start *slugging*, buddy," the big guy said. He was a weight-lifter and ate three pounds of food every meal. Before this, I'd always sort of admired his great, ugly strength.

Everett hovered up, and the big guy let me go, and they both came in on me with fists, while also trying to hold me in *arrest* in a formal way. I got a feeling of soft clubs falling on my head, then something sharp arching up deep in my stomach, and I passed out.

I woke up by the lake in front of the house. Tonnie Ray was with me, wearing an aqua swimming suit that I could see in the bright moon of the night. It seemed terribly cold to me. Cold gray sticks were set around us—the May willow trees on the bank. There was a group of ducks just now putting out in the pond right below us. Tonnie Ray was so wretchedly pale that she glowed. Thistles, I was lying on a carpet of thistles. The shore mud and pond scum gave off a fertile odor: like Coca-Cola poured over a heap of new cow manure.

"I thought you were dead," says Tonnie Ray. She has been keeping watch over my *corpse*. Then I start seeing the yellow-greenness of the willow leaves, little things, on the limbs, and a hump of weed the same color in the pond, and hints of the same yellow-green color in the grass around us, in the inch of it right next to the ground. A huge fish or serpent wallows in the water under a willow tree for an amazing five seconds—some creature waking up and crazy, strutting like fury on the margin between the water and the air. Quite something to hear, this something with scales tearing, sloshing. Makes you afraid.

It's wearing, it's horrible to feel this. I have a nauseous, chalky sensation in myself, and I'm waking up with nature, and *Tonnie Ray* has my head in her lap and is holding me with her arms, telling me that Everett broke his hand when he missed hitting me and hit the wall and the other guy was ashamed of the way they beat me up. They became concerned about my having passed out, and Tonnie Ray came out dressed in her bathing suit all ready to go and told them

in so many words that they had made a horrible mistake,
and then she and Lala Sink had walked me around the yard
many times.

"Lala?"

"Yeah. She just now left when she saw you were all
right."

I turn around and see little Lala, indeed, walking up the
slope and just now making the hill in front of the picture
window. I see her little body striving, and the hearth burns
pink on the window. There leaning against the window is
Sherry, her natural blond hair and her full but lean hips
pushed out on the window, alone, the Tulane romeo is not
with her and her backside looks lonely and broken off from
that *National Geographic* scene with him I had seen earlier.
I chuckle, and laugh, "Ha ha ha ha ha ha!"

Yet agony too. Lala goes into the house without a look
back at me. She only wanted to make sure I was *alive*.

And I'm stuck here seeing spring come on yellow-green,
the ducks, the smell of manure and cola, the writhing of the
unslumbering creature, and the waking of the earth, with
Tonnie Ray, falling on me with her plastic aqua swimming
suit, tickling me with her roach antennae.

"You are such a *character*. Who else could be beat up
and wake up laughing?!" she says.

"I don't feel good at all."

"Oh, don't you?"

"I feel worse than I have in my life."

"Oh, do you? Now, now. We've hit it off so good together. Listen, Harry. Let's get married." She made some kind
of Southern twirl out of that word *married*. I'm sure she
wanted to sound fetching as a siren. Bless her heart, after
all. She wanted me forever, something awful. And it was do
or die for her. She was not going to college. She smiled,
knowing she'd failed with the voice; then, clutching her underlip in a desperate bashfulness, she tried the last bravest
thing, and eased her hand under my trunks with trembling,
awkward fingers. By the way I looked at her, she must have
known it was No all the way. She bent her head down,
squeezed me lightly, and fell into a crumple into her own
lap.

I got up and went walking up the slope. We were in the
gray of the rising sun. I made it halfway up the slope and

110

looked back at her. She rose up and really shook. God knows what new self she was putting on, but she got straight—she had put it on, whatever new self this was she was coming back with—and I grabbed her hand.

We went up and had pleasant conversation between one another while we ate that greasy house-party breakfast of burned undone pork. I remember Tonnie Ray held her piece out and squeezed it like a sponge, and we saw the grease drip out in an unbelievable amount, on the rug. We thought it was very funny.

10 / This Boy Sheds Dream of Pines

In 1960 Dream of Pines began turning into plastic. The Sink boys put up a corrugated aqua fiberglass fence around the mills. The tracks ran in two lanes into and out of the mill yards. The sun was scalding that summer. It boiled out the heart of everything you looked at and you could sense the hot ooziness of innards breaking out of wood, brick, and even glass. Intestinal slime burst out in tears on the steering wheel of your car if you left it in the sun any time.

What had happened to me? I lived in a woodsy glen in a nice wet shade, where late in the afternoon the deep cane patch and the overhanging oaks manufactured their *own* breeze, and strange blasts of almost frigid air blew through our house. I never had to suffer. I could lie in bed all day, naked, and will myself into one hard-on after another, detumesce (an unstudied pleasure all in itself), maybe go over to the desk and write my name over and over, lift up the stack of records and let them go again—Cannonball Adderly, Miles Davis, Gerry Mulligan, Mose Allison: new heroes—or take a cup of coffee, sit at the kitchen table, and wait for Tonnie Ray to call. She made out like every call to me caused her a crisis. She always took up five minutes apologizing for having called. Was I busy? She would just

111

die if she were interrupting something. She must've called a hundred times that summer. Oh, Tonnie Ray knew we were not lovers, but couldn't we be *friends?* I never agreed to anything.

Fifty times she wanted me to assure her everything was going to turn out right for her. She had some secretarial position lined up in New Orleans. She was going out with a business-major greaser from the nearby junior college who was after her to "prove her love." What should she do? What should she do when her brother Lloyd stared at her for a whole minute one morning, then went outside the kitchen, down the steps, and came back with a teaspoon full of *soil* and dumped it in her coffee? What was her life turning into, that . . .

One afternoon she asks me, "Harry, do you think God is really keeping up with me? Most of the time I feel like I'm just not . . . watched."

"There are so many trillions of people on the earth," she told me. Her self-esteem increased considerably when I mentioned, by way of fact, that there were really only a couple of billion. This was generally the kind of smart-aleck consolation I gave her. Her calls were a bore, but on the other hand, they weren't. When nobody else was in the house, I'd come to the phone wearing nothing but a sheet draped around me, like a monk-bard. Why? Just for the irony and fun, I suppose. I'd hold the phone out and peel off a shattering belch while she was weeping away at some story of crucial disappointment; then I'd come back to the speaker and make a tiny faraway voice, like at the bottom of a well, reading names passionately out of the phone book. Sometimes I'd hang up, flat. *Nothing* turned her away. She was always so concerned that she'd called while I was *practicing my trumpet.* I waited for her call, lifted the receiver off the hook, put the bell of my horn over the speaker end, and blasted off several bars of "On Wisconsin!" I answered then with a mild hello.

"Were you playing your trumpet?"

"No. Not today."

She said something had harmed her eardrums. I got an inspiration. "Say, is old *Lloyd* around? Put him on a minute. Don't say who it is."

Lloyd answered. I heard him make a nice couch out of

112

his ear. Eased the receiver down to the end of my horn and
blatted into "The Marines' Hymn" for all I was worth.
Tonnie Ray picked up the phone over there.

"Oh, you really *got* Lloyd! He is holding his head and is
turning red! Hee hee hee hee hee! Ow! Lloyd . . . now!!
Lloyd is *hitting* me. He is using *fists!* Oh, oh, awroh! He
has his *fists* made! unnnngh! . . . Oh, Harry, he hit me on
the face! Can't you do something? Can't you say something? Harry!"

She kept calling me. Tonnie Ray amazed me, how she
kept on, and kept on. I never had anything to say. Then I
realized I was God to Tonnie Ray. She was using me as
God. I was the closest to handsome that she would ever
touch; I was Music and Higher Art; I had fought twice
with her old boyfriend in her presence; we had drunk the
mysterious vodka together; I had put my finger into her at
the moment she thought she was at her loveliest; she had
had her spasm with me hovering over her like an angel.

Yes, I could've just hung around the house and lain naked in the sheets, caressing my own paps, hearing Mose Allison on the phonograph, and being cool, and being Tonnie
Ray's God all summer. I could've locked the door, a little
ashamed, got out my old faithful Daisy BB gun, set up
some rubber soldiers from the closet where my boyhood
stuff was kept, put them on the bookcase, lain behind a pillow and potted the soldiers, ducking the visible BB's from
the old, not-so-powerful gun, as they ricocheted off the
wood back at me. The word *ricochet:* what Frenchness,
what powerful romance; I remember when I first heard it
back in 1951. Pick up the phone from Tonnie Ray and
catch her frantic stream, then intone the cynical boredom
of God or act out something astonishing and cryptic to her.
Or at last resort, pick up my horn and practice it. (After
the first six months on that horn, I was sick of the whole
concept *practicing.* Maybe I should've known I was done
for as a serious musician then. But I heard Miles Davis,
and wanted to be like him. And every time I brought the
horn to my lips wanting to be big and original and have
some *style,* I felt Dr. Perrino's dick lying on my shoulder
blade. Oh, Mother, the funk; the sticky feeling of some
merciless expert lying on your back.) Or I could've spent
the whole summer mooning over Lala Sink. I never called

113

her because I was afraid of her answering the phone, very kind, very sweet, very soft and tiny, and telling me No, don't come by tonight around six-thirty, thank you so much for calling. I learned through Tonnie Ray at the end of the summer that Lala had been in love with me for about two months; that she lay sick the last week of her love with my annual photograph in her little pink fingers. Aw, Christ Jesus! The Sink millions! The Sink Mansions! The rooms with pink fur floors. Lala . . . Away to Stevens College in Missouri, and I never set eyes on her again. For that matter, I never laid eyes on Tonnie Ray all summer either. Strange, but true. She never even hinted trying to see me again.

Or I could've been a cool slob in other ways.

But I wasn't. I was drawn out of the house. I drove downtown and saw all the sweaty Jaycees in the streets. The way I see it, people in the subdivisions of Dream of Pines started noticing the pine trees were beginning to grow up a little bit in their yards from that devastation twenty years ago when the Sink boys hit town and went into the lumber business—the Sinks had everything but the stumps razed in five years, then they turned on the stumps themselves and made a fortune making them into paper when the war broke out, but of course pine cones fell off everywhere and accidentally there was quite a new little forest coming up in the subdivisions now—and these people in the subdivisions became very self-conscious about there being Beauty, after all, within the city limits of Dream of Pines. All of the younger men, some of them even Yankees and Midwesterners, turned into Junior Chamber of Commerce personnel. The entire basketball squad graduating from Dream of Pines joined the Junior Chamber of Commerce. They met, and did all that parliamentary procedure hockey. Garbage cans looking like green stubby policemen began appearing on the streets and on what the new signs called *avenues*. A monthly Yard Award was called into being by the Jaycees.

A bunch of beery good old guys went out and hacked away the vines and trash from a monument. It was a monstrous boulder with a tiny, almost unreadable brass plaque up front. Three soldier's names. Lost in World War I. Back in that heap of blackberry bushes and ancient rotting pine needles behind the high school. With the cool snakes, the

114

slug slime, cobwebs, and the rock moss and ferns hugging it close. The Jaycees found it. Earl, Bob, and I always knew it was back in there; we hadn't read the plaque and didn't want to. We knew it was to the Dead, back in there; somebody's Dead. It was . . . gloomy, gorgeous, and deep: oozy, even. With the Dead dignified with the spookiness they deserve. With the spiders and scaly, repugnant creatures, back in the mossy shadows and sordid growth, touching it, wrapping around it adoringly. "Its ours, ours," they hiss. Not everybody knew it was there. It was in the bottom of an odd scoop—as if real bodies were in the ground in front of the monument—which appeared in the old thicket that scratched us as we passed on the sidewalk from the gym to the classrooms. Earl saw it first one morning about ten. I stared a long time before I picked it out. "God damn. It's a tomb," Bob said. I saw the boulder go on back in the shadows, and I knew it wasn't a tomb; I could see the chisel chips all over it—a scaly living thing, itself. "We won't tell anybody about it." "You know everybody's seen it." "Nobody's ever said anything about it." "Why's it next to the high school?" "It *crawled* up here." "Monroe, you dopey fucker." I can tell you that I didn't walk that walk alone at night, even when I was eighteen.

One night I couldn't get to sleep thinking about it. I thought of how nice it would be to disappear—Lost!—into World War I and then come back underground to lie under the noses of the high school students, back there in that serpent gloom. To get *out* of Dream of Pines, and yet to *haunt* it! This was the best idea I'd ever been given.

The Jaycees found it, peeled off the moss, killed the snakes, poisoned the thicket, and the monument lay at the bottom of the hill now like a big bone in the sun. I read only the first name on the plaque—something Smith. I was sitting on the stone at noon and the sun was like a fluorescent lamp leaning against me. The temperature was a hundred degrees. I tried to feel something. God of the shade and sleeper that I am, I did open my eyes wide as I could and try to feel something here on the stone of the three lost men. I got a hot profound nausea and a headache.

The Jaycees put triangles of shrubs or flowers around some *new* green brass historical markers. I was all for it.

Wanted to pick up on this new history of my place. One of the new plaques was set on the median of a hot intersection; tin cars were flying everywhere and reflecting sprays of plastic colors like crazy. Ten thousand folks lived in Dream of Pines now; taxes in the parish were low, and three factories had set up in one year. This plaque was on the north side of town; perhaps I'm the only guy who's read it. It remarks on the fact that just thirty miles south of here used to be this fellow of the late 1700's, this Frenchman, Pisroin, whose accomplishment was . . . with all his heart . . . against a wild jungle . . . being French. Being *French.* That's it. Damn, if I could make out anything else. That's all they could dig up for Dream of Pines.

Well, still I was drawn around town, down to the old center of commerce, with the old one-story red brick shops from 1915, neither ugly nor beautiful, as I saw it, and the red brick streets, the same, all fading now with a brownish grime that I always took to be rather charming—easy on the eye, all the angles rounding, bending. Ladders were standing thick in the street. Negroes were ganged around watching. The shopowners were putting up striped aluminum awnings and fiberglass false fronts, at three in the afternoon, in front of everybody. Bricks were falling onto the raised sidewalk and crashing down into the gutter, where I was. Some workmen inside were getting rid of these bricks with a machine that went off like a shotgun. I jumped out of the way of a few powdery brick fragments from 1915. Finally I understood what was going on. The merchants were having the brick blown out of their front walls to make room for show windows. A week later they had them, and the drugstore on the corner where I charged cigarettes under the name of milk shakes let out a huge banner photograph of a Revlon model in its show window.

This Revlon model picture stung me in the guts. She was a skinny thing lying supine in a silk outfit, with a high-heel shoe dangling off her toe. Her face was big and just this side of weird, in her silvery Revlon eye and mouth make-up. She was lying on a pillow of sand and behind her, in twilight, was the whole Sahara desert. The top of one breast stretched above the neck of her gown; one thigh lifted under the dress, so you saw she wasn't all that skinny. She was playing with a piece of her own black hair. I had to

116

have her. What kind of cruelty was this to have her *photograph* lying there? What did I have to do to get her? Her eyes looked as if they bragged on all she'd seen and understood. I would understand, I would learn all of Culture, if that's what it took. Tears came out of my eyes. I would go to college and study Culture.

God *damn* Madison Avenue . . . New York! Why do you have to make every woman you work on into an *idol*? Why does she have to be silver? Why does she have to be lying out on the Sahara desert like only the smoothest Arab who knew everything in the world could possibly deserve her? You made me marry her, that luminous teenager down at Pascagoula, Mississippi. That pubescent Arab-looking girl, Prissy Lombardo, the girl who had kissed everybody! She was an underdone fascimile of the gal in the Revlon photograph. I admit it heartily. The sand, the silvery shoe draping off her foot, the eyes as wide and cognizant as animated black pearls. I *had* this scene with her; asked her to marry me. Prissy didn't have quite the body of the Revlon gal. The beach was white and rippled, but not the Sahara. It was the beach of Biloxi, Mississippi. However, this beach, stretching from Pass Christian to Biloxi, was then the longest manmade beach in the world. It may be still, for all I know. Doesn't take away any of my anger.

One last time I drove into Dream of Pines to see how the aqua fiberglass fence around the mills was doing out in all this sun. I drove over the tracks and noticed that Ann Mick's house had disappeared. The old shack wasn't with us any more; there was only that hideously pounded-out earth where it used to be; a few dozer swaths, crushed wine bottles, dirty newspapers, flattened and yellow. I haven't seen Ann or any of the Micks since then. Don't know if they went to another city or straight to hell. Mr. Mick didn't show up at work, and poof! The Micks were our only outright slum. My heart was out there in that hot field. I remembered my dream of Ann, of our love, of Malibu; I was still under the spell of it. I was a little ashamed of it, but it still had me; I always trusted my dreams before anything else. And now the vacant field, with the terrible noon sun above it and this plastic sweat on the steering wheel dripping on my hands, was bringing me awake, miserably, horribly, like somebody waking you up by pouring warm

117

molasses on your eyes. Hell, I didn't want Ann any more. I knew I could do better. But the *familiarity* of her in that hypnotic dream . . . The aqua fiberglass fence was running through the middle of their former shack. Through the middle of my dreamy heart. I could've coughed up a portion of that fence right out of my chest at the time.

I got out of the Chevy and looked up the hill in time to see a loaded train chug into the mill yards. Then I saw the boxcars move on in; I saw it through the hot, translucent aqua fence. The boxcars had their hump of pulpwood—the stump corpses of pine trees. These look like dead octopi, groping everywhere, strangled in the daylight. Then I got a big whiff from the wooden fart fog of the mill stacks again. Saw the aqua fence trying to shield me from the oily gears of the mill that I knew so well, and I said, "Jesus."

"Jesus, take me out of this place." I appealed to the divine Jesus of my church.

My mother comes in waking me up, waving a letter she's already opened. I gather up the sheets around me. Have been sleeping naked, as usual, and my own body has become an immense bore to me. I have red welts all over me from standing nude with my air rifle and firing it against the wall almost pointblank, willfully suffering the riochets when they come back.

A distinguished little denominational college in Mississippi is offering me two years' tuition on the basis of my musical talent. I've heard enough . . .

Mother, I don't care about the rest, that a Dr. Livace, the chairman of the music department, happened to be sitting in on my performance last year at Shreveport with Mr. Medford. That this college is strong in music—believe me, says Mother. She was born in Mississippi and is wild for anything decent going on in that state. No, I've heard enough.

Never mind telling me . . . Mother confesses she wrote a letter to the college indicating I wanted to attend. She's worried that she has intruded and has done too much in forcing me toward this one college. Not at all, Mother.

For, after all, the letters from Columbia, Harvard, Yale, Princeton, and Juilliard just haven't been pouring in, have they?

I grab it. I kiss her and thank her. I'm going to Hedermansever College, near Jackson, Mississippi. It sounds *exotic* to me. It means I am not going to be in Dream of Pines
next year.

BOOK TWO

1 / Our Lady of Mississippi

I made it to Hedermansever College, driving a Thunderbird which I'd been awarded through pressure on the old man by my mother. The car was three years old, a '57, navy blue. There was a mashed fender on the right, and the interior was like an old garden glove, but it was tight and fast. It had a cockpit top you could unlatch, take off, and store in the dorm basement on good days, for the open ride and the sunglasses.

I felt very precious in the oily leather seat; I was a pistol leaking music out its holster. My horn was in the well behind my seat. I had an intense suntan and scorched hair. There were California license plates on the T-bird which I hadn't bothered to remove: Malibu Harry. It was all right if boys and girls thought that about me. Sneering, using the car radio music as my own accompaniment, I thought I was quite a piece of meat.

I liked the shade and the neatness of the curbs and the olden greenery of the place. General Grant had been here in 1862 or so, and liked it enough to stable his horses in the Old Chapel, that beauty of Georgian architecture. That was in the days when the Yanks were getting fed up and a lot of edifices were being burned up. The Confederates at Vicksburg were starving, the city of Jackson was on fire, and Grant was coming back west at last to meet Pemberton in Vicksburg on solid turf, and swallow him.

There Grant was, for me, half-drunk, slouched in an ashy-blue jacket in a room of the Old Chapel, interviewing petitioners—flushed nubile belles of the South ding-donging back and forth like flesh clappers in their hoop skirts. "Please, Ginral Grant, spare, oh spare . . . I'm in my last and only dress, and it's just so smoky-smelling. I feel like a smoked ham." She steps back, opens her knees, and a Minié ball rolls out from her petticoats. She stares at it as it

123

rolls on the floor; Grant sees it. She is all marvelously eye-lashed wonder. "Someone must have shot at *me*. Oh, I did not expect *this*." She faints, with careful rustling of petti-coats and outflung arms. Other women seek him, all of them using the word *Christian* on him in different ways. "You *are* Christian, then? No, I do not mind if you smoke. Now, I have made *my* concession, I have allowed you to smoke in my presence, so you can make your own decision about burning us down." They all want to know if he's fight-ing harmless family houses or fighting a war in Christian gentleman style, Grant behind the desk badly wanting to use the spittoon. Grant is hungry for whiskey, food, every-thing.

A blond teenage sultreen appears around lunchtime—and Grant is starving—and means to lay it on the line about his keeping soldiers and fire away from *her* mansion. Her mansion is her dead daddy's and she and her big sister are trying to have a small Christian women's college in it. They do not want to give it up, not even during the war. This little college, back in 1826, gave the first degree to a woman ever in the United States, the blond girl, Lady Love Deuteronomy, declares to Grant. It had its history—early poverty but always Christian culture. There were only *girls* out there, Ginral. What else? Grant still holds his face in that spittoon-seeking screw. Lady Love Deuteronomy sees she's getting nowhere, and becomes, in desperation, a leg-end. She steps back and shuts the door. (From above in the chapel come down the soft knocks of horse hooves.) "I see," she says, "your lunch is waiting for you on a tray in the hall. You're having a steak and, I believe, dumplings. It's nice you can have steak while the girls at the college are having field peas, pork rind, and water . . . Now though, Ginral, regarding your appetite, how would you like to have, well, *this* . . . *me?*" She raises her dress, uncovering a succulent white ankle, a fine calf, a naked stark knee. Grant whimpers and heaves up out of his chair. He creeps, he flaps his lips; a vile breath of whiskey and tobacco rolls off him; his unfastened suspenders, like the tail of a beast, trail him on the floor. Grant *grunts!* But suddenly Lady Love Deuteronomy releases the hem of her dress, stiffens her breast, and from some corner of her waist which got by the shy soldiers in the hall, she fetches out a pistol, a silvery little snout that means no play. "Did you dream that I—

124

You tragic Union hog. Have your *shame,* yes, *be* shame, Ulysses S. Grant! I have had my moment. Now *dare* burn our harmless women's college." All this while, Grant was disarming her. But he never dared, out of shame, to give orders to raze that Christian women's college. He passed the very mansion, riding at the head of his columns on the way to Vicksburg. Lady Love herself stood on the porch and curtsied to him, Grant, the deflated punk, slinking toward Champion's Hill and his seat as President of the U.S. While in her basement, attic, in cupboards and closets on all three stories, under the beds and in the kitchen out back, Captain Hannah and fifty mean lean horse corps guerrillas of the Confederacy lay perilous, breathless, and safe. Hannah and his men had run through Union lines, coming from the siege at Vicksburg, and having eaten at the women's college, they were poised to do great attrition to Grant's supplies. Only they were all sick. They had eaten rats, and moths and crickets and grass in Vicksburg, and every one of them had dysentery, so they did not become a thorn in the guts of the invaders. They couldn't even crawl away from their own odor. Nevertheless, Lady Love Deuteronomy had saved them. She was the legend.

So it happened that Lady Love and Captain Hannah, after blushing intimacies as she served his illness, got married and were president and wife of the women's college through the dire years of Reconstruction. New students had to know all details of the anecdote concerning General Grant and Lady L., along with other directives about playing cards and what to do in case there is an atheist in the group or dancing is suggested. Both Hannah and his wife were Baptists. Lady L. D. Hannah was hallowed in those days when the sad folks of the South didn't have much to live on but a good joke pointing up Federal stupidity.

She was put to earth one day in the nineteen teens. Her funeral took place just before her captain, husband, college president—who was so robed and hooded and encrusted with state, Southern, and even national honors in education he could barely raise his hand—bought the Old Chapel and its environs with funds from his denomination. His denomination loved him. He established a coeducational college here. But mainly, he now owned the Old Chapel. He taught in the room where his wife had had her moment with Grant. And perhaps, lecturing in Grant's very footsteps, he

125

saw the rising hem and the leg of the nineteen-year-old
Lady Love revealed, time, time, time and again.

The name Hedermansever was given the college when it
was saved financially in 1920 by the first of a long line of
gloomy rich jingos by that name. No more was it Hannah
College, though President Hannah still lived, and his denomination loved him.

Academically, he taught the Old and New Testaments.

He stood staunch against the short skirts of the coeds in
the 1920s; and most of all, against automobiles. Surely he
looked with horror upon the time when it would not matter
a gnat to anybody which leg his wife had shown President
Grant.

He saw students of his leave class and get in open cars
with young women with bald knees and bangs, and he saw
the automobile despoiling the family and community and
church. He could imagine but one place for these couples
to go in their automobiles, nowhere except to the peak of
lust in some shade off the gravel road, with cigarettes,
which he had also come out against after World War I. His
denomination loved him.

And he was right. A farmer who could draw sent him a
picture of a couple parked under some willows, on his land,
he complained. The couple were mating in the car seat
while cigarettes smoldered in their mouths. Hannah recognized the car, which was drawn unearthly well.

His age was eighty-six then. His heart was broken. He
knew the young man who owned the car. He had taught
him St. Paul on the afternoon in question. He recalled how
beatific the young man had looked taking his notes. He recalled his dear wife, who gleamed with the treasure of the
words he spoke to her—while these young gas-car people
came alive only when he cleared his throat (or broke wind
—the old deaf man never knew how loudly) or otherwise
sounded like an automobile, pulling the lectern over or sliding the tin waste can with his foot.

He began raving. In his office he said, "They can send
me fools to teach, and I will send them back educated
fools; nobody can teach the fool out of them!" very many
times the last week of his life. This statement bit and lasted.
They had it cut into an epilogue on the marble tablet of the
stone arch at the exit of the campus drive.

That dreary antique word *fool* lashed at me every time I

126

drove under the arch. The tablet was muddy with veins now. Some days I was on my way to playing snooker over at the Twentieth Century Recreation in Jackson. Tuesday nights I was on my way to rehearsing with the symphony. Then there were the afternoons when I rode with a hag or roach: lonely, tacky girls I picked up in the coffee room or in the hall of the Fine Arts Building, girls wearing Ivy League outfits from Sears, Roebuck, girls with odd fannies, queer noses, and strange legs. Then one time, a positive beauty, begging to come with me and crash the Twentieth Century, where no women were ever seen, and then she opens her mouth to laugh and shuts it immediately, very sad now, looking out the window away from me, knowing I've seen them—her teeth, a brown nest of grubworms. "Take me back to the dorm," she says. Then in front of the dorm she explains that her family had once lived in an Arkansas town where nobody knew the water was bad until their children got their permanent teeth. "It could have been something worse," I said. Later I wanted to hang myself with shame. I wondered if I had begun some rotten subconscious habit last year with Tonnie Ray Reese. Why did I even approach these girls? Who was *I* to give them my backside when they didn't suit my needs? How had I known there was some huge spoiling defect when I picked up this beauty with the teeth? I was sure I already knew, somehow, when my eyes took her in. Well, I was a fool, as the epilogue told me.

But the alternative to being a fool, and maybe a bastard, was staying on the campus of this forlorn asylum and being conscientious and being dead. Such choices, I think, have broken over this head of mine whenever I stopped to think.

I filled my space in the desks. I was looked through and talked through by all the Pee Aitch Dees, and I turned around to see just who they were looking at and talking to in the back of the room, and saw they were talking to nobody, but a thing: out there was the lawn, the olden greenery, the slow quietness, the recumbency, the ancient brick and the long, long history—everything you need for a cemetery.

We were dragged into Chapel three times a week to hear speakers of such interest as to make flies change place on a corpse. The Pee Aitch Dees checked roll for their sections and then sat down and slept the old eye-open snoozes of

127

scholars. Up on stage would be a millionaire Christian from Texas, dramatizing life to us as a tennis game. There you were with the net of dread in front of you; but you had to keep serving; you fended, you sweated, you looked to see if your partner was still there and He was. It was Jesus. (The Savior favored a dogwood racquet with lambgut strings—a cheap joke on my part, but it matches the allegory of the millionaire evangelist.) Another morning we heard the anti-beer and anti-promiscuity specialist, a limp bachelor of fifty who was a huge personality among the denomination. He clung meekly to the lectern, paralyzed us for five minutes with memorabilia about vivid prudes we had never known, then he affected a madness like Hamlet's and cannonballed—dry limp hands flying, wide stiff suit reminiscent of an iron lung—into a case history of two "young people" on a Saturday night. Hands wrapped together now, coming to it with dire breathlessness, holding the vowels in his mouth: "A dark night, a parked car, a can of beer, a fond embrace . . . a wandering hand . . . and *sin* entered the lives of these young people!" Oh, the dizzy sick mauling of it; oh, the vague sweaty pre-coital commotion; oh, the breaths of beer, that drink "akin to rat urine!" (so he pronounced it)—all we students perking up when he said that. Then he told us about seeing the rat swimming in the beer of the vat of a brewery down in New Orleans. The student body and I sat back then. We had thought we were going to hear about the whole act of love, but no, and we lay back in the seats. The boy right behind me was a famed athlete on the Hedermansever football team. They called him Mole-Digger. Mole-Digger struck me on the back of my head. I turned around. He leaned up on the back of my seat and whispered, "Why'ont you raise yo hand and ask him would he go on about them lovers . . ." Another athlete, sitting next to Mole-Digger, had a big, living snake in his hands. Covertly, he rammed the writhing thing under the back of Mole-Digger's tee shirt. So Mole-Digger fell back, clutching his back, grinning, and that was my only contact with Mole-Digger, forever.

But the ministerial students, who were about thirty per cent of the student body, stood up and clapped for the bachelor at the podium who was such a great name among their denomination. In their ranks were the hard-lipped scowlers for Jesus and the radiant happy gladhanders for

Jesus. You had Jesus coming at you in all styles at Hedermansever. You had people full of Jesus who dressed very costly in Ivy League and you had people full of Jesus who looked like they just ran out of a fire.

At eighteen years old, trying to come on strong in that herd of backs and cowlicks, female pageboy hairdos, pants-butts, bouffant hair, bare girls' ankles in brown penny loafers, and skirts flairing up to show stocking latches, all of us making out of Chapel in our congested warm dumb way, I smelled in that crowd the odor of flowers and fish, together, the effluvium of real women somewhere in the crowd. The heavy magnolia and the sardines. I held to my books, becoming the very nose of lust.

I am a gift, so someone take me, I thought. Someone record me. Don't lose me. What with my talents on the horn, my car, my suntan, my musician's hair, my execution of the Vivaldi piece just recently in my music room . . . well, what about *that?* But carrying the slippery books alongside my hip, and sweating tactlessly like a slug snail, I looked in the face of a belle, some gal in her negligent blouse who had found a cool nook for herself and was leaning back as if saying, What can you show me, boys? She looked just as annoyed by Chapel as I was, but in some way I could not possibly touch, my hands were so full of sweaty books. The belles were there at Hedermansever, about ten of them in the two thousand of us there, and you would see them poising like statues in the alcoves, the shadows of the halls, and they knew how to lean, and how to be mildly reckless with their legs, cocking them out of their skirts so you saw, could imagine, both knees raised.

But the belles had learned to *ignore* by the time I got there. They knew how to look blissfully by one. What they were looking for is still unclear to me. I followed them up in the newspapers later and saw they'd married men like Air Force lieutenants and stockbrokers from Dallas and once-married rich lawyers from Atlanta, who seem like second-rate interlopers to me.

These belles were expert at ignoring me. They had developed such subtlety that my gleaming face did not occupy them. So there I was left with my books, yearning for my trumpet to play that Vivaldi strain brassy and direct into this belle's face, working down her until the bell of my horn was perfectly crammed by her breast, the song going

129

right to her heart; then moving down to the cup of her navel to delight her at the place she snapped off from her
mother, making her tickle as she receives food there again,
in the form of music this time, from the brass throat of my
horn . . . But the belles looked away, and I was shocked to
think suddenly how drear and antique the Vivaldi tune
would seem to them, just like another Chapel meeting,
sleepy, with another baba on stage drinking glasses of his
own words, a wind blowing in and out of the cracks of
dead Italian castles. So I removed my cold horn from the
navels of the belles.

Thirty per cent of the student body was studying for the
ministry or work in the church somewhere. You'd see every
now and then a boy or girl—sometimes two together, holding hands—with unbreakable scowls, or on the other hand,
jolting glassy smiles, looking like they had just set off a
bomb in behalf of Jesus Christ somewhere.

In the dorms, the dorm-mothers watched the girls going
out and called them back if their dresses were too short.
Short dresses had come back in style, and it was President
Hannah's crisis over coeds' knees all over again. The
dorm-mothers were generally widows, and a couple of them
were true monsters of piety. I know of one who borrowed a
convertible, drove over to Jackson to a curb-service tavern,
even lit a cigarette and ordered a beer to seem appropriate,
and watched for girls from the college coming in with boys,
and craned her neck to see whether the girl took beer. She
couldn't get the girl expelled for that, but she could get her
confined to her room for a few weeks except for classes and
meals. But this dorm-mother widow picked out the trashi-
est, dinkiest tavern for whites in Jackson, where nobody but
roughnecks went—out on Highway 49—to watch for the
girls.

I should say nobody went out there but me, and my poor
date, a girl from Holly Springs who had had polio in one
leg. Bonnie had one shriveled calf, but the other one was
lovely, tan and firm. She was turning up a quart bottle of
Busch Bavarian when we drove into the place and worked
on it seriously the rest of the time we were there. And the
widow saw us, my top down, her top down. I waved to her
and yelled, "Have a ball, honey. He'll get here soon, he'll
look like a Greek god" (thinking she looked like an old
whore on the search). "You just have to wait on your
130

prince, babe!" I'd been here before with Bonnie, and liked the place because it looked like the end of everything, a little upsurge of tin and asbestos shingles on the edge of a city dump, like somebody's desperate artless hands had made a *place* just before everything turned into rubble. I hoped that one of the times Bonnie had to get out and walk through the lot to use the restroom, I would see just one of the clientele in the cars so much as raise an eye toward her slight limp and her small calf. I would jump on that son of a bitch with a sublime fury, I didn't care how big he was or if he drove nails with his head; I wanted to pit the good I had left in me against him. But it was never that way with these folks of the lot. The guys noticed her and then looked straight at me with a nod of pity for her, or they ignored the bad calf and rubbernecked, watching her all the way, their eyes on her like she was any other piece of tail. These people were pretty bent and annihilated sorts themselves, even the teenagers, trying to look like *hombres* east of *hombre*-land with their hair greased and swung over the forehead, sideburns slick, sometimes combed down lower than they actually grew. Bonnie was all for the place, too; we'd talk and drink pleasurably, supping upon that air full of the smell of thousands of other beers served out here on the lot with every sip we took.

Bonnie was the best one I had, really, for a long while. Out there on Highway 49 I would be telling her something like "I don't think anyone is old enough to perceive God until the minute they die," and she would be dressed in a green fall outfit with a necklace and high heels, dressed for everything she was worth; she never went casual with me. And me in my jeans, tennis shoes, but still a white shirt and necktie, for her; Bonnie smelling like a magnolia in spite of her weekend quart of beer, weekend after weekend with me. Some nights she would drink more than that and get really in love with me, and also get very sick. I'd pull over on the grass off the highway and she'd ask me to put my hands over my ears, then she'd sob and retch in the weeds pitifully and come back with a handkerchief, looking bright although not pretty, smiling, ready to be returned to the dorm . . . Bonnie dressing to the hilt and doing the rest to *go* with me, to keep up with me; Bonnie tight on that beer she loved but couldn't keep down, deliriously receptive to me, telling me I was truly profound, I was too smart for

131

Mississippi and maybe the entire South; Bonnie and her tendency to cry briefly after every sentence she said—and not a blessed thing in her head (her head covered with heavy wonderful black hair which she had "frosted" with a bleach which gave her a look of champagne over licorice), nothing in that head but details of the romantic life of her late teens in Holly Springs, Mississippi. She told me she was a make-out in Holly Springs and had been the cause of a lot of breaking up among couples. She was the confidential friend between a lot of boys and girls, and the boys would take her out parking and begin describing to her what was wrong between them and their girlfriends. But before Bonnie knew it, this fellow would be glued on *her* lips, trying to force his tongue down her throat, while still trying to carry on a conversation about his girlfriend. For it was inconceivable that he be doing anything earnest with her, she was accepted so generally, in her crippled condition, as the go-between of Holly Springs; and she accepted this. She wore glasses then and didn't have contact lenses as nowadays. But things always went cold with couples for whom she was the go-between. She had a certain appeal to the boys, she found out. She could kill the love between them and the fiancées, and she began to like it. Even the strongest, most fixed loves, even loves since the fifth grade. The boys took Bonnie out and fell on her like a buoy in the deep blue water of love. She became a regular witch at murdering love, but always very gay at it. (And she was gay and tearful with me in a new way, because for the first time in a long while she was out in a car with a boy who wanted no love destroyed.) Oh dear, she had had to do things eventually back in Holly Springs, things that would make the boy unable to look his girlfriend in the eye come Monday morning, things that would leave him barely able to look *her* in the eye Monday either, things that left the boy trying to ignore her and see her at the same time, so that his face was jig-sawed, fractioned apart oddly. One boy she told me about was the class secretary. When they had talked in the car awhile, he got bold and said to her that he didn't see why Janine wouldn't give him the whole hog when she knew they would be married the coming summer. Bonnie worked him up on the subject of sexual love very easily, and at the height she stroked him, as she had stroked others, but knowing this fellow wanted to undress and all, and wanting

132

not to allow him the regular thing, not wanting to be pregnant especially, she waited until he was mad for rubbing anywhere and after feigning pain to her leg every surge he made, she turned over and told him if nothing else would content him, he could rub himself into joy on the contours of her fanny; anything else would kill her, she lied to him. Then she gasped and faked intense pain and at the last of this cold farce, she fell down to the floor with the pedals and the transmission hump in a seeming coma of injury, while he begged her to wake up and live and forgive him. He did not think he could live with his shame, and the broken romance with his sweetheart was the least of his worries. He was "too good-looking to live," she said. She gave others the same scene, with the same ending. She saw hearts of the sweet and handsome crash in hot shame, saw the old boy of love sink like a rotting dummy; saw the boys themselves the rest of the year, lonely and mute with a sense of unconfessable crime. She limped a little more for them when they were near.

She was shyly proud of having vanquished love. I can't reproduce it, but believe me, there was a way she told her history which made it not so perverse and unlovely as it might sound. Her face was too close to mine, the beer was too good, for me to remember well. "God forgive me, but I do believe all young love is wrong and I can't say I mind about destroying it. But here I am eighteen years old and in love with you, Harry." She told me that one night. I do remember that. Bonnie laid her left hand on the seat so our fingers touched, giving me a bare naked shock. She felt cold and brittle, she held her hand against the nerve-marrow of my bones; she did not sweat, and I felt like a damned walrus touching her, this odd sort of virgin. "I wouldn't care if . . . well, I just wouldn't care at all if I was with you. You rat. You think some girl better than me is out there in the future, don't you? You're in love with her already and I can't do anything about some little priss-ass in your imagination. If I met her, I could do something about it." She licked her teeth, the virgin crippled witch, so deadly sure.

Then she recognized the woman in the convertible next to us. It was her dorm-mother, the widow, who was a total success pretending to be an old whore. She had the country-and-western station up howling on her radio. She held her cigarette like a torch, this widow. Bonnie screamed to

133

me who it was, and I backed out. The ride back wasn't pleasant. Bonnie said she was done for at the college and wanted me to turn off at every dark road. What the deuce, she said; she might as well get pregnant by somebody she cared for, and live in some swamp hut with his infant, because, what the deuce, what was living going to be like now? Look up at the stars, Harry. There were so many of them out that night they seemed like an electric dust over us. The stars were urgent and careless, and the black air of the universe was advertising sheer rapturous multiplication. A man could imagine the million little people of his sperm lit up like that in the wide black endlessness of a womb. One could give in so easily and combine with the carelessness of the universe. I don't know if Bonnie was thinking all that, but it was there to think of. I took her straight to the dorm. That ended Bonnie and me. The dorm-mother locked her in for half the year, and I got only one phone call from Bonnie telling me what it was like being at the mercy of the widow, who sat on the bed next to hers and taught her morals by exemplums from the life of her dead husband, the thirteenth disciple.

2 / Bobby Dove

But I do not readily admit that I had come to the wrong place. Hedermansever was ruesome in many ways, but I confess it was not all dead. There were a half dozen members on the faculty who did teach me there were alternatives between being a corpse and being an ass, and who bragged on me for very small feats—my poetry, for example. About D. and S. and the L's. and Miss J., my teachers, I still give very much of a damn. There are others around the campus who'll say I was honest in all the wrong places in this book. Bad shake to them.

My first roommate was a freshman preacher from South Carolina who wore quadrafocal glasses: Blind Tim, the

Pastor, already a pastor at age eighteen, ordained by his church at sixteen. He woke me up more than a few nights listening to this late radio broadcast from Arizona. It was the sincere, true thing, he said. The man broadcasting was a college-educated Navajo converted from the medicine men and then from Roman Catholicism to a cult of angry Protestants in Phoenix. My roommate had a transistor radio with an aerial that let out two stories high. He'd hear a fragment of the sermon he wanted, cease thrusting up the aerial, and jam his ear to the box with its blue-lit band. This poor boy lived by his ears; he might have been going blind, in truth, with those quadrofocal glasses that weighed half a pound. When he got his radio sermon, though, his eyes boiled like grease through a hall of mirrors. His morguish white cheeks hung off his eyes and were covered with whiskers that sprouted like some sort of filth; you thought of a grapefruit rind somebody had used for an ashtray. He had the voice of a sissy nightwatchman.

"Navajo Ben is *right!* America is walking on cellophane paper over the pit of hell! For Americans there awaits a worse hell than for any people in the world. 'To whom much is given, much shall be required!' "

He was packing in his aerial and glaring at me. I told him Navajo Ben didn't know his butt from a tom-tom. I didn't care for that fiery educated voice piercing through the static two thousand miles, nor for whoever had the money to build that powerful a radio station to air Navajo Ben's message every night of the week. The fact is, that faraway Indian voice was unsettling me; there was a torment in it that cut too far into me. It had me facing life like I was plastered against the side of a stone cliff in Arizona and inching my way along a rim of rock a half-inch wide. Navajo Ben had gotten to me one night when he made a sermon on the body scars he'd received falling down nude at a peyote-eating ritual back on the reservation, and by the time he whispered, 'God, the gentle Jesus Christ of scars, calling to me late in the evening to go out to His garden and compare scars, . . ." I was ready to go with him. And now I resented Navajo Ben and his testimony of bruises; I did not want a male telling me about religion, because I can cut through male cant too easily, my mind hacks it like razors against hair; I know at the bottom of every male voice, no matter how detached- or firm-sounding, there is an old

135

bald idiot screaming, "Save *me!*" But Navajo Ben almost dragged me out there with him.

Tim the Pastor and I broke up and he went to another room, with consent of the dorm-master. When he left I went about being wanton. I took my mattress off the bed frame, slept with it on the floor, taped up the pictures of all the models in *Esquire* magazine, girls dressed in silk and fur and slips and reckless sandals. My phonograph was always wailing. I brushed my teeth once a day and took a cigarette freely on impulse. On the back of my door was a picture of Maynard Ferguson, old scar-tissue-lipped Ferg, with his trumpet and wearing a purple sweater. Out of his mouth I had drawn a speech balloon enclosing the words "Practice, you bastard." And all this is what passed for being a beatnik at Hedermansever. I'd already been thrown out of the student center twice for playing jazz with a few musician acquaintances. We drew a crowd of coeds itching to dance; the ex-preacher who had an easy loft here as a student dean came in to tell us loud dance music wasn't the right thing at Hedermansever. This man held an office and drew a salary for such services. Like a social disease, he showed up on such occasions as involved clandestine pleasure; showed up, a raving, red-faced symptom, wherever joy became too unconfined—in his natty orlon shirt and loafers and his Ivy League crew-cut and his failing youth, just one of the boys, but God knows whose boys.

Two weeks went by before they threw in Bobby Dove to live with me. He took almost a week to truck in all the books and machinery that went along with him. His correct whole name was Robert Dove Fleece. He hadn't made it with his roomie either. One thing I could see: he dragged in so much clutter that there wasn't really room for anybody else to live with him. Fleece said little to me the first week. Then one afternoon I walked in on him and he broke open.

"You're some counselor they've hired to live with me, aren't you?" I had interrupted his reading at the long plywood table he had for a desk.

"No. I'm not. I'm in music."

"Are you a genius?" Fleece asked me.

"No. I've never considered being a gen—"

"Just going to clog up the field of music, are you? I understand, I guess. I'd hoped we'd have some ideas transpiring around the room. I *am* a genius. I'm going to bring

136

something *forth,* my brains are going to *come up with something.*" He caught me staring at him. "All right, rube, stare at me. I've got skinny limbs, I'm not Mister Muscle. Want to see me look like a puppet?" He stood up and formed himself into a slump which made him look exactly like a pale marionette out of work and hanging. Even sitting back down to his chair, he seemed to be worked from above by some cynical puppeteer. "Did you notice that fulgurant mother of a forehead I've got, though?" He tapped it. Then he put his little finger in one ear and hooked it upwards lovingly: *"Brains* up there," he said.

"I've got ideas. I don't mean I don't have any ideas," I defended myself. "There is a lot of idea in music, you know. When I play the trumpet, for example—"

"No, I'm afraid that music is *not* idea. Music is instinct dignified by instruments or voice. Music is howling in tune. The guts come first, and there is no disinterestedness, as in actual Idea."

"What would that be like?"

"Idea? An idea is something which exists already and does not care a shit whether you like it or not. You probably haven't had any ideas, rube, not fonking away on a horn. Sorry. I have ideas, I live at the top of my brain. You look like somebody who's looking out his navel. Oh ho! You want to get me don't you, Ruben? You want a *fistfight!* You peer meanly at me! Oh yes, attack! Thinking I look like a limp dry pea-pod or the like, aren't you? Some sort of fragile *herb* with hair on its arms. Go ahead, have a blast at me. Everybody else has. Easy stuff! Just one thing: I am a meatball at heart, a red meatball."

"I wanted to get along," I said.

"No matter how much you pound me, you can never defeat that meatball inside me. My manhood is sewed up inside me, courtesy of the Baptist Church. My mother cracked me over the head with the Baptist Hymnal. But my head *grew,* see. I won the State Science Fair . . . I surged, hating God and His house, which meant, you know, that I was *insane.* (Did you notice, rube, I said *hating,* not *disbelieving?* I never took the easy way out.) I let a few swearwords drop around the house. I was noticed to be standing in our open garage in only jock shorts by some women driving in from the grocery store who saw fit to call my mother about it; women astonished at how raw I had looked. If I'd had

137

muscles and a tan, they wouldn't have said anything. But not so with noodle man and all his thigh hair crawling out. Someone must be told. It's so easy to call a frail man crazy. But you already know all about me, don't you? Sent in here to practice *psychology* on me . . . you would've hit me by now if you weren't hired to counsel me."

"I don't know a thing." I didn't know that the voice-major in hymnology had asked him to leave after a month of life with him. Fleece's conscience did not hurt because of any of his crimes, such as threatening to alter the hymnologist fellow's voice pitch by an operation deft and silent while he slept (Fleece with his early knowledge of medical arts could do it, as the sleepless cantor knew), or ripping out a page of his expensive soft-leather Baptist Hymnal several times for use as he passed by his desk on the way to the commodes. What Fleece was concerned about was that his mother was close on his heels, consulting with men who had the power of throwing him in an asylum. He was always seeing her car around the dorm. Her car was green and black, and every time we neared a car with those colors, no matter what the make, on the way to the cafeteria or classes, Fleece hid behind me. He trembled, jumped up and down on his cigarette, and grabbed the collar of his shirt and buttoned the top button. He'd had bad bronchitis all his life and thought she'd catch him and have him shipped away on, say, three counts of inability to take care of himself. On the positive side, Fleece was sure he could forget all this once he'd "stolen pleasure" with a girl. In the meantime, his imagination was about to do him in.

"My mother can drive to this campus in five minutes if she wants to," he said; his head rolled like a melon on a stick over his desk. "If you were wondering about my father, my biological father was killed on Tarawa. I have a stepfather who's high horse in the National Guard; that's his job, being Field General Creech standing by for flood, tornado, race riot, or direct attack from North Korea. The emergencies for this man are always doubtful in coming, but immense if they do. He and my mother love God but don't really believe in miracles. Me, I hate God but believe in miracles, very much.

"Sixteen years old, I saw my box garden of cacti bloom out with quills overnight. I was awed by what these plants could do in nothing but sand and quite ready to believe in
138

dew-fairies or the Sand Man or any kind of heavenly inter-
cession that could've made this possible, then in comes my
mother, who *scraws,* 'Now doesn't that prove that God was
here in this room? Oh, Bobby Dove, your little sand garden
is a small Holy Land in Mississippi!' She picks me up by
the handle of my spine and rubs my face in the sand
around the cacti, as much. Creech is near; he hears her.
Thirty minutes later, I'm still in bed, thinking of miracles,
reading a paperback *Lady Chatterley's Lover.* Creech
comes in, in uniform. He eases the book out of my hand
and reads the pages I was reading. He keeps the book folded out like I had it, turns it over, and lays it pages down
over my five cactus plants in the sand garden. He says, 'I
know you smoke even though she might not.' I admit it.
'Where are your matches?' I give him the box in my dresser. He doesn't ask for the cigarettes. 'What the Lord giveth,
He taketh away,' enounces Creech, striking the match and
setting fire to the book. That's the only scripture I ever
heard from him. The book takes fire, like a burning roof
over the cactus plants. They throb away eventually, little
crumbling hairy little bulbs. The book collapses among the
brown stumps, the blackened sand . . . the ashes puff up a
little, as if Connie and the gamekeeper might still be humping away under them; pussy, with interludes of cigarette-
smoking and studying of history and biology—that's what I
dream of. To steal pleasure like that, have it in spite of
them that want to coop you up for good. Oh, after the fire I
began hissing and they let me crawl off with a book and
play with my doo-doo in the corner. That's what they
thought of me reading doubtful Christians like Joyce Cary,
Aldous Huxley, and William Faulkner. You couldn't get
Henry Miller in Mississippi then, with which one mastur-
bates feeling like an intellectual snob.

"I dream of my mother escorting me to an amphitheater
crowded with castrated singers. Around my neck hangs a
white tablet with my negligence and sin shown in black
checkmarks. The crowd sings at me in wrath. My mother
cries over me. 'Mercy!' she wails. She prevails, and we walk
down to the bottom of the amphitheater, where there is a
cave of exposed muscle tissue between two great male paps.
This is God, His Bosom, just set there gigantesque. A
wound, harsh, deep, and puckered. My mother and the
crowd begin a humming of one of the church hymns they

use for Invitationals, meaning that I should go on down into the wound and walk into the raw flesh of the Supreme Being. "But Mother, this hymn I despise is echoing in the wound-hole. This *hymn*, Mother, I heard it so much at the church, it got into my ears like an infection. I can't go. I've had God speaking through those hymns so much, I've been immunized against him. God God, God, you always said to me at home. Is he simply this gruesome *slit?* You were so sure of Him, the hymns were so sure of Him. Look at the 'no-smoking' sign at the peak of the wound. Just like you said. And the bouncing ball over the words of 'Amazing Grace'. You know I won't sing the hymns."

"It's night. Too late to get to the cafeteria now," I said. Fleece ignored me.

"Did you know, Monroe, there are damned few dull moments reading the Bible? You can't say that for many works its size. I couldn't put the Bible down; I read it between when I was fourteen and seventeen and hid it from my mother just like all the other books."

Suddenly I was wary. "Fleece, you aren't after all just another kind of preacher, are you?"

"You just can't regard an idea, can you, Ruben?" He fell in the bunk, which he had placed behind a bamboo screen room divider. I heard him sigh, invisible. "I'd really like you to come beat me up like you want to," he said. "I'd like to show you how I could live through it." He sat up and put his head outside the screen. "You think men of ideas are going around trying to catch farts with a hook, don't you? Come on, mash me. I'd like to show you how an idea, an essence, *me,* can emerge whole in spite of punishment."

"You're some sort of flit, aren't you?" I knew this was stupid the minute I said it, remembering the episode with Lloyd Reese years ago. "I don't mean that. I mean, what idea would you be if someone came over and—"

"Laid waste to me," he broke in. "What would be remembered now as I'm twenty-one years old, free and white. What would survive me worth thinking about for long? Some idea, some essence . . . Well, honestly, I haven't quite come up with it yet. But I'm on the verge. When I steal pleasure with a woman, probably, then . . . ."

"Aw, look at all the billions of idiots who've done that—"

"Yes!" he shouted, holding his finger up next to his face. *"Idiots!* But look out when the man of ideas takes off his

140

underwear! He is a log jam of throbbing pieces. He is Robert Dove Fleece, hearing his mother scraw through her nose about God at him; he has heard God scratch His fingernails across the blackboard; has heard those dirge-tune hymns curling out of the mouths from people moaning in that red brick church . . . with weeds and young kudzu vines up against the foundation, the old yellow pianos in the basement assembly rooms. The nandina bushes standing around the church with their berries that the little redneck kids rip off to throw at one another, leaving only the raw wood fingers of the nandinas . . . the leaves moldy and pissed-upon by all the dogs owned by people in asbestos-siding houses nearby the church. I slip out of church one night during the last hymn. 'Just As I Am,' the hymn, comes to my ears for the thousandth time, one hundred-odd dead hums of the buried from inside a cheap red brick sarcophagus, and I decide to become more detestable to God, Christ, the Holy Ghost. The hymn is running in my blood like a poison. But—"

"Stop talking . . . That's enough, by God," I came in. I didn't want to hear *all* the throbbing pieces of experience.

". . . I allow myself to come to Hedermansever because my mother says Syracuse University, where I had the scholarship for winning the State Science Fair, is too far away and too cold. She'd rather write all the checks for me here. Then they room me with a guy who's a major in *hymnology*. Is this to drive me into a barrel? Get me in there long enough to where, when I tumped it over and made a break for it, there would be a lot of them to get a shot at me."

Fleece stood up out of his bunk and folded back the bamboo divider. There was nothing between us now. He was in a profuse sweat, very yellow around the collar of his white shirt. "Believe me, Mississippi is so boring you will find a lot of people doing with their noses what canines do to other canines. *Studying* you, *understanding* you, getting some smell off you, nodding their brown noses over you.

"You called me a flit a minute ago," he said, looking at me warily, taking off his glasses and dropping them with his hand slack to his thigh. "Fuck ideas, by damn, I'll fight you over that."

"I didn't mean it." I really didn't want to crush the boy. Right now I could see my fist go into his head as into a cantaloupe, and there was no victory in it.

141

"Sit down, then. What are you? Who have they put on me now? You play the trumpet. What do you play? *Hymns?* Do you play 'There Is a Fountain Filled with Blood' with that special tone like a zombie underwater? . . . Never mind. I'm going to sleep. Now, don't you leave. You go to sleep, too. This is a fine damn time to go to sleep."

Other nights Fleece explained to me how he had declared himself—he was going to be a doctor and study how "one suffers in the meat." "I was always a meatball," he said. "I'm going to be the best doctor Mississippi ever produced. They'll bring in some whore whose boyfriend has shot her in the cunt pointblank with a shotgun and alongside her her boyfriend also, who thought he commited suicide putting the last shot into his navel, and I'll put on my mask, wave my hands with some instruments, and bring them back Romeo and Juliet."

Fine dreamy ambitions, but Bobby Dove had taken some insulting liberties with me and what used to be my room. Besides the plywood desk, he had brought in three cases of books, two lamps, a fishbowl into which he dumped cartons of Salem cigarettes, cigar boxes with pens, various single murdered insects, newspaper clippings, photographs, and, mostly, the letters. The letters were written by an inmate at Whitfield, the state sanitarium. In the stacks on his desk were some childish sketches of the police arresting Freedom Riders at the Jackson bus station, done by Fleece himself, who was on the spot and had had his camera grabbed off him and smashed in the dock; then there were marijuana leaves, which Fleece, as a former State Science Fair winner in botany, supposed he could keep with academic impunity; 200-proof lab alcohol in Dr. Tichenor's Antiseptic bottles; and antihistamine tablets and cough syrups. Further, he had a stork in flight, made of iron, with two incense pots hanging on a chain from its beak. Set under the window was a hip-high radio console owned by his biological father. On its top was a wooden planter containing cactus plants big and vigorous like cucumbers with steel pins forking everywhere. The room was twelve by eighteen and his cargo occupied seven-eighths of it. About all I had was my bed and the telescope. Fleece had given me the telescope.

For a couple of weeks at the beginning of school, he had

had some luck spying over at the girls' dorm with it. He had seen some towering girl do the Twist naked in her room, but he said he was tired of only looking. He told me that late one night he had taken the scope down to the urinal intending to drop it out the window, but had noticed something odd down in a urinal on the first floor of the other wing. He pulled out the scope, looked, and there was old Leon, a boy he'd gone to high school with, flogging himself, sitting on the pot, in complete apathy. Fleece became ill watching Leon practice masturbation so casually. Leon had no pride or rapture; neither happy nor sad, he was simply getting it out of him. This sight depressed Fleece gravely. He threw the telescope on my bed and said I could have it. The vantages of the voyeur were bankrupt.

The equipment in the room made it hard to get out of bed and dress. My room was another man's entire *home*. He meant to leave his family for good, taking everything which had ever touched him.

"Fleece," I finally said, in October. "You know I'm paying, or rather my scholarship is paying, for *half* of this room. Now look where the screen is. Three inches from my bed. And I can't get to the lavatory without knocking over something of yours."

That evening I came in to find he had somehow drawn in his materials so that I had more than half of the room area. The bamboo screen was clutched around his tiny space. I heard Fleece rattling at his desk. His gear was stuffed and balanced to an extreme height behind the screen. On my side of the screen there was tacked a note: YOU WON'T LEAVE, WILL YOU? I looked around the screen. Fleece was huddled over a foot-square working area on his desk. His possessions were hurled up around him, trembling—the metal stork, the cigar boxes, the easel (Fleece did hidden art efforts, in Crayola, I believe), the books. He turned toward me, his study lamp shaking the light over his hands. He was angry.

"I have to beg, *beg*, to keep a rube like you to stay with me. *Me*. You know I have to keep you here, I can't afford to break up with another roomie. They'd come get me. There would be reason."

"I'm not concerned with that. I wasn't saying I was going to leave."

143

"You weren't?" he asks sincerely.

Then we went ahead as normal. The screen crept over toward me inch by inch, day by day. He read by day and wrung out his thoughts on me by night.

"I want to do a little subjective-response quiz on you tonight, Monroe. I've written down some words: *tallywhacker, dong, peter, dick, tool, prod, root, member* (more literary!), and *dork*. What *adjective* describes the whole set?"

"*Silly.*" He had read them in a prolonged Southern nasal way and there was no other answer.

"Right!" he cheered. "Or better: *condescending*, or *mocking*. You think *men* ever gave themselves those names? Never. Women named us. They saw it down there begging for lubrication from them. The woman sees him hunching beneath the throne of meat and fur, I don't care if he's Alexander the Great or Eric the Red, with some random shepherdess—she sees him, she names him. Caesar had to have it, Napoleon stooped for it, J.F.K. with his millions is not immune. But we look *up* when we see women, any woman. *Cunt*, we breathe out . . . delirious, obsequious to her . . . *fuck*, both words going deep, maybe all the way to the heart."

Fleece took a breath and rubbed his glasses on his sleeve.

I told him what he had said was rousing and eloquent but doubtful. Fleece loved the noise of the words of his latest thoughts; I was always holding back because I didn't have the words yet. I had the music, but not the words yet. As a matter of fact, I expressed myself so badly, Fleece ignored me completely.

"I think of writing my mother," he went on. " 'Well, I've done it with Judy Rut, a white whore over on Mulberry Street in Vicksburg. It's done. I'll be hard to catch from now on.' She receives the letter during the day, while Creech is away rehearsing at the armory. She calls up the Dean of Men. This is one of my favorite dreams. The Dean of Men has me sewn up in a beanbag. Just *captured*, you see. In five minutes my mother is over here walking around the beanbag. I hear her footsteps. I'm lying in the bag they've stitched me up in, amongst *hills* of dried beans, utterly nude, having let nobody bathe me, no, madly satisfied with Judy Rut's oil still on me. They've made a mistake. The stitching of the beanbag has been done *too* well. It's

144

unbreakable. They've captured me, but can't get *to* me. My flag is in the air, my tally is stiff, trustworthy and cheerful as a lighthouse. I roll in the beans, creating harmless light avalanches upon myself. Just every now and then my mother's voice gets through the cloth. 'Are you telling God about this, Robert Dove? What is *He* thinking?' I stop moiling in the beans and I *do* think of Him. 'What do You think of a man lying naked in dried beans?' I ask. And as usual complete silence socks me in the ear. I shout out, 'Where is General Creech?' I know this will send her away, wordless, creeping, drooped, down the dormitory stairs. Creech must never know about me.

"I believe she saw it as her duty to hide my exceptional quirks from Creech even more than she saw her duty to God. I had to seem normal when he was around. I saw him the night Elvis Presley appeared on the Ed Sullivan show. For some reason, we weren't at church that Sunday night. Creech hated all music and couldn't really tell any of it apart. But he wanted to crawl into the television and choke Elvis. Things I thought were just curious, Creech wanted to kill. He finally kicked the On knob off the set. . . . But it was secrets about *my* life that Mother and I were supposed to keep, such as the fact I was two years older than Creech thought I was. I pitched some fits I don't even remember the first two years she tried to enroll me in school. I'm twenty-one now, freshman at college. But we kept this from Creech.

"She married him in Florida where she was in the subdivision close to an army base. She was a church-going widow; a card-carrying Christian. Met him at a dinner in the church basement; found herself romantic with bachelor Creech, who asked her to marry him before he'd ever looked in the house and seen me. Don't think I haven't meditated on that young postwar girl who has been molded by panic ever since she was nineteen. I'd get bronchitis trying to hold the tears inside. You didn't cry in this house. We even kept my botany project for the Science Fair a secret from him, because she wasn't sure how my excessive interest in plants would impress him.

"Some nights I even combed my hair and left the house on supposed dates, showing the normal interest in the opposite sex that comes to all good boys. This drew a wink out

145

of Creech and thrilled my mother. She whispered to me at the door to go up the street and introduce myself to some awful sixteen-year-old girl whose body looked like frozen oatmeal. Some nights I would sense that Creech just wanted me out of the house. These nights I'd put on my whole brown suit, water down my hair, and leave the house with enthusiasm. Run out in the dark and beat off.

"The noise of my turning pages in my room drove him out of his mind, and also my whamming the slides of my microscope together. It interrupted Creech in drinking his gallon of coffee every night while pursuing his own original art form, that of violently ripping to shreds the newspaper of the day after reading every particle of it, about nine P.M. This had nothing to do with the contents of the paper. It was the theory put in practice that one should live each day as it came and forget, or in his case, destroy, the past. I wish I were kidding you.

"Creech is from northern Florida. Let me tell you how mean the town he grew up in is. We went down there one Christmas with him. In the history of this town, there had never been any snow. But it snowed that Christmas, about two inches, at night. I looked out the window the next morning and saw that already the kids on the street had scraped up the snow from four yards and in a vacant lot next to this defunct service station they had built a huge snow statue of a man having relations with a dog. Merry Christmas. What was it some professor said about Florida? . . . That Florida was unique in going straight from barbarism to decadence without an intervening period of civilization.

"Getting back to my mother: I told her goodbye, wearing my suit. I went around to the dark of the back of the house and rang true as a normal adolescent by dropping my pants and having at it. Then I would fall asleep in that tall grass next to the house that the lawnmower never could reach. Wake up in two hours and stroll in mimicking the afterglow of a fine time with a girl. I had on my mind one of those dancers fom the Jackie Gleason show—a big-legged girl in jeweled brassiere and net hose, panting, at last contented by me her hero who was a sort of surprising churn upon her; her nipples still hard in excitement, lifted toward the moon. In those hours I had absorbed an arro-

146

gance, a privacy, a self, with crickets jumping around me. I could finally ignore Creech. I won the Science Fair, and in a little excess of pride, I appeared in the garage in nothing but my jock shorts. Proud of the hair on my body as if it were a fox coat. Then the women call and tell my mother."

While Fleece was behind his screen, seeping out the biography, I was lying in bed eating an orange. Suddenly I noticed the screen had been pushed almost flush against my cot. Fleece was looking at me through a tear in the thatch.

"I said, Ruben, that I appeared in the garage in nothing but my jock shorts, and that the women called and told my mother." He put his eye up to the hole closer. "But there were mitigating circumstances. I had been reading Walt Whitman. 'Song of Myself,' you know, the poet, Ruben?" I was weary of the Ruben theme.

"I know about Walt Whitman," I said, lying.

"Lookie here." He crooked his index finger through the screen hole, its end searching stupidly.

"What?"

"Man-root," he said in that crimp-nosed redneck way.

"Oh Lord. This is diseased," I said. "This is sick, an obsession!"

"Yes!" Fleece brayed, doing the finger lungingly, mashing out the hole.

"What would your mother say?" I was really wondering. It was the wrong thing.

"She would say, 'Aaaaaaaa!' " He jumped up on the screen, shrieking, and he and the whole affair fell on me. He hit me through the screen on my face and back, me trying to squirm out. "Nasty boy! Ugly, ugly!" he said, hitting me. "Out in the garage, after all those years in God's house!" I smelled the lab alcohol on his breath then, through the screen. I took account of this, and really it was a wide relief that he might be mostly drunk. "Monroe!" he hit me on top of the head a last time as I was turning him and the screen back. "Life is long, and so messy. I *had* to grow up, didn't I? I get a chance to be messy too, don't I?" I had knocked him over by then. He scrambled to the door. "I love it, I love life!"

Fleeing, he begged me, "Please don't tell them. Don't tell them." Then he wavered swiftly down the dorm stairs. Who could chase that?

147

3 / Mondo Porno

Fleece was sharp of bone. His back almost cut through his shirt. He was my height, five ten, but weighed somewhere near 120. At twenty-one, the boy was losing his hair. He was left with the high, bald intimidating forehead of, well, of a genius. Already he was reading the *Merck Manual* as if there were patients calling him. Fleece was never bored by pain, his own or that of others. I presumed he'd make a good physician, but there was this cornered spider-monkey style of his that might give him some trouble at bedside. Also, he was prone to an attack of what he called Hudson Bay flu about once a month. Mucus would harden like antlers in his head and chest and he couldn't get out of bed. He'd just lie down, smoking one Salem after another.

It was then that I would hum softly and earnestly one of the old hymns of the church, and another. I would become an endless seepage of fine old hymnal numbers. Fleece would turn his head on the pillow and look at me with his red flu-stricken eyes. "It takes a sorry white man to treat a sick genius like this. You bastard. Go on off and suck your trumpet, you bastard." Then he'd cough like somebody raking out an iron tomb. I hummed on, sweetly smiling.

A day in December when I was at it again, he whispered to me why didn't I smoke some of his marijuana, or drink some of his lab alcohol? Everything that was in the room that was his, was mine, he croaked. Why didn't I read some of his terrible books? I could even read the letters. On his desk he had *Justine, Fanny Hill, Lady Chatterley's Lover, Tropic of Cancer,* and *The Blind Mistress.* But I went straight for the letters. He had been clutching them significantly now for a couple of months, and sort of patrolling the room with his eyes as he clutched them.

I took them out one by one from the three cigar boxes, sitting on my bed, reading right down to "love-milk" (the

148

writer was strong on using quotation marks around anything he considered reckless), "the curlyfur purse of love's jam," and "the tongue that laps the yolk of your precious egg." "Remember (said the writer) when we played early morning breakfast and you said, how sad we don't have any cream along with those lovely eggs of yours under Sir Silly Limpness who was, shame on you, such a Bully Be-Hard last night. We could have eggs poached in cream, but I know you are too tired to go to the store for it now, and since necessity is the mother of invention, I'll just . . . then Beloved you tittered and threw your head down full of your glorious hair—there is just no expression for your full lank hair lying in a thousand soft pricklings on my stomach, Oh how many gentlemen have felt *that* ever? And breakfasted upon it with your lips, then your whole drawing oralness, making your soft direct assault against the object you had been shy of before, with precious tears streaming down your cheeks, the meal so full, and so surprised was I, I spewed irregardless of your sacred throat or former earthly laws of love-conduct, Beloved. You sat up and laughed the laugh of wiser freedom that good God had given us. (me dropping this page, opening another envelope, finding) . . . the magic grape-heaven of your nipples, darling rare nipples and puckered buttons, the only things I know of that God has put on this earth that swell, widen and grow daily the more one puts his mouth to them and sups thereof. Was I too greedy the last opening of your bosoms? Splendrous sight! greedy at the brown buttons covering half your ideal breasts. Yet still you pushed them up with your hands—ah memory, memory of your fingernails painted heart-glow red which you always kept polished along with your toenails whatever hour I awoke and declared the timeless want of man for woman—true Beloved, you demanded of me I give you that hour's 'sucking' time that I never not one day since I knew it was your sacred desire deprived you."

(Me, lifting out another, reading into further sacredness, heartness, Belovedness) ". . . can you Beloved like I can away from you, can you have that holy liquid 'Coming' when you *think* of me, as I can as I imagine you postured upon the violet sheets of our marriage bed, what did we care if every window, every door of the house were wide open, having the north breeze wind upon your my Be-

149

loved's soft thin legs, your eyes, elfin eyes, hoping unselfish-
ly that this might be one of the times when you 'pulsate'
too? Can you think yourself into love's undeniable 'release'?
As your husband can do now? Last letter you said it was
impossible. Beloved, you must believe in the psychic power
channel between us. You must *concentrate* on me and find
me in our most wanton duets of yesteryear. Picture your
ecstatic flanks rubbing me, your little feet interlocking and
kneading the base of my spine, that sitting position we assumed when we could spy more completely on one another's mounting course of pleasure; picture me mounted, eyes
greedy and agleam . . . I know so many of your thoughts
must of needs be dismal by the mere existing day by day,
but you must think *through* these weak chains of boredom
to me, think through 'impossible'—that's a word a nigger
would use. Beloved, don't use it again. Let yourself into the
deluxurious habitats of our psychic channel, and 'COME,
Come Please.' "

(Next letter.) "I have not been getting your letters. I
have discovered that two of the doctors are Jew rascals. I
cannot doubt they have made something happen to them. I
couldn't tell you what I have suffered at the hands of the
niggers. If I thought one of their hands had ever touched an
epistle of yours, or that one of those Iscariots had breathed
on your precious script. . . ."

(I keep opening.) " 'Doctor' Eis thinks he has healed
me. He asks me if I am keeping my hands off myself now. I
said to him, unspokenly, keep your hands off me you unin-
cinerated curd of Jezebel's milk. Why don't I hear from
you? Send your letters Special Delivery, Darling."

(Spotting the next one, losing desire.) "Can one look anywhere without seeing crowds of nigger orderlies? They
creep through these halls as if they were in a haunted
house. They peek in to see poor white men flat on their
backs. Their eyes are like muddy eggs. They laugh. They
are such things in their white uniforms; they cherish cleaning up the vomit of men who would thrash them if the odds
were even. . . . I can not tell you (Oh, Beloved, now I
don't know for certain that you even hear my epistolary
voice!) how I have suffered by these prissy niggers this
Eternity, from the first day a year ago when one of them
tied me to the bed with raw hemp rope, and told me to be

150

ashamed of myself. But now that they know I'm getting out, they don't come near me."

(On into the last half of them.) "There is something devilish going on. The niggers are moving to positions of authority. The Jew doctors cavort with them and trust them. I have been silent for so, so long. The other afternoon the black scoundrels were running in the hall drinking beer. In a psychiatric hospital, celebrating Christ's birth. There was a group of intoxicated black orderlies gathered around the bulletin board at the middle of the esplanade. They had a jackknife and they were throwing it to stick up in the bulletin board itself, piercing the official state and federal information sheets thereon. White men were close with them. It was 'Doctor' Eis and 'Doctor' Clyde, the Jews. They applauded when one of the bucks stuck a knife in an announcement sheet from twenty paces away. Foremost in congratulating the nigger was 'Doctor' Eis. I made as if I hadn't seen them and was walking up to see the week's menu on the board, but a biggish nigger wearing the badge of a nurse, turned me around with his mealy hands and said, 'See you later, alligator. You got to wear some pants when you come out on the porch.' I shook him off, knowing I had on my gown. I was furious to know what 'Doctor' Eis would do with this nigger 'nurse,' as I saw him coming on. 'You have to watch yourself,' Eis said. His breath was also revolting with beer. Then he drew out my gown and dropped it, and I realized that I had had the edge of my gown caught up inadvertently on the top of my penis, which I had not known was in an erective state. I am not now such a freak as to come out with niggers throwing jackknives, in such a condition, consciously. The suetty demons. The Jews abetting them. I was excruciatingly embarrassed. But there is some accounting due me too."

(Reading another, written in the fastidiously brittle old ink like the rest, with the letters slim and high, as if someone had dipped a dry eyelash in the inkwell and gone to work) "I will undergo electricity this week. Not at the behest of Eis or Clyde. I do it on the advice of a marvelous Christian psychiatrist who hails from Raymond, Mississippi. He seems just a boy to me. Would you believe it, he studied at the University of Massachusetts, the same as yours truly? Then he went to Johns Hopkins and to Tübingen, as a Fulbright Scholar."

(Letter after the electricity, apparently) "I have made investigations. Eis is a voluptuary. His wife is a nurse here and he can't keep his hands off her. I've seen other things, such as at the Coca-Cola machine. Eis was making change for a colored woman custodian. I could tell he had designs on her. I gave the black slut her dime. I wouldn't take her two nickels. I slashed Eis with a sneer. He wasn't my doctor any more. He couldn't keep his sexual 'projections' out of the public eye. I do hate Jews. I do. One of them invented this hateful psychoanalysis, you know. God damn him! and all their interloping, their prowling, their secret-killing. Oh, Christ, to strangle, to torture! Christ! that I could personally have assassinated Sigmund Freud. The Jews cannot live at peace with anyone they can't put their cancer to. They will raise up the nigger, and teach him power and pride of position, and somehow too they will have to deal with that barbarous voodoo 'christianity,' and they will fail. They will succeed only in making hordes of niggers atheist warriors. They will be too 'kind' to deport and dump the niggers back into Africa and make it again the continental monkey-house it was intended to be, as we were too 'kind.' We let the cannon be set against our skulls, while we smirked vainly at having unloaded it and made it a phantom with our 'humanity.' And there we will be, looking at armed phalanxes of those mumbo-jumbo blackamoors brought over to my green and golden America by fools three hundred years ago. But I will not be of those whining insects of inevitablists who would let this happen. I am pointed to action: TO TREAT EVERY NIGGER AS IF HE WERE A JEW AND EVERY JEW AS IF HE WERE A NIGGER.

". . . I now know, Catherine, that you have been hearing me in every letter. I have heard also, in the cold tones of Dr. Eis, of your plans. Be out of the house, then, by Tuesday, since you will not live with me. If you have preserved my letters, leave them. I will enforce. Do not write another check on my account. Do not use my name in any transactions. You *must* burn our marriage bed. Take everything else you want with you. I beg you not to engage lawyers. Believe me, you would not want the sordid fraction of lucre you might desire after I countenanced you even at the distance of one corner of a courtroom to the other. I would be civil, not, as you might wish, frothing in manner fit to be reinserted at Whitfield. You would see me tearing you to pieces with a little smile. You were ever shy of the public eye, Catherine. You know that. Even the postman. You were made for existing in that drear rodential shade of lichens up in the New Brunswick rocks. As a Quaker girl, you were always hiding your 'inner light' under a bushel, weren't you? Take what you are offered and run, run all the way back to New Brunswick, and take what's left of your life with your parents, the shade-mongers, the coolish, the tapwater Quakers of the four-room house, where it will be safe to speak of me ever again. The Same [He always signed this way], Peter."

As I put the last letter back in its envelope, I noticed my friend was asleep, his eyelids gathered together in a great creasing. I felt alarmed, nasty, tired, and most of all, curious. I shook Fleece.

"Who is he?" I asked.

"A man."

"A real man? Is he out of Whitfield now?"

"I'm not going to tell you. You hummed those hymns, you bastard."

"I won't do it again."

"All right. He lives. And he's loose. The day I went down to take pictures of the police arresting the Freedom Riders, he was there at the bus terminal. I didn't know who it was then. Two years ago. A man wearing a big almost sheriff kind of hat ran over and grabbed my camera out of my hands. The strap was around my neck, and he jerked it off, snapped the strap, and hurt my neck. He smashed the camera on the pavement in front of the bus. I was just getting ready to be very indignant, but the man then comes after *me,* very indignant. So I ran. And he chased me, through the bus terminal and out to the street, yelling at me. I thought, God, for sure, he's one of our Mississippi lawmen, with that hat and all. But the moment I knew he wasn't was when he unbuckled his *belt* as he ran after me and whipped it *out,* coming for me. There was something too unofficially *personal* about that. And you know what he was saying?"

"What?"

"He was saying 'Stop! Stop! Stop!' while I was saying 'Why? Why?' legging it, knowing it was simply between me and him, him being of some odd independent strain of

153

creature. Well, I outran him. I couldn't see why he was angry, what interest *he* had. The police whose pictures I was ready to take weren't being too vicious with the riders when they arrested them. Not yet. They beat them in the jail with rubber hoses later. Ralph, my friend the police station clerk, told me. But later. Other camera people were at the scene. He must have noted *me* as unofficial, too young or something. Came at me. The man was Peter the letter-writer himself. Whitfield Peter. I didn't know. I hadn't even seen the letters yet.

"Two weeks later I did. My teacher in botany was always seeking field trips for our class. She wrote letters to landowners down around the coast, over in the delta, and she wrote to one real estate baron up in Madison County who had a spot advertisement for 'Canton Harbors' on television. He wrote back saying he was overjoyed to let students use his property for hunting specimens. He'd seen some very interesting specimens himself on his acreage, had yearned for them to be classified by botanists. Being the leading brain of the class, I was shown the actual letter by the teacher. Written in skinny tall glances in brown ink like the ones you've just read."

Fleece and the group went up to Madison County, near Canton, looked around in the fields and woods, and gathered at lunchtime around a big house, which was unlocked. They went into it, out of the sun, to use the commodes and water. There was only a little furniture in it. Fleece climbed up in the attic. There was a big crate full of letters. He had a field bag, and after reading a few, crammed in as many as he could. He backed down the attic stairs, dizzy as if from snakebite. He was on fire and the rest of the kids and the teacher were eating bologna sandwiches. Then out to the fields again, where there were some really rare flora. But what did he care. He picked up a four-leaf clover and spent the rest of the day trying to keep himself from ripping out of his shorts, rereading the letters in forest holes, getting himself amongst gloomy bushes, the words of sex memorizing *him*, it seemed, rather than the other way. Getting back in the bus a dangerous bulging thief. Getting a seat to himself, which wasn't hard. The rest of them had long since given up on Fleece as a social being. (Fleece hated all the males in his class because of the irrational hope in their faces. He disdained the female for the reason that none of

154

them was a goddess with whom he could fall hopelessly in love.) He jerked the tops of a few letters out of his satchel. "Oh Catherine, Catherine, you are my naked breakfast, lunch, dinner. Well do I gain again that day, noon, as the language of your body aroused you helplessly to climb upon the table from which I was eating, open your robe, and lie back supine, your thighs begging me to perpetuate the holiday of love with you, forget my mere plate of food. And of course you won. Intercourse with you versus trifling food-hunger—never a contest! What did I care for politics, my inherited wealth, the possibility of being a senator in the state congress of Mississippi? Oh my lost sperm in you, oh happy, happy spewing away of ambition and power."

I read this letter, finding it in the heap of thirty or so in the cigar boxes. Fleece's voice had left him. He wanted to tell me, but the flu was on him too grimly for him to continue. Fleece's eyes, as he lay back down, bubbled out as if in a hot yellow pie. He was in an alarming passion.

"So somehow you found out this Whitfield Peter was the same man who broke your camera and chased you?" Fleece nodded. "And did you find out why, or how, he got put away in Whitfield?" I asked, but I already knew, partway. "It wasn't on account of his hating Jews and niggers, if he did before he went in. It was sex. She turned on him, Catherine."

Fleece had found a pen and was scribbling on the flyleaf of a textbook. He gave me the book, and I read "Right, rube. You don't get Whitfielded for hate in Mississippi. Apparently she gave out during the honeymoon sometime. She made a phone call, one would guess. But *I know* by his other letters that when the Whitfield squad got to his house, he was upstairs, naked, hunching every crease he could find in the pillows, curtains, his own torn-off underwear." Fleece finished another note on the back of one of Peter's letters. I took it. "Peter speaks proudly of this in one letter. Like he thought it was marvelous for him to be continuing on in passion for her even when she wasn't even there any more. Maybe he didn't go crazy until they had him in Whitfield itself and he became sane enough to know that he didn't even have access to the proximity of sex with Catherine. If you can believe him, one unfortunate thing did happen when he got to Whitfield. A couple of the Negro orderlies were cruel to him. They tied him to a bed with raw hemp

155

rope. He was still going to town on the sheets, still trying to simulate sex in any given crease once he woke up again, and the orderlies let these colored maids come in to watch the white man straining at it regardless of the ropes on him. Peter lists this as a grievance he will never forget, the Negro eyes beholding him in his compulsion on the sheets. He had one bright horrified sane eye on all that happened to him in Whitfield, along with his blind, squirming insanity."

It was four A.M. and I was muddy of sight myself, sleepy, but exhilarated. I was glad I'd stuck it out with Fleece.

"She wrote him, too, I guess. I'd like to see some of *her* letters," I said.

"They must be down in that crate in his attic," whispered Fleece. "I want them. If you've got the guts, we'll go steal them."

4 / The Theft of Her Letters

Bobby Dove was better the next day, coming out of the flu. He could talk again, when I saw him in the room at noon.

"Sure we'll steal them, Monroe. We'll whiz over there in your little sports car, we'll be up in that attic, we'll steal them. This morning I was lying here thinking: *every* thing good in life is stolen. Knowledge is stolen, pleasure is stolen, all art is stolen from time; ideas are stolen from events. None of them wanted us to find them out. Life has done her damned best to keep us away from her secrets. She may be *afraid,* you see, that when we know Her too well we will hate Her. She is afraid of the master thieves, like me. Yes, we'll steal those letters!"

I had never thought of it in such large terms, but I was ready to go steal the letters. I had never stolen anything that I knew of. Except, briefly, perhaps the trumpet that night with Lloyd Reese. I held the trumpet in my hands and looked at it anew in the afternoon over in the Fine Arts Building, with Dr. Livace instructing. Well, indeed, it was a

156

fine new wound-up golden thing to me. I could steal music
from the dumb muteness of the air. What did Adolph Sax,
inventor of the saxophone, what did he think when he
made *that* instrument, wonderful thing, that finally made it
into jazz and let loose the rambling reedsweet moan we
needed? Stolen, stolen. The reed growing in the swamps,
the metal ores underground, and between them the buried
dead who had needed the sound but never knew it was possible, needed the Master Thief, even if he never knew he
was a Master Thief. I myself was letting loose on the subject of theft. I believed in theft and could almost sing a song
to it. And so I got back to Fleece very ready to steal almost
anything.

"When do we go after the letters?" I said.

"We're not going after any letters." He looked at me
coldly and stood up to study the dreary iron skyscape out
the window. Today it had been seeping a little cold mist.

"This morning we were going after the letters. To steal
them."

"But since then I've gotten afraid. You see, he offered his
fields to our botany class. If he looked in that crate in the
attic, he would know somebody in the class took the letters.
The house was open, but he never said we could go in it.
The teacher didn't know we were in the house until after I
took the letters, and then she ran us out. The next Monday,
he was over at her house. He was polite but very angry.
Something had been stolen from his house. She knew I'd
been in the house and called me to come over. A friend of
mine drove me over to her house. He wasn't in the house.
She told me he was sitting in his car out front and wanted
to see me. I walked out and leaned on the car at the window across from him. The street light was barely catching
him, and the fear I had already was nothing like what I had
when I recognized him, vague as he was. He wore the same
big hat, leaning toward me. The same man who broke my
camera and came at me with his belt. His name was Peter
Lepoyster. He had wavy tan hair. 'You were in the house.
Do you know what I want?' he asked me. I said I didn't.
'Well if you are the class leader, I tell you, you'd better get
what has been stolen back to me, and very quick. I think
thieves and their collaborators should be shot.' I was so
scared I suddenly got bold. I asked him who he thought he
was. I told him my father was a general of the National

157

Guard who would come against him anytime he showed force against me, and would cram him so far back into Whitfield he'd never see enough light to find his own dick. He stared back, his teeth apart like some big biting jackass, and he drove away with my hands still on his window. Did you ever see somebody fifty years old who wanted to kill you? Christ, what a mistake I'd made. He knew I'd seen the postmarks of Whitfield on the letters, but I knew he knew who I was and could find out where I lived."

I took this into account. Fleece, feeble and nervous in his robe, seemed to be looking around the parking lot for Peter as well as for the old demon, his mother.

"Did he ever come around?" I asked him.

"Never. I suppose the threat of the National Guard held him off, maybe."

"But now there are two of us against him, Fleece. If it came down to it, we could *beat him up* and steal the letters. We could wear masks. We could disguise our whole bodies, even."

"No. I didn't want you in on it. It's all mine, whatever it is. I was sick. I don't want you a part of it. It's mine."

"I have the car."

"You have the car, but you don't have the address."

He made me mad, letting me down. I went behind the screen, took the three cigar boxes off the shelf, and stole them from him, the letters.

"You saw what I did. I've taken them. Now they're mine. There's no way you can get them back. I'd hurt you if you tried it."

Fleece looked amazed at the boxes in my hands.

"You don't even know what you have," he said. "You can't imagine how . . . *snorty* you look holding those boxes to your breast."

"Well, I have his address now, on every envelope. I'm willing to steal her letters. I want them."

Fleece was shocked right in the eyes. He seemed not to have thought of the envelopes.

"They're *mine*. I love them. I love the old brown ink on them so much. Those quotation marks around *lush vigilant digit, your clitoris* . . ." Fleece paused reverently, cutting in with a smile of pure glory.

"I know," I said, smiling also.

"The anguish of the joy of the words . . ." Fleece eased

158

the boxes out of my hand. I had made my point and didn't care. He seemed to absorb a nervous power in the repossessing of the letters, holding them. I would never have denied him that.

"What I want to hear is the woman speaking back. We're going to steal those letters, Fleece," I said.

He laid the boxes in place on the shelf. "I guess we have to. But you know what I want more than the letters from her? They could be dull little notes. I imagine they are. What I want is *her*. *Herself*. To steal pleasure with her, or *from* her, I don't care. Somewhere in New Brunswick, the lush vigilant digit of her clitoris, I don't care if it's forty years old, which is about the age I'd make her, somehow."

5 / Mean Times

However, nothing happened. Fleece became concerned again about his classes and labs and his medical career, I saw little of him, and I—well, God, there was nothing else to do—was becoming an intellectual. This gave misery a little class. I became concerned, concerned, concerned. I went to the library and checked out *The Sound and the Fury* and *War and Peace*, hiding the books from Fleece, because I knew he must be long beyond these. Also, while in the library, I thought it might be true to the manner of a scholar to pluck off two or three random plums which caught my eye, and what caught my eye were two books on Geronimo, the Apache. I went for the name, *Geronimo*, for one thing, and opening one book I read this piece of advice from an Apache father to his son:

My son, you know no one will help you in this world. You must do something. You run to that mountain and come back. That will make you strong. My son, you know no one is your friend, not even your sister, your father, or your mother. Your legs are your friends; your

159

brain is your friend; your eyesight is your friend; your hair is your friend, your hands are your friends; you must do something with them. . . . Then you will be the only man. Then all the people will talk about you. That is why I talk to you in this way.

The passage came alive in my hands. You must do something . . . your legs, brain, eyesight, hair, hands are your friends. You must do something with them. The father himself saying even he is not your friend. At the same time my eyes fell on the word, name, *Geronimo*, again and I realized that *my* last name could be found mixed up in it. It was silly but true. Monroe could be found in Geronimo. I was delighted—even more so because I didn't know what the hell was giving. But it was all a high throb.

My condition as an intellectual became even lonelier. I wanted to read the Geronimo books straight through, but when I saw the photograph near the front of one of the books I stopped cold. Geronimo was the least-favored hero as regards looks that I'd ever seen. This man was really just a bit too ugly. He was furious. He held the rifle with a terrifying claim on it. There was no glib negligence here as in the portrait of your ordinary romantic hero. There were no stars in his eyes, only a narrow cross-focused anger. His mouth frowned, and here it was uncertain whether he meant to frown or frowned involuntarily through loss of teeth. And there at his neck the filthy scarf. The single handsome thing in the picture was his left knee, brown and bare above his boot. It was a good knee. He propped it up, had his elbow resting on it. (*My son . . . your legs are your friends,* I remembered.) Perhaps his legs were the only feature which hadn't betrayed him. But then back up to the face. It was too akin to senile lunacy, too much the old desperate male idiot we would all come to. So I put the books away, disheartened. I knew Geronimo was a part of my private, intellectual life, I couldn't imagine who else would be interested in him besides me and the authors of these books—I even went over and checked out all the other books on him, although with no special happiness. Fleece saw the books stacked up by my bed and assumed I was writing a term paper on Geronimo for English or history. I simply shrugged. I didn't know why I had them. Having the books—it was like being related to some mad bore in town whom you would have to visit sooner or later.

Yet, from reading that piece, the father's advice to his son, I was drunk with freedom to do *anything*. I sat on the dorm steps among this pack of other miserable boys. Some of them were like Earl and Bob back at Dream of Pines High and a couple of them were intellectuals, and there was one twenty-year-old alcoholic—I mean to the extent that he would pour a shoe-polish bottle full of bourbon over his slice of watermelon and eat that for breakfast. The alcoholic always suggested things we could do, while the rest of the group discussed his proposition for thirty minutes, the intellectuals coming in at the end to discard it as worthless. Essentially they held that all motion was worthless. There was nothing possible to do. The others were beaten down, since they could not get their thoughts into the King's English. Some days Zak, the drama teacher, would drive by in his Edsel station wagon, see us out there, and join us. Zak was about thirty and had grayish-blond hair. There was a rumor that he had been a beatnik somewhere and also that he was engaged hopelessly to a beautiful crippled girl in Denver. One evening he was out there and organ music was coming out of the auditorium across from us, Bach, I guess—something sacred yet mathematical—and we were looking across the yard beyond the concrete pool with the defunct fountain and the slimy water at the unlighted windows of the auditorium. I was thinking of the organ-player alone in the ranks of seat shadows of the huge auditorium. His music at this hour of the day was enormously depressing. It was like gloom in little shrieks. All else was quiet—suppertime. I thought of the organist, he or she, thinking of himself or herself as so grand and prissy with the loneliness, and the Bach, and, who knows, God. I couldn't take it. Neither could Zak, apparently.

"Damn that organ!" he said, in a sudden blast. "This time of the evening." I had seen Zak express a lot of phony emotion in the drama class, but now he seemed to be real. *"This* time of the evening . . ." He held his hands to his ears and burst out, "This time of evening I tried to make love to her in the wheelchair . . . oh, it's all just a horror and a gloom! . . . and she *farted*, dear sweet Linda. What kind of earth is this?" Even as he said this—and I was shocked along with the others—the organ shrilled up in a

161

torrent, triumphant. It *mocked* Zak, his sudden confession; it drew the gloom out of you and then mocked the gloom. I made a decision and ran in the dorm up three flights of stairs to my room.

I pulled out a drawer and yanked aside the tee shirts. I hadn't seen the pistol, the one the old man gave me, since I'd put it in the bottom of the drawer the first day at Hedermansever. It was a joy to find, a brutish little Italian hero. I got my raincoat, dumped the gun in the pocket, and put on the raincoat. Before I left the room I picked up one of the books and looked again at the photograph of Geronimo holding his gun. Looking at the filthy scarf around his neck, I wanted it.

When I made it back to the front steps, Zak and the others were saying nothing to each other. The organ was still going, and the group was still paralyzed in depression by it. The night had almost come down. Then I saw Fleece walking past the auditorium, coming from his lab, toward us. He was looking backward toward the windows of the auditorium. As he came up to us, his face was full of pain.

"Who needs that goddam *organ?*" he said.

"Let's stop it. Stop him, whoever it is," I said.

The alcoholic boy rubbed his hand through his forlorn crewcut and stood up and assented. Zak, with all his biography, began walking, Fleece joined us, and the rest of them fell in. By God, I thought, we are in motion, this pack of misery all together. I couldn't feel the ground under my feet. It was trancelike. I thought of what Zak had said about his lover in a wheelchair. Thinking of the wheels themselves, I moved along at the head of them, rolling. In the auditorium windows I could see the tiny light of the music viewer of the organ. The player was still fingering zealously and to my mind the sound was like monstrous dominos of tin falling. I told the group we would go in by this side door, and we did. We went by the basement classrooms and climbed the stairs, went to the left through a door, to the stage. The organist was undulating, by himself, below the other end of the stage. We drew up, over him, and saw him waddling away on the pedals in his sock feet. We were in the total darkness of the stage and he was down there alight from the tiny lamp over his music. I put my hand on the pistol in my pocket. I knew then I would use

162

it. The pistol felt so automatic. And mechanically, it was. I felt high and loose. I took a book out of Fleece's hands. I pitched the book onto the keys of the great wooden organ. The organist was in a fit of holy music and barely recognized the event.

"Stop," I said. He stopped and looked up toward us. "Get out of here. Keep your eyes down. Or you'll get hurt."

"I have permission," he said.

"You didn't get permission to depress us with that damned organ." I spoke; the rest were completely silent. "You'd better stop. We can't stand the organ."

"Can't stand Bach, well, I . . ." started the organist.

"I know it's Bach. I know you wanted it to sound like it was coming out of some cathedral. I thought about you in here thinking you were so lonely and holy. I was thinking about you looking at your own fingers moving on the keys. You thought you were the final word."

He picked up his music, stepped into his shoes, and flicked off the music light on the organ. Still, he really didn't want to leave, not seeing me yet, trying to see the rest of the group on stage too. He was dallying, I saw, even in the brown gloom. I really couldn't stand him. I saw him put his hand on a seat and turn to try to discern who we were and my patience was at end. "Get out!" I told him. I had forgotten the pistol. I was ready to leap off the stage and grab him with my hands. This time of the evening, like Zak said; this time of the evening, that organ falling down on you like the wreck of some old tinny car, the gray tin pieces of it going right in your brain, releasing, God knows, all the horrible streams of your life. Gaf! Oh, me!

The organist was nearing the doors of the auditorium. I saw his wobbling shadow near the windows; there were lights in the lobby outside. His form was nearing the lights. He was reaching the end of the auditorium, where we all were commanded to sit down three times a week. Where in the seats and on the floor were the fingernail dirt, the plucked eyebrows, the scratched-off scalp particles—the germy castoff of the bored, during those speeches; where now, I saw, pulling out the pistol and aiming it at his back, the gloom came in brown as your very sweetheart's fart. At the last second I pulled the gun over to the right and shot the wall next to the door, as he went out. *Pooooooom.*

Then all the echoes, a screech in the lobby, a sort of trance filled with clangs for me.

"Monroe had a gun!" someone behind me yelled. Then I heard them bolting for both wings off the stage. Someone took me by the arm. It was Fleece.

"If we get out of here quick, it'll be all right. He couldn't have recognized us," he said. I noticed Zak was still on the stage too. He wanted to run, I think, but had been frozen. He was very concerned. We passed him going out. Fleece asked him if he didn't want to leave too. Somebody would be back soon, and it would be curious to see the drama professor still on stage, with his arms frozen in a posture of flight like that. He touched Zak.

"Monroe. You weren't aiming *at* our organ friend, were you?" asked Zak.

"No, no, no." I shook like the devil. I was cold.

"He had *left* the organ. He had stopped playing . . . yet you pulled a gun, you shot . . . after all, a harmless organist . . .," Zak said.

"Was not harmless," I chattered. "Don't forget . . ." We opened the basement door and were out of the building. I grew warm suddenly, lying to Zak, all flushed out in a false cause. "I had to. I did it all for your fiancée in Denver."

Zak himself was a harmless queer, and believed in heightened moments of friendship. He looked at me with ineffable gratitude as he went off to his car. Zak had a lot of grayish blond hair which he tossed around emotionally, true to drama.

Another day, a week later or so, I was still tingling in my head, feeling that I was in danger. My mind pounded, for the first time in my life, as if it was a thing distinct from me. And in my body I experienced cold sprays of nerves. Life shot through me as if existence really meant something. Before pulling the trigger in the auditorium, I seemed to be only verging toward life—say, like a man eating color photographs. But now the excitement was hounding me. I was thinking about Adolph Sax, the inventor of the saxophone, listening to Sonny Stitt on the phonograph. Then I heard David Newman, the sax-player in Ray Charles's band. What a thing, to have invented, finally, the horn that actually *talks?* I shouted. Fleece looked over at me snidely.

164

"Sounds like a nigger who's been made into a bagpipe," said Fleece. Thinking back just then, I realized my old friend Harley Butte might've said something like that. I remembered that Harley and I were in the same state. He was directing some band somewhere, surrounded by pine trees. I wondered if he had them out on the field now, under his baton. By now he had had several months with them. Were they as good as Jones's band in 1950, ten years ago? How could they be? The bursting dust, the blue Napoleonic spades.

"Fleece, there's so much that you don't know. Let me take care of the music. I've been at it for ten years. A decade."

"You can *have* music. Outside of a few very soft things on the piano, I hate almost all of it. As far as I'm concerned, you could take all your clarinets and operas and hymns and flush them down the commode."

"What a narrow . . . what a *bigot* you are. You stupid bastard. I'll tell you something. All art aspires to the condition of music." I had heard Livace, who taught me trumpet, quote that the other day. In my case it was a grand thing to believe.

"All life, to which all art is at best a whining stepsister, aspires to the condition of sex," said Fleece. I suspected he was also quoting, but couldn't call him down for it with a very clear conscience.

Ashlet, the drunk, who had discovered Fleece kept lab alcohol in the room, looked up from his Pepsi-Cola highball.

"Hail, I'll take sittin' on the front steps over this. The *wisdom* around here, you could drown in it." He went out the door with his drink. Then he came back in the door. "Monroe, you could get your gun out again. Now that there was entertainment." He winked merrily.

Eventually I went back out to the front steps too. Fleece thought the front steps crowd was depraved, and it was. They told a brand of joke out there which was a true revenge attack on taste, beauty, and human emotion. They used sex only as a sort of springboard into horror and slime. From there on it was all scabs, fornication with the hairy nostril of a crone, the sow with the chastity belt versus Picklock Ned, and all that. The idea was to poison the

165

audience, make them ashamed of having heard the thing. Then came the muddy laughter, the closing of the eyes. Then came another joke more meticulously vile than the last.

"Shoot him for telling that joke," begged Ashlet, looking at me. You never knew how serious his despair was. The rest of them were not certain of me, either. Nobody would venture a joke right away. Came the pall, came some belle driving by us in a green Cadillac convertible, all of us—if the others were like me—wanting to jump on her windshield spread-eagled and beg her to let us in. Fleece walked in from his lab once, right in the midst of a pall. Ashlet was abjuring me to shoot something, *anybody, anything*. "Hit something! Knock it over!" I wore a kerchief around my neck now, and my raincoat, in whose pocket I indeed had the pistol. I thought all of it lent an air of handsome danger. Zak was there. He was all for the kerchief. I was making an A in the drama class, no sweat. Fleece beckoned me with his finger. I left, walked to the room with him.

"What do you think you're *doing* with that crowd? You standing there in that kerchief like you were their hero."

"I *am* their hero. They need me. I have this pistol." I drew it out and clumped it on the top of the chest, taking off my raincoat. I had taken the pistol with me a few times to chapel and to class, looking at the Pee Aitch Dees and dwelling on the enormous possibility that I might use it again. Ah, one wished that his enemies were less boring and more violent. I tugged the knot out of my kerchief and laid the kerchief across the pistol. This set a provocative little still life on the chest.

"Now off with the spurs," said Fleece.

"Ah, no. I'm an Indian, not a cowboy."

He hissed. I lay down on my cot with my raincoat. The coat I liked very much too. It had a certain secret amplitude to it, like a cape but not that wanton. The high calf boots, I confess, grew heavy as the day wore on. It was good to be off my feet.

"Goddam *knee* boots with his pants stuffed into them," Fleece derided, observing my footwear. "Listen. Do you think you'll ever get any pussy wearing *that* outfit?"

Fleece was exasperatedly taking off his jacket, one of those old shiny Occupation affairs with a luminous yellow map of Japan on the back. At the shoulders *Japan* was stitched in the same luminous thread in that choppy style which evokes the Orient. There was a smaller rendering of the same idea at the front breast pocket. He wore the jacket constantly. It was a little big for him, but he had got his hands on it somewhere, and wore it, I think, to commemorate his true father, who had died fighting the Japanese. Otherwise, he wore white shoes—in the dead of winter—pleated pants which, since he hadn't gained a pound since he was fifteen, he'd worn for six years; and usually, white shirts and blue or black dingy ties under the jacket. Another failure of style, I noticed as he began to undress for the shower, was that his socks had been drawn down almost out of sight by the backs of his shoes. The revealed ankle was hairy and chafed.

"With his *pistol* too." He picked it up like it was a smelly thing, then opened my drawer and flung it in. "Hero of the criminally stupid." Fleece pored over me again. "I ought to call the cops. I really ought to call the cops."

"By the time they got here, I'd have put on my loafers and combed my hair. The pistol wouldn't be in the room. I'd call your mother and tell her you're berserk. She'd be here faster than the cops, and when they all got together, you wouldn't stand a—"

"You deliberating, taking-advantage son of a bitch. You know my mother must never, *never* come in this room." He meant it very seriously. I was sorry I had pushed it to this degree. He went on, "What do you think you're up to? Please. Don't think I haven't seen the picture."

He reached under my cot and pulled out a couple of the books. He opened the right one to the photograph of Geronimo. His dirty fingernail lay right against the soiled kerchief. The old chief seemed to have taken fresh offense at this new finger upon him. He was cross-eyed with rage. I hadn't seen him for two weeks. I was absorbed by the rage.

"Get your fingers off of him."

Fleece let the pages flip by. He looked at the check-out slip in the back. "This book is two months overdue. You idiot."

167

6 / Fazers

Driving home for Christmas, I passed the fields like dead palomino horses—winterset in Mississippi—the sun a cold bulb; and later, over the Vicksburg bridge, saw the river: a snake in throes, its belly up.

The raincoat, the scarf, the boots, the little pod of iron lying against my thigh—I was sticking with them. I had nothing to lose.

At last I was in Louisiana far enough and I picked up WWL in New Orleans. Bobby Blue Bland was tearing it up with "Letcha Light Shine!" Now what has happened to Bobby Blue Bland? He used to deliver enough raunch in one tune to get me through a whole day. But at this time, the Blue Bland band also rang up a sense of disgrace in me, for playing fourth-part trumpet in the Jackson Symphony Orchestra. This was really the hind tit of music, even if you were playing Beethoven.

I needed some solo Beauty in my life. There were my secret poems, all right. I would write out a whole ink cartridge in one night. I had tried them on index cards, on yellow paper, on unlined paper, on flyleafs, on onionskin. I had tried green and red ink, black, blue. In the mornings it was astonishing to find all those poem-looking things. Nothing had helped. It was all miserable. It was like visiting a site where ants had been killed—the dead flat sprawl of the words, the small kinked bodies of the letters.

The old man may have looked a bit dismayed at the scarf and the boots. I'm not sure. It began as a happy time, this first Christmas reunion. Harry is back.

Uncle Harry. My nephews are waiting for me with the football. I'm the passer and the star. There isn't any telling how much I love my nephews and nieces. Ah, leaping for the high pass and crashing in the cane for a touchdown. Son of a gun. I remember my two little nieces on the front

168

steps, at twilight, calling us in for the Christmas Eve supper. Inside we go for the oysters, the duck with sherry, the turkey, the ham. Afterwards, my nieces flock to me and sit in Uncle Harry's lap. They're wearing tiny maids of the Alps outfits. Their tender bottoms—the softest, most innocent flesh on God's earth—are on my knees. I begin feeling like Jesus telling the parents to let the kids come to me. One of them kisses me and I know how unsullied and just slightly moist love can be. I wonder will it be like this when I marry. "I can count," says the baby. Then I watched them all tearing apart the presents. There's nothing like seeing a kid yank his prize out of that colored paper. "This thing is *mine*, free and clear!" the eyes seem to say. Turns your old soiled heart around. If somebody could've stopped it there, it was my peace on earth.

In honor of *me as a college* man, there is beer in the refrigerator, for the first time ever. My brother, my fosterbrother, my sister, and their families are here. The house is crammed with wonderful people and greenery and candles, the children are surging, and my old man is about to crack with pride. It's *me*, it's old wild Ode Monroe that filled this house up like this! he seemed to mean, wearing the Christmas sweater from me. I loved him. I had a four-beer glow on, but I would've loved him anyway. I loved him in his age. He had put on five years in the four months since I'd seen him. But he was a man. He could bear it.

My mother was pretty all over again. But though she still looked something like Elizabeth Taylor, she had aged and was on the down side of Liz Taylor's beauty. I trailed her. I saw her in all the lights and shadows of the house. I couldn't quit staring. I became long and rude in my stares. She didn't understand me. She lowered her eyes, embarrassed at me. *I* was embarrassed at me. She sighed, she told me that smoking cigarettes made me look like a hoodlum. The fact was I couldn't stand to see her lose out to that old simpleton Father Time. I hated it. I hugged her and hugged her, at every decent opportunity.

When the rest of them left, and I was still there, it was hard to make talk at all. I took the pistol out in the back yard, and before I knew what I was doing, I was shooting at birds. The birds—robins, sparrows, thrushes—alit on the bare gray limbs. They weren't used to being shot at. So even with the pistol I killed three of them. They would stay

169

on the branch after I missed a shot, not understanding. I was learning the weapon. The last one I killed I hit him shooting four times from the hip. He burst apart in feathers and fell ten feet from me with feathers floating around his corpse. I reloaded and shot at the corpse in rapid fire from the hip. The corpse jumped about, its head vanished, sod flew up. I had the scarf and boots on. The old man had come up behind me sometime during the blasting. I never heard him.

"I believe he's dead. *What* do you think you're doing?"

"There's nothing else to do," I said.

"Do you realize that bullets travel? You shoot a twenty-two bullet in the air, it goes a half-mile until it hits something. I just got a phone call from Oliver Sink. One of your bullets came through a window in his dining room. Now isn't that nice? He's just a little damn bit upset."

"Oh, God. I'm sorry. God knows. Listen. I'll just leave. I'll leave, go on back to the college."

The old man told me he didn't want me to leave. This was an accident; he never meant for me to *leave*—looking at me uncertainly. We could *talk*. We could get along fine. I drank beer and skipped supper. When he came in the den I was tight enough to call Lala Sink, see if she was home for Christmas. I was at the phone when the old man came in. The Sink's phone was ringing; but I hung up.

The old man told me a couple of whore jokes. I thought they were corny, but I laughed. Missy and her missing husband, Edna in the barrel at the dude ranch, etc. The tone was ribald, words and laughter were passing between us. I told *him* one. It was one of the jokes from the front-steps crowd back at Hedermansever. After the punch line, I looked at the old man and knew I had crossed the line.

"*What* did she say?" asked the old man.

I knew I couldn't do the old woman's line again, and the trembling voice was important. I repeated the line flat: "Them weren't no sack of potato chips. Them were scabs off my—"

"You think *that* is funny? My lord!"

"I didn't make it up."

"Think of this: your mother was in the house when you told that story."

"But . . . aw, Happy New Year, Father."

"Are you *drunk?*"

170

Since then, very little has passed between us except money.

Fleece was late coming back to school. We were well into "dead week," the free time before final exams. A boy from Morton whose father was a pharmacist was selling amphetamines in the hall. He wore a canvas jacket with the hide of a yellow cat—house cat—sewn on the back. Above the hide, written in Magic Marker, was "Dead Cat," with quotation marks, just like that. Morton, Mississippi, was a nasty mudflat where they killed chickens and drove them out in trucks. So I don't guess the fellow could help it. He pointed to one vial of yellow pills bigger than the rest. They cost two bucks. "Them are the Cadillac of bennies," he said. Truck drivers were known to take one of these and drive from Morton to California and back without shutting an eye. I bought one of them off him. I was behind in everything except drama class. He noticed me eyeing him. He stunk, as a matter of fact. I don't think the cat hide had been tanned well.

"I don't smoke nor drink," he said.

"You killed that *cat?*"

"My front yard right at noon Christmas day. I hate a cat. Now I love a dog, but I hate a cat."

"Did you shoot him?"

"Naw. I choked her—it's a female—I choked her with my hands. We had two birds, two bluejays which we made a feedbox for in our yard. She killed one of them birds which my mother *loved.*" He saw my disgust. "It didn't hurt. I didn't choke her all the way. I hit her head on a phone pole. She was scratching me something terrible. *That* did her."

"It was a pretty cat."

"I know it. I sewed her right on. I know it's pretty."

I was looking out the dorm window when Fleece entered the yard. He carried his suitcase. The rain was drizzling down. His suitcase broke open. A gift in Christmas paper tumbled out, with some clothes. He cursed and hurled the clothes back in. The gift he kicked. It scudded and broke apart, trailing the ribbon. Leaving it, he sloshed on into the dorm.

"Your present is getting wet," I said to him. He didn't

171

even say "hidee" like he used to. He went straight to the
bed, snorting and hacking. The Hudson Bay flu was on
him. "I'd better go get your present."

"You can have it. It's your sort of thing."

I put on my raincoat, went down to the muddy lawn.
There in the rain was the mess of cardboard and ribbons
and poking out of it, a .22 long-barrel revolver, black as
coal. I presented the gun to Fleece. It was the kind of gun
which if you missed your shot, you could go over to what
you were shooting at and whip it to death.

"I don't want the bastard. My grandmother gave me fifty
dollars for Christmas. We went to Florida again. General
Creech hauled me downtown to buy something with it. The
pistol seemed to be the best bargain in town. It's of some
faultless German make that pierces the heart of a chip-
munk from eighty feet. I tried to look fulfilled when I gave
them the fifty. The goddam Christmas carols on the store
radio were donging my head off. I finally made it as a son
to General Creech at that moment, I did. Lucky me. I'm
sick. I've been faking good health for six days so my mother would let me come back."

"I can't just take the pistol."

"Yes, you can. I don't want it. I'm sick, but I'm happy,
in a way. Listen: When we were in the house in Florida,
Creech's glasses fell off in the commode. He was drunk and
didn't know it; he sat on the pot, flushed it, and the glasses
caused a stoppage. His own horrible sewage backed up on
him and filled up the bathroom. He wouldn't let any of us
know what was happening. He said he was taking a shower.
I saw his fingers covered with toilet paper wiping up around
the slit under the door. The odor coming into the house was
dreadful. He was completely blind and didn't even know
where or what he was wiping up. But all the while he was
yelling to us that there was no trouble, he could take care
of it, even though he was blind. And he did. He found the
PineSol in some cabinet, reached down the commode and
drug out the clot, including his glasses, put the glasses back
on, and by the time he opened the door, he was standing
there normal as ever. The bathroom was clean as a pin and
threw out a vapor of PineSol that would murder any germ
from a mile away. Go ahead and laugh. I myself had to *admire* him a little."

Fleece's green irises lit up with a sort of bleak cheer. I asked him if any of his stories ended any better than that.

"Yes. I have some other endings now. I was looking at hairy Allen Ginsberg, in *The New York Times,* thinking of myself in the garage, naked, seeking ecstasy like him, about how publicly I sought it, what Creech would've done if my mother hadn't taken such care to quieten it, even while calling one of the three psychiatrists in Jackson, who later called the house because I didn't show up; add to that the minister that I was at *least* supposed to see. I turned off the lights in the living room, loving the dark—it was three in the morning—although catching a cold; it was chilly. I drew out old pedro and let him lay in the air on my thigh in a sort of warming-up ceremony to the second anniversary of the afternoon in the garage. The thing perked up halfheartedly, while I was thinking about Bet Henderson, this huge girl who takes the zoology lab I teach; she—at first, I didn't think it could be true—seems to be making a play for me. . . ."

I turned to my wall. At the wall I grinned and winked like a fool. I knew who Bet Henderson was; had an English class with her. I saw her in the Fine Arts Building, too. She was taking private voice lessons. The girl was one of those larger-than-life statues of a woman, at least six feet two. Perhaps if I called on her with Fleece riding piggyback, there would be enough man for her. She smiled at me; the moments passing her were full of puny wanting. Fleece, I pictured then; he would drown in her breasts. She went around with a group of three troubled-looking small men, one of them a real auntie sort, who seemed embarrassed that you might think they were adventuring with her in a romantic way. Her shoes, I'd noticed, were in the mode, but were such long, huge things they looked like some specially manufactured travesty of the mode. The same thing was true of her dresses. Me oh my! Right in style, Villager prints of geese and weathercocks, but an almost absurd expanse of cloth. I don't mean Bet was a laugh. She was well-made; her ankles were dear long things; her lap, when she crossed her legs, was a trim valentine of muscles, which the cloth could not hide. She had narrow, damp eyes, and gazed mainly at her own lap during classes. Her nostrils were large and exciting; and her lips pouted out like a red cushion some fevered boy could lay his head on. She was

173

shy! And she was an agony. It was as if, being horny, you had had a chance to blow up your dream-object of lust in the form of a balloon and blew it up, what a shame, just too big. I remembered particularly the day in English 101 when I saw her smile at me with a sliver of tongue between her teeth. As a matter of fact I had thought of calling her up to meet me at some withdrawn place. Fleece was ruminating on about her making a play for him.

"I know who she is," I said. He was explaining her to me as if reporting on the wilds of some lost geographic scape. "Don't be overexcited. She smiled at *me* the same way, tongue between the teeth. I think she wants a *team* of us." He ignored me.

"I didn't encourage it at first. I thought she was simple-minded, this huge girl making her need for me so apparent. She'd stay late and watch me smoke a cig. Then one day we found out talking together that that naked girl I saw doing the Twist through my telescope was *her!* I perspired. I knew then she was saying take it or leave it. I left it like that at Christmas. But *back* now, if I can get hold of this conversation: I was thinking of Bet in the dark, catching the Hudson Bay flu in only my pajamas, concerned about ecstasy, how going for that big girl was as public an announcement of seeking ecstasy as one could make. I stood up and I was dizzy. Stars were in my eyes and I accepted them as the stars I was *among,* being in a rocket of desire. I couldn't breathe well. But I took this as a symptom of being in the stars above the atmosphere.

"I took a chance, Monroe. As I left my house, ill, I shouted, 'I am on the make, Mother!'

"Either you have to live in the uterus, or you have to slam it shut with an uppercut," he said after a pause.

Fleece told me a new story during finals about an "upper cut." I doubt if he'd swung his arm ever in his life in anger, but he was taken by the image of an uppercut, and I think he wanted to drag it back to his past to see if he could get some theme out of his miserable life with it.

The time was a couple of years ago at that red brick Baptist church that he was expected to attend. The invitational hymn started, and he sneaked out to the front steps in a sort of adventuresome hate of the music and everything. He fell upon these redneck children who had sneaked

174

out of church before him. Their shirttails were ripped out and their hooked-on neckties were barely hanging on, because they were going crazy tearing the berries off the nandina bushes and throwing them at each other. Fleece took offense and demanded that they stop, but they wouldn't. One of them threw a wad of berries in his face. He could not help himself. He dove at the child and crushed him with a tackle. The others came up, thinking it was a game, Fleece all dusty with one shoe off, but he was for real. He hurled a smaller one back in the bushes, and, spotting some long white neck, he drew back and hit this boy's chin with an "uppercut" in a full wheel of his body. As he did that, church was over and General Creech and his mother were the first out on the steps. Hence, they saw him socking heedless at the children. The pastor came out and separated the angry parents of the children from Fleece. Fleece maintained that he would fight for the beauty of the nandina berries, and that he would hit other children and their parents if anybody wanted to tear off any more berries.

When he finally got to the car, with his lost shoe, his mother was crying piteously. She wanted General Creech to leave her and Fleece at the church so that they could see the pastor, who might, she cried, if it was not in the realm of the spirit, arrange a psychiatrist for Bobby Dove. It was then that Creech came through on Fleece's behalf, suddenly and strangely. He explained to her a rule of life; number one: *Contention is always going to break out.* Number two was a point of legal description: there were many against one. True, Bobby was almost an adult, but opposing him had been at least seven human beings, small, but army ants are small and so is the coral snake. His mother dried her tears to this speech.

"And here I drive in that priceless free 'uppercut' to that kid," said Fleece. He demonstrated the actual "uppercut." It was a stilted, finicky gesture, but there was great passion in his eyes. His glasses had slipped down to the end of his nose, uncaging the happy evil in his eyes. I thought he looked like a puppet, again, some renegade puppet which had begged for human life so persistently that he got it.

Then later, in February or March, all clear of the Hudson Bay flu, he brought in a bottle of Mogen David wine— tart & greasy—and some paper cups. We drank the first glass, and he took off his Japan coat.

175

"Why are *you* here? I thought you practiced your horn this time of the afternoon. As a matter of fact, I didn't want to share this wine. Didn't want to *open* it yet, really."

"I hate it, practicing any more. Give me another dip there. It's not good but you feel it already."

"I *can't*. It's for later tonight, with someone else."

"Gimme some, you bastard. I need it. We finish this, then I take you out and I buy something else. I know I was rude last week when I said I didn't want to listen to you any more. And listen, you're *not* a bore. You're *interesting*. C'mon, gimme. I think the problem is, you . . . speak *above* me. Hand her over, swear to God. You can say anything. I'll just listen and drink." I'd been thinking for an hour, all dry and bored.

He was holding and shielding the bottle from me. He'd given me the telescope, the pistol, the marijuana (which I was afraid of and hadn't used), and, in fact, the freedom of his 'lab alcohol which was right there in one of the cigar boxes. But the wine was a more kindly thing and I was enraged that he wouldn't give it to me. I darted at it, Fleece holding it high and low.

"It's for her and me! A rendezvous at midnight. An actual *rendezvous* . . . to sip."

"I'll *hit* your little ass, then!"

He turned his back and I hit him angrily. He huddled over the wine. "She approached me today." The huddling little coot was speaking on, and rather evenly, while I pounded his back like a spike. "She was in a wasted condition, wild and desperate. And, Monroe . . . stop beating me!" I stopped. "She asked. And I said: 'Yes!' I said 'Yes!' "

I began pounding his back again. I told him he was a liar, a bag of hot air, that he lived in the realm of boring snot, etc. He only huddled there, uncomplaining, so I came to a disgusted rest, not even wanting the wine any more. But of course he spoke.

"I pity you, Monroe. Such a sad person. Just a violent drunk. You could take your place at any roadhouse in Mississippi and nobody would even look up. Just a violent *tight* is what you are. A one-cup-of-wine gladiator. Mississippi really *needs* more people like you. You could join the Ku Klux Klan and ride around at night beating up girls who teach the theory of evolution, or maybe stab a Negro imbecile in the back. Oh, and you've got your *scholarship* practi-

176

cally paying you to be like this, you're such an *investment* to the college, because all the Hedermansevers and the other trustees of the school want out of you is that you become a weapon for the Lord, and you for sure with your *style,* with those kneeboots and your scarf and, oh certainly, carrying that pistol around, looking at it like it was a scientific breakthrough! and all this alongside that half-ass lease on music you think you have, being a creature of moods, you're just more of a body than Mississippi could invent."

"Leave me alone. I've been mooning around for a month. I don't know what to do."

"One thing I still say," said Fleece, capping the bottle, at ease. "You aren't going to attract any nookie if you wear those boots and scarfs and costume. Now that I've got a little on the line, let me give you a little advice. Be a doctor. There isn't any trade outside of being a minister that attracts nookie like a doctor. You could quit mooning around wanting to hit people. You could put all that mean funk of yours behind a microscope for a few years. It takes no great mind, really. Look at all the stupid doctors."

"Thank you very much," I said.

But I took the advice seriously later.

7 / "Fight! Fight! / Nigger and a White!"

—ANONYMOUS ALARM, c. 1956

In April one day I went to the post office. Every now and then there would be a free sample of soap or hair oil or the Dream of Pines newspaper, which I had never asked for. But I got a surprise. It was a formal invitation on a gold border.

The Beta Camina High School (Colored) Marching and Concert Band solicits the honor of your presence at

177

Capitol Street, Jackson, Mississippi, for review of the
Gladiators in formal parade competition, April the ninth,
nineteen hundred and sixty-one, ten o'clock ante meridi-
an.

> H. J. Butte, Director
> The Gladiator Band
> Beta Camina, Mississippi

That prosperous-sounding middle initial gave me a pause.
Then I knew who it was. I wondered who else he had
mailed these fine invitations to. Who were the big followers
of jig bands in America? I thought of Harley penning that
note, and I pitied him. The time he'd spent. Yet who gave a
fig?

Fleece had been home the past weekend. When I saw
him I invited him to go over and see the band with me. He
told me that if he had to pick out the one variety of music
he despised the most, it was Sousa. It was all just a wad of
Prussianism and trombones. Then I told him that it was a
Negro band which ought to be awfully good; that they were
marching in a contest on Capitol Street. He perked up oddly. He took a newspaper clipping out of a book on his table.

"Look at this. I ripped it out before Creech got to it the
other afternoon."

The piece was a letter from "Our Reader's Viewpoint" in
a Jackson paper:

Honorable Mayor and City Council:

The parade permit you have granted to the Afracoon
marching bands is a mistake. Mr. Mayor, you with your
degree in Greek should of all people know that Jackson
cannot *do* with having the projected parade and the
swarms of irresponsible young negroes it is bound to attract along Capitol Street. Every sighted scholar of history and that race knows what an Afracoon festival generally turns into before the day is over. I am not so nam-
by-pamby as not to mention that the cooties and lice will
be fighting it out for predominant pestilence, which will
linger behind for weeks, you can be sure. They will be
hopping in our socks on the very steps of the grand Old
Capitol we citizens reached in our tax-pockets to restore.

I wonder if even the Governor's Mansion will be
spared. I wonder if the Afracoon "fleamales" would not

take time out from open fornication on the street and the Governor's lawn to storm the doors and find the guest chamber and the pillow upon which Senator Kennedy once laid his head as a guest of Governor Coleman, (For once, don't we Mississippians regret our famous hospitality?) so they might kiss this memento of their "celebrity" president. (Or has some official of integrity *burned* it, hopefully?)

I suggest incidentally that the Kennedys use their whiskey-millions and buy our Afracoons their own island and construct a swine-wallow the size of Capitol Street down the middle of it for parades. Perhaps some of our *"Nee-gro"* bandsmen and their camp followers would march on into the deep blue sea. I am confident that a navy of the Orkin exterminators could deal with the raft of cooties and louse-ridden banjos remaining afloat. Of the resulting slick of Royal Crown hair-straightener, we could only hope the wretched pollution would eventually find its way back to the beach of Hyannis Port, Massachusetts, and that Bobby and Jackie and Johnny and Teddy would see what it is like to sailboat in the voodoo sewage with which they want to drench this land.

With those who would rise and say "Never,"
Col. P. D. Lepoyster

"It's Whitfield Peter," said Fleece. "Of the letters."

"You never said he was a *colonel*. Colonel of what?"

"Oh, he was an honorary 'colonel' in Fielding Wright's governorship years ago. I guess he gave money and influence to the campaign, whatever. When I saw his picture in the paper, this was explained under it."

"What picture?"

"A picture of him making a citizen's arrest on some group of sit-in demonstrators outside of Walgreen's, Capitol Street. He was just holding them until the police got there; as a matter of fact, a cop was advancing in the edge of the picture. Peter was planted there like a rock, rather statesmanly. Oh, he's quite a citizen, when anything 'racial' comes up. You'd think he'd had an operation where they put a police radio in his head. But do you realize this is the first time *since?*"

"The first time *since?*"

"That letter is the first time I've heard him speak directly

179

since that night in front of my teacher's house he threatened me about having the letters."

The day of the parade we drove over in the morning and made a little affair out of it. Fleece had his camera, a Japanese mistakeless thing that looked damn near like a typewriter. I was carrying my hardware also, the pistol. I'd had a wild hair about the day, and so I'd brought it. I wasn't sure why Fleece had come. He bit his hands. We were passing the Hickory House on West Capitol. I told him really, Harley's band ought to be good. He could stand it.

"Oh, no. Oh, *simple* ass," he said. "I was thinking about my camera. I was thinking about where or when I might see him to get a shot, looking around at the goddam miserable light in case I could get one anywhere, and I just saw *that* bastard." He slapped my coat pocket. "Let me out."

I pulled over and stopped the car. I didn't care. It was all right with me just then if I never heard the moaning or the disgust or the imprecations from Fleece ever again.

"You can't walk around with a *pistol,* you rube."

Then I told him to get out. He seemed surprised, but tried to hide it by slumping carelessly in the seat. He wasn't getting out. And when he spoke, after I drove on, he changed his voice into a more equable tone.

"The pistol is just *there,* Fleece," I said. "I don't have to use it. It makes me feel like something may be coming any minute. I walk around, you understand, watching out turn after turn, like I was in a wild country. It sets a light on the things or people I see. I see what I see in the light of what it might be if I pulled out the gun, and what things would do, how things would change."

"You talk like you want to *discover* a country, is the hopeless thing," said Fleece, in the new tone of an impartial observer. "You've been reading about that Indian. But, although it's true you look like Hernando DeKotex with the swamp boots, you ought to know that Mississippi has already been discovered, and that . . . it's enough of a rectangle of poor woe without you putting on that costume and pistol roaming around out of some *pageant* of gunslinging. They could use you in the United Daughters of the Confederacy as a salute-shooter at the cemetery in their birthday of the Civil War service. I thought it was funny you scaring that organist with a pistol. But I don't think it's funny you carrying it around ever after."

"Another thing I want to settle," I said. I was fed up. "Whichever tone of voice you take, I don't want to hear so *much* of it, for godsake."

We'd just passed the King Edward Hotel. Fleece had been almost deathly quiet. Suddenly he said to pull over. I could go where I wanted to but he was where he wanted to be. I found a parking space. Bobby Dove took out a pair of snap-on sunglasses and fixed them on his regular hornrims.

"All right." He urged his nose up to test them, and I could tell he was unable to see much. As he'd complained a few minutes ago, the light today was dismal; there were odd cloud strands the color of coal in the sky—odd for April, I mean. "I bale out. See me at Al's Half Shell in an hour if you want to see a scared mother."

"Where do you think you are?"

"Just beyond Peter's real estate office. There was an 'open' sign on it. He might remember me, but I want a shot of him head-on, to go with the letters. I've almost forgotten what the old pecker looks like." Fleece embraced the camera and opened the door.

"He ran at you with a belt, Bob," I told him, getting out myself. Fleece looked terribly small with that elaborately sensitive camera clutched to him, and in the sunglasses.

"No gunslingers. Go on."

I sat back in the car, took out the pistol, put it under the seat, with Fleece watching. All ready to escort. I wanted to look at the man myself. Fleece began walking toward the narrow box of glass which was Peter's office front, and I came up. In the window was a showcase, with reading material laid on a display board. One item invited you to buy a lot on a lake in beautiful Canton Harbors, Madison County, and here is the number you dial; to one side of the other display literature was the front page of a newspaper called "The Paleface Roll-Caller." Nearby it was an outstretched page of the Jackson paper with the letter in "Our Reader's Viewpoint" circled in brown ink, the same shade as in the letters from Whitfield, but I'd already read the newspaper letter and went back to "The Paleface Roll-Caller."

Half of the front page was occupied with a history of "The Paleface Roll-Caller." The editor was a simple gentleman farmer from Alabama who had never thought of putting a newssheet together until one winter he was at a convention of Big Dutchman farm machinery dealers in Chicago

181

and was walking along minding his own business when a Negro dope addict asked him for five dollars, and when he refused, in his natural Alabamian accent, the Negro pulled out a sharpened "church-key" on him and called him a "paleface." The Negro told him to call his friends too, because he wanted to cut them up as well. The Alabamian began shouting for his life, but, though the opposite sidewalk was covered with white citizens, no man came to his aid. The Negro laughed and told him he had no friends. He told the Alabamian that he wasn't worth cutting, and, leaving casually—this criminal—he told the Alabamian that he knew some "intelligent" palefaces that, before the day was over, would not only give him the money he needed, but would, one of those women palefaces, remove his sordid rags and kiss him all over the duration of his heroin spell. This was in Chicago, U.S.A. The editor had never seen the Situation like this before. He'd been too simple. Now he had seen the Situation. Even though he lost money on "The Paleface Roll-Caller," it must appear.

It was time to go in if we were going in, and we did. Fleece had the camera up ready to snap and run, but there was no one in the front room. There was a carpet and three chairs and a table, with more reading matter on it, but no Whitfield Peter. I sat down and took up another copy of "The Paleface, etc." The same history was on the front page. Apparently a permanent space was given over to it every issue. On the rest of the front page, I read about JFK, how Secret Service men had to drag him out of one Harlem brothel after another; and about a "certain gynecologist" in D.C. who had performed a number of abortions while Jackie was a gadabout reporter, pre-JFK. Other articles spoke of grassroots upheaval in the Catholic Church if it continued to hang the threat of excommunication over certain white patriots in Louisiana. Another harked back with some incoherent curse against Eleanor Rooseveltstein. The last returned to Jackie. Her nose was as "Semitic" as the nose of Lady Bird Johnson, wife of a key traitor among the Democrats. There was some bad spelling in the paper, but it was a wonder of consistency. Bobby Kennedy, who had so many children he didn't know what to do besides dance and sleep with Jackie, had recently met with Negro "leaders," and made a secret promise of billions to them. Jackie had had her influence.

182

"Somebody's back there," said Fleece. There was a room off the narrow hall in the back. I hadn't noticed the light. A shadow burst out against the opposite wall. I was frightened too. I started bellowing, putting it on.

"Shit*fire*, finally the truth! Everything in this paper's the real god rightout *trooth!* All of it, ever shitfire comma!"

Peter came out in a wide, lank wool suit colored like a speckled eggshell. It was in a style which had never either come or gone, as far as I knew. At last I saw his face. There were locks of grayish tan hair, parted high, and the actual face was flushed like a doll's, red cheeks and lips and also the ears. There was the mask of a pretty, babyfat boy behind the whiskers, the crow's-feet wrinkles at the eyes, and the liver spots; there was a vulgar trapped boy in his face, and he horrified me. I couldn't move. I saw he was thinking that we were rednecks.

"The truth always has good manners," he said. This was the first time I heard him speak. He was scolding me. But his voice was so pleasant it would put you to sleep. There was none of that hateful Southern yap in it. We got up and left, in fact, to the soothing ring of it.

Out on the street, Fleece was shivering. I was such an amateur about cameras, I thought the camera might've worked somehow by itself. I asked Fleece if he had gotten the shot.

"Hell no. When he came in, I turned the thing upside-down."

I drove up to Lamar Street, couldn't find a space, and finally found one on Pearl, behind the post office building. We walked around the porch of the building. Being on Capitol Street again, we sat down, on the post office steps. On the curbs it was solid spades, young and old. Fleece was wearing his camera in case he saw something, but he was not hopeful. As for me, knowing his mind was still on Peter, I'd slipped the gun out from under the carseat and dropped it in my raincoat.

I'd never seen so many Negroes together at one time. You could smell a high character of smoking fish in the air. We stood up when the first band came down. On the steps like this we could see. The colored girls would walk with the bands. They had on sweaty bobbysox and pointed witch lace-ups like the fad at Dream of Pines two years ago. I was looking at their ankles as they tried to break into the

183

line of spectators to see their band. Some just followed the band on the sidewalk. One group was four-across, doing the skip-and-kick for school spirit, and they created a jam coming down the sidewalk.

The first four bands had snaky ranks and played very loud, with majorettes desporting on their own, each a star in a separate audition; and this held true for some of the musicians too. I saw a tuba man doing a private jazz ballet and skiffle to the march, his eyes closed, and dancing off into the spectator ranks before he opened his eyes and found out where he was. Then we saw him and his huge instrument running after his band. A small boy ran after him slapping his pants like he was a stray dog. The crowd in front of the post office put up a cheer. Up till now it had been Count Basie set to march-time, and shallow in arrangement.

"This is awful!" said Fleece. "You hear that a nigger has rhythm, and these bands are making a fraud out of *that*." I was absorbed in the way the bands kept tooting away and falling apart. One drum major who was using his band as a moving, undulating yellow backdrop was hopping and slithering and even doing flips on the pavement, grinning, and confident that we were seeing him in black relief, as we were. At the peak of arrogance he would throw his baton.

There were quite a few whites standing on the steps with us. That arrogant drum major's baton shot up some forty feet in the air, spinning, and we watched it come down at his skinny body, wishing—if the crowd was with me—that it would crash on his teeth and take some of that prissiness out of him. But he caught it mid-twirl in an even more arrogant act, looking sideways away from it and catching it in a strut, as if ignoring it altogether.

"Look at them jump! Look at the niggers jump!" said a man on the higher step behind me. This man wore a big felt hat. The hat seemed to have started out as a full cowboy venture, had a wide brim, but it was crushed deep across the crown like somebody had slammed it with a crowbar. It was beige with a gray band. The fellow's suit was a speckled beige sort of wrap. The pants rolled out like curtains. Then I caught the face. I jerked my face away. Then I nudged Fleece.

"Look behind me."

"Great God. Him. How fast did he fly this far up Capitol

Street." Fleece put on the snap-on sunglasses again. "I'm going to step up two steps and see if I can shoot a profile. Don't move or look his way."

Peter had been hollering all the while.

"Give that coon a spear!" he called, about the drum major. "Did you ever think you'd see Jackson so full of jungle bunnies?! I'll tell you what the problem is going to be. The problem is going to be getting this trash *out* of town once this honky-tonk jamboree is over. It's going to be dogs and hoses, my friends. . . . You call that out there *marching?* What we're looking at is a Mau-Mau rehearsal. These Afra-coons have been given *dope,* you can tell by their eyes. You know who's in town?" I felt his hand brush my shoulder. I felt ill. Kept my face forward. "Martin Luther Coon, that's who. Don't tell me I didn't see a black Cadillac full of silk-suit jigaboos riding up and down Capitol this morning," he challenged me. I did not swerve. Out of the corner of my eye, his hat and suit seemed frighteningly large. The suit seemed to flare at me. All I could tell was that he appeared to have no special friends on the steps. But there was a cop leaning on the pole at the curb, and he turned around, looking over the Negro heads at the bands. Peter made a motion and the cop gave him a smile and put his hands up to his ears.

"You know who that is?" Peter had drawn right up to my ear, although I looked away. His breath touched my neck. "That's Victor. He knows me."

"Magnificent," I said. By then Victor was not there any more. Peter stood on the step directly in front of me. Over his big hat, I could see the hats of the bandsmen and little else.

"I got old Pete. Twice," whispered Fleece, stepping down next to me. "Once he took his hat off and I caught him. The fruity-cheeked old soldier of Eros, bellowing away." I pointed to the hat in front of me.

A band came on with rowdy syncopated drumming and choreographed trotting and sudden oblique marching, with the majorettes doing swaggers and shimmies that they would never repeat the same way again. I moved over to watch them. There was a fellow with a clipboard kneeling on the pavement. I suppose he was a judge. When the end majorettes saw him, they went berserk, doing the mashed potato, rearing up and down so as to reveal faded sateen

185

panties under their uniforms. Peter howled something charged with revulsion, took off his hat, and waved it back and forth across my field of vision, as if to knock down the musical notes like flies.

A small black-uniformed band came down then. They had the American flag, the Christian flag, and the Mississippi State flag flying out front. They were a meek little unit, all boys, and they gave out a lonely, thin sound, "Onward Christian Soldiers," stressfully, but flat and wheezing. Fleece elbowed me.

"A *hymn* on the march?! I'm absolutely limp. Where's the organ? If my mother ever led a band this would be it. Look at that slave playing oboe! That's her musical dream of *me!* This has to be the Gladiators. You ass. I don't think they're funny."

"No, they aren't."

Whitfield Peter was standing at brace, following the American, Christian, and Mississippi flags with his eyes. He held his big felt hat over his heart in the layman's salute. I had seen earnest old fellows do it when the flag appeared in the Shriner's parade in Shreveport.

Peter was braced there, nobody around him owned a hat, and his pants whipped as a cold wind blew downstreet from the Old Capitol. Somebody laughed at him. There was a long gap in the parade, then along came some more bands, sincere but puny. You could imagine them as the heralds corps for a Moorish children's crusade. Peter had apparently been preparing a speech to the crowd of whites on the post office steps. He dropped the hat to his side and addressed himself to the right, where the laugh had come from.

"No, gentlemen, I am not ashamed to salute the flag of my country. The heartbreak and the shame is that you and I have less of a choice every day about who *holds* that banner. Yet we stand here. . . . Yet we are constrained . . . we are the constrained . . ." Either he had been weeping or his eyes were purple with emotion. He put a handkerchief to his mouth. From this side he looked older. His left hand was hanging down at his watchchain like a punctured udder. I was sure I could knock him around if I wanted to.

"Another letter to the editor," said Fleece. Then we forgot him.

Harley's tremendous green band swung around the cor-

186

ner in front of the pinkish bricks of the Old Capitol. That's three blocks from where we stood, but up a slope, and I saw Harley with them, like a tan lollipop in an all-white suit and, sweet Jesus, a short-billed British helmet of canvas. Easy, easy, they came down, the lazy dragon-body of them almost never finishing its turn down toward us. The shakos and the plumes stood ten across. Spectators on both sides of the street had to retreat to the sidewalks, and I saw Harley using his arms to spread the crowd back as the band marked time. There was no music from them yet. Just the drums. The patient boiling holocaust of the drums. They went deep into the concrete and you could feel them through your shoes. I noticed the fine sand of the street gutters rise in a sheen. There were three other bands in front of Harley's, knocking and tooting their hearts out, but his drums were going right through them and under them.

Then the Gladiator band had its way cleared free and wide. Harley made a motion to the drum major, and the band oozed down towards us, no hurrying this green monster, still leisurely, eight steps to five yards, the drums still holding back, *but like a hungry tiger in a rotting net;* and yet no music. Harley walked with them on the opposite side from me. He was not in step, this being the director's privilege. Neither did he seek any lead or spotlight, merely escorting the head rank of brass in this green-suited musicians' army. We saw at last its people and its beaming metal. Brass mirrors in phalanxes, and on back in the multitude, waves of tubes at arms, three lines of every kind of percussion and behind them the three lines of tubas, like caves about to spout fire, walking toward you. They had the faces of a dead-eyed Ethiopian corps, so damned certain about the outcome of whatever they were marching toward, or against, that they hadn't even raised their weapons yet. You did not think of sixteen-year-old boys and girls of the colored high school when they came down.

All of them were snobs. They were such snobs a delicate judge might have counted off for it: they were too stiff, too certain, too proud, and too callused from being proud, riding too casually along, too confidently with that corps of drummers bombing down on what sounded like a hide stretched over the Grand Canyon.

My eyes went back to Harley. He had brought them down to the head of our block now, still their humorless

187

lackey, Director Butte. But—maybe his white suit and helmet put this across—you saw his short red-brown beard and the mouselike cunning in the eyes, and you saw now the control he bore over this green immensity of snobs: the control of a mouse over an elephant, say. Then he proved it. He put his right hand in the air.

A piece of chrome jumped up in the air, some cannons erupted down the mouth of a cavern, the brassware pipes stood up all at once, and we were looking up throats of gold and silver as far as we could see. The bottom fell out of the street.

I had that lonely, stranded, breathless feeling I'd had once before, watching Jones's band from under the bleachers, when I was a sneak and a twerp, in 1950. But it was much changed now, now that I knew music, now my heart had room for it, now I had grown an ear that could pick out mistakes of technique and tone, and I could not be washed clear off my post by fear of music as in the old days.

I tell myself this fraudulent blab about my musical progress. The verities are that I was washed away again, ripped off, out, away, and that for me even to *name* the march they let loose is impossible, the same as it's impossible for a man drowning, waves blasting him, to pronounce the name of the ocean he's in. When I got back to my post with my mind, they were half through the march and almost upon us. One resents being knocked out by musical teenaged children when one has earned oneself a purchase on cool, and I came back very skeptical about the Gladiators. But still they were a scare, a magic scare, even if you hated Sousan music. They were not overcharged or too tinny or loud in the brittle way bands are when they're trying to make up for shallow talent. Talent went deep in this band. The third-part harmony boys were making it on trumpet and trombone; the clarinets, saxophones, and flutes were all making it. The basses were making it, way under everything, with restrained mastery, so you never heard them pumping at the notes but sensed something moving wild at the bottom of the world. A few trumpet men played a melody of sixteenth notes an octave over everything, and all in tune (which H. Monroe, trumpet man, would have been hard-pressed to do, sorry to confess). They were cutting Jones's band. They were as thorough an orchestra as I've

188

ever seen or heard off the stage. Music so big; and they were, incredibly, *carrying* it down the street with them.

"The idea of a contest is a farce with *them* here, isn't it?" Fleece said.

I was concentrating on Harley again. He was a bit forward of the band. *How,* Harley? I wanted to know, what kind of threat have you hung over them in so few months to get these pubes to play like this? Harley was less nonchalant than he had been. He had his eyes closed; in fact, he smiled, and was enjoying the hell out of his band.

The gallery on his side was solid black skin, five deep. The smallest children were in the front row, and they were scared to death but having a fine time. I observed a big strange hat moving up behind the kids. Next thing I knew there was Whitfield Peter, with his hands over the shoulders of a tiny Negro. The child shot out of the spectator line at an odd angle, turning like a top. He knocked into Harley's legs and both Harley and the child went down on the pavement. You knew the kid had been pushed then. The big hat of Whitfield Peter rioted up and down and I saw him trying to get back through the blacks, but he was held there by the mass of them. In fact, he was bounced out in the gutter, and by that time Harley was on him, head to head, he knew who had pushed the child, and he back-handed Peter in the face, knocking the big hat a long ways back into the gallery, then stopped abruptly in the middle of the next blow. By then the band cut us off from the scene, but they gave in our direction, marching around the fight. Then a euphonium was raised by a player on the other end of the line, and the thick horn fell like an ax. I saw the eggshell-suited body sprawl at the end of the euphonium line. Harley flashed out ahead of the band, double-stepping and adjusting his helmet. He had sooty marks on the back of his uniform. I looked for Victor the cop, who was not at the pole any more.

Fleece and I caught up and began walking alongside the Gladiators, as I'd planned anyway, so as to meet Harley at Parade's end in front of the King Edward. We were hustling. Fleece told me he'd shot twice at the fight, but he didn't know what would come out, he didn't have the shutter-speed for an actual *fight*.

About at the Heidelberg Hotel, I looked across the street and—I'd thought I caught something disturbing the gallery

189

—there was old Peter walking parallel to Harley too, screaming. Peter had found the hat, but his face was botched and you could tell he'd been wocked by that horn. His suit was smudged and ripped. Peter got in step with Harley and mimicked his posture, but Butte was the heedless Prussian. Peter couldn't stand this. The gallery was much thinner now, and I saw every move. Peter was gathering his mouth to shout something at Harley but just then the band lit into "Washington Post" inhumanly, a drastic sound that blurred sight and made human voices into a squeak. I thought I could pick out Peter's squeaking across the street, as he stayed even with Harley.

All at once Whitfield Peter put his hand into the breast of his coat. I knew he was going for a gun; it did not occur to me that he could be reaching for anything but a gun, my forehead was hot with knowing this; but something could be done because he had missed yanking his gun out the first time, whereas I already had mine out and was almost to the middle of the street since I knew I could hit nothing from the distance I was from him on the sidewalk, and if I got there in time there might be no gunfire at all. Then Peter saw my gun out, and his not even drawn. Fleece was right with me—"Don't! Idiot!"—huffing away. It was a mistake. Peter had nothing, or only a big handkerchief, on his second draw. Fleece knelt and pretended to be getting some camera shots of the Gladiator band, and I passed the gun very subtly back into my coat pocket. Apparently no one had seen. We faded back off the street. Fleece's trifurcated chrome-ringed instrument aided in the ruse. He seemed to be railing technical observations to me, when of course what he was doing was scolding me to blister a slut. I had nothing to say. There were cops all over down here at the end of the parade. They had billy clubs at the casual. Whitfield Peter was gone.

We made our way to the front of the King Edward. The Gladiators treaded time to the drums, whose volume ballooned out into the Illinois Central overpass. Finally they cut off, *whoooommmpp!* and you could've sliced the silence with a knife. Harley signaled the disbandment. The players turned toward us and massed at the hotel door. I couldn't believe how ordinary and small they looked. They pranked around and barked at each other in that private nigger English you couldn't understand. There were several girls

190

among the Gladiators, too, jammed into green pants and double-breasters with the rest of them. The sweat on a couple of necks was another surprise. Then Harley came up. He held his helmet. With the other hand he had a euphonium-player in tow. The boy was telling Harley, "I gan outa control," almost crying. "You little sonuvabitch, you'da been watchin the music . . . you don't mind about me, you hear?" The boy was a head taller than Harley. Harley cast him away violently, and the boy ran ahead to the door. Harley turned back to look again.

I told Harley we'd seen everything. "He's crazy. He's been in Whitfield." He seemed consoled a bit to see me. Then we went through the hotel door with him.

"Wherever he is, his head ain't any better now. That boy busted him on it with his horn, I mean hard, and he fell down on the road and right on his head."

"*You* hit him," said Fleece. "I took a picture of that." Fleece was only making a technical point, as he often did. But Harley looked at the camera distraughtly. "No, I mean he deserved it. I guess," said Fleece.

"What the hell you mean by *I guess?*" I demanded of Fleece.

"I didn't know he was a white man till I hit him," said Harley.

"All I meant was that a fight is unfortunate. Somebody'll carry it on," said Fleece, trying to make up. "This damn place was *built* out of long memory."

"He knows. That boy knows," said Harley. "That Whitfield man followed me for a *mile* screaming at me."

"What'd he say?"

"Ah, all about my daddy, my daddy, who was my daddy? Everybody thinks they're the first sonuvabitch to notice I'm not a true nigger."

The pause after this was charged with gloom all around. Harley's beard was almost black with sweat. The helmet seemed to hang at his leg like a wilted trophy.

"He was so crazy he was stone-deaf, that man," Harley broke the gloom. "Anybody that heard that band, they couldn't . . . You heard my band." He smiled dreamily, beyond me.

"Yes—"

"Aw, my ass. Look in there." He put the helmet on. What he meant was that his bandsmen were standing all over the edge of the lobby and jamming up the hotel walk-through instead of moving on to the buses waiting outside as they were supposed to. The Gladiators, tubas set on the floor and brass and woodwinds jabbing around, brown faces wandering, were crammed everywhere, back to the plate glass of the souvenir shop and down the granite hall flush against the registration counters, on back to the airlines service. We passed some white couples holding newspapers who were getting out, in a rage. Some of the girls sat in the old plush chairs and couches; a few bandsmen were flirting with the water fountains—for whites only, like the whole hotel. Harley found the drum major, a big boy with his fur hat still on, dragging his braid-wound baton on the carpet. He dressed the boy down in some quiet gnashing language. The boy blew the whistle and made an epical gesture with the baton, shagging toward the rear revolving door. The Gladiators gathered into file quietly; there had never been much noise, anyway. Now they were a sagging retreat of children barely able to hold up their brass. Harley seemed satisfied with them again.

We were next to the men's room. The door flew open and Peter rammed out. He'd cleaned himself up. His hair was oily with water, his nose was bright, but he was purple about the forehead and an ear. The big hat he fended about was more of a bag now. I wet my pants when he came out shouting.

"You fellows help me get these cooties out of this hotel. Do they think this is Washington Dee Cee? Kick into them. Thrust them!" he said, doing unfinished demonstrations of these acts. Then he saw Harley, whom he had overrun. He jerked back.

"Mutt! Treacle!"

He began swatting Harley with his hat. "What did you say, you banjo?"

Fleece was at my ear, hand on my arm. "Don't," he said. The fact was it seemed like a sissy theater performance. Harley waved at the blows glibly, as if Peter was a gigantic gnat, but only a gnat. Some of the bandsmen were looking back and halting. At the height of the attack, Harley somehow jerked his head and they shuttled on.

"What did you *say?* Liar! Smuthead! Coon-beard!"

"I said if you would turn around you could see my band was nearly 'bout out of this hotel and I said I never meant

192

them to stop here. And if you'll put your hat back on your head, I'll put mine on too and we'll never see one another again, Mister White Man. I'm sorry that we ran in—"

"*That* thing?!" shouted Peter, sneering at the helmet. "Yes, do put that fancy thing on your head." Harley did. "But did you hear the *ed-u-kay-shun* squirt out of the high-yellow tadpole? Would you look at that helmet? Look at that beard. This one's hardly left a place for being a nigger." He struck off the helmet with his hat. Harley caught the helmet. Six or seven white people were looking at them from the Delta Airlines booth. Harley began edging away. I looked beyond the people at the booth, and here were two cops coming in the front, being led by one of those women with newspapers. Peter saw them. He reached out and caught Harley. "No, sir, Mister Neegro. I believe you'll stay until the police—"

"We can't stay," Fleece whispered to me. "You won't keep your mouth shut and they'll get you with the pistol. We can't."

I told him I was staying. Fleece hightailed it along the edge of the hall, then rode the revolving door out, disappearing like spun-off slat from the door—a hilarious thing, actually. But my own nerves broke with the cops approaching. I felt the gun was murmuring like a toad in my pocket. I couldn't wait here, not even silently. So I did much the same thing as Fleece, even more breathlessly, because I knew the cops were closer on my back. I was thinking about being caught by them in the slat position against the revolving door, maybe being unable to detach from the door and whirling around again, pistol slinging out and clattering right under their feet . . . but I got out free, and by the time I was out there, I was feeling utterly lousy about the whole thing. Fleece was nowhere around the rear driveway. I decided, all right, I'll stay here. No further.

Five minutes, and a new black Cadillac full of colored men in suits drove out of a lot across the street and entered the hotel driveway, coming to rest in front of me. The glass went down, the driver spoke.

"Did you see a colored man with a helmet and white uniform, with a beard? Look like a band director?"

"He's inside with the law and another man."

"That white man with that hat?"

I told them yes. They rolled up the glass. After a minute

193

they drove back across the street and parked at the mouth of the lot. Deeper in the lot sat the four long yellow buses full of the Gladiators.

Harley finally came out, by himself. He saw me and he looked miserably weary, with a tiny sneer, like that was all he had left. He flicked the helmet; some snap of disgust for me in that, I thought.

"I wanted to stay but I couldn't—"

"I didn't need you, little Harry. One of those cops, named Victor. He saw the man push the kid at me, and he *told* it. There wasn't anything to it. That was all, except for that Whitfield man." Harley smiled. "He went crazy all over again when I told that cop, Victor, I understood this man had been in Whitfield and I was ready to call it even. That man went all to raving, swinging that hat, wanting to know just how I thought I knew that."

For the first time I got Peter's face together with the Whitfield letters in my mind: the purple bruise of the forehead, the severe hat, among the lines of brown ink prose, and there, his wife lying on the prose as if on thorns, tortured all to moving every which way.

"—but you just think about that horn. You don't need to get in trouble," Harley was saying. That black Cadillac in the parking lot honked. I walked over with him.

"That slick one, he owns that car. He's the principal of the school. Now you know what he wants? My band, he wants my band. The man couldn't find the key of C if it came in a bag, but he sure do want this suit I got on. We drove a hundred miles up here with the air conditioning on, all us freezing, while that genius was explaining the principle of why we needed it, said science dictated that a number of bodies together gave off heat which the air conditioner was equalizing, and he wants to take over my band."

When we got to the car, they were holding up their hands for us to be quiet. I could hear the radio announcer out of the rear speaker, recognized the station as WOKJ, the colored station in Jackson. You could get B. B. King and a lot of other fine pluckers and honkers on it, and on Sundays, "Ain't No Flies on my Jesus," "Little More Jesus, Little Less Rock-and-Roll," and "Crazy Stranger, Where Yo Home?"

While the announcer was still going, Butte whispered, "I *made* the band. Now he says he wants me to go off for two

194

years to earn my Master of Music degree so as to *deserve* this band. Try to get a hold of that. He took a correspondence course in music over the Christmas holidays, so he says he could fill in, in my absence. He also told me I might be outlined for a better place than Beta Camina."

"I think he's right, there."

The people in the car began applauding lightly.

"The man said it. We won again," said the principal. The radio had been announcing the parade winner. Harley got in the back seat, crowding over. One of the men shook hands with him. The principal, with his arm crooked over the door, looked me over before they rolled off.

"Who is that?" he said, speaking right at me.

"He's from my home. A musician friend," Harley spoke from the back seat.

"I thought it was Roy Rogers. He got boots. He got a pistol pokin' out his pocket."

I had been cramming the gun down in my raincoat so long to assure its secrecy, I guess I made a hole in the old thing. The whole barrel was out. The principal drove off in distaste, carrying Harley; then the buses rambled past me. In the back window of the last one, two of the Gladiators were giving me the finger.

I walked the long way up to my car. I cranked the motor and Fleece sat up in the well behind me.

"Guess what?" he said. Something precious was coming.

"No, you guess what. I couldn't help it. They came for me. I cut them down in flame, Peter first. Peter crawled over to the wall and wrote *fuck* on it in his own blood. It seemed to be an ultimatum."

"Ass! . . . but not bad, though. 'An ultimatum.' I was lying here telling myself, if Monroe gets back, we've got to steal the rest of his letters. Because I didn't get him."

"What?"

"I got no pictures of him. When I was running out of the hotel I was trying to take the roll out so no matter what happened, I'd have the pictures, but the spool got away from me and unrolled out on the sidewalk."

"That wonderful camera, and you drop the film."

"But at least we'll get the rest of the letters. I don't want to get close enough to him to take any more pictures . . . but we'll figure out a day when he's away from his house . . ."

I remembered that, in the hotel, I had avoided looking at Peter as often as I could. In fact, I'd held my hands to my face when he was there. It was too embarrassing a horror to see him directly, all beaten up, the face of the letters.

8 / Sliding

I was being faded out of music, "serious" music, I mean, and didn't know it. The professors were running me out of the field. I bought a new coat made out of reptile leather over at a sale at Gus Mayer ($150, even so). And I wore it, it was full spring and getting warmer, but I wore it, thinking *now I am ready*. I didn't know for what, quite, but I suspected there was evil weather ahead. Fleece attempted to ignore the coat for a week. I did wonder about the figure I was cutting, and asked him what he thought. He told me I looked like an endlessly mean queer, which he had been patiently waiting to say that week, I bet, knowing I was uncertain about the coat. However, there was a bleached-blond girl who played flute in the Jackson Symphony who was excited about the coat and declared to me, during the symphony recess, that I looked like an Indian prince. This was Patsy Boone, a freshman at Millsaps College, and she was nobody's beauty—after the popping blue eyes and the nice teeth, just a piece of skirt, it seemed—but she had pleasant, stunning things to say about me. I took the solo of the "Habañera" once, in the absence of the first-chair trumpet. During the recess she found me and pressed my arm. She said she almost couldn't stand it while I was playing. Something had happened to her, body and soul, which she couldn't discuss just now.

So, at the next rehearsal, I was playing along at fourth part, swelling with new zest, and I got in trouble with the violist who sat in front of the trumpets. He was a professor of music at Belhaven College, a girls' school in Jackson. He told his other violist friend that I sounded like a cow step-

196

ping in its own pies. I heard this, and told him I would get him for it. He had a loud voice and others had heard him. The jackass was six foot three and could've beaten me to a pulp just defending himself. But he called the police about my threat, and I got a call on the floor telephone in the dorm from the captain at the Jackson police station telling me this violist had bolted his doors and was trembling in his house with a shotgun.

He never showed up at rehearsals as long as I came. Manino, the conductor—a lean sissy who'd made a reputation down South on the violin—decided he needed the violist more than me and kicked me out with a quiet explanation about how, if the truth were known, I did every now and then sound like a Mexican calling the bulls. I packed up and told symphony work goodbye. I walked out of Murrah auditorium, heard the orchestra plunge into "Polovtsian Dances" without me, and with no lacking in the brass section; heard no dismay over my absence; everybody was bright on his notes, the percussion were ripping and jangling in my bones so I felt like a drunk gypsy, the French horns were husky and Slavic, and the strings carried the dances with that sadness strings still carry, no matter what gay dance they play.

I lay down in my T-bird. My eyes were wet, and I had to drag out the old handkerchief, looking out at those silvery streetlights on Highway 51, and over at the Ole Miss medical center, its new spring campus rising toward the lights, its big lazy trees, its rolled green. You felt that the moon in the blue was the old drawing master of it all. Goodbye Bach, Handel, Haydn, Beethoven, Manfredini, Mozart, Vivaldi, Purcell, and Borodin, I was thinking. Then I sat up and told all European music to go to hell.

I had jazz and miles of blues and an endless trek of rhythm in me. I got my shades out of the glove compartment and put them on, even in the night. Then I went sailing away, in a thunder of leaking mufflers. Let the gas and the ass spill, no top on my car. The young May wind took all sweat and all tears off me, and Jackson was a deep greenery with intersections of orange and gray, by what showed through my shades.

I didn't tell Livace about being kicked out of the symphony. He was my instructor and he'd gotten me the place. He used to be first chair with the symphony, but now he

197

didn't have the time. When he sent me over, he told me what I ought to do was *listen* for a couple of years. I asked him why I would need to carry my horn over with me. He said I should finger the notes and *think* the tones. I could actually play at *forte* markings and above. This was the way he had learned, with the Minneapolis Symphony, and when he'd begun actually playing, he never missed a note or was out of tune and moved swiftly up to first chair. Among the musicians of Minneapolis, it was known that he had never missed a note or tone. I thought of Livace as a statue of a man with a trumpet to his lips in some cold Minneapolis park.

At first I couldn't figure why Livace didn't have the time to play with the symphony any more. He was another Italian who dragged his darling fathomlessly intricate culture around with him, like a tail; he was Catholic, he had to drive to Jackson for mass, since there was no Catholic church near Hedermansever, and his weak old De Soto stalled out on him perpetually, but further than that, he was *scared*, and I knew it. One day in his office, he was so scared that he spoke to me as if I was his last friend. To get his doctorate in music he had borrowed money from the Mafia. Now he had a family and could afford to pay back, at the most, only two-thirds of the monthly note they wanted; there was quite an interest on the loan. He knew he wasn't sending his payments to people who sat around in offices writing letters to him about how much he was lacking. He expected that, at the least, one day he would come to this office and there would be an angry muscular creature laying for him. Livace kept one of those giant economy bottles of aspirin on his desk and ate from it—he always ran a fever, you could see it in his ears. He looked something like Sid Caesar, the comic, and like Sid, sweat and fever were his realm. One afternoon he wanted me to take his monthly payment to the post office; it was a heavy envelope, packed with green cash, I could tell. After I got back, he asked me if I knew what I'd done. I said I'd mailed a lot of money for him, is what I'd done.

"What you have just done is mail the money I needed to pay for a hernia operation on my baby son."

Aside from this sort of thing, though. Livace could play the fanny off a trumpet. He's the best straight virtuoso I've ever heard. When he taught, it was by a glib performance

198

by the one and only Livace himself. Try to match me, he said. His eye would lie on the music like the dead eye of a fish, he would take in the music by that one eye, and out the end of the horn came a spray of notes not only correct, but sweet, spangling. I'd be in the practice cell across from him, blasting away at a passage, and hear steps coming my way. He'd have his own horn, a Bach Stradivarius, and give me the courtesy of a chuckle, then bend that dead eye down and render the passage so well you wanted to retire to comb and tissue paper.

But one day I'd forgotten him, tooting away, thinking I was lovely, I was in the stars in my own Milky Way. Some-body grabbed my ears and jerked them outwards painfully. I could smell the aspirin on his breath.

"Aren't you hearing all those bad notes? Don't you know you must have *ears* to be a musician? You've been out of tune on every note above middle C for the last fifteen min-utes."

"Get your hands off my ears."

Then there was nothing between Dudi and me. I didn't care if he had believed in my promise ever since hearing me at the contest in Shreveport, that I was supposed to transmute into a genius under this care. Just no more hands on my ears, please. Stuff his care. Some afternoons I sat in the cell and stamped out as many cigarette butts as possible in front of the wire stand with the page of music Livace set up for me. Sometimes he'd insult me by putting up some whole-note exercises from the Baldwin primer; next it would be a piece so black with runs it was impossible, in a freakish key, five flats and such. When I felt like it, I'd just play jazz, play the blues loud and watery with the door open. Dudi gave up then. I'd hear him locking up with great assertion; lights went out in the nearby rooms. When I heard him on the stairs, I moved out to the top of them and bellowed and blatted to give him a fine sopping echo —"La Cosa Nostra Blues," had he asked me. Probably he was afraid to ask about my progress in the Jackson Sym-phony.

Patsy Boone had not given up on me. I took her out. One night in the parking lot of the Dutch Bar, having kissed most of her visible body and bored to tears, I was lying dis-mally face-down in her hair. She told me how she missed me at rehearsals, she told me she wanted me and me only

199

in her hair. I poured off some of the beer over her head. "Oh, my valentine, anything!" as I fell into the matted strands.

I was Romeo of the Roaches again, eating the lamb patties of her hands, licking her yellow hair. I grabbed her thigh ruthlessly, put my hand around the ankle of the other leg. I *need* you, I said. Bored, but having at it as the male of the species. I'd been trained. My owner was crying, Get out there and perform, you simple hairball; finger out of the nose, now, no lifted hindfoot, no dicking off! Everyone's paid to see you! Up on the trike! Ride! Be a man. Flick of the whip there about the scrot to give yer a little spirit. El Humanoido, the trained link of evolution! I'd fallen into the floor pedals and was sprawled over the gearhump of the T-bird, yanking at her skirt. Not here in the parking lot with the top down, she cried. Besides, it was starting to rain.

On the way to her apartment, she had second thoughts. She told me she was virginal and wanted to have passion with me in the clear light of reason. It should be no drunken thing like this. Touching was too precious. I should come to see her on Sunday. The light in her room would be on and she might bring in other lamps.

It seems I exuded an exotic melancholy—her words— that undid her. When I'd played the "Habañera," sob, she'd kissed my heart. How long she'd been trying to meet her eyes with mine! She'd gone out with another boy who sort of looked like me. But he had no heart like she wanted to put her tongue on.

"And then many nights I'd think of you while I was lying in bed, and I'd have an erection," she said.

I just turned my face and looked up in the blue night when she said that. I didn't know about going to her place Sunday, although I was flattered to the point of torment by her confession of love. I let her out at an old white house on Titpea, off North State, and she ran, like an injured lark, alone, to her apartment, as she said she wanted to.

Back at the dorm, I asked Fleece what possibly she could have meant. He was so avid to know everything he didn't even laugh. I think he sort of fell in love with Patsy, hearing about her. He said she was just a little mixed up in her terms, was all.

200

"Do you remember in Peter's letter, 'the lush vigilant digit of your clitoris'?"

"Yes, I do."

"Well then."

He gazed off amazedly. "She *said* that?"

Exam time came around the next week. Fleece's parents went to Europe for four months. General Creech wanted to live in all the places he'd helped shoot to pieces, said Fleece. He imagined Creech all blown up like a toad with his memories. Fleece's board was paid for at the college through summer and fall, and the house was locked tight, but we broke in and set up. The grass was already high in the yard, high around the cool mimosas, which were everywhere. It was a ranch home, with bricks and green boards. Fleece felt terribly good, at first, being in the place. He read like a monk. We had the air-conditioning and the free telephone. For me it was free board for the summer. I was finished with college music and thought I might indeed try medicine. Fleece made it sound easy, and at the same time glorious. The idea was that his own knowledge was so large that just being around him, enough would rub off on me to make the basics, even starting from scratch. Beyond that, there was only memory work, and my memory had always been fine when it needed to be. So I was going into chemistry, German, and algebra this summer, and I felt like a swashbuckler of the mind.

Saturday evening I called Patsy and Fleece was on the extension.

"I'm going into pre-med," I told her.

"My baby a *doctor?*" said Patsy. "Then you can come right over and cure me! I've got bruises everywhere where you grabbed me the other night. Honey . . . no! . . . I love all my bruises. You were my poor drunk Harry . . . I love you more! When I see your face tomorrow."

"Darling, do you want to have intercourse with me?" I said.

"Yes! Yes! I'M FAINTING WHEN YOU SAY THOSE WORDS. Oh, darling. I didn't know you loved me enough to say *intercourse* and *darling* to my face!" I was doing all this for the benefit of Fleece, of course. She was a great joke.

"Now that I'll be in medicine, and thinking of what you

201

said the other night about our act, you know, in the clear
light of reason, I think now I *should* say words like *intercourse* and, well, *vagina* and *penis*. *And feces*, even, certainly!"

"Oh, yes! And our children, too, we'll teach them that!
All of the Latin words! My honey Harry. Let me ask you
this. Will you *not* smoke, will you *not* bring your cigarettes
tomorrow? I don't want those clouds of smoke coming
from my darling's mouth. We don't want the room cloudy
or smoky in any way, do we?"

"For you," I volunteered.

"Would you let me call you something that is not very
scientific? I saw a movie once, I know it's girlish, but you
with the horn . . . when I saw you and heard you playing
that Mexican solo—please, I know, I hope you'll go on
playing your horn. But—"

"What?"

"My *Apache Valentine!*" She sighed. "I've said it." She
hung up. Now, I knew what Fleece would do with this, and
I did wish she hadn't said that. She had peered in so close
to me that she'd gotten as close as the right tribe.

I waited a while, but he was still in his parents' bedroom,
holding the phone. He looked askance at me through his
horn-rims. His sideburns were wet and curling.

"Ain't she keen? Does she come on strong?" I said.

"That was wrong for me to be hearing her. She's real.
You don't deserve her. Shut the door."

I read a bit of my chemistry and went to bed in Fleece's
room, a brown room with varnished pine, black knotholes
in it, thinking of the queer blotches around me. I woke up
with my cheek hurting. A thick book was lying on the
sheets. Fleece had hit me with it.

"Open the eyes. Don't be mad, now. That's *The Brothers
Karamazov* you're looking at. I could've stacked all the
books I had to leave behind in this house on your chest, and
you'd be crushed to *death*. So, see, you're alive, and don't
be mad. I want to talk about my girlfriend, Bet."

"I've seen Bet at least once a day all semester and I've
never seen you with her. I don't believe in this; I think she
barely knows your name. Don't *ever* hit me in my sleep like
that."

"She's from Rolling Fork. A Delta woman. She is six

202

feet, one inch. Her father is taller, her mother is even taller, and she is *little* Bet to them. She has a brother who is taller than all of them who played basketball at Mississippi State. Her daddy was a Marine in the Pacific in World War Two. He lived through the same battle my father died in. I really do have to make a choice. She has several strikes against her. Don't laugh, but she sings *hymns*, spontaneously, with all her heart. Our first date was up to the Hilltop Theater. We were walking to the movie under that arch of oak trees, neither one of us could think of anything to say, and she breaks into 'Amazing Grace, how sweet the sound, that saved a wretch like me. . . .' At the moment I was taking mark of the white insides of her toes where her suntan hadn't covered. She had sandals on. I can see her feet by the lightning of the spring storm that's breaking over us. Her dress was blowing between her legs. I let go of her hand when she started 'Amazing Grace.' I went over to the side of the road and looked at the weeds; I almost threw up. I'd taken in some lab fumes that afternoon. My body was throwing out an alarm. I told her I was dizzy, I hadn't eaten supper. 'No supper!' I'm quoting her. She stroked the back of my head. How can I tell her it's the hymn that really made me sick? But it was good, really. She said she hadn't even made the concert choir, but screw you people over in Fine Arts. It was good. For the first time in five years I felt like I was a sinner, when she sang. We went on up to the movie, and I took hold of her hand about midway through. She liked that . . . I'll tell you, to sweat hands together in the Hilltop . . ."

I appeared at Patsy's apartment on time. She met me, clutching together a purple robe that looked like a piece of rented costumery for a male actor in college Shakespeare, and she did tell me she'd been in two campus plays, showed the photograph taken under a proscenium which revealed her as an inscrutable female extra in Elizabethan wraps. We had such common interests, she said. The lights of reason were truly up; there were extra lamps. On her wall was a fishnet holding all her flute music and other things meaningful to her—menus and stolen wine glasses and her diary. She pulled the robe apart and sailed it away, and leaving no moment for examination, she was nude, hurling herself on the bed.

What a feast of sight I'll make, I thought. I peeled off. I went over to the old dresser with the tall three-way mirror and picked up the pistol she kept, a ten-dollar .22 revolver for protection against rapists. What a laugh. I had pity for her. I glanced over at the wire screen of her window. He breaks through there, a raw pink craver, and the dyed-blond horrorstruck princess of the roaches shoots blue holes in his stomach. Then claws out his eyes if the bullets didn't stop him. Saving herself for me. I pitied him too, maybe more than her.

I'd done some push-ups every other week, and knew there were some muscles apparent on me. I turn, blinded to her by the effect of my own body. Look what you are getting for free, Patsy.

"Lord! Wow! You're so *ugly!* Men are so ugly, at last I see! Doesn't it *hurt* to be like that? Don't you dare turn away, though. Get on the bed. My lord, it looks like you've been wounded! Something they rammed through you from behind . . . I have to help that swollen thing, don't I? Yeah, ah, yeaaaahasssss! Aw, is this right? Is this it? Aw. *Be* ugly in me, be ugly . . . Don't you quit!"

I was fed up with her calling me ugly. I quit and dressed. The window screen seemed the right place to go out. She began sobbing; she drew up the yellow sheet around her. It was all very well to me that I'd quit at the time she started needing me. I didn't like that loud screech calling me ugly, ugly, ugly.

She sobbed, unfulfilled, teats abob. As I was leaving I caught sight of her kicking off the sheets in some sort of fit. Then, the first time, I saw her nude and whole. I'd never seen the whole body of a female from this range. The lights of the room seemed to jump up even brighter. A magical flare-burst is what it was, over Patsy. I saw her lovely waste of breasts, even though they were small, and her navel, a pink whirlpool of flesh, her pale brown cup of hairs, her thighs and her toes all together. Her hair was glistening wet and thick. My word, I wanted another chance at that, but I was one leg out of the window already. I fell out, on the nasty stems of a hedge. Oh, let me back, but I was too much a fool to climb back up.

My mouth hurt. She had sucked my tongue when we kissed. And I had that stupid wilt of pain below. But I clambered back to my car, as if the ham muscles of one leg

204

had been cut. My face was hot as the rash. And behind me, in the yard, I could feel something yet to pull into the car, like a kinked tail, as if my ass had unraveled off me and was caught in the hedge under her window.

9 / The Theft of Her Letters

Fleece could not drive a car. When he went out alone at night, he called a taxi. Sometimes the taxi would back out of the driveway and head west—toward Hedermansever—and sometimes east—toward Jackson, about which he was mysterious. Bet was at Hedermansever, I knew. But what was in Jackson?

"I'm going diving," he said about one trip. I thought he might be swimming at the YMCA to build up his body. This was possible. He took no swim trunks or towel with him, and at the Y, you swam in the raw. I was trapped in one weekend and found that out. It was in Shreveport, the night before the solo contest. Old Mr. Medford—who was going to accompany me on piano—and I thought a swim in the heated pool might be nice before supper. We went out and bought us some swimsuits. Then we went down to the pool and everybody was in naked. This put me off. Old Medford didn't know what to do, and I felt for him. For him it had taken guts to even get in the swimsuit. I told him it looked damned odd to me. We forgot the swim and went out to supper.

But this had nothing to do with Fleece. He meant *dive* in the sense of *tavern*. What Fleece was doing was going out to meet and talk with the people, I guess for the first time in his life. I found this out later. The fact was, Fleece told me sometime during college, that he wanted to be a doctor for about ten years, then he wanted to run for governor of the state of Mississippi. It seems his ambition increased after he met Bet Henderson. However, Fleece was no drinker. Three beers almost took him away. His drinking partners,

205

angered by the line of debate he took, would often spit at him and strike him.

It was nice to sleep late every morning of the weekend in Fleece's house, to have your coffee at noon. I think I was made for that. I'd been up an hour one morning when Fleece came into the kitchen. His hands were locked in front of him. He told me it was time to visit the king cat's house. We had to steal Catherine's letters, had to, soon. Somewhere in the house there must be something from her.

We drove to the house the next day, Monday, around ten in the morning. Peter would be at the real estate office in Jackson. I had the hard top on the T-bird. At Canton, we turned off on a gravel road. The house itself was two miles down this road. It had an overgrown gravel turnaround in the yard. The house was a large thing; the white paint was falling off its boards, and it had a swollen gray aspect. I kicked through a window, and we climbed in with no trouble. We were looking for the attic, but I noticed that the downstairs was sparse of furntiture, the floorplanks were bare, and there was a desk standing right out in the middle of the biggest room. At the top of the stairs, before you got to the attic stairs, there were other rooms on both sides. I saw a made bed in one, and a pair of aqua-blue nylon fur house slippers resting by the front leg of it. A woman was living in this house, now.

We had two duffel bags. The crate was there. We pulled all the rest of the letters out. They stunk, like a mixture of spice and dung. They got yellower toward the bottom. My hands were rancid, with flecks of orange on them. We had them all and it was time to go, down the attic stairs, past the room with the house slippers. We were in a hurry, but when we got to the main room downstairs, I saw some more envelopes on the big desk in the middle of the room and ran over to them. I saw one with a letter in it stuffed into one of the cubby holes and took it. We were at the front door going out when I saw the back door of the house opening, hard. I caught a glimpse of Peter and then showed him my back. Peter hollered out. "Yaaaaaaaa!"

We barreled for the T-bird, but I saw there was a white Chrysler parked sideways across the drive right in front of it. We threw the bags into the well of the car and I tore down on the key of my T-bird. I would have to back up

into some huge growth of briars to get out of here. The car
wouldn't start. I bent the key again.

"Here he comes around the house!" said Fleece.

Then the T-bird reared back on pure fire into those
briars, the back end of the car rose up in the air, I was getting no soil with the wheels; then the wheels came down
and I steered out of the yard, framming his car with gravel
and red dust. Fleece said he was in his car now, coming after us. We made the hardtop on the outskirts of Canton,
then got on the four-lane of Highway 51, and he was still
trying, though way back there. I put the accelerator down
the last quarter-inch, and left him out of sight. Fleece
thought he might've taken down the license plate number.
But I still had the old California plates on the car. I'd take
them off and get new Mississippi ones.

The letters, the yellower they were, the more unspeakable. The last one fell apart in your hands. It was still Peter
writing to his wife Catherine. There were no letters from
Catherine in the crate. The last letter set another scene, this
time out on the front porch of the house, in the open air.
The two of them seemed to have gotten out here from the
upstairs room in some method which allowed them to make
their way while at no moment uncoupled. There was a potted fern on the porch which was a sort of shrine and destin-
ation. Around this fern they emitted climactic fluids, blood
included, and somehow they collected most of these fluids
into one offering, which was poured on the fern in the last
gasps of exhaustion. The letter ended in an undiminished
mating call: "Let us see, beloved Catherine, how the fern
will *do!*"

All over Fleece's house lay letters. The duffel bags sat
tumbled over on the couch. The house smelled like swamp
gas. Your hands were brown from handling the last letters.
It wouldn't wash off. Your hands stank; you couldn't eat a
sandwich with your hands that way.

Fleece handed me a page which consisted of nothing but a
crescendo of spelled-out grunts.

"It's not fun any more," he said. "He doesn't have any
style any more. Let's build a fire. Get this filth out of my
house. I do believe I'm going nuts with him, Monroe."

The other letter, the one I'd gotten off his desk, was post-
marked last year—

. . . taken poor me unner you wing like this I caint har-
dily thank you eneough, Uncle Peter, I just do hope Im
sharp enough for college.
                    Love,
                    Vinceen

What was this? The postmark was Mobile. Looking again, I
saw the date was August, exactly a year to the day ago.
"Who could it be?"
"Thinking is making me sick. I said help me with this
filth," whined Fleece.

10 / Shades of the Belly and Bean

Bobby Dove meant it. Exams were on, it was not a good
season for it, but he was having a dark fit again. He slept in
his mother's room and opened her drawers and held her articles. I saw that accidentally in the door-length mirror. I
also saw him standing in front of his mother's closet, peering in, for an overlong period. He went into the closet and I
think he cast himself onto the clothes on the hangers.

After exams I let him have the house and left for Dream
of Pines. He hadn't spoken directly to me for two weeks. I
didn't want to become implicated in his mental condition.

The old man had been playing golf all summer and he
was suntanned, with the gray hair a little longer than usual.

"A doctor in the house," he said.

"If I can keep it up."

"Do you think you're finding your way? You know, you
could *still* play your horn, all that wouldn't be wasted. Doctor Israel plays the drums in his basement, you know, even
as a G.P. Music can be a lifelong hobby."

Ode was really betting on me as a doctor, and even
though we had little to say to each other, it was fine with
me to give my daddy that happiness. While I was at the

208

house, my grades from Hedermansever came in. B's in chemistry, a D in hateful German.

My mother had the beer in the icebox again. She wanted to know if I had a sweetheart. I told her I'd been casual with a few. She told me how important it was to meet someone with Faith. We were sitting at the kitchen table. I had never drunk liquor right in front of her before and was holding the can as if I weren't interested in it. She told me to drink it, she knew I drank beer in college. After two cans, she looked at me. She wanted to know if I felt easier about talking now. Her eyes were moist and she had turned slightly breathless of voice. She asked me whether I thought they, Ode Elann and she, had instilled me with any things of the spirit when I was growing up.

"N—" Then I saw the trust she had in me, how hopeful she was, and said, "I know you did."

"You're bored here, aren't you? All your college activities. You shouldn't be always scowling though. You're a nice-looking boy. Don't spoil your face." She'd seen the other children come home during the vacations from L.S.U. Their lives were not lived in her house. They had their sweethearts. They were on the phone or waiting for the mail, their lifeblood was in the telephone wires and the post office. Now I was home, but without a sweetheart, so she could talk to me.

"What's wrong with her?" I asked Ode.

"She's gotten holy." He talked to one side of me, as if some person next to me would understand. He didn't like it anymore than I did, I don't think.

"Your mother and I have read these magazine articles about how fifty-five is just middle age. That's a lie. Even if you feel good. I feel good. But when you look down the end of the path, 'Let this cup pass from me.' You know who said that?"

"Jesus."

"Even Him. He didn't want it any more than I do. Let it pass on down the line to the other fellow who hasn't taken care of his health and deserves it. It just isn't fair that once you get fifty you have to worry about death any second. You start listening to sounds in your body. You see how lonely it will be. So you want a friend with you, you see. You have your children, you, your sister and your brothers. But a woman with religion, she wants much more sympathy

209

than that. Even more than her husband. A woman hurts more times than ten men could ever take notice of. I can't say anything about it."

My mother was still a beautiful woman. There was either a great new absence or a great new presence in my mother. Her physique was perfectly fine, but now I looked at her knowing she was not eternal, was considering the possibility of her own death. Something slid out from under me.

"You pick out a rich girl, now," said the old man the last day. "It's all the same in the dark."

I left Dream of Pines by the old greasy highway, seeing the new motel courts and a few pale boys on the diving board of their swimming pools. It was mid-September, and almost cold. They were having a good time. But everything and everybody was ghostly to me now. They were ghosts, they knew they were near death and they were having fun anywhere they could take it. Their old man had taken a job in a place that was still warmish in September and they were living here until they found a house. They stayed underwater as long as they could to get away from the stinking air of the paper mills. Their old man was back in the room using the motel ballpoint to figure up on the motel stationery how long they could last before the paycheck. I thought all this under the influence of my old man, who had told me how Dream of Pines was booming. "Booming!" I saw the swimmers in my dreams later. They were skeletons, shivering, smiling hugely with their gums, the last flesh left to them. Death was everywhere in Dream of Pines, since the old man first mentioned it. I didn't even trust my own youth. My youth was an old sick pirate; there was a boy back there lying on the reefs, bleeding. The lad's throat had been cut. I had cut it. "Push off, push off!" came an odd voice in my ear. I had no hometown, and Hedermansever was not my home. There was no real bed for me, not in the bunk at college, not in the gray stone house, not in Fleece's house.

I knew Fleece would not be back at school and I was wondering who they would stick me with in the room. But there he was waiting for me, healthy as a berry. He'd put on some weight, in truth. I had an impression, however, that he was only simulating health. He was a mite frantic to cut a healthy figure, like a man skating casually while

210

trying to balance a cantaloupe on his neck. He agreed with everything I said, everything I wanted to do. "Hell yes, Monroe!" Want to play some poker? Want to bet on the Colts? Want to play some snooker? He didn't know how to do any of those things. "You bet, Monroe."

Then his mouth became restless.

"Do you understand when I say that by the time it counts I'm afraid I won't have enough energy to get my genius across? There are two people, professors on this campus, who once *were* geniuses, you can tell it in their faces, walking around with their wives and families, these men altogether sapped of power, with their caved-in smiles." He was out late frequently with Bet. He acted as if he had just run a long way.

"One thinks he can play with his own energy forever. Then she comes along, giving you every indication she means to be only your hobby, just wants to trail along as long as you let her. Always the *flirting*. And before you know it, you're pouring your brains down her cunt. She isn't smiling any more, nor flirting. She's serious as death. She ought to be. Half your self lies in a pool at the backend of mons pubis."

This went on the whole fall. Then in 1962, he wouldn't get out of the rack for classes and slept like a rattlesnake hibernating in winter. One night the last of January he got out of bed, put his shoes on contrariwise, shut his eyes, and walked right into all his stacked-up material—the books, the cigar boxes, the metal stork, everything, it all tumbled over. I cannot define for sure what state he was in. He plunged sightless through the debris, kicking at it. He mounted a pile of books and stood there on top in blind idiocy. The books would not support him. He crashed on the end of my bed.

"I'm a dirty boy. Hit me."

I tapped him. His eyes were still shut.

"Hit me hard, Ruben. You know how fed up with me you are."

I punched him. He slunk away and crawled back to his bed over the foot-high rubble. He put his hand in the plate I'd brought him from the cafeteria.

"I'm a dirty boy, dirty, dirty, dirty boy. Get me a preacher."

I closed my book. "All right, I will."

I went down two floors and got that Baptist from South Carolina that I used to room with. He was already asleep, nine o'clock at night, and came to the door in a brown robe. He couldn't make me out. I went in the room to help him find his quadrafocals. A Chinese boy was sitting up sleepily on the other bunk. This was Don Thing, the poet from Hong Kong. He wrote a sort of timid new English set to poetry in the *dart,* the campus literary magazine. His poems were printed on the slant, with lines wide apart, so as to de-emphasize what utter banal coonshit they were.

"Don and I have taught each other a lot," said Thomas, my old roommate, going up the stairs in his cloth skids. His tiny black eyes were so lost in his glasses, he seemed imprismed, and you thought he probably couldn't hear you, either.

"I've brought Thomas," I said to Fleece, who lay stiff on the bed, like an open-eyed corpse. He hadn't eaten in two days and had seldom smoked. I was the one who had to explain to his professor in the lab. I backed to the door and told Thomas Fleece was ready for him. Thomas made his way over the collapsed library and knelt by the bed, being unable to find a seat. I shut the door as if I'd left, easing at the same time into the plaster cave of the closet. Thomas never even looked back.

"Monroe said you needed me."

"Pastor, when you get as much as I have and you can't quit getting it, but you know you're robbing your mind—"

"Is this about a girl?"

"I won't say her name."

"Have you made her pregnant?"

"No. I want you to read the letters that led me down this sorry road. Pick up one of them. Look around the room for letters written in brown ink."

Thomas bent around the room like some huge exiled rat with goggles. He waddled over a cigar box which was tumping out the letters we hadn't burned. Then he picked up a wad and sat down to read. This took ten minutes. There was only the study lamp on, upended.

"This paper smells like a restroom. Is that the joke, that now I have smelly hands?"

"What he has done, Pastor, I think, is make an intellectual preoccupation out of sex. You see how much good grammar he spends on it. Sex wasn't made for thought, was

212

it? It's only instinct and touch. As intellectual matter it is a swamp from which no man comes back whole. You go into the swamp with your mind—there seems to be so much to contemplate. And you come back, if you get back, with a few pubic hairs in your hand and a shriveled-up backbone."

"Why do you need me here? You aren't going crazy like Monroe said."

"Yes I *am!* I've been theorizing on sex every minute since I found out it was possible that a lady might smile when she spread her legs. I get flashes of sexual visions as fast as you can open and close your hand. I read books and see flickering pictures, not a movie, but still-life photographs that . . . I know that when the mind plays variations on the same theme, you have lost part of it somewhere—"

"Well, you do have a lot of theories for everything you say, don't you?" says Thomas. "Wait. Now you say you are getting it regular?"

". . . I have had too much in too short a time. My brains are turning to mud. I need to put my foot on some rock, and you may be that rock, Thomas."

"What are you wanting to *tell* me?" demanded Thomas. "You've got genius and you're getting it regular and you're lying in your bed moo-cowing? Why'm I kneeling here? I got a ninety I. Q., I been wandering around in a funnybook for six years being hooked by every sharpie in the pulpit, I got *this* looking at me in the mirror, I couldn't find twat if I paid for it, and I'm led down here by a guy that hates my guts to babysit his roommate that can't live with his own luck, well I'm getting back to sleep and that for your information is the only fun I have!"

Thomas waded out of the room and smashed the door to. Fleece let out a prolonged swoony sort of groan.

"Look who was here!" I said, leaping out of the curtains. Fleece started in fright. Then he tried to settle himself into a sort of corpse stiffness again, his back to me. "I heard, I heard. He would not be your rock, the rock ran, eh?" Fleece would not respond. "I was surprised. Thomas. My God! I can foresee the day when *nobody*'s a pastor any more. All the rocks'll be wandering around in a funnybook. Matter of fact, they'll be pissed-off when a simple soul comes to them with his guilty little diary." If you know Gleason, with his Reggie Van Gleason the Third voice, I

213

was talking like that, the dandified baron with a cold. But nothing from Fleece. I knew he'd been serious with Thomas, that he had not known I was there. "Why don't you get your ass up, Fleece?"

There was another whole day of silence yet. I came in at a late hour. Fleece was sitting on his bed. He had brewed himself a cup of instant coffee with hot tap water from the lavatory. He gave *me* advice.

"You need to have at it with one girl for a length of time, my friend. Buy presents, work her delicately. Hold hands in the movies. Pet. Neck. Begin begging. See her slip her underwear off with tears in her eyes . . .

"Be understanding yet press on. After some days, hear *her* beg with another kind of tears in her eyes. She has built her house around you. Meet Daddy, who thinks you're someone she's hired to take up her luggage to the dorm and is surprised to find out you are her spark, as Mommy calls you in letters to her daughter. But know the reality (outside, the mob howling that you can't have this girl); minutes after Daddy and Mommy have driven off back to Rolling Fork, she can't wait for dark to fall. Drags you across the highway along the path laid out for the cross-country team, by the orange markers on trees and cloths tied on limbs, your shoes hitting all the roots in the wood-path. Down a hill to the pond. Through the blackberry bushes on the dam, seeking the smaller path veering down on the back of the dam, in moonglow. Through the rotten leaves, the snails, the snakes, to a shelf. See and hear the dress fall lightly, see that movement of hands to her back, see the brassiere cast afloat, watch her bend, pull off the wispy hose from her legs, the brilliant white panties torn up off her feet, because she's lying down now. See the long fingers on your belt buckle. Have that, my friend. Have the zipper zipped down for you. See your watch taken off, feel your pants clink down with the wallet and your belt buckle weighting them. Feel air on your thighs, my friend. Then *save* your woman, cover her moans, fill her. Be an eel in waves of soup. Try to swim until you evaporate. You were her hero. Then the next morning see her all crisp, combed, new dress, sprayed hair. Glancing by you as if the competition for her had not been settled. Other men might make a play. So she tries to look pretty because they must all hurt knowing she is owned by you."

214

Fleece seemed enchanted, telling this. It was so strong that, a couple of nights after it, I went to sleep trying to dream of a loved one. I forced it, I got the dream, but she was a woman at the bottom of a swimming pool. She wore hose, nothing else, and she was giving a lecture on sex. With a pointer she rapped on her sex and pushed it out a bit. You could barely see, because she had hair like a sheepdog, but you could see, as through the eye of a needle, two cooked hamburgers rammed together. Your eyes went up in horror to see her chest, where there were two suit-buttons sewed on her, bleeding. Her lips were moving in a cold lecture all the time.

It was a stunning dream I couldn't do anything with. I think I almost always sleep too deep for dreams. Then one comes, like that old dream of Ann Mick naked, and it does nothing but ruin my waking time for a month.

11 / In Vicksburg

On a clear warm day I told Bobby Dove I was driving over to Vicksburg. He said wait, he wanted to go too. It was a Sunday. Fleece was still inching out of his mental spell. He had wanted me to hit him in the stomach again, and this time I did not hold back. He spat up a peck of odorific gobs and passed out. But he wanted to go out now. He'd also lived through another bout of the Hudson Bay flu. He put a towel around his neck.

We went west on 80—the top down—past Bolton, Edwards, Bovina, and into the deep-slit hills and trees covered with kudzu vine. Eighty was a thin, cracked road full of tar repairs. There was a big sun, but the wind was so cool it was like taking a fine spray of water on your skin. I dialed the radio, was going to pass by a white church service, when Fleece hit my hand. They were singing the invitational hymn. It was noon.

"Can you hear her singing?" I slowed the car to hear.

215

"Whatever church it is, my mother's there. She wants to go down the aisle. She thinks whatever is wrong in her home might come to her when she's in front of the congregation."

"My mother might be there too," I said.

"I can't hate her. I can't hate somebody who starched and ironed all those shirts for me. (This isn't your mother, god damn it, it's *mine!*) All I remember are the light blue ones. They had so much starch in them the arms stuck out like wings. I had to strike through to get into them. I went out to the bus stop feeling like a kite. The wind actually moved me around, I had to hold on to the bench. That damn button up against my neck to ward off colds . . . It would be easy to wish I *was* a kite, I'd take off, with my mother holding on to the string. Kick those fluffy clouds with my shoes, stay up there and just report on what the weather was, all my life."

I told him I was glad my mother would never have been satisfied with that little baby blue dream of me.

"There's a sweet wolf in everybody's past," he said.

"You're quoting somebody."

"Me. Myself."

I parked below the Illinois Memorial, and started following the markers. We went into the marble halls, saw the busts and read the bronzes, saw the bas-reliefs of the armies squirming flabbergasted, the pretty long-haired bullies they had for officers; the sober yet flamboyant colonels on their bronze horses rampant; the green vegetating bronzes worked on by the rain. I pitied the idiots who cared for such scenes. I was among the idiots who cared for such scenes. I lay my head down on an old brass hoof. I bit it when Fleece turned away. It tasted like my useless trumpet mouthpiece. We saw the names of the dead, we saw the kudzued hollows and walked the fields where the earth was still low in the old trenches.

"The South isn't dead," said Fleece, beginning to run down a hill.

"Hot damn! Gawd no," I said.

"We'll strike in the deep of the night!"

"The deep of the hot damn night!" Fleece was having a good old time. He whipped off the neck-towel and slung it around.

"Follow me!" I ignored him. He ran a ways, then came

216

back. "I said follow me! I'll break you ovuh the code of the Confedrasee, boy."

"I'm sitting down."

"Bull*sheeit*. Follow me!" Fleece really meant it. *"Run* for them, cocksucker. We over the ground of General Pemberton's Rebel boys. They ate *rats,* right heah! Right heah they finely threw up their hands. Mortified by the stomach, but never licked by the gun!"

Fleece knew the history of the battle, which irked me. I didn't know beans. He ran up the hills like a goat. At the top there were cannon sitting in concrete, facing the Mississippi. A mile below was the dull old snake herself, with barges creeping along, sand bars streaking here and there, and the bank of mud and scratchy-looking trees on the Louisiana side, while Fleece was explaining to me about when cotton was king in 1850, and what we had here was the struggling remains of riverside Pharaohism—the restaurants advertising fresh river catfish, the plasticolored motels, the antique shops, the bait and snack stores, featuring a rubberoid worm which kaught fish kwik; the four-story whorehouse on Mulberry Street, whose parlor Jayne Mansfield had visited, thinking it was "cute," who, in fact, bared her breasts there for the house artist, on her way to Biloxi; and Louisiana, in a low strut of trees and mud beach, calling to me like she had missed me, even though I didn't give a damn for her. Fleece held my arm. He told about Grant finally dragging his gunboats out of the Yazoo River and into the Mississippi, told me how the Rebels just laughed and tried to sink the boats with mortars for a while.

I noticed you could see much of the town of Vicksburg. I spotted the white banistered house of my grandmother. She was dead and this house was no longer a part of her. But that was where my mother had grown up. I told him this.

"She was the most-adored piece either side of the river. That porch was where she and the old man fell in love. He was . . ." I just thought through the rest. He was the Louisiana State handsome, but running out of money, wearing a straw hat and widepants, my old man thinking of taking this soft sweetie, Donna, back to that lovely village with its lake and towering pines, so many pines that the streets and walks were quiet with the needles they dropped, and children and lovers could fall down pleasurably, that Dream of Pines, Louisiana; the old man thinking he would

217

take *any* job if he could take her there with him. She had a
high skirt and beads, but she was shy: a caution and ski-
doo. She's thinking about going to college. She's backwater,
a know-nought, and she's pretty as a doe. He wants her to a
degree nature or luck couldn't refuse. She comes to him.

Here I was seeing the house she left behind her. Here
where my grandmother stayed and died. Died remembering
the birthdays of such jerks as me and mailing dollar bills in
cards which cost fifty cents. Died of receiving the hurried
ballpoint pen thank-you's from me. She lay near a church I
could not see.

There was the *Sprague,* an old paddlewheel they had
made into a floating theater, which showed a melodrama
with a trailing cancan each year; harking back to the really
good times, the 1850's, before the war. Come aboard. Don't
be a stick in the mud. Eat it. Lick it. This is Old Man River.

Fleece began singing "Old Man River" emotedly. This
was a rare surprise. I'd never heard him so much as whistle
before. He sought the tones lustfully. No wonder he despised hymns and most all music, if this is what he heard.
But he was joyful as a hunchback jumping up and down in
a loft with the bellrope. "Tote dat barge! Lif dat bale! Gets
a litl drunk and ya lans in jail O!" trying to be the operatic
nigger, but puny, sorry, afflicting me like somebody was
scratching my teeth with a piece of aluminum. I asked him
to stop, but he wouldn't hear me.

Jesus mercy, I was sad. We went and saw the last sight, a
football-field-sized green full of white graveblocks no more
than six inches apart, with a gravel path which separated
the Union from the Confederate dead. By then I was drool-
ing blue. Close to the cemetery, a family was having a picnic. They threw the wrappers and the paper plates meekly
into a barrel. It was almost the centennial year of the fall of
Vicksburg. The strange *silence,* then, is what got me—as if
you walked in a dream of refracted defeat. The horror was,
I could think of nothing to say. I couldn't think of even
anything to think. I could not get "Dixie" or "The Battle
Hymn of the Republic" to play in my mind.

Vicksburg simply weighed on my heart like lumber: all
the old history, all the ravaged gun-toters, all of contempo-
rary Vicksburg; Grandmother's house, how it seemed like a
boat rotting up in a bayou nobody would ever find.

218

We were walking back through a sparse line of trees. Fleece collapsed to the ground. I thought he was having a relapse. He was wrestling with something.

"Help me, Monroe! Let's pull this boy out. Ufff!"

"What is it?"

The clod came up in his hands, shooting dust and grass. Fleece twisted his fingers around it. Something was showing through the turf.

"Mine, mine. You didn't help. It's all mine!"

It was an entire cavalry pistol. That lucky, needlessly lucky scoundrel. On any other given day he would have had his nose in the air, gabbling away. He was *averse* to pistols. Whereas for me, I'd love to put my hand around the dirty handle of it. I thought some feeling, some sense, might come to me if I did.

"Look. *U.S.A.* Sherman's cavalry."

"He was here?" I tried to grab the thing.

"Of course, Ruben. This is where he sharpened up for Georgia. Let me alone, it's mine. It won't shoot. You wouldn't want it. On my soul, a whole gun!"

This pettiness—I hated the son of a bitch. I'd show him some petty. I took off running, for the car. I knew his lungs would kill him; I'd leave him.

"monroe!" "monroe!" came the tiny faroff shouts behind me. The last leg was a vertical slope. I got in the car dying for breath myself. Perhaps his heart would burst. In my own heart I felt the hard little tick of pettiness. Well, this was something, this feeling.

I thought of the organic chemistry lab, how I hated it, hated it even more than histology, or invertebrate anatomy, because Fleece was the instructor for it. Bet Henderson took the lab too. Fleece would drift into the big room, as if on some pompous unicycle, in his lab coat, his mental life so far beyond this room, with its cruddy stone canals and fumes; ignoring Monroe, who had expended so much of *his* imagination on excuses to the professor for Fleece's absences; but deigning to hover around the shoulders of Bet to say the tritest, namby-pambyest words that ever came to my ears. "What are you doing, tee hee. Need some help, tee hee?" whispering, "Are you still my Bet-Bet? tee hee?" With me trying not to hear, but dragged up into it like some involuntary nauseated peeping Tom, since my set-up was right next to hers. Really he deserved to die of a rat bite.

As he appeared on the ridge, practically strangling, I began to ease the car away. Out in the road, I saw him limping after me in the rear-view mirror. How much can he take? I wondered, easing on faster. When *will* his heart burst? I suppose he gave a last effort. It must've been something. I was shocked to see him holding to the door handle, being dragged along. He simply heaved over, face-first onto the seat. I stopped the car. I was outraged.

"Damn you! You know everything about Vicksburg, *have* it! Stay here and own it. Choke on the place. I didn't want you to come over here. *I* had things to see. . . ."

"Marrrk!" he said.

"What?" Some sound, the beginning of some word.

"Maaarrrrrrrk!" He threw up all, *all* over the car—and me—trying as he was to wheel the spew around toward the road on his side. I suppose I sat there a minute in the vile after-puking calm. Then I ripped that towel off his neck. My life seemed so bleakly redundant, an amplifying farce. Here the boy had been *wearing* the towel, the exact thing you would carry if you knew your life was going to be a cycle of puke.

In the dorm halls we passed by those rooms here and there with the queer and the hapless in them: Thomas, Don Thing, Ashlet; a boy whose stomach swelled up periodically, a boy whose face had been jerked askew by polio, a boy with an enlarging wen whose head bucked, a boy with purple acne, a dwarf, a pale giant; then there were the sissies, the religious maniacs, the homosexuals, including the compulsive ear-to-tongue man of the Hilltop Theater, and last —I don't mean there weren't a bunch of good fellows and honest scholars around too (the *president* of the college was an honest scholar who learned my name and always wished me well)—last there were the ones who looked so *ordinary* it was morbid. A number of people seemed to have come to Hedermansever so as to use the college as a sort of proving ground for their afflictions, wanting to know how far they could push into the world before it spat them out. I hope they all had good luck, and I don't feel heroic even recalling them but they were there, and I lay down to sleep a few cells away from them, perfect of body, good wind, good arm and leg, afflicted with a nervous gloom, feckless. I dreamed about old Geronimo, peering out miserably from a cage in the zoo of American history.

When Fleece left the next morning, I walked over to his radio console and picked up the cavalry pistol. I looked out in the dorm yard. I recalled that, back in the fall, my German teacher had announced to us that the Cuban blockade was on. Soviet ships were making toward it, lower Florida was full of soldiers, and only divine intervention could help now. So she led the class in prayer. I looked around; most of the class had their eyes closed. A special prayer service in the chapel had been called. I myself had on the reptilian coat and was fondling the pistol in my pocket. I felt no dismay. Let them come, let the Russians hit the coast, take Gulfport, up Highway 49, overwhelm Hattiesburg, Collins, Magee, Mendenhall, D'Lo, send a corps over to conquer Hedermansever, building by building. A few of us meaner men would get our share from the windows. I saw all the scurrying brown raincoats in the dorm yard, sighted down the cavalry pistol. It would be all quite keen and simple.

12 / Return to Vicksburg

I rubbed off all the green. I slipped a handkerchief through the slides and yanked them loose. Then I rubbed them with Vaseline and treated the valves with Conn oil. I ran water in the bell and that ancient ferny sludge of '58 to '62 washed out. Now I had a horn again. In with the Bach mouthpiece, on with the lips. Not bad. I did a few exercises I'd memorized from the Arban book and then went straight to jazz. It seems I could put more notes to the measure than ever before. I could play higher and brighter. Fleece wanted to know if I intended to practice in the room. I told him I had nowhere else. He checked out.

A drummer I knew down the hall, who was in the marching band and was a corny sort of fool, actually, heard

221

me and brought down his snare drum, sat down, and began hitting for me. I couldn't go long the first night. But by the fourth night I had built up a lip, and Joe the drummer from Texas was giving me time on a complete trap-set he had borrowed. A fellow from Yazoo City was doing the bass part on a cello. The cello was owned by his roommate, a student evangelist who wanted eventually to use the instrument as a part of his appeal, and who was out of town now on a revival circuit. Silas, who had the cello now, had learned his strings on country guitar and wasn't very good plucking the thing, at first. But by the fifth night he was sounding the rhythms well enough and hitting a note every now and then. The sixth night, the hall people got Dave, the dorm counselor, and he pounded on the door. This man was blind in one eye, but enormous and hairy, a cycloptic wrestler sort. I never knew he was a physical coward until he came to the door.

"Nothing but crap and corruption comes out of this room. People are trying to study and sleep! Look at these crayon marks all over this door! I'm getting you for room deposit! What's this, drums in here?" He didn't see well and I think he thought he was screaming at Fleece alone.

Our cello man, Silas, stood up and crowded the door. Silas was also enormous. He was an athlete who had failed at Yale, his father's alma mater. He lived in a constant rage over the general piety of Hedermansever and toadies like Dave, who kept the locks on it. His father had given thousands to Hedermansever, being a millionaire in chemical fertilizers and also a big Baptist. I suppose Dave knew some of this at least.

"We're sitting down playing jazz music. This man"—Silas stood aside and pointed to me—"has a mute in his horn and is playing wonderfully. We are keeping it as down as we can. You . . . shitbound cocksuckers . . ." Silas dragged the cello like a piece of gorgeous trash, as Dave and the hall complainers minced back. "Who haven't ever heard anything like this—"

"Get him for room deposit, I have to," Dave was murmuring.

"You see this crayon picture on the door, Dave. That's abstract art. You know why these boys made this picture? I'll bet they did it because these white walls and halls and rooms were looking a little too much like a hospital for

222

sanctimonious one-eyed fuckers, and for all the rest of you maggoty little finks around that one-eyed fucker." He had lifted the cello.

"There are rules," Dave said, against the other wall.

"I hope you mention some rules to me again, Dave. Me and you're the biggest two men in this dorm. You mention rules again, I want to crack your cocksucking bones and let these little maggots watch me. I want you to make a phone call tonight, after you go downstairs, so somebody else will see me about some rules."

It was amazing. Dave and the others simply rambled back to their rooms, stepping on each other quietly. I liked Silas. I liked his power over the college. I'd seen him up at the Hilltop a number of times and thought he was one of those football players who hadn't made it at Ole Miss or Delta State and had come to Hedermansever for action in the small college league. He wore tee shirts with numbers front and back, and floppy jeans; he was freckled, his nose was broken or beaked, and he sprawled about. I found out he had not failed at Yale because of hate for it. I got the idea that he was so excited, being there, that he couldn't write down anything in the classroom. On Yale, the East, Connecticut, and New York, he was still all babbling awe. He had had such Jewish and Polish and Greek friends. At Hedermansever he spent a good deal of his time lifting barbells, playing soccer with one other guy out on the football field, and searching for, as he said, meaningful group things. Never in my life had anybody taken up for me like he did against Dave and the hall people.

By, say, the eighth night, he was making a curious sort of progress on bass-part cello. He got a ripping, thrumming sound out of every note he made, no matter how fast we played, and I began dipping the tones, traveling with the bends of the cello sometimes; Joe the drummer fell on the tones and the thrums with great hustle—and Joe indeed could play. So I thought we might have something, just us three, no piano. It was odd, with no chording as you played. I suppose I thought of it as brave. It was *intrepid,* is what it was. I thought we were ready for the applause and the money. And I knew the club in Vicksburg. I wanted to have another chance at Vicksburg. The hills were fat and green, the ditches were steep, the houses hung on slants of old gloom, and the river was a rich ooze, like tears and

223

whiskey. It would be fine to be happy in the cellars of this town, cutting away with some buddies on horn.

My school work was not going well lately. But there was a new kind of exhilaration in writing your name on the top of a mimeographed test sheet, handing it in blank, not having to sit there with your head in your hand. Back to the room. Silas was already there trying to do some phrases on the cello. Get the horn, the taste of fruity silver. Joe comes down at six. Ti-tat-di-ching, dinga, chingdingachingdinga-ching, di oomp oomp. To blues and to jazz.

"Like, what we gon *call* ourselves," said Joe. I told you he was a corny fool; also a bit of a liar. He said he'd studied at the Texas Conservatory of Jazz, which sounded like a place where cowboys play Glenn Miller.

"Call—man, you can't *name* this. This band is too close to the *truth* to give a name. We are three *individuals* with a hell of a lot to say," said Silas.

"Right." Looking at the cello, you noticed Silas's huge confident fingers on the neck.

"Well, like, will we phone up to warn them, like? Maybe we should."

"That would take the sting out of us," I said.

"We come as a surprise or not at all," Silas agreed.

Bobby Dove came in at midnight. We musicians were sitting around, tired but merry.

"How's that Amazon nookie?" Silas asked Fleece.

Fleece was sullen. After they left, he lay disgusted on the cot for a while.

"What does that big farthook Silas *do*, by the way? He looks like a jock but he doesn't play sports. I hope to God he doesn't think he's playing that cello, either."

"You wouldn't know. He has some ideas on cello. I think it's good, played like a bass."

"I think you ought to fire Silas, then think about how infinitely bad you still are."

"Silas said I was terrific."

"Well yes, compared to him. Has Silas asked you anything about Bet?"

I lied. Silas had told me he was calling Bet, but I didn't want to get into this with Fleece.

"He's telephoning her, you know. I hope you're not sitting over there being an insect about this, thinking Silas is her secret telephone-lover. Don't you think she told me?

Don't you know how we laugh over what he says? Tell me this. Has he ever said anything about me? C'mon."

"Why should I tell?" I must have been smiling.

"I'd like to hear some of that farthook's wit. Then I'll leave you alone."

"He said that you had better marry her quick so she could have some document to prove that you were making advances toward her."

"You think that cheap little ·vision is very funny, don't you?"

The club seemed to be three hundred Negroes, couples, packed up into an old butane gas tank. Perhaps it was a quonset hut of narrow dimensions. The façade was shingles with a peak arch and a Falstaff beer billboard off its stand, lit up by craning lights, waiting for you at the bottom of a hill steep and parallel with the nearby river. The façade looked landlocked, but once in the club, you didn't know. The thing shook as if on weak stilts, and you could smell fish. The sign at the door mentioned a dollar cover charge. Because the Mean Men were playing. The hotshots and their dates were flocking here from all over Mississippi and even from Louisiana. The Mean Men had made records in Memphis and everybody knew it. All I knew about them was that they had been charmed to have a musician friend of mine back at Hedermansever sit in with them once.

We eased in, Silas and I carrying our cases, Joe hoping to use the traps of the Mean Men. We paid the dollar. The man in the box wasn't certain about this. He just let the dollars pile up there and didn't move his hand for them. Silas went right up to the stand after the number and explained to the band—all of them Negroes—how we thought we might take the stand and spell them. I saw him shake hands with the singer, and he seemed to've procured an introduction all round. The band had just finished a hot pinpointed arrangement of Negro-Latin jazz, eight instruments full, and my faith was sinking. But the singer took the mike and introduced, *named* us and our instruments, and we had to step up quickly so as not to seem like immobilized pink hams. The Mean Men broke by us like a school of dark cheerful fish. Joe the drummer proceeds to drag the traps nearer to center stand; I stand there with my horn out. The bandstand is aflame with pink lights, above and

225

below, and I'm looking at the veins of my arms, thinking how bunny-nose pink I am, and how *few* men we are, above this crowd used to the Mean Men.

The fans were not hostile, but they weren't going to cheer for just any noise. I looked down at them—restless cocoa pods of their faces, all of them drinking beer in two feet of space per couple. The waiters couldn't reach the tables and there was some anger over this fact. We three had on our coats and tennis shoes—the I Vee League demands —but the crowd was much more casual than that. We seemed stiff as dolls. I was frozen up and barely made squeaks on the horn tuning with Silas. Silas's cello clonked like a banjo, and Joe rapped preparatorily with doubt, like the drums were turning to oatmeal on him.

"We are ready. Sting like a wasp," said Silas. He was sure of us. Good man, Silas. My throat grew warm and wet. Joe began sounding like a drummer suddenly. We were standing by for an advent into "Sweet Georgia Brown."

"Toot," said a spade voice. So I went right to it.

We'd never been better. Coming in tight, I hit the flatted seventh of what I meant to hit, way up there, and came back'down in a baroque finesse such as I'd never heard from myself, jabbing, bright, playing the pants off Sweet Georgia, causing them to flutter in the beer and bacon smoke of the place. Silas began the dip-thrums and I unified with him while Joe locked the gates on the measures, back-busting that beautiful storm of hides and cymbals. Harry had found it and he began screaming with glee through the horn, every note the unlocked treasure of his soul—and things he had *never* had, yes, he hit an F above high C! What a bop the three of us were raising in there, what a debut, what a miracle. My horn pulsed fat and skinny. Oh, Harry was stinging them, but stinging them mellow. Didn't I see out the corner of an eye that some spades were moving to us, see some eyes blissfully shut, heads pumping, grooving, digging us, seeing Sweet Georgia shriek after her panties? I gave Silas the solo bars, seeking that F again. Joe lowered the storm, and Silas, was he coming forward, was he backing the cello up the wall, did he have some ideas? Yes. The pianist of the Mean Men slunk by me with the devil's own grin on his face. He wanted in on this, must have it.

As I lay out, I glanced over at the rest of the Mean Men,

226

who were lining the bar, a glass of beer in the right hand of each man. I heard the pianist behind me ease in with Joe and Silas, still looking at the Mean Men. When I saw that even line of Negroes it came to me, a vision of Harley Butte's band. They marched perfectly, those fifteen-year-old kids molded into impeccable musicians. Harley on the side in his white helmet, the years of band-work behind him displayed in the wafer-colored face of the man. The Beta Camina Gladiators dressed in green, as glorious, prosperous, confident, free, and arrogant as they would ever be, under Harley, keeping to that dream of perfect Sousan music for so long, under Harley, the hater of blues for so long; keeping that flame at Beta Camina, rehearsing those black germs without mercy, for the pure joy of having faultless geometry and faultless music at the same time. I did not want to get sappy about this, did not want to *think,* aw God, but I felt shoddy, unrehearsed. The applause was a fraud, the spades were drunk. I knew I had been at the peak of what I wanted, I might still be on the peak, but I couldn't, *couldn't.* It was my time to play again, but my horn was stuffed up, it was crammed with green uniforms, and I was *smiling.* I was not embarrassed.

"You just quit, didn't you? What did you, why did you *lay off* when we were hotter than we ever were? You were *stinging* them. I was *getting* it on my part. I was sounding like the mother of music, then you fart off!"

"The back of that place was like about to shake off! I was playing real drums like for the first time in my life. The niggers were jumping up and down in that tube thing," said Joe.

"I tell you what. I tell you it's a good thing that piano man came up and finished the number or it woulda been total fucked ruin. Those people were *kind* to us to let us step and play. I made some *friends* in there."

"It's like forty miles over here to Vicksburg."

Listen, Harry Monroe, I was thinking. Listen to these good men you brought down with you. Why why why in hell did you have to become a thinking person, what kind of baba are you to be thinking right in the middle of the best jazz you've ever played?

"Knowing of your big weekend appearance, I was inter-

227

ested to learn from this source"—Fleece was mild and clinical, always drawn in by pain—"that you folded rather mysteriously during the first song in Vicksburg. Believe it or not, I wanted you to make it over there because you wanted it so much. And being honest, I heard you through the door one night and thought you were pretty good. I like that mute-thing you played through in the end of the horn. It had a certain sound I was beginning to like. Fuzzy and sorrowful, in a darting way."

"The whole night was fuzzy and sorrowful."

"You say you've put up your horn for good?"

"Probably."

"I wouldn't do that." He was perched on his rack like an owl.

"I think I should get back to thinking. On the books. Since I can't quit thinking. The estate of the world never sleeps." I repeated something I'd heard. "I got some catching up to do. Tomorrow I've got to smoke some graphs for my EDTA and ATP stuff."

"You ought to keep up the horn, or something else. Because you don't seriously think you'll ever see the inside of med school, do you?"

"I'll bet you one hundred dollars that I do."

"I'll give you a hundred dollars. I feel guilty. I know I got you into pre-med. Look. Sometimes I don't think *I'm* going to make it. Have you added up the years? I mean lately."

Well, I did win the bet.

13 / Rambler

I used to hang around the snooker hall in Dream of Pines, especially during those months when I was practicing trumpet so hard and wanted a couple hours' breather. By being at the snooker hall I thought I was allaying some of the doubts that the guys had about me being the fabled queer who had molested Lloyd Reese. I played some fairly tough sharks and learned the game by needing to win, having my sexual reputation at stake. To be a queer in Dream of Pines was to be like an alligator wearing panties. I was an athlete in the snooker hall and defeated many a mill hick and rube, who could not really afford to pay for the games they lost.

So you see I was taking Fleece over to the 20th Century in Jackson three times a week and coaching him, giving him thirty points, just wanting a semblance of competition out of him, beating him, making him pay, until he got hooked on the game and *had* to play me, for money, a beer, for Bet, probably, if I'd pushed it. People of intelligence get hooked on snooker very easily. The pockets are so small they seem impossible. They notice all the red balls and the peculiar configuration of the snooker set; there is an ideal lawn of space—the felt—to their eyes. There is an invitingness in the problem of spheres and motion, there is little dumb luck as in pool. Compared, once you shoot a few games, pool seems a game of fat men hitting bowling balls with ax-handles. Fleece even broke dates with Bet to shoot with me. He bought himself a two-piece cue stick across the street at Hale and Jones. We finished up the evening by eating the red beans and rice plate at Al's Half Shell—65¢—which Fleece generally owed me, plus up to four Millers. Tabasco on the rice, an extra sausage, and you had a fine growling meal inside you. These afternoons I played as if I had enemies watching me. These enemies were there back at the school. I could not name them, could not make out their faces, but there was a gallery of them in my mind, and it was swelling. Finally I saw two faces: Dave, the counselor, and Patsy Boone, whose face was in her stomach, with her breasts above it like a twin-peaked jester's cap, and the scorning beard of light hairs on her chin. Patsy I had dreamed of like this, Dave was so ugly he had to appear, but there were others, swelling.

We were coming back one night when we hit the stoplight by the library and I thought of the books all of a sudden and jumped out of the car, telling Fleece to take it on to the dorm.

"I can't drive," he said.

I shouted for him to just ease down on the gas and keep a foot on the brake, everything was automatic. Bobby Dove

229

flapped and protested, but I saw the car buck around the campus turn all right.

There was a mean gloom in the library; huge plaster rooms, green tiles on the floor. There were a lot of older night-school sorts here. I was about to burst. I wanted the basement restroom primarily. However, it was my idea to swoop across in the basement stacks and pick up the books on Geronimo, take them into the restroom with me, read about the old rogue in the ecstasy of relief, then perhaps climb out the restroom window possessing the books forever.

By the time I went down to the right row, I was humbled by agony. I gimped down the row, holding on the tier, and started parting the books. They were gone. I wanted Lieutenant Britton Davis's *Geronimo* and Betzinez's *I Rode With Geronimo,* and *Geronimo's Own Story.* Somebody *had* them. I broke wind incredulously.

"My word," says a prissy voice from one of the carrels at the end of the row. The sound had not been moderate. I was in sublime comfort. I mean the comfort of a wiener who has been a balloon. I made my way toward the voice.

"And who are *you?*" said the round monk graduate student. You knew none of the graduate students were any account or they wouldn't be at Hedermansever.

"What kind of person are *you?*"

He had my books. The red beans and rice had resurged with a little pain to me. I told him the books he had were mine. Including that one in his hand.

"I happen to be entertaining myself with the exploits of an Indian who may figure into my Master's thesis. As a matter of fact I think I *will* use him."

"Give. C'mon. I'm in a hurry."

"Shall I see Mrs. Finger about graduate student priorities?"

"I'll hit you in the face unless you give me the books." Fair deal, he seemed to agree. He handed them over in a wise flabbergasted way.

"One bully after another," he sighed. With this I knew he was queer. Just about bald, ring on his finger—a wife, kids, all of them bullies. Taking the Master's degree just to get out of the house. Being argumentative in class, being as British and sardonic as he could be, trying like hell to abolish his Mississippi accent. I didn't know all of this then, of

230

course. But I sat down with the same types in my later schooling.

I had my thrill in the restroom, climbed out the window, stole the books. A campus cop would've had a nice shot at me as I was wriggling out of that roll-out window. That was hard. I got down and ran through the Fine Arts parking lot. Livace's old DeSoto was there. I spat at it and crossed the highway. I think this was a high point in my physical health. I felt clean, fit, and mad as an elk.

Up a hill was the century cedar, a dull evergreen hanging shaggy, as seen in the lightpost glow in the middle of it. Underneath was a stone lovers' bench. I burst right in on a couple, who were going to it with all the lust a mouth can get at. They got up and ran off together. The girl, Blakey Newman, so I saw by her name inside, left a book, *The Story of the Old Testament,* on the bench. And on it was a flattened Doublemint wrapper, which I used as a bookmarker later along with the book, and made a B in the required Old Testament course.

I did have quite a pile of books in my hands now. I seemed to be gathering an energy from them as I sat on the bench I'd won by ambush. I turned to the picture I hadn't seen in a while. There he was, captured by the camera. Preserved by the saltwind off the Gulf in Fort Pickens, on the island of Santa Rosa. I put my face on his outraged face and looked cross-eyed at him. Hard as it was, I bent my eyes and laid them on the rifle in his hand. It was close and dark with my face on his picture like this. In this dark there were no friends, no women, no speaking, no songs, no tobacco, no drink, only the cheated anger, the unused bullets, and cutthroats and spleenstabbers in every corner.

What I especially liked about Geronimo then was that he had cheated, lied, stolen, mutinied, usurped, killed, burned, raped, pillaged, razed, trapped, ripped, mashed, bowshot, stomped, herded, exploded, cut, stoned, revenged, prevenged, avenged, and was his own man; that he had earned his name from the Mexicans after a battle in which he slipped up close enough to shoot their senior officer with an arrow; that the name Geronimo translated as "one who belches" or "one who yawns" or both at the same time; that he had six wives all told; that his whole rage centered around the murder of his first wife and three children by the Mexicans; that he rode with the wind back and forth

231

across the Rio Grande and the Arizona border and left behind him the exasperated armies of the moonlight. I thought I would like to go into that line of work. I would like to leave behind me a gnashing horde of bastards. And I did have on my action boots.

I stood up. The campus was meek and depopulated. Then I saw the cars packed along the curb outside the auditorium. Something special was going on. Lights were on inside it. The bigwigs, the trustees, and the constant preacher-saviors of the college, the ashen-cheeked deans, were in meeting, I thought. But the administration office lights were not on. Only the auditorium was lit. I thought I heard a piano inside. I was standing beside a skyblue Cadillac. You pretentious whale, you Cadillac, I thought.

I jumped up on the hood of it. I did a shuffle on the hood. I felt my boots sinking into the metal. "Ah!" I pounced up and down, weighted by the books. It amazed me that I was taking such effect on the body. I leaped on the roof and hurled myself up and pierced it with my heels coming down . . . again, again. I flung outward after the last blow and landed on the sidewalk, congratulating myself like an artist of the trampoline. I spun to the next one, a Lincoln. With my boots only I stove in a fender, *flamp, flamp.* The paint came off in flakes. Once more to see the top of a car. I was dancing for real now. Doing the spurs. The dance floor bent and gave through, raw blades of tin reared up. I pounced off all the way over to the grass. The Lincoln looked diseased . . . caved-in, speckled with leaden marks. Hundreds of dollars' worth, already. I hiked along jubilantly. I simply walked over the Buick. I mounted it at the rear bumper and tramped into the back windshield. The safety glass popped out in a web, no shattering, just a hole and a burst of crystal. I gained the top. I had another floor. My boots did their duty. The steps that cost. Five dollars a heel and toe, at least. And at that rate, I planted my boots down on the top and held my books to me, looking at the stars. There was no paint left when I sprang off the hood. I kicked out the lights with happiness and faced the next car. It was an older Chrysler, white, dirty, with sailfish tails and a sunken trunk, a '59 model. What did *it* deserve? What could I treat it to? I was a little out of wind, but stepped up on the trunk. I squatted down. This trunk was a little sturdier than the others, with the sunken continental kit.

A good thing I looked through the rear windshield. Somebody was on the front seat, asleep, perhaps waking now. I slipped off the trunk. The man was already looking around. He knew someone had been on his car, damn everything I could do slipping off the trunk. He opened the door, and there we were looking at each other across the roof of the Chrysler. I spoke first, in fright.

"I'm the campus police."

"Would you know what time they usually end the rehearsal? I'm waiting for my niece. She's in the musical. I know I'm parked in a faculty place, but at night, I thought . . ."

My frozen eyes and ass, it was Whitfield Peter. He stood there with his head full of tan hair, under the streetlamp. I took off running.

"You aren't the police!" He yelled. He also demanded, "Stop! Stop!" and he was chasing me. I made it to the bellhouse next to Crestman. They had this bell that they rang when Hedermansever won a football game, and this is what I was behind. I kept to the shadows and reached the basement of Crestman. I ran through the game room, the TV lounge, past the milk machines. The athletes had ripped all the phones off the walls and had turned over all the candy and drink machines upstairs and if they saw a sluggish man, they would attack him, so I ran. At the steps on the other side of Crestman, I had twenty feet of grass between me and my dorm. I kicked it. Safe! Home free, with all the freewheeling strange sorts of my dorm. I loved all of them. Safe, walking by their rooms, I saluted them, at their desks, playing cards, hunched on their beds, looking regretfully into their mirrors. They seemed strong in their afflictions. And the ones with the completely ordinary faces—all these were my friends. They all formed a thick sanctuary of bodies around me.

I got up to the first floor and there halfway down the hall, talking to Dave the dorm-counselor, his hat off, seeming perfectly respectable, was Whitfield Peter. He was raising a hand to indicate my height. I took to the stairs.

Fleece was at his desk. The room was cleaned-up but crowded as usual. He had a glint in his eyes.

"What a machine that T-bird of yours is! I've learned how to *drive* tonight, my friend. You didn't care if I took her down Raymond Road a ways, did you? Monroe, I took

233

that whore up to seventy-five miles an hour! She responds to the old foot, doesn't she?"

I got back my breath. Opened the top drawer and gazed at them, cold and oiled and wrapped in towels. I plunked them down on top of the chest to see if they were still loaded from the day of the Cuban missile crisis.

"Whitfield Peter's in the dorm. He saw me sitting on his car. He and Dave are coming up here. I know it."

"Sitting on his car?"

"What's going on in the auditorium? His niece is in it."

Fleece locked the door and turned out the light.

"Put the guns up. What'd you *do* to him?"

"I jumped on the trunk of his car. He was in it. He scares the hell out of me."

There was some time to talk before someone came to the door. Fleece told me they were rehearsing for "Oklahoma!" in the auditorium. He knew this because Bet had tried out for it and hadn't made it and had been melancholy for a week. The spring musical was a big thing at Hedermansever.

"Well, his niece is in it. She made it."

"I don't understand. Now you . . ."

The door rattled. The lock was old and the door-facing around it was splintery and rutted, and I was thinking about this because the door was being kicked, once, twice, and who could've expected *this*? Fleece crawled into the closet in a low swift silhouette. I didn't have the guts to release the safety on my automatic and just quavered, standing up, pulling on the dead trigger, the gun aimed at the floor. The door broke and swung in.

"Hi, weaselfuckers. I knew I heard you in here. I have something very, very damn happy for us!" It was Silas. "Is that a *gun*?"

Some explanation had to be made. Fleece came out of the closet. Silas turned on the light and closed the broken door. I told Silas the complete history of it. He really caught on fire with the story. He demanded to see the letters. Fleece cursed. But I felt very safe with big Silas in the room. Fleece, of course, detested Silas and squirmed and smoldered, and sat in a rage the whole while. I went to the cigar box to get the letters. He told me to keep my filthy hands off his possessions, but I took them out, reminding him that I had stolen my share of the letters and it wasn't

234

my fault that we didn't have the hundreds of them that
went up in the fire behind his house. Silas sat there three-
quarters of an hour, reading. Every once in a while, he'd
look up and stare like a bursting demon at Fleece, who
looked away.

"Have you men ever seen ten actual inches?" he wanted
to know, standing up with the last three or four envelopes
in his hand. He unsnapped his pants. I looked out the window. Then I glanced at Fleece. He was looking right at me,
wagging his head in sick dismay. I agree it was a very perverse surprise.

"You people ashamed of the human body? Thinking I'm
a faggot? You poor prig-trained people. I wanted you to see
a real phenomenon, in and for itself—what letters! *what*
letters!—and now it's gone. Never have it like that again.
Oh my, you two people. You read these letters in your dark
little dirty minds. Giggling, I bet. Won't look at the flesh of
a man who *loves both of you!* Never wanted to see the actual red flesh, did you? Couldn't bear it! All your little rules
say I'm queer. You'd love for me to *be* queer, wouldn't
you? I'm all dressed now. You can look at me."

"I get ill enough looking at you with your pants on," said
Fleece. "Who *are* you, anyway? You look like somebody
who's taken exercises all his life so he could finally bend
down enough to suck himself off." Fleece was such a frail
animal to be saying this to Silas.

"You expect me to haul off and hit him for saying that,
don't you?" Silas asked me. "That was honest, that was
brave, what he said. I like him for it. I mean more. I know
he's a genius, I already respect him and like him for that.
You people just can't stand being *liked,* can you?" Well,
there were some more friendly accusations from Silas.

He told us what he came down for. He had found us a
cheap but extraordinary boarding house off North State in
Jackson. Its landlady was Mother Rooney, an old Catholic
widow who didn't cook badly and stayed out of your way.
He wanted us to move immediately; he meant tonight. Over
at Mother Rooney's, we'd have a separate room apiece, the
rent was near nothing.

"We'll be citizens of the world and not pigeons in this
goddam roost," he said. "I've got most of my stuff in my
car already. This has to be fast, because these medical stu-

235

dents want the rooms; Mother Rooney said she'd give us till
midnight. I can get a trailer for all your stuff."

I began getting my stuff together. Silas left. Fleece
watched me packing and sorting. He was still snaky and
sour. I told him we did need a new address, away from the
college and Dave, and I was for it; told him that the place
seemed fairly close to the medical school. I told him that,
after all, Silas was not so bad. He'd made it so easy for us,
he'd found the place.

"You son of a bitch. You know I won't stay here by myself," said Fleece. He packed his clothes. Silas came back to
help us with all of the cargo of artifacts and books which
Fleece owned. It was five in the morning when we got it all
in the trailer, which was hitched behind Silas's Pontiac. Fog
was all over the road to Jackson. Fleece hadn't said a word
for six hours. This was almost a shock to the ears. One
thing to Silas's credit: his presence caused long spells of silence in Fleece.

The house was on a little dead-end alley full of weed
clumps. The alley was named Titpea; we passed the apartment house where Patsy Boone used to live. Our house was
situated over the state fairgrounds. It leaned a little off its
foundation, this house, toward the back yard, which didn't
amount to much and ran to a high cliff all grown over with
kudzu vines that saved the back yard from further erosion.
Nobody ever promised me or any of the other boarders that
the house wouldn't fall and crack apart as it tumped farther
over the lip of the cliff. It was a preciously weird house, anyway. It amounted to two high silo-like towers attached to
both ends of a two-story bungalow. The towers had yellow
wood shingles; the middle bungalow had the same sort of
shingles, but they were chocolate-colored; it had a porch
with a banister, steep steps, glass doors, and white Victorian
edging—grills and windows—like a fudge whorehouse. We
would room in the southern tower. The old lady was already up when we got there.

"Now let's get this straight. You do allow private nookie
in the rooms. And we could practice music without fear of
complaint," said Silas to Mother Rooney.

"Music? Of course! I love music. I had hoped someone
would room here who could play—"

"Never mind going on and on about it. Listen, I don't
want you even close to the south tower, don't be dragging

236

around when we're over there. Leave this door open. We're moving in."

"Silas, God knows!" I implored.

"Now this is Sunday morning," he continued. "We're going to be sleeping all day, probably. Don't wake us up making the sign of the cross or knocking your beads around and don't slam the door leaving for Mass. You be a good girl and tonight Monroe here might take you down to the Royal for a movie and kiss your neck."

"Lookahere," I said. Mother Rooney was seventy.

"The *movies?* I love the movies," she said, gazing at me fondly, which made me think she only heard certain hard nouns you said to her, especially the ones she wanted to hear and cherished.

"Let's move in, men. Mother Rooney, you grab Fleece's trunk. Watch the old arthritis. It weighs a ton." I grabbed the trunk up quickly myself. The thin old lady was actually moving toward it.

On the way over to the tower, Silas, with his arms full of clothes, turned back to us.

"She loves me."

"What *is* this place?" said Fleece.

"You just keep a smile on your face and peer into her eyes with concern. She puts her hand on your shoulder. Let her do that. She loves that most of all."

Silas went straight to bed. Fleece began yammering.

"What are we doing here? What is this place? We're in the inside of a three-story tube. He forced us over here. We came over yanked along like damn puppets. He's smooth. He's mean. You heard him talking to that old woman. We have to pay extra money. How's your old man gonna like that? You have to write a letter home just like me. But not that rich bastard up there!" Silas was in the top room, me in the middle, Fleece below. The rooms were perfectly round, and there was a light and double bed in each of them. I asked Fleece why didn't he go down and enjoy his big bed like I was fixing to do. He went down the unpainted wood planks which were his stairway. The stairway to Silas's room was planted in the north corner of my room. It was a narrow thing, had a wrought-iron banister, and hugged the wall.

But, say, if Fleece wanted to visit Silas—an unlikely wish —he would come up his stairs, walk to the right three feet,

237

in full view of me if I happened to be in, to get the stairs to Silas's room. I could see Silas descend, similarly, and go to his right to catch the stairs to Fleece's room, which had a back door giving onto more black iron stairs that put you in the back yard. This is the route, these iron steps, we all used coming to and going away from our quarters.

The stairs coming through my room, I was fixed worse than anybody. I awoke on my bed and had to observe Silas escort his drunk hags up to his room. They were always little women, and I saw in the moonlight that they weren't even as good as the roaches I'd been with. I think they must've been nurses and beauticians. We were near the nursing school and the beauty college. It was well known that the girls from these institutions would tear off their pants for anybody who gave off a hint of making ten thousand dollars a year. Silas's bed walked all over his room. I thought of the tiny little mermaid he'd taken up there. Almost always, you would hear the girl weeping; hear her bare feet sliding. The ceiling was thin and the stairway was completely open. Silas would speak out, broad and jolly. What he liked best, I gathered, was for little girls to break into tears when he undressed. He would call them to sit on his lap, they would do this—I guess—and he would lecture them about how he would never force himself on them—I heard one of these talks—because he didn't want to soil their plans to marry a smaller fellow with high principles. She must understand that she was only a naked pygmy on his lap, and that the kisses he was giving her were only for good luck.

Then they would come down fully dressed, Silas handling her with one wrist.

Silas read certain magazines and sent away for certain uncensored underwear and a bottle of red oil. He called me up to his room and explained this. The room was so bright you felt heat. He had two sunlamps on; the curtains were tied back so anybody on Titpea could see him. He wore this bikini which amounted to two strips of leather attached to a bandage covering his genitals; the idea was a sling made into a jockstrap. He talked, at ease, sitting on his bed, as if he had on nothing unusual.

"This is me. I can't change it. It hurts me to put on a shirt. It hurts my arms. It hurts me to wear pants, it binds me. And oh God, shoes. Nothing fits me. When I put on

238

socks, it's like, my feet, somebody's twisting a tourniquet on them."

"Fleece got in trouble wearing his underwear in his garage," I said. I asked him if I ought to call Fleece up to talk it over with him. Yes, yes, Silas wanted to hear what Fleece had to say. I yelled down. Fleece wasn't there. I'd told him he could use my car, and he was out with it now.

"I have to wear tennis shoes," Silas was explaining, "and they're bad enough, but if I wore leather shoes, they would strangle me. They'd kill me."

14 / Catherine

It was nice to be in the double bed all to myself, nobody else in the room. I read several books in this bed that I would never have read in the dorm: *Billy Budd, Pride and Prejudice, Wuthering Heights, The Sun Also Rises,* and *The Great Gatsby,* all of them pleasures which inflated me and upon which, on the exams, I could write for hours. I was taking a minor in English and was making A, no sweat, in the courses where these books were assigned.

One morning Fleece was coming up and Silas was going down. I was too sleepy to get what they said to each other. But I know the word-knives flew and the low blows of the tongue were traded.

When I was fully awake, Fleece was pulling out the drawers of my chest. He was looking for the gun he'd given to me. He said, One night when Silas was asleep, he would go up and shoot him through the head. I told him that would be cowardly. He said, No, it would be beautiful. He would come down and turn the gun over to me. I would make a citizen's arrest on him. I didn't know then that Bet had agreed to go out with Silas that night, on the terms that he would quit calling her.

Next day it was bright gray in the room. The windows were small octagonal portholes, and you had to turn on the bare overhead light to see anything. I hadn't smoked for three days. When I woke up, I was ready to meet the classes I'd missed and attack them with the facts I'd memorized. One look at my twelve pages of histology and I knew it cold. I felt so healthy I could learn anything. I could swallow the world.

But then they showed me love, the love from afar that hurts the worst. Silas and I went to "Oklahoma!" and sat beside Fleece and Bet, who were holding hands. We all knew that Whitfield Peter's niece was in the musical. I bought a coat for the occasion, a wild red madras plaid. I looked around for Peter in the audience. He didn't seem to be there. I carried the little automatic in my coat pocket.

The student orchestra took the overture surprisingly well. I could've done better on the first trumpet part, but you can't go through life adding up regrets like that. My old friend Livace was conducting, and Zak, the drama teacher, had coached the cast. Livace was waving the baton with big romance, his black tuxedoed back to us, and you saw he was conducting nobody but himself, saw he had forgotten the orchestra and was dwelling on his own histrionics. I thought of shooting him in the back to get him in line. Because he was what was wrong with the musical. He was not one to follow the singers on stage. They followed *him,* they sang to *him.* The singers kept their eyes glued to his baton.

Whitfield Peter's niece was a minor dancer and chorus member. She was mama's little darling. That's how she looked. She was lithe and restlessly shy. Her hair was brown, pinched back, but strands fell over her ears in the heat of the dance. Just pretty enough to disturb you after a third look, and by then you wanted to take her to your chest and have her breathe on it. She was the one you came home to. She was your helpmate. I fell for her before I was certain who she was. You could tell she loved being in the musical. I felt sorry for her. The musical was such a wreck. It lunged on, a robot dream above the heads of the orchestra; people appeared and fled like costumed metronomes. Good old Livace.

Fleece passed a program down. He had underlined her name in the cast. *Catherine Marie Wrag.* She would be anxious to have her last name changed. Fleece had encircled *Catherine.* Yes. I'd read it often enough in the letters. His estranged wife. My stomach went cold. But her last name

240

was not Lepoyster. I still loved her purely. My imagination was going crazy, but I hung on to my love for her. She held herself like she was accomplished in innocent talents that the musical was not making plain.

"Wouldn't you love to tie that nice brown-headed piece across a barrel and work the old will?" Silas whispered in my ear during a scene that had her out front.

"No. Leave her alone," I said.

When "Oklahoma!" was over we kept seated and let the crowd get out. A photographer was popping away at the cast. He told Catherine to move a little closer. I was even jealous of him. Watch your hands yanking her, you, you jaded bag.

Catherine ran off into the wings, and then down the aisle came her uncle. Peter had been waiting for her. He was a young pink fifty now. His hair seemed to have been waved and veneered by professional aid. And his profile—a matured fruity cupiedoll. I almost lost my supper when I saw him.

Catherine came back out with a little suitcase. Peter was at the footlights and she stepped down to him with his help. I was in the orchestra pit by then, losing myself among the musicians packing away their instruments, so I could observe her up close. I took time out to grab Livace by the elbow and tell him what I thought of his directing; Livace, still lost in his maestro-fever, was accepting it as praise, not recognizing me. I saw the first trumpet, Derrick, who used to fear me for my talent, and I clapped him on the back and asked him what he was playing nowadays. I tore his Conn Constellation out of his hands and ran my fingers over the keys, and poised there, because Catherine was just then coming by the pit ahead of Peter. She did look at me and in my eyes she must have seen the gravy of pure hopeful love because she kept looking at me until she went by. I kinked my head around then, not wanting to see Peter. When Peter passed, I set the horn down and followed.

"It was every bit simply lovely," I heard Peter say to her. I was at his back and listened for her voice. Silas, Bet, and Fleece mobbed out into the aisle around me. Bet spoke in my ear, leaning down a bit. She had on long ear-drops and smelled like vanilla—ah, woman—which deterred me a moment.

241

"Bobby says to tell you 'Please!' He says you have a pistol, don't you?"

"I forgot the pistol. It's the girl."

She asked me why we were walking so fast. Go to Silas's Pontiac, quick, everybody, I said. Peter led Catherine down the sidewalk going east, and I noticed the fins of his goosey Chrysler in a slot in the alley between buildings. I could catch him then. We were down the row just a bit. I asked Silas for the keys.

Peter eased out, and we gave chase.

On West Capitol, just beyond the Overhead Bridge, he seemed to notice us. He cut over to Woodrow Wilson, going by Livingston Park, and on the fly. But no, we sat behind his bumper, stopped at a light, and he nodded his head up and down talking delightedly to his niece. He didn't know we were there. He was just in a terrible hurry to get home. With her.

He went over the speed limit getting up to Madison County. We hit the rougher blacktop. Then his lights swung left in a flurry of gravel. I stopped at the inception of the gravel road, pulled off, and cut the motor. The house was a half-mile down there, over a hill.

"She lives with her uncle," said Bobby Dove.

I asked Silas wasn't there anything to drink in that car pocket over there. There wasn't. Well, I said, I'm going to walk on down there and see what I can see. I felt sickish and bespooked.

"I think she might need me."

"I think it's just great that Harry's in love with that girl so much he'll walk down there to see if she's all right," said Bet. Being an enchanted-tower sort of challenge herself, I guess she was bound to love high plights and things like that. Trysts.

"I think he's more in heat," said Fleece.

"Oh, uglymouth! Jerry, you go with him and don't let anything happen to him."

"No," I said. "Alone is what I want."

"Oh, marvelous," cried Bet.

"We don't want him to stay here," said Fleece, meaning Silas.

This made Silas surly. He came with me. He asked me if I wanted to know a secret, by God. It was that Bet had promised to go out with him some night if he'd quit calling

242

her. He told me it was hard to like that brittle little monkey, Fleece. I agreed. He could see that Fleece thought he had Bet trained. He wasn't happy about their slobbering on the seatcovers of his car, whatever they did for lust together. I told him to please go back, then; he couldn't imagine how much I didn't want to hear about other peoples' love careers.

"That's all right. I'm shutting up. That's the shrine of love, just around the turn there, isn't it? The honeymooners. What . . . a bat? We're really in the sticks, aren't we?"

Yes, we were. The blackberry thickets hung on the road ledge. The moon showed foot-high corn sprouts in the field beside us. The land spoke of meager, desperation farming; of people who could not afford the machinery they did it with. We saw a weathered board house, leaning, empty. It held the souls of some sharecropper family who were burnt out to zombies before they left. We made the gate of Peter's house and turned in to the yard, with its circular drive, high shaggy grass in the center, and otherwise the rabbit tobacco bushes, the neck-high milkweeds, and clover. We flushed out a covey of quail. Other creatures snuck away.

"What is it you want to *see?* There's his car. All right, they're here," says Silas. Both stories of the house were alight. There was no light on the veranda, but the living room lights made it visible. "We're not going up and knock on the door, are we?"

I told him I really did wish he would leave, now.

"You think they'd be going to it with all these lights on? What, you want to *see* them. That Catherine—"

"She was a sweet, teenage child. You saw her," I said.

"She was older than that. I thought she had a good bit of knowledge how to move her body."

I sunk down and sat in the weeds when he said that. We were in the shadow of the hedge of the veranda and, as things turned out, too close to it.

The doors opened and out came Peter and Catherine into the warm night. They were holding glasses. I heard the ice tinkling. We had got caught under a sort of single bush of the hedge. What I had already noticed on the veranda was that potted fern, of the letter. It was a thriving giant, with arms falling all over the veranda and the banisters. They came out by this fern and weren't ten feet above us.

"Now this is what I used to really enjoy, this porch," said

243

Peter. "Your aunt and I spent hours out here from May through September. Now *that* was leisure. Your generation is so busy, you will never understand that leisure. A musical tonight, another interest tomorrow. You bounce from one event to the next. You will piece yourself out, I fear, Cathy. You will not be able to set yourself still and focus. I'm not capturing your interest any longer, am I? You aren't having a good time in this house."

"Naw look, some days I get homesick for home and Mobile, but you ain't . . . it isn't you Peter that has anythin' to do with it. I couldn't ever forget how much you've did for me. This house is just fine, there isn't nothing wrong with it. I mean there isn't *anything* wrong with it."

"I need to cut the grass. I was always one who hated to harm the greenery. Tomorrow I'll get a nigger from Canton." The ice tinkled above, again.

"This is a strong drink of gin," Catherine said. There was a long pause. "I wonder don't it make you sad to think about Aunt Catherine?"

"Now what did you say?" Peter corrected her. "It should be 'I wonder, *doesn't* it make you sad.' No, it doesn't make me sad, as long as I have such company as yourself to talk to . . ."

Silas and I were hunched practically face to face under the bush. "She uses bad *grammar*, doesn't she?" Silas whispered, loudly. It sounded like a scream to me. He'd given us away. I brought out the pistol in hopes it would give me some strength of position when Peter discovered us. Silas could not speak quietly; he tried, but that wasn't his talent. "Not a *gun!* Sssssst! You aren't going to shoot him, are you SSSSSSSSSSST!"

"Somebody's right down there!" Catherine shouted.

I stood up, holding my pistol. I was on the border of the hedge shadow. Silas was crawling across the gravel like a crab, making for the deep weeds. I was stiff as a cork. My mouth and tongue clung together. To Peter and Catherine, I know, I must've seemed a wild pop-up dummy—thinking back on the scarlet plaid madras coat I had on. My hand went up in the air. I shot the gun twice straight up, and heard the two weak *tark* sounds it made. Then—why?—I yelled, "Stop! Stop!"

"He has a gun!" Catherine screamed.

"In the house, the house!" shouted Peter. Peter backed

through the porch doorway, as I did the same across the gravel drive. I heard him tell her to bring him something. Then he came right out to the banister again. This was damn brave. He threw out his arms, and began making a sort of speech. I was in the dark, but I had fallen in a coil of those same bushes in the middle of the driveway that the back end of my T-bird had been in.

"How many of you are there? Do you know there is a young woman here? What can you want? Show yourself! Are you such cowards?" and so on. I ran across the other side of the driveway then and got into the trees near the fence. He was still declaiming, framed perfectly in the light. He was in shirt and tie and his legs were far apart and his pants were baggy. God help him if there'd been somebody in the yard really wanting to shoot him. Then he met Catherine at the door. Her little arms were full of guns. I'd always known he had them. He came forth with a shotgun in one hand and a pistol in the other.

He began shooting at the hedge right down from him, and then toward the gate. I hoped Silas had made it out of the yard. I heard the bullets skinning the road outside the gate, nowhere near me. He snapped the pistol. He was empty. I think it was a .22. Then he walked off the veranda and pounced into the yard, in front of his car. I ran out the gate then. I'd waited too long, wanting to see her again. But I was always fast on my legs.

First thing I heard was a triumphant shout and a blast from the big gun, then another and another. Two more. *Rooooooom, Rooooooom.* Then there was a bigger *ruff* sound, and I looked around to witness a rose-shaped explosion of flame in the yard. The Chrysler seemed to lift, on fire. The flame was twenty feet high and awfully close to the veranda. I was making a dash, but even running I could guess what had happened. The bastard had shot the gas tank on his own car. There were more shotgun blasts. He'd reloaded. He was taking care of those of us who had not fled the light of the flames. He was flushing out the last coward.

The Pontiac wasn't there when I got to the blacktop. Then it came toward me, from the direction of Canton, slowly. Silas was driving. I was hacked. They seemed on the verge of not even letting me in.

"Harry, Harry! What did you do?" asked Bet.

"Nobody was expecting this, with damn guns and fire. What'd you do, throw a match down the gas tank of his car, didn't you. You killed him, you shot . . ." Silas said.

As we drove off I looked out, and what a scene over the little hill—there was a pulsing orange glow fifty feet over Peter's house. They had been looking at this for several minutes. The house was burning.

I swore I had not done it. Really, honestly, believe me, trust me, I begged them. I told them they had to be on my side in this thing.

"Fleece wanted to leave you. He was the one. He said we should forget your damn name," said Silas.

"He set it on fire himself," I said. I stared at Fleece, and Fleece stared murderously at the back of Silas's head.

While we were deciding what to do, the fire truck from Canton came screaming up the road behind us and Silas took us away.

"What you've got to do is simply forgive me for a simple act of cowardice."

"I don't have to do that. No I don't."

"I never said forget your name. Silas embellished that one on. Don't just sit there on the bed cleaning your gun."

"What would you do?"

"Throw it in a lake."

"Nope."

"Do real *hombres* say that? 'Nope'?"

I kept rubbing the gun. If I rubbed long enough, Geronimo appeared in my head, like a genie. He sat down and lay back as if in some chair of my soul and said, What can you show me? What have you done with your hair, your leg, your arm, your firepower, your firewater? There was a fine, private, steady security having him there. How have you exasperated the man or men you despise? How are you going about getting your woman? He watched me, leaning back in his chair with the pleasure of an old ghost who had nothing to lose. And mainly he said: *brood*—that's it, your natural state, not *think*, you know what a fraud that is for you; brood, and take my shape. Brood on the despair of *not* being me, that too; and brood on the fact that even though you ain't me, cheap fame is *some* fame.

"Well, you do have this," said Fleece, picking up the

246

pink edition of *The Jackson Daily,* where on the second page it read

gunman or gunmen he routed after a molotov cocktail type gasoline explosive was thrown on his porch, said Lepoyster. Lepoyster said he replied at first with his own pistol and then took his shotgun to the front yard, which was afire. "I revolved amid fire seeing that the house was an inferno and rushed back to assure the safety of my niece. My last act was to telephone the Canton fire house. Thank God the wires ran in back of the house and I was able to make fruitful connection. My niece and I withdrew to the old well with naught but clothes on our backs, myself armed, I assure you. They had taken to their heels, whoever they were."

Lepoyster said his niece was upset and unavailable for comment. He said she saw a man "of indefinite race" in a bright multi-colored garment near the porch and sounded the alarm.

"Our home is half gone in flame and it was the home of fond memories for us both. We could not buy it back. I shall not mention our future quarters."

Asked if he had any idea as to the identity of the attackers or their motives, Lepoyster replied, "I shall remain alert and armed."

"That's right," I said. "No one can take that away from me." I was beginning to feel easy in the cheap fame and the fear of it. I mean the fear of the police, and the fame of having ignited this baroque stream of fraudulent melodrama in Colonel Lepoyster. Getting his sentences all together, Peter had probably not had time to touch his niece for several days.

"It's even nice and pink, for your scrapbook."

"What more could a gunman or gunmen want?"

"You say you fired first, but up in the air. You just popped up and shot, twice. You didn't say anything."

"I never said that." In truth, I'd just recalled that I had said something. "I yelled, 'Stop!' twice."

"You don't mean *Peter* yelled 'Stop! Stop!'? Now *he,* that's exactly *his* variety of . . ." Fleece held up a finger.

"I know. But it was me."

"Stop *what?* Was he pawing her?"

"No. Or not yet. But he had her under his wing, and that fern, that damn fern, was so large, spread out, it looked like they were in a jungle alone from where I was looking at them. They were drinking liquor; she could hardly drink it it was so strong, the girl. Remember he'd just seen her in the musical like I had. Remember the speed he drove over there . . ."

"Would you forgive me if I said I could understand all that? You love the girl, don't you?"

I avoided that one for a moment. "No, I can't forgive you for wanting to leave me. If I forgave you for that, where would it end, forgiving you? Vomiting on me, damn you, and—"

"Ah shut up! I don't have to beg. I don't have to apologize to *any*body! Silas heard that stupid slut you're so hot for. He said she was a real spelling-bee queen."

He stomped down the staircase to his room. I heard him rattling around, shaking the pieces of his portable Fleeceiana museum—the metal stork, the big useless radio console, the cavalry pistol, the framed, newer thing—a decree of high taste and decorum, a *degree*, in fact, which he had typed and awarded to himself, affixed with the seal of a prophylactic foil, Bet Henderson's signature on the dotted line beneath, as she was the only attestor possible. Seeing the foil, I'd stopped there, not reading the document. I think it was intended for Silas, anyway. Well this man of such staggering couth was down in his room, knocking around, having slandered the girl *I* loved.

But yes, that *love*. How was that doing? My Catherine! I couldn't quite get those words in my mouth. There was a flinty little crab running over them: *her* words, her voice. I had been crouching there under that hedge bush, ready to hear anything she might have said and hide it away in the pleasure of my heart. She'd just come off the stage from singing and dancing, and I was waiting for the lazier sweet notes in her voice, and then came this bad whining illiteracy, not even good Alabama English; a sound, that if I had seen her speaking, I knew she'd be raising the side of one lip to get it out. And, damn me, I'd read so much good English poetry and prose and had developed such a sense of the exquisite—I thought—in grammar. James Joyce and Scott Fitzgerald were my masters then. I'd read *Ulysses* blind and knew about a fifth of what was going on, but the

248

sentences stuck in my throat, spread like a cold to my ears, and I was diseased by elegant English sentences. Some days I had such a sense of the exquisite I wouldn't speak at all. So, I asked myself, does her speech finish her off, murder her? This is how thudding stupid being literary can make you. Of course, she was alive. Don't even think *of course,* ass. She has her arms, legs, breasts, and hair. She's not waiting for anybody to say *of course* for her, like some combination obstetrician-grammarian giving her a spank on the bottom. I went up to Silas's room, Silas being out: away with the curtain and you could see the lights of Jackson. I could see no rooms higher than this one in town. I was thinking about Catherine's red bottom, what man spanking it? What parents waiting for her? Was she living within these lights? At the same time seeing her little arms and hands push outside the porch door with those guns, Peter grabbing them from her, I had her right in front of my eyes, in handwriting—

> taken poor me unner you wing like this I caint hardily thank you eneough, Uncle Peter, I just do hope Im sharp eneough for college.
> Love,
> Vinceen

had Vinceen, her own leaky ballpoint pen self in my hands, holding her letter; the rest of the letter was even worse, but what do we care, Vinceen? I know who you are and want to know at which point you became Catherine Marie Wrag, and what exactly you gave away when you gave away *Vinceen,* unless you have four legal given names knocking against one another, say, Catherine Vinceen Marie Wrag, four heavy boxcars like that. And so what? You live, my Catherine, and you were so much when I first saw you, language couldn't do you right, and you're worth four different names, at least, if language tried.

I looked out at Jackson a last time and went back down the stairs, God help me, still trying to make those names into some audibly sweet order.

15 / My Catherine

But she could not be found on campus. The semester was ending and I decided she had quit, or had been pulled out. I had an unendurable need to see her. I couldn't read, sleep, or pay attention. I had an edge on constantly; I knew if I saw her I would touch her and she would look into my face.

Fleece was cleaning his room one day, and he yelled up to me, If I really wanted to break the law, why didn't I smoke some of this marijuana he was throwing out? So I did, I smoked it in rolls made out of notebook paper, did it through the phase where your lungs hurt with a sagebrush fire that does nothing for you, to the phase when it takes hold, and you are an irresistible hero saying "Hot Dog!" and things like that. I would try to meet Catherine and eventually there she was, allowing herself to be caught in a green pasture. I am your rag, my name is Wrag, she said. Then the stone-deadend of sleep.

Fleece was in the Roman Rituals and Religion class with Ralph, who worked at a phone in the Jackson police station. He called the night Medgar Evers was shot in the back. Medgar was a field secretary for the NAACP. Some champion had killed him, in the dark, as he was walking from his car to his house. I suppose we were among the first in the world to hear about the murder, if that gains us anything. After Fleece put down the phone, he told me about it. He told me, if my gun was loaded, keep it that way. Silas came down to his room asking what was going on. Silas, when he heard, said he just wanted to be in the same room for thirty minutes with that champion, that champion shitlicker who could aim a gun in the dark at a man's back. And the champions who were the bombers of the Sunday School in Birmingham could be this new champion's managers; they could advise him what to do when

250

his eyes were ripped out, when he was strangled with his own guts, and while they were thinking of what to advise him, the champion, Silas would already be falling on them, tearing each man's stomach out and holding it up for his observation for a moment before he slashed their eyes out and they could not see their own selves dying. I liked that idea, and still do. Since then, the FBI has arrested the lead suspect, the champion-suspect has been freed in two hung jury trials, and the champion-suspect has run for Lieutenant Governor of the state, getting an insignificant vote of thousands.

But what Fleece meant about keeping my gun loaded is that Whitfield Peter was the first one the local police called up. Ralph had seen him at the station. The police wondered if he knew anything about it. Ralph didn't know all that was said. Peter did a lot of laughing and came by Ralph's desk clicking his mouth and looking sublimely amused. Ralph got up to stretch his legs. He'd already seen Catherine sitting in the car in the dock. It was a black Buick now. He saw Peter get in and saw his niece draw over to sit nearer him. He had Peter's new address. It was a house in Jackson. They were in the same city with us.

"They let him go," I said.

"Yeah. They don't think he did it. They just knew how much he wanted to've done it. And who knows; he might *have.*"

I saw her. She came in by herself and sat down on the other side of the brick divider with the rubber foliage across the top of it. I was in the grill. She drank her coffee and went out the glass door by herself. She had a huge stack of books in her arms. She looked meek. The load was killing her. I followed her, saw her calves; just under the skin behind her kneecaps, she had a shadow of baby-blue veins. I caught up to her.

"You don't know me, do you?"

"Nart!" She made a surprised sound.

"You were good in the musical."

"Wasn't anynothing especial. You uz with the horn, wuzn't it? I uz just hardly *in* it."

"Let me carry some of those books. Listen. We could have a *date* this Friday night," I beseeched her. She jerked

251

back the books I'd taken from her. Nothing mean in the action, just panic. Like a fox you tried to pet.

"Nart!" She shied off with her burden. I opened the door of the Student Union for her. She didn't appreciate it too much. She made anxious squirming sounds.

What a piteous animal Catherine was, and so lonely. To class, and then home to Uncle Peter. Ralph of the police station had told us where they were. I'd driven by the house already—an old Spanish plaster thing near Meadowbrook Mart which we could see any night on the way to the Dutch Bar. And what did Peter say to her in that house? What did they do when the books were put away and Uncle Peter was home from the office?

As I watched her going across campus I wanted her still, with a trollish spasm. I loved her fear and wanted to bring it to me. And I suppose—I'm not sure—I thought if I could love her I would be a nice boy like my mother always wanted me to be. Perhaps, say, if I could kill someone who insulted her.

I whistled, *wheep!* Another day. This time sitting on the steps of the Education and Psychology Building, and she was coming down them from class. She wanted to be a schoolteacher.

"You have to give me a chance."

"Now let go my hem of my dress." I saw a paper sticking out of her book. It had *D-* on it in red. She pulled loose but didn't go anywhere.

"You waiting on your boyfriend to pick you up?"

She looked at me with an expression of tearful horror. Catherine looked a bit like Claire Bloom at times.

"Is this serious, between you and him? Don't you get any time off? And Catherine? . . ."

"Aw *whut?*" Such a delicate hug-able thing until you heard the voice.

"Would you say your whole name for me?"

"I cain't."

"Why not?"

"I ain't got time."

She stepped down to the sidewalk, and I saw she was watching the black Buick turn toward us around the horseshoe. I stood my ground. At least I had on my sunglasses and they gave me some confidence. Catherine walked out in

252

the road to get on the right side of the Buick. Peter was behind the wheel, studying me from ten feet away as he stopped. He had a cordial grin on his face. I'd seen his face since the night of the fire. Silas had a television in his room and we watched a broadcast of the funeral march for Medgar Evers which showed Ralph Bunche and other dignitaries, like old Peter himself, standing on the sidewalk of Farrish Street with his big hat most positively *on;* a little riot broke out later, as was telecast. We didn't see him then.

By the time he got a good look at me, I was being a complete and craven chicken-ass thespian. I had drawn in my lower lip and a good bit of my chin to my mouth, and I let my top teeth hang out bare; I also dropped my shoulder down and turned out my hand in the posture of mournful dystrophy. I beat my teeth on my chin and ran my tongue around as if unable to say the passionate thing I wanted to say. I nodded up and down and stamped my foot. Peter became embarrassed and turned to his niece in the car.

"Who is that young man?" I heard him ask her.

"That's Harry Monroe," she said to him. Peter nodded to me hesitantly. His rival. So she had found out my name! Catherine saw me being the muscular dystrophy pretender on the steps. What awful humiliation. As they left I saw them in conversation with each other and saw them craning around to look at me as the car went down the hill to the highway. I waved to them then, bending out of the guise. I vowed then that Peter would never frighten me again. The next time he saw me, he would meet Harry Monroe and all that that boy really was.

16 / Oh My and Again

We sat at Mother Rooney's evening table. She had served us fried chicken with mashed potatoes and dark pan gravy, with turnip greens and a lettuce salad, plus her own rolls, and there wasn't a crumb left in the room. The pharmacist,

Delph, had left, and we were lying forward on the table, just mumbling. Silas had eaten two entire chickens and Mother Rooney had loved it. For a while Mother Rooney had sat at the end of the table, watching her food being eaten, taking nothing herself. She'd been lightly chiding Silas about the other evening. He'd sent her to the Roy in a taxi, telling her there was an epic of the Catholic faith showing called "The Blood and the Cross," which was an Italian vampire movie featuring the indecent exposure of five women just before the fiend bent them over in silhouette to slake his need, with an old coughing priest and his crucifix the hero at the end. Silas was so stoned with food he didn't even answer her, or perhaps he did. He commenced heaving out long rending belches, and she got up and left.

"What sort of parents would let her stay with Peter?" I said.

"They aren't alive. Either that, or they're so low they can't afford to think. My theory is," said Fleece, "they don't know he was in Whitfield. If somebody wrote them, and if they can read, what they read was he had tuberculosis or something all that time. They think she's with some man who has recovered because he's such a fine man he deserved to recover. They think he's weak but has a lot of money. She's in a Christian college. She's in their dream they never ever thought of hoping for."

"That's something like my theory," I said.

"I'll tell you. My theory is . . ." said Silas. He was dead with food, and belched again. "My theory is that the *meat* of *Pete* is her *treat*. And that was a poem, mothers."

"I want to go over there and stay in the yard for half an hour and see what I can see," I said.

"I'll go with you," said Silas, with no enthusiasm.

"*I'll* take you over," said Fleece. He stood up.

Fleece had just been issued a license from the State Highway Patrol. Silas lifted a hand and fell asleep.

It proved out that Fleece and I hadn't eaten so much that we couldn't do with a six-pack at the Tote-Sum. We parked in Peter's front yard and finished it off—ten o'clock by the clock of the T-bird. The T-bird was getting to be an old car, and it was surprising the things that still worked in it.

He got out with me and we walked right up to the show window of the right rear of the house. "This would be a living area," said Fleece. He was drunk. He suggested that we

254

climb up on the roof and dive down the chimney together and land in the fireplace and show them something. He called me by name several times, afraid he would forget me, I suppose. "Zersus? Zersus Christ? What was his first name?" "Jesus." "Jesus Christ!" We were looking at Peter and Catherine and they were popping corn over a fire in this huge room. Catherine held the wire contraption and Peter was leaning on the mantle, expressing himself blissfully. You could tell he was using some art in whatever he was saying. It was long out of season for a fire, but there it was, going. Catherine was covered with a chaste robe of turquoise flannel, but, nevertheless, you could see her thigh-line, and her breasts sat forth very plainly in it, though she was buttoned up to the top. What seemed really compromising was that she was barefooted. Peter was getting to see the line of those pretty ankles and feet. Catherine, holding the stem of the popper with both hands, moved away awkwardly from the fireplace suddenly. Some of the corn seemed to have taken flame. Peter swirled around and leaned over her shoulders with his arms around her, to take it. His head fell to the side and he was a long time at the back of her neck.

"You can see what he has on his mind!" said Fleece. "What's wrong? You've got your pistol. Shoot him! Look at him, still on her neck! Give *me* the gun!"

It happened that Catherine broke free of Peter, or the handle of the popper, and went hurriedly out of the room just then. Peter, still holding the contraption, mooing at her with a spread cupped mouth, inched her way. I brought up the pistol and shot through the window, into the fire. The window was made of twenty little panes or so. *Patuda, patuda, patuda, patuda, patuda, patuda, patuda!* Shot out all but one shot. A number of panes fell away. Peter stood there in his robe and slippers, in full relief twenty feet from me, the center of an erupted shower of popcorn. He was trying to do something with the black pistol he'd pulled out of his robe pocket. "Let me take him," said Fleece soberly. He was drunk but very serious. I gave him the gun and got out of the way.

Fleece aimed on Peter. Peter seemed to be making a lot of racket inside. I heard Catherine scream. Then I picked out the gunshot noises. Peter was blazing away from inside, and glass was flying past Fleece, and Fleece seemed to be poised there in the glow of the window light forever, a steady hand and pistol five feet off the ground. Then there was a yell as if a horse's throat had been cut. Fleece walked quickly over to me and we were in the car before you knew it.

"I took him. It was fair. He saw me. I saw him. He shot at me nine or ten times. I took him down in the kneecap."

"How you know you didn't kill him?" I was trying to keep the T-bird together while we did eighty, hitting left from Northside Drive on to Delta Drive, which is very slick and bounded by ditches and greasy parking lots.

"I aimed at his knee for a whole minute, is how I know. And then when he fell I saw blood spurting outa his knee and he was holding his knee with both hands, is how I know."

"He yelled like he was murdered."

"I know he yelled. . . . You forgive me now for wanting to leave you at Canton, don't you?"

"Yes. Yes. Fool."

"All right, so you keep your motherfucking mouth shut about it."

Such a hard all-square man then, Fleece. You should've seen him the rest of the week. He stayed in bed. He couldn't eat the crust off a piece of toast; when he began starving, I brought him a piece of light bread, right out of the sack. Even this was too much; he couldn't even nibble. He wanted me to keep a watch on his window. One afternoon a police car came up and backed around in our alley. He saw me stand up. "Who?" in this tortured gasp. I didn't tell him. I thought he might be dying. My own heart had frozen seeing them.

I was in his room at the end of the week when Silas came through on the way to his own room.

"Dirty boy, dirty boy," squeaked Fleece.

"Is he talking to me?" asked Silas, stopping.

"Somebody better hit me in the stomach hard, or I'm gonna die," squeaked Fleece.

"He needs somebody to hit him in the stomach?" asked Silas.

"He's said that before," I said.

"He has? Well, let's see . . ." Silas went over to the bed. "You want something to bring you out of this?"

"Wait—" I began.

256

Silas raised his thick fist over his head and slugged Fleece in the belly so hard it made the bed move. I think it took the mattress down to the floor. Fleece's tongue jumped straight up. I went on up to my room; I was shy of seeing what remained of the living Fleece, if anything. Then I heard Fleece calling me. When I went down, he was up walking in his pajamas, pointing up the staircase toward Silas's room.

"That son of a bitch has *had* it!" he said.

BOOK THREE

1 / The White of His Eye

Some days it seems to me I never knew any of them. I get sleepy thinking about them. It seems I was encapsulated in a dull glass ambulatory unit, and they were too, and we just happened to knock against one another and squinted through the glasses to see if the other was still insisting that he, indeed, existed. You see the arms pressed on the glass, and see their frowns squashed against it, and remember their flesh as if it appeared only in pink splotches, like a rash.

"When you think about it, it does shine forth as a little chemical miracle of rare device, doesn't it?" Fleece was fondling the long pistol he'd given me, and looking wry. He was letting his hair grow out like Trotsky's on the sides; his forehead was even higher; the brains up there seemed to burst his hair away to both sides. "I believe I'll take this one back." He glanced out the window and then up the stairway. "A side arm makes one feel downright *shrewd,* don't it? And my buddy-roll, we must be shrewd now, eh? What say?" He hadn't asked about the bullets.

"You see *her* at school today?"

"Saw her yesterday. She didn't see me."

"She look worn out? She look eaten?"

"She looked like she was just plugging away at college like it was killing her. She was holding a copy of *The Sound and the Fury* and *The Waste Land and Other Poems,* and another book called *Statistics and Appraisal.*"

"You looked at her good, didn't you?"

Poor Catherine. What was she possibly doing with "The Waste Land," with *The Sound and the Fury* and *The Stranger, The Brothers Karamazov* in sophomore lit? What was she going to do about the junior English proficiency essay? With statistics and appraisal, with audio-visual education, and child psychology charging at her like monsters out

261

of the fog. How, my Catherine? What will you do, what will you write, what will you say? At Hedermansever, which was so "rigid" and which they called the Harvard of the South, seventy-five per cent full of Pee Aitch Dees whose lives consisted of bringing bitter news to people like her—the dumb. Those Pee Aitch Dee people at the front of the room: "Look here, I'm Doctor so and so. The people that gave me the degree, *they* knew I'm not as narrow and stupid and boring as I seem. I spent years proving this!" Her bright black eyes on all that. Did she ever raise her hand in class? Of course not. I'd talked to Zak the other day, too. Catherine was assured of a place in the fall musical. So now, with also learning the tunes and the dance steps! And with Peter. How much could she keep in her mind!? I must've been showing my concern.

"Damn. You do care about her," said Fleece.

"Care about her and don't dare let her see me. I got the feeling if she saw me again, she'd remember who it was with the gun by their porch out there."

"She didn't see your face. They've got *nothing, nothing.* You know what he said."

Fleece alluded to Peter's statement in the article "Local Citizen Attacked Again" in the green edition of the *Jackson Daily,* which appeared two afternoons after Fleece shot Peter. Peter was quoted from a bed in St. Dominic's Hospital.

I do not know any person or persons who should want to shoot me. If I have offended anyone in my public stand I would offer him debate and not bullets. Please let me meet you in the open.

I only hope that now that I am crippled and will be forced to make use of a cane as I walk, that person or persons will be satisfied. I have confidence in the Jackson police, who will be stationed at my house until they break this case. You ask me if I look forward to violence in the future, and I say if they get through the police, they had best creep softly because I carry now a stick of large nature in the name of two loaded automatic shotguns with double zero buckshot in them. This would tear a telephone pole apart. I am only protecting myself and my own. The villain or villains who attacked me know already that I shoot back. If you are quoting me, let it be known that I am not inviting them. I hope they are satis-

fied by crippling me. But let them know I am now armed
to lay waste to them if they have ideas of sneaking about
my house again.

He was whining now, like Fleece said. He might have his
double-zero armory, but the guns were shaking useless in
his hands. He was begging the villain please not to come
again.

"I think I've made a sedate old racist out of him," said
Bobby Dove. "Nervous and absolutely immobile. I put age
on him. I'll bet he doesn't reach for your sweetheart any
more without thinking of bullets coming in the window. I
bet she's been dry for two months. The Jackson police, 'until they break this case.' Sheeit. He knows as well as we do
that in Mississippi, all you have to do is be sure, when you
strike, you strike by night, and you can do it free. They, or
he, or it, shot Medgar in the back, that person isn't ever
going to see the wrath of the law."

"Really," I said, "you ought to realize how damn awful
lucky you are even being alive, saying this. It was a miraculous *fluke*. I watched it."

He smiled like a possum. He drew his hands back
through his bursting Trotsky hair.

"I was so drunk, and it was so, so *perilous*. He saw me
and shot at me, I could see a cloud break out of the end of
his gun, nine or ten times. Then I pulled on him, the very
first time I ever shot a weapon of any sort. I got him. I saw
the puff on my gun, and I saw the bullet travel out of it and
strike him."

"You saw the bullet travel out of the gun?"

"Right to his knee. It was so certain. And all mine."

It passed into autumn. We saw nothing in the newspapers. I'd been avoiding the house all summer, still a bit
leery. I tried to do well in my studies. I'd get concerned
about midnight and read my books until three or four, and
leave the house at eight, feeling miserable, but passing the
quizzes. I have a beard which grows exceeding slow but is
thick when it finally gets out. When it was out, I thought
the time was ripe to ride by and see the house again. I took
Silas's Pontiac. He wanted to go too.

There were no policemen staked out around the place.
The car tires crackled over the red and yellow leaves in the

street. The wind was lukewarm. The house itself was surrounded by maples and oaks. It was a big stained Spanish house with a red tile roof and green wainscoting and a driveway of clay-colored rocks. Growing close to the house were yucca plants—green sharp Mexican-looking things. There were a number of Los Angeles villas like this in Jackson, but none of them quite so grand. It was furnished with a garage that also had a red tile roof and a steeple, altogether useless except for esthetics.

On the third trip by the house, around five o'clock, I saw Peter and Catherine getting out of the Buick in the garage. She had her books and he had his cane. He still wore the tall smashed cowboy hat. Catherine had her hair trimmed to pixie style. I hadn't seen her for a month. I was driving the Pontiac. She dragged behind Peter slavishly, arms full, through with Hedermansever for another day. Her head hung to one side so that her throat was bared.

"The tires are on the curb, man! Get us off the curb!" said Silas.

"Did you see her?"

"I never thought she was such a cutey-pie."

"She's delicate."

"Aw delicate, delicate. She reminds me of a TV dinner. Put a little aluminum foil around her. Can't you see the old boy beating his cane on the floor in ecstasy."

"I don't need any help with my imagination."

"Anyway, it was Whitfield Peter I was looking at. I've seen that old boy before somewhere," said Silas.

"What the hell do you mean? At the musical, under his porch."

"I didn't see him good, though. I mean another time. He had on an overcoat like he was wearing just then."

"At night? When? What was he doing?"

"I can't tell you. Where *was* it? Come on, mind!"

When we got to Mother Rooney's, supper was ready. The whole rear of the house glowed red and gold through the windows and you could hear merry-go-round music screeching away like an accordian run by a locomotive engine. The Mississippi state fair was in session right down the cliff in back of us. On the grounds nearest us were the cattle and swine exhibitions, with their dense stench. It was the same Royal American Shows fair that I'd seen back in Dream of Pines, and I felt right at home, though the others

264

were cursing it. You could see the "Harlem in Havana" club, way over there to the right of the ferris wheel, could see the musicians playing on the balcony for the girls in their wraps on the stage, in the five-minute spot they did to invite you in to the real show, $1.50. Mother Rooney's house sloped even more now, it seemed. You might sit down on those slick dark planks of the entrance hall and slide right through the house, out the back, and be hurled over the cliff into the fair like a tumbling angel; the sawdust and the hay of the animal barns would catch you. Then to hit, I thought, and roll briefly, bouncing up on the fly, being right in the middle of Dream of Pines Royal American Shows, 1957.

Mother Rooney was not at the table. I was the last to finish. The others had left. I took my plate to the kitchen and saw her. She was sitting in a chair next to the back window, which was open although the weather was very cool. Her hands were up to her ears and she looked distressed. I asked her what was wrong. Then she put her hands over her face.

"He's dead. But last year when the fair came and now again, I hear his voice calling me. I don't want to hear it but I have to."

"Who?"

"Hoover Second, my son."

"That was killed in the airplane crash?"

"I loved him so, but I never said I wanted any ghost calling me."

She told me someone or something was calling to her, "Mother!" Over and over. She couldn't stand to go in the back yard and see who it was, and she couldn't stand *not to* hear the voice, either. It scared her, but she had to hear it. I gave her my arm and walked her to the ledge of the cliff where the kudzu began. Below us fifty yards was a truck with a ramp leading off it. There were a few cows in the truck. Some boys in blue corduroy FFA jackets were trying to drag the cows down the ramp. I didn't know what she could be hearing. Then one of the boys hit a cow with a stick and yelled out, as I later explained to Mother Rooney, one of the graver profanities, denoting incest and including the word *mother*. She was disabused, but she didn't seem overly relieved.

On the way back to the porch, she kept her eyes on my

265

face. "Why would anyone find it necessary to use that word?" she asked me.

"It's as old as the Greeks. It's a cruel world, Mother."

Her eyes were weak, but they shot wide and angry just then. "Don't *you* tell me how cruel the world is, Mister Monroe." I apologized. "Young men who learn a lot of knowledge should not be prissy little scholars." Then she apologized. "I do thank you, dear. I thought I was losing my mind. Do, do thank you."

I asked Fleece what he knew about Mother Rooney's son. I felt wretched. Fleece had talked to her privately several times. He told me her son was a hero of almost suicidal bravery who piloted a B-25 bomber on deep flights into Germany. He'd come back home in 1945 with his legs full of shrapnel, but in Jackson he couldn't stop. He bought a Piper Cub from the Civil Air Patrol, stole several boxes of toilet paper out of the basement of his old high school, St. Joseph's, and flew over such things as the state capitol building, the governor's mansion, and football games, cutting the engine and screaming something, as he cast out the toilet-paper rolls, which unwound and plummeted and scrawled in the air over these places. When the newspapers found out he was a famous veteran, they thought he was beautiful, with his sense of humor. He was Jackson's high jolly aerobird. Then they found out he was not jolly, as Mother Rooney knew well, seeing him rush out to the airport every morning with only a half-cup of coffee in him for breakfast. He came down on some girls who were playing tennis over at Mississippi College, right at them, they said, and crashed against a practice board on the courts. Mother Rooney and her husband Hoover Rooney were called over to the college to see the black wreck.

"And her husband, if you can trust her, I'll bet it's been a cruel world for her. He was a plumbing contractor. His father and he had come from Ireland to Jackson. When his father died, Hoover was so crazy disoriented that Mother Rooney made him build this house so he could look at it and not mistake it for any other place in the world. And we're living in it."

I heard Silas coming down the stairs to my room. He called me. I went up, and Fleece followed.

"I'd like to speak to Monroe alone," said Silas.

"We were talking," said Fleece.

"Yes, you're always talking, but I have something to *say*."

Fleece framed Silas a moment with his glare. Then he went back down to his room.

Silas was almost berserk with information. He'd just recalled where and when he'd seen Whitfield Peter before. It was early in the morning at Oxford, Mississippi, the home of Ole Miss. It was the morning after the night when the FBI brought James Meredith, the first Negro to enter a white college in Mississippi, on the Ole Miss campus. Silas had driven up to see what was going on. Two men had been killed in the riot during the night. Random cars were burned. There was nothing especially new about what Peter was doing: Silas saw him dropping crossties off a rail bridge onto military trucks. Or rather, Peter was supervising the act. The story only made me want to see Catherine more. I'd been spying at her now for four or five months.

When my beard was out full, I got myself a pair of cosmetic spectales from Sears.

In early December I stood on their lawn. The trees were bare and looked outraged. I looked for the cops around the palm trees next to that garage with its bell tower. I carried no weapon. The house was as white as a bone and jarred out at me. It was Saturday, the deep edge of twilight. I felt all mushy and electric inside, this near it again. I had a *keen* feeling, too. I felt like only the eyes of a face hidden in ambush. Then I felt the presence of another face, not mine, waiting with me. I closed my eyes.

"Who is it?" Nothing moved. I thought for certain some person had the drop on me. A voice spoke in my head: "You've made one mistake. You may get in the door, friend, but you should never believe in yourself so much that you leave your weapon at home." It was Geronimo. I hadn't seen him or heard from him for months. He'd been lounging a long time inside me, and now he stirred. I loved him. The grunting old pouch-face. "Get on up to that door." His voice carried with the melody of a raunchy old chum.

Catherine answered the door. I smiled and tried to be droll. At last she recognized me. She wanted to know what had happened to me. I asked her what had happened to *her*. I told her a friend of mine over at Hedermansever had given me her address. She was stunned.

267

"What friend?"

"I can't tell you. Somebody who's been sweet on you but didn't have the nerve to come himself."

"That's some larkey." She was teased. I told her I'd tried to look her up in the phone book but couldn't remember her last name.

"All I remembered was *Catherine*. That was so pretty I couldn't remember the rest."

"Wrag," she said.

I closed the door and we were in the dark vacant front room. There was a rug, and pieces of furniture sat twisted the wrong angle to each other in brown wet shadows. I followed her through a gangway to the rear of the house, passing over a furnace grate in the floor. The house was overheated. It got even warmer toward the back. We came into a small library sort of room with only one tiny window in it. Peter sat on a couch away from the window. The walls were palate-smoothed plaster, showing swirls and solid drops. This room, with the tiny window in the corner, looked like a fort. Peter lifted up a leg and put it over the other when I came in. He wore a yellowish robe but had on a white shirt and a black tie at his neck like a snake assaulting him. His hair was a shock of lightning gray-tan thrown back so as to make the face come forward like a wooden mask. I couldn't look at the face yet. I saw his feet—thin socks in orange leather house slippers. He got up and walked into the kitchen.

"Who was that?" I asked her.

"My uncle."

"Is he upset?"

"He's been sick. Listen, did Gillis Lock tell you my address?"

"No. Who's that?"

"He went to Hedermansever one semester. He known me. I had a speech class he was in. He calls me up all the time." We sat on the couch Peter had left.

"Catherine, I've missed you so much. I've seen you."

Suddenly her uncle was at the door again.

"Fidel?" he said.

"Sir?"

"Are you kin to Fidel Castro?" He thought this was rich. He was holding in a giggle. He stepped on into the room. He meant my beard and glasses. His hands were on his

268

stomach. He was about to break a rib, laughing. When I caught on, I looked up smiling, but he was gone.

"Do I look like Fidel?" I asked Catherine.

"Naw. You look smart."

Then he came back and stood in the door again.

"So you're Mister Lock," he said.

"No, sir."

"He's Harry Monroe. This ain't Gillis," said Catherine. "That scoundrel has telephoned us. I finally told him off, myself. I said, 'Boy, if you don't have spunk enough to let us even see you, you'd better hang yourself up for good. I suggest a pine tree and a good rope.' That's what I told him." He crouched, laughing again. I got the feeling he would drown you with jokes like this if you ever gained his confidence.

"I'm from pine country," I told him.

"Fidel?" he said. "I grew a beard once at the University of Massachusetts. I wanted to look like my professors from Europe. I took myself to the barber within an hour of being apprised that the Jews and communists made themselves known by wearing beards."

"I know what you mean," I said. It seemed the thing to say. I looked at his face straight-on, getting courage, and saw the friendly smile out of the bleached hawklike features, with purple around the mouth and eyes. Then he left again, using his cane. "You finish supper, child. I will be back after I've had my medicine. You stay for supper," he said in the next room, which was the kitchen; we could hear him creeping stridently away.

I went with Catherine to the kitchen, where pots were on the stove and the oven light was on. Some greens and peas were smoldering in the pots. She saw to them. I mentioned that home cooking was a wonderful new smell to me.

"I do it out of them frozen plastic bags." She held up a dripping plastic sack from the top of the garbage bucket.

"He said for me to stay, but do you want me to stay?"

"I's thinking I wouldn't never see you again."

She spoke with her back to me; she was at the sink. I was looking at her small shoulders. The dress she wore was a neat brown thing that touched her bottom alluringly.

"I'd be a boll of cotton if they made me into your dress," I said.

"Oh lissen at Mister Mouth." At least her voice was softer than I'd remembered.

"Your uncle stays on the move, doesn't he?" I heard him easing around through the doors.

"He's scared to death. Somebody likes to shoot at him. It was in the newspapers. Last year they shot 'at window in there all to pieces and hit him in the knee. Did you see his cane? The police didn't turn up nothin' at all. If somebody is drawin' a bead on you, there isn't nothin' the police can do about it. The first house we lived in, they blew up his car and set afire to the house."

"What did *you* do?"

Peter entered the kitchen. He dragged his knee behind him nimbly. He was adept at shooting the point of the cane out to hoist himself along. He passed into the forward room and threw a hand out to flick on the light. A plump round dining table sat in there. He caught me staring at him.

"I was *shot* in the knee, son! Shot! I'm a casualty of my convictions. I'm a victim of 'peacetime' America." His eyes seemed gorged and red. I noticed on his finger, the little finger, he wore a dainty ring with a black pearl set atop it. I couldn't linger on his face long.

"Just set two. I can't eat now. Excuse me. You two young people . . ." he trailed off, leaving again for another part of the house.

The supper was quiet. Afterward, I asked Catherine to go with me to a movie at the Capri tomorrow night. I wasn't sure I wanted to ask this, but I was nervous, and my visit to the house would seem pointless and more, suspect, if I didn't pursue it. Catherine was pretty eating, her mouth shut. After a while she said all right, about the movie, but rather cautiously.

"What's on?"

"Something European. I forget."

"I caint even talk English well." She smiled. Something between a joke and an abashed confession. I smiled. "You could be in one of 'em. Your beard, you look Victrolian." I'm sure my smile drooped, but I brought it right back up. Peter caned into the dining room again. He said he would see me to the door, and Catherine went back to the dishes.

As I touched the doorknob myself, he began speaking softly at my back. "We know she isn't bright of mind. But yet I know what a dear little *self* she makes altogether. I

270

don't want anything sly. Not to be presumptuous. But I imagine you might find her willing, hot."

"Sir?"

"*Passionate.* She's near twenty-seven, you know." Peter's own breath struck me.

"My Lord." I was shocked. "Why?" I don't know what I meant. I was being an idiot.

"She didn't have the best start. Don't ask her about that. Another thing is you must not talk about the violent events which have transpired within the last year. I can tell you she had nothing to do with them, certainly, and I will tell you I . . ." I was in the light of the steps; he was within the shadow of the foyer, his robe like hanging wings. But his voice began to constrict, became tiny all of a sudden, an airy sort of reed. "I am not dead yet. I am stubborn. I have ideals. I have had . . ."—he continued on as if unconscious of any change of tone, but his voice was even reedier, like the voice of a rodent in the movie cartoons—"have had . . . a wife. Hence I know the unutterable burning filth of a young male's mind. You'd put yourself between the legs of a clock if you could." Now the voice was coming back to a thin growl.

"The legs of a clock? No. I didn't come here—"

"Horsepiss!" I turned to leave. "Please! I apologize. To presume . . . wait!" He inched the screen door open. "Your beard has made my head swim. Do know that you look ruthless, lad. Believe me that I'm not . . . that what I said . . . my undue sexual . . . eh, realism. At best. I've a mind which has sometimes frightened others." His hand clenched on the door.

"I saw her in the musical. She's pretty. I came by to ask her for a date. She said she'd go to the show with me tomorrow."

"Certainly. But know this. You were the first."

"She hasn't had dates? She's twenty-seven?"

"That boy Gillis Lock has called her on the telephone. But he is no college student. He could not 'make the grade,' as you youngsters say. He's merely a clerk in a Krogers' store over at Pearl. You have no competition. Perhaps that's what alarmed me about you. So tell me something and I will remember it."

"What?"

"What is your address?" I was offguard and gave him the

271

right street, but thought in time to change the number to the one of a block which didn't exist on little dead-end Titpea.

"Your telephone number?"

Now here I was together enough to lie. But I didn't lie well enough. I gave him the number of Fleece's parents' house, which was the only number in Jackson I'd ever memorized. This was an insane inadvertence too. If I'd been Italian, I'd have torn my hair on the way home. This girl, this girl, whom I'd seen, finally face to face for an hour. The minutes ticking by, my care for her turning to an impatient desire to yank her around until her secrets were out.

I didn't tell Fleece or anybody I'd been over to that house. I was horrorstruck that Peter knew the street I lived on; couldn't tell Fleece I had been so stupid, had bowed like a thoughtless chattering tongue to old Whitfield Peter's urgent commands. Damn me. Now, to carry on with the girl seemed the only thing to do. I took her to that foreign movie. Wait. First, I stood out in their yard and held my beard and looked the place over again. I could sniff the brass pepper of fear, feel it reaching in my head all over again. Perhaps they'd remembered me from under the porch and in the shadows of the window. He had those shotguns and was so fractured and anxious he might pull the trigger on anything moving. But I rubbed my beard, thinking I was imperceptible and safe in my fur. And the spirit of Geronimo was still there with me, saying, "Push on in, push on in. Love what you can find and kick what you can't." As a matter of fact, he suggested I drive out to the wilds around the Ross Barnett Reservoir and ravish her until she admitted that, sure, Uncle Peter was quite a sport at lust, but she'd never had anything like this; then change my address and keep moving, making an impossible target.

I knocked on the door. She appeared alone and was all dolled up. She had her own true loveliness, still. She was thin, her limbs had their own soft glow, her eyes had their shy sparkle; the small fruit of her mouth, the two cool doves of her hands, the melted china of her throat. And she'd been all this in "The Boyfriend" just weeks ago, in her silk shimmy—shy, even in the wide-mouthed everybody-on-stage finale. You would take her to your breast, defend her. Hardly daring to think of making babies in her.

272

Thinking of that as an incidental event in some far-off purple glow. I took her out for two years. Not regularly. I
would time the dates so as not to create embarrassment
over the length of time between them, and so as not to risk
a phone call from Peter. I let it be known that, being in
pre-med study, I had absolutely no time. And I pretended
well. I did study. And oftentimes I'd pretend again that I
loved her, when she was in the car. Pretend that, while attempting nothing physical with her whatsoever. It caused
no special anguish to resist. I heard Peter's voice in my
mind while I was with her, but that isn't why I was so
chaste.

Even beyond her pitiful grammar—which improved over
the months (she'd say words like *apprehensive* and *verita-
bly*)—she was just another roach, after all. I knew the
breed better than any. She had some tremendous incurable
fault, even though at times she seemed perfect in make-up.
Something in her being, something that made her slump her
body walking across campus; something in her mind that
made her fall away slack from the fine little body she had;
something which some days made her so careless of her
looks you would see a whole soapflake swashed over with
makeup sticking on her skin; something in her, off the
stage, out of the musical, which slunk, that I couldn't ignore, told me. God knows how long it took me to see what
every man on campus had seen first time he saw her. You
should have seen the girl shrink, practically out of sight,
into the corner of the seat of my old oily-smelling Thunderbird. Like a whipped rat. Like a roach with all its exits well
remembered before it ever ventures out. My dozen nights
with her never approached romance, never approached
anything. It would've been the same if I'd picked her up on
the street. I had never met a roach that I couldn't get a good
bit of my marvelous self across to. I wanted to ask her all
sorts of questions, of course. Sometimes I'd become excited
over the fact that she was twenty-seven—and twenty-eight,
twenty-nine! I never even saw my way clear to asking about
her age. You'd look over there, and she'd be like a per-
fumed roach on its back, seeking its legs so it could flee to
a crack in some filth, and all chance of intimacy would die
choking.

Peter I didn't see for over a year.

She was at the door, opening it. That was fine with me. I asked how he was, on and off.

"He's better. Everyday he's better. He's heavier. He's put back on weight."

"What does he say nowadays?"

"Like what?"

"Like anything."

"He's saying almost everything."

"What does he say about you?"

"That I'm going to cut the mustard."

"You got your hair fixed nice."

"Cut it out."

"If it's fixed for me, I appreciate it."

"It's just fixed. Spray net."

2 / Heart on the Tilt

I think it was at a time when I'd memorized so much, I'd smelled the hydrosulphur effluvium so much, I'd seen those green concrete canals so much, that my face and head were hateful to me. This was my senior year. I knew so many facts I never wanted to know, I'd seen the back of my dead cat stretched out on a board, I'd learned to lift out muscle layers with a scalpel, I'd made slides over and over, and never wanted to keep this in my head, but I was desperate and had to, so what I got was a week-long headache, and all I could see for relief in the future was me, picking up a book of Bobbie Burns's poetry—the only poetry that ever took me in college—and pouring a glass of Scotch to seal myself with and celebrate the mind, body and soul of old Bobbie Burns, who brought them all together and made them sing—in a choir whose members are mad at one another, but who sing nevertheless, together—and I could see myself reading that book in some future office as a general practitioner, when my day was over, the lovely women of the town had all been naked before me revealing their hurt, and I had to brush the dollars out of my chair to sit down. But in the meantime, I had such a headache. And turned to simple beer at the Dutch Bar, with Silas next to me on the stools.

"Silas, you rich bitter disconsolate bulky hod-carrier; what're you going to *be?* I been worried about you. Even rich bastards got to be *something.* I'm seeing three of you, and I been worried, what exactly you going to be. For instance, I'm going to be a doctor."

"Monroe, my friend. I'm going to be in Art. I'm taking a position in Art. The only good course I had was with Sam Gourd. Art."

We came in very late. Silas had been talking about how Mother Rooney flushed her commode every morning at six, on the minute. He was right in saying it made a detonation like the house was splitting; all the plumbing around us shuddered, and our tower shook. I woke up in fear many times myself. Well Silas was sick of this. He wanted to teach her. I followed him into her bathroom downstairs, and he turned on the light and stuck his finger down his throat. He threw up a flood of beer and something the substance of grits and whole dissolved fish. It was awesome, the amount of stuff he'd taken down this day. An entire boiled egg from the Dutch Bar. He vomited on the tile floor and never even tried to use the pot. I couldn't bear it, only he'd told me to watch, so earnestly. He shaped up the mess into a pile and then worked from this source, with his foot. He made a big curved smile; then he dragged off some pieces and made two eyes. The pile became the nose of the face, with the egg at one nostril. When he was through, he had rendered a jack-o-lantern mask, with a yard-wide smile: a hideous culprit of one dimension, not counting the odor.

"She'll think twice about that six o'clock tee-tee," he said, pointing to his work solemnly. The secret gleam of the artist was in his eyes. He staggered past me.

"This is taking it too far," I said. But I wasn't going to clean it up, and I turned off the light. I followed him over to the tower. In my room, he stopped and grabbed me by the collar before he went up to his loft.

"You can't say I've taken it too far. In matters of art you can never take things too far. Lurk me in the eye. You know it?" Then he rose up the stairs haughtily, but missing a step, falling; he rose again, with his solemnity intact, like a lord at the head of an expedition.

I was not awakened by the plumbing sounds that morning. Perhaps Mother Rooney just held it awhile after she saw the bathroom. Perhaps she just lay down in her bed again and pained away until a decent hour.

Then Fleece and I gave her the high-lace leather sneakers, to make up for it; because the house was tilting back even steeper, and I'd seen her come in the front door and almost skid down the lobby in the black slick-heeled patent leather ones that looked a little young on her. This takes us on into the early days of med school, when I seemed to be making it, and spent my spare time in being aware of possible injuries and hazards to everyone around me. I'd quit smoking, and was a regular health officer with my head full of air. But it was Fleece who found the shoes. When you're a freshman in med school, the big thing is to hang around the emergency room and see what they bring in on the ambulances. I myself never sought this. I went down a few times and saw some poor women who'd waited till the last minute to give birth, but it wasn't my cup of tea. Fleece was there the night they brought in the dead lady wrestler from the city auditorium. Her feet seemed to be about the right size, and Fleece brought back the shoes. We told Mother Rooney they were refined orthopedic models, already broken in. She popped then right on. She expressed a little concern about their ugliness, that her feet didn't seem to breathe very well in them. But the next day she said they did make her feel stabler in the world. I was awed by their perfect fit on her. Silas saw them on her one night at supper.

"Where did you get those old-timey goddam *pugilist* shoes? Are you wearing your husband's shoes? Are you going loony?"

She told him where she got them. On the same night she announced that there would be no more open consumption of alcohol in her presence, since Mississippi law forbade hard liquor. Smoking would be allowed. She said she would like to hear someone, if he could, play the piano in the room, and the rest of us would gather around it and sing. This would be a good thing to do after supper every night. Her spirit was on the rise.

"Shit," said Silas.

Then she said that some days she heard so many bad words in this house that it gave her a headache. Silas told her to take an aspirin. She took a sort of stance and declared that she had never taken an aspirin in her life. Silas clapped boredly, but I was impressed. Later, he wanted to know, "What did you *mean*, giving her those shoes?" I left him groping.

Once a month, an old priest with a look of off-balanced kindness and patience would visit Mother Rooney at the house. He came in at supper once and the two of them sat on the divan. I was eating, always the slow man at a meal, left at the table and trying not to hear the two of them talking. Then Silas walked in from the tower with only his jockey shorts on. He knew damn well who was visiting the house. He went and opened the front door, asking loudly where the evening paper was. In a minute he came back in with it, opening it. He looked at me as if trying to find Mother Rooney.

"I tell you! Have you looked at that crack between the porch and the foundation lately? Six inches of black humping air! Have you smelled what's coming out of there? It's *sperm* under there's what it is! Nature will always scandalize. Damned *sperm* is what I smelled!" He pretended to just now see them on the couch and ran away, dropping pages out of the paper. A slice of the old priest's tongue fell out through his teeth, and he had become more intensely cross-eyed.

"Mister Silas is an athlete," chimed Mother Rooney.

"Of what game?" said the priest. He had a cranky worn Boston accent.

"He lifts barbells," I said.

Then came a voice from the area of the tower. It was Silas again. "Help! Help! Mother Rooney. Please!" She got up and excused herself, padding away in the leather sneakers.

I couldn't think of anything else to say to the old Catholic man, so I began discussing the assassination of the President with him. I'd liked Kennedy, as you might like a shy handsome foreigner you saw at a party, and I always imagined that he might like me, and I told the priest this. The priest said, Ah, yes. I could hear stone-deaf cross-eyed clerics all over the world saying this.

Mother Rooney padded back to us.

"Mister Silas said he had found a fish-eater crawling in the house."

"You mean a silverfish," I said.

"No. He said a fish-eater, that he saw a fish-eater crawling in the house, that he would strangle him if he found him in here again."

"That he would *mangle* it . . ."

"No, his arms and hands . . ." She held her frail beige arms out and clutched her fingers in and out. "But of course his arms were so full of muscles. He's such a nicely made boy, but what could be in his mind? What . . ."

"Some use that as an epithet, against Catholics," said the priest. He was leaving, hurriedly. "As a joke."

The next time I saw Silas, he was well gone at the Dutch Bar. He worked at Wright's, a music store on Capitol Street. Being in the arts, you know. He was in conversation with a flushed old drunkard at the end of the bar. As I sat down, he told me he'd *run* all the way from Mother Rooney's to here for punishment. He explained to me that he had taken out Bet Henderson two times this week. He held up two fingers. I asked, How was she? He reiterated that he had taken Bet out two times. She worked in a surgical supply house in Jackson now, and he had taken her out two times. He said he felt luck was coming to him now, but his conscience was sore over Mother Rooney, how he'd treated her, and he wanted to clear it up because he had an omen his good luck wouldn't stand if he didn't. Silas then talked to the sinking old fellow to his right.

"This is a lonely intelligent man. He says he doesn't want to sleep another night alone," he turned to me. "We could, see, just introduce them tonight. I already told him she was a beautiful older rich woman. Meet them together, see? Happy old people."

"I'm not in on this."

"Whataya mean?" He grabbed my tie. "You got the car!"

At twelve I opened the bar door and Silas kept the old man in ambulation to the car. Silas bragged on Mother Rooney some more, and the man seemed to sober up a bit as he listened. He said he wanted to go by a service station. I stopped at one, thinking he wanted to vomit in the restroom, but when he came out, he had fluffed up the Hollywood kerchief at his throat, pulled his pants up, buttoned

278

his coat, and combed his hair with water. He had age spots around his hairline. Now he wanted just one more slug, and Silas gave him one of the quarts we'd bought. We got to the porch together, with no help from me. I was only tight. I thought about the hour of the night, Mother Rooney tucked in her bed. There were no lights on downstairs, not even for the porch, and this was strange because Mother Rooney always kept this bulb on for us late voyagers. The old guy was scared stiff. He kept swabbing at his mouth and his hair and edged behind Silas. Silas told me to go wake her up. I entered the long vestibule and switched on the light. She was not asleep. She was lying on the slick boards, hurt. A grocery sack from the Jitney Jungle lay ripped and strewn over to one side, as if there'd been some violence. I locked the door, hearing Silas protest on the porch.

"Finally you get here!" she said. She'd taken off the wrestling shoes. Her bunions twinkled through her stockings. She was wearing a floppy silk dress with blue flowers figured on it. Her hair, yellow, was in the wreck of a bun. "I'm gone. I've been in this state since five o'clock . . . afraid to move and make it worse."

She had fallen coming in the door with the groceries. A brooch the size of an Easter egg was standing out at the cleavage of her breasts. The dress was pinioned by it. I saw that the whole length of the pin of the brooch was buried in her chest. It had unclasped and stabbed her as she hit the floor. On entrance it made a nasty purple slit. There was only a little Blood. God knows how long the pin was. "You were the right one to come in and find me, unless Bobby Fleece . . ." she said with a meager hope for life.

I stared at the wound. I didn't know what to do. I was in medical school, and it was disgraceful, but I couldn't remember what to do, if I'd ever known it. I ran over to the tower and got Fleece's *Merck Manual* off his desk. I turned the pages and tore them trying to get to the Punctures section.

"Is that Jerry Silas out on the porch?" she asked. "I'd like to see him. He's such a nicely made boy. He could hold my head." Then she sat up and glared at me. "Don't you *know* what to do?" Either the page for the incised wounds had been torn out, or I couldn't find it. I found half a page which discussed débridement, ". . . making the depths of

279

the wound ideal for the propagation of infective . . ." I
turned to Gangrene, anything. Then I went and made a
phone call to the University Hospital, to the same building
where I was going to school.
"Isn't that Jerry Silas out there trying to get in? Open the
door." I could hear him twisting the knob and battering the
door. I didn't want her to see the old guy. The door to the
porch was a double-winger with no middle frame, and I
knew that if Silas rammed it much more, it would give.
Mother Rooney began to stand up. She was hissing, as if
losing air right out of the lung. I rushed over and brought
her back to earth. I took hold of the brooch and jerked it
out, stood up, and threw the thing at the back shadows of
the hall, slipping down on those slick boards as I did so.
"My heart is tilting!" she cried. I thought I'd killed her.
Then I heard the siren yawling up Titpea. Silas made a last
attack on the doors, and they broke apart. He staggered in,
crouched over. The old man was riding piggyback on him.
The old man had closed his eyes in fear.
"What's going on? I have the lover here," Silas demanded. I hauled back and hit Silas square in the eyes. He went
down, and the old man abandoned him and crashed on the
boards of the vestibule. When Silas stood up again, he was
raising his hands to kill me. I had my arms over my face.
But nothing came. I stole a glance down. Silas was watching too. The old guy's body was slipping down toward
Mother Rooney. He was such a red ancient drunk, his white
hair had popped out like a sparse wig, his Hollywood cra-
vat had flown apart, and he slid down the boards, out cold,
his head coming to rest on her knee, his rough-out Hush
Puppy shoes retarding the slide.
Then Mother Rooney really let bellow. She couldn't
stand him. She hipped away from his touch and shook her
hands.
The ambulance crew—I knew one guy—thought it was a
family fight, and took the old guy out first. I walked Mother Rooney out through the front yard, although Silas wanted to lift her along all on his own. The boy I knew looked
at her wound in the red lights of the back end of the ambulance.
"Did the old man stab her?" he asked me.
Wouldn't you know it, I had to go back in the house,
turn on all the lights, kick the furniture around, until I

found the brooch. Drove with that czarina's bauble to the emergency room, to furnish proof that we didn't need an inquest, walked around like a wondering queen with the jewel out forward in my palm, until I found the right doctor.

Then got back, landing on Fleece, Bet, and Silas, all standing with arms folded on the porch, Fleece and Bet having arrived recently in Fleece's new Renault. I suppose Fleece was taking Bet to his room, but met Silas on the porch waiting for my return and exploding with the tale of Mother Rooney and the old drunk. I heard Silas reeling off a monologue and went right through them to my bed.

3 / Age 22

I got out of my car in the north parking lot and pulled my microscope box out of the back seat. Rain was threatening. The Choctaws were sitting on the grass between me and the door of the school wing. The Ole Miss medical center lifted up like a monstrous sandy brick. Saturday the same group had tried to collar me, but I ignored them. I didn't know anything. I was no doctor and they saw my jacket and thought I was.

The women wore dresses that looked like the flag of some crackpot nation. I'd seen two Choctaw women come in at the last minute to deliver. When they had their legs in the straddles, you could see the dye rings on their thighs which came off the dresses. Their vaginas were fossileums of old blood. Their babies came up in a rotten exhumation; then the baby was there, head full of hair, wanting to live like a son of a gun. It almost belied the germ theory of disease. The mothers did not cry out for Jesus like the Negro women. They bawled in shorter shrieks, but higher, as if in direct, private accusation against some little male toad of a god. It made my blood crawl.

The men on the lawn wore big soiled shirts of red and

281

blue. These Choctaws would sleep together on the lawn until whoever they were waiting for came out or died. A woman came up to me with a bunch of papers in her hand. She motioned toward the back of the cafeteria, and I saw the pick-up truck parked in one of the slots. She said a sick man was in there. I took out my pen. What she had were BIA forms. "Have you applied for BIA medical aid before?" Questions like that from the Bureau. I made several jag marks on them and signed my name at the bottom, *Harriman Monroe, M.D.* She barked to the group sitting on the lawn, and two men got up and walked toward the truck. I was late for class already, so I waited. The men pulled a limp man out of the front seat and carried him toward us. His arms hung down to the ground. The squaw told me that the man had eaten a dead terrapin he had found in the woods near the frontage road at 51 Highway. They thought he was poisoned. She was very thankful, this squaw. "Docotor," she called me. I agreed that he was probably poisoned and then hurried off. The hospital treated him and cured him. I checked that out. My signature had helped. Sometimes even now, I'll put *M.D.* after my name when I sign a check and get a warm old kick from it.

I went straight to the basement lounge and got two milks out of the machine, which I drank for my breakfast, as I sat in the ping-pong room. The serious players were there, and they noticed me. They were all residents, two of them from Japan, one from South Korea, and the big slammer, from Germany, who was a head in the field of cervix cancer. With them was an M.D. from Malta, of unknown function in cytology. He didn't play the game, but like to call the points, with a deep bold British accent. He was almost a midget in a small lab coat, but he liked to hang around and shout out the scores, for hours. "A point, a clean point! Eighteen-fifteen." Since almost all the points in ping-pong are obvious, you might think it was silly to have him around. But not at all. When you made a big shot—a blurring slam, an unreturnable english on the ball—he would practically *knight* the damn thing. "An absolutely clean point!" If Dr. Eaver were still calling the points, I could do nothing but play ping-pong, today. Apparently he was not much needed upstairs. I was in the same boat.

The finest game, competitively, was between Dr. Völl and Dr. Shibata. Völl (Verl, we said) would slam the ball and Shibata would return it with a kind of apologetic scoop, so the ball dropped just over the net and flung out to the side of the table like a ball bearing dropped out of a jet plane, and Völl would have to leap out to get it back. I said the finest game, competitively, because when I was there the game was not competitive. I could slam Völl's *slam*, I could put stuff on the stuff Shibata hit at me. You get this good with practice. Nobody could be quite this good and be serious at anything else. My heart was in the ping-pong room. I was winning nowhere else.

In anatomy, I had Monique, my female cadaver, whom I had fought for down at the vat. There were few girls of any sort in the freshman vat. In anatomy I was taught by a stately old buzzard named Potter who had slugged up out of the Depression in Mississippi and let us all know how proud he was of his situation as anatomy professor. He was a humble man. He had an immense respect for the King's English. He talked very slowly and seemed to be recollecting some rule for every word he spoke. I impressed him with my English. I was working late one afternoon on Monique, and Potter saw my shoes under the curtains when he came in.

"Who is it?" he asked.

"It is I," I answered.

After a while, Potter drew the curtain back. We were alone. I was hacking away, too lazy to change scalpel blades.

"I like that," said Potter. *"It is I*. You've had an education, haven't you young man? I've been grading the quizzes, Monroe."

"No good news for me."

"You're the type who won't write down an answer unless you know it perfectly and can spell it perfectly, aren't you? What you got, you got right with an exact veritude that I admire. I wish you could have answered more of the questions. But there was a high certainty in the answers you had, though there were only three, that I can see in your handwriting. What kind of pen do you use, by the way?"

"A Scripto."

"It carries an authority with it. I can't deny . . . I refuse to fail you. I am going to let you take the trimester test."

I thanked him. I tried being literary in other classes, but it didn't work out so well. In pharmacology there was a

283

poem in the textbook where the author had attempted to be witty—"Histamine/The knavish son of Histadine"—which I pointed out as execrable, but the professor and the class ignored me. For better or worse, the chairman of pharmacology seemed to take to me, though. He was the one who came to my aid when all the chips were down—when I didn't make my probation the second trimester—and gave me a job injecting granulated nerve gas into dogs and let me in the pharmacology graduate program. Dr. Holland was dedicated to reconstructing such M.D. dropouts as me into doctoral candidates so that we would not be lost to medical science. And he was a good man, as was Dr. Briggs, my professor, who treated me as if I were not a fool and a loser. This is always nice. Holland's charity was so immense, I took the English Oval cigarettes out of the tin in his office when he was out, feeling that he'd want me to have them anyway. My apologies, but now, for the first time in my life, the money press was on. The old man was not sold on my being a Ph.D. in pharmacology and the money tree at home was drying up. Nobody ever told me how the old man took the news when I got the boot from med school, but I had to write the letter about it, and I could imagine him going into his study for hours, holding my letter up, and writing me a check, carefully, for $125 —what he figured this letter was worth, to the dollar. His signature on the check was limp, like a wet shoelace draped on a fence. So there were the days of deciding between a hamburger out at T-Willie's and a pack of Marlboros with coffee downstairs in the cafeteria. And my hundred-a-month job, recording the respiration, the pupillary responses to light, responses to pinprick in the lumbar region and the other regions I've forgotten, and the more obvious physical dispositions, of hundreds of dogs, after you'd pumped up the femoral vein and let them have it, which wasn't always easy when you got a big rowdy animal. Invariably, right after injection the dog would wobble around pitifully, evacuate his bowels all over the room, and faint, lying dead for a whole day. I proved that they did this in my reports, incontestably. At five o'clock they woke up. I'd take them to the freight elevator. They looked normal, but the ordeal seemed to have increased their affection for me. You hated to turn them back into that reeking catacomb of pens in the basement, beyond Experimental Surgery, where
284

there were ten other dogs lying on stainless steel tables. These dogs, eyes closed, were trembling to pieces; they had long sutures along their stomachs, which I asked about. The experiment was to open up the dog, wound him internally in subtle ways, sew him up, and time him as to how long it took him to die. Herdee, a graduate of Hedermansever whom I had hated particularly, told me this. He had this neat summer job of holding the clock and marking down the expiration times to the minute. If another man had told me about it, it would have been better. It's pointless to mope around animal labs with your hands on your heart. But here was Herdee, having finished his first year of med school, so neatly, with his neat summer research job. He was using his time so wisely. He had acquired a hard sage smile, very serious, although all the hell he was doing was walking among the tables and holding a clock. He was stupid and had been compensating for this fault terrifically all his life. By all rights, he should have been lying sutured-up on one of the tables while one of the dogs held the clock and looked sage.

One day Herdee wanted to sit by me in the cafeteria.

"Sorry, I'm waiting on my friends."

"This table seats six. You have a *lot* of friends."

"And all of them hate your guts."

He sat down, with that same smile. He was uninsultable. One of the ways these sort of people make it is, they have absolutely no pride. Fleece came over with his tray and sat down.

"What's the nerve gas doing to the dogs nowadays?" Fleece said. I really was interested in just how stupid Herdee *was*. I whispered so he could hear.

"You know well that this is a secret. We aren't even supposed to know this is nerve gas. If the army heard me, they'd jerk my thirty-thousand-dollar grant right out from under me. Fleece, they really have something. As soon as I inject, they, their fur becomes gray, then white, then *clear*. In sixty seconds, the animal simply isn't *there*. Only its *functions* are left behind. And the functions, *per se*, are tripled. A mound of dung two feet high appears within the hour; you can see the saliva dripping out by the pint, and every thirty minutes the unseen animal urinates, so the floor is a damned wading pool of moving liquids, and you smell rotten dog *breath* all in the air. I just sit there with my stopwatch and my pin, searching for the animal, who *can not* be found. Long hairs begin falling in the room on the flood and defecation. I'm still looking for a *corpus*. Eight hours after injection, this tiny, whimpering semblance of a dog appears, rubbing against my leg. He is *wild* with love. When I pick him up he hugs me with his paws around my neck. I take the dog down to the basement and put it in the hutch. When I come to see it the next morning, its little heart has burst."

"Same as last week," says Fleece, who sees that Herdee's ear is driven toward me, and food parts are hanging on his nether lip.

I stare into my cigarette coal. "I think that is what Man is: a ghost with amplified *functions*, a body stolen away by its functions, and discovered at last as a tiny cur, crazed with impossible affections."

"This man makes all of medicine his allegory, Herdee," says Fleece.

"No. I think he's actually brilliant at it. Unless he was quoting Shakespeare or somebody. You weren't quoting Shakespeare, were you? You keep it up, Monroe. We need people like you too."

"What do you mean, *too?* Kiss my ass."

A second goes by, then I pitch the live cigarette over the table into Herdee's lap. He rears up bowlegged and swats himself about the crotch. "This is something you'd expect from a . . . a . . . a!" but he won't finish. I'd love for him to tell me what I was. Yet he wouldn't quit stuttering.

"Nobody likes a thug," says Fleece, after Herdee has taken himself away. "That was a hell of a fine moral, but it was a stupid jerk-off story. Oh, it took in Herdee. It was worse than Edmund Spenser, for an allegory."

"I didn't ask you for literary criticism. I do all right on my own." I got up and left to dump my tray, but I caught Fleece looking, well, concerned about me. I think he was still feeling guilty about having drawn me into med school, and I confess I played with this guilty concern the few times I saw him.

The lined record manuals that I used on the job were rather splendid little logs with pale green sheets, faint rosy lines, all bound in fake purple morocco leather. The pages yearned for a Harry who would raise his pen and come down with everything he'd always wanted to say. There

286

were long vacant hours in the lab waiting on my dogs, hearing the eels slosh around in the tank across the way, where a team of two doctors from Chile and New Jersey were adding tiny solubles of this and that to see how the eels would take it. And I would write in the logs.

Fleece came down one afternoon when I was out for ping-pong in the basement. He was sitting on the stool reading the log, in my specially partitioned room which I was supposed to keep locked at all times, as the stipulation in the army grant said. I was working with the same #227 with the dogs, and the room was full of costly luxuries of research, like the five-hundred-dollar mixer, which was only a deluxe milkshake-making apparatus with a built-in heater to make solutions out of compounds that resisted being soluble, like #227. Fleece had a summer job in biochemistry, a couple of floors away, but I hadn't seen him much since June.

"What're these things on pages by themselves? Hey! These are *poems*, aren't they?" I reached for the log. Fleece was overjoyed; he had a smile on, the size of his waist. "This one is really creamy. Like 'diamonds lying in gravy,' huh? And this one is *dirty*, ha! Let me get on my muff-diver goggles. No, let me read it!" He turned a page. "An *acrostic* poem! A poem written in the shape of a trumpet! Gawd!"

This one did embarrass me. I tore the book away from him.

"What's the army going to think about your poems? Some of them you've got written right in the middle of a report. I guess you'll rip them out. Or you could just cross out the poems, or something. What *are* you going to do about them?—is what I mean. The 'diamonds in gravy' wasn't bad."

"You aren't supposed to be in here."

Fleece looked over at the black drugged dog in the corner. Dung and dried urine were all over the floor. "You want to go on observing what the nerve gas does to dogs for three more years, till you have the Ph.D.?"

"Hell, it's fine with me. I don't mind helping the army develop this. It's better than shooting a man with a bullet. They wake up *alive* . . . not a one of 'em has died on me yet."

"I'm not talking about the nerve gas. I mean *you*, do you

287

want to sit here watching what it does for three years? I just don't know, can hardly wonder, what a person like you would do with that Ph.D. in pharmacology when he got it."

"I know one wonderful thing about it. The army won't draft me into Vietnam while I'm here. If I get out I'm one-A."

"You'd go if they drafted you?"

"Sure!" I said. That was in the days when I thought they were bringing in American soldiers to help shoot communist fanatics who were blowing up children on school buses and walking into harmless restaurants in Saigon with explosives strapped to their backs. I don't mean the Viet Cong never did that. I mean that at the time, I thought that was all the war amounted to. My dream was that, if they got me to Saigon, even unwillingly, I would see some skinny bastard trying to place a bomb under a school bus full of children and be possessed with enough knowledge about my machine gun to sight on and scatter that champion all over South Vietnam; that the children in the bus, helpless darling little black eyes, would blow kisses to me, and I would show them the wizened smile of old democracy on the march, reloading. A simple dream, taken right out of the movies. But that's what I had in my mind. One boy, Anderson, had been drafted right out of the pharmacology graduate program by the army; Anderson was slow, squat, and had bad vision. If they wanted him, I knew they were thinking about me. I'd thought about the draft a good bit.

"Monroe, you've got to get out of here. I *know*. There's nothing here for you."

I'd known that too, for three or four months. But it was hard to quit. Things were rather easy in the department. Everyone smiled at everyone, as a matter of form. We had thousands of dollars of equipment around us, and there was a technician, Jimmy, who could make any harebrained dream of an experiment into a reality—glycerinated guinea pig uterine fibers, chick embryos, damn the cost. There were two secretaries transmitting it all into publication, reading the earphones of the pocket-size tape recorders: "Caffeine on Rat Tongue" and " 'Retreating' Magnesium in Rabbit Skeletal Muscle Suspensions Treated with Violin Lacquer." It had all the hum of a factory, and I was sure I'd be cast out as a Ph.D. within the decade.

But I knew the day I walked out a Ph.D., I would drive

home, hear the old man call me Dr. Monroe, then come back to the lab and shoot myself full of #227 itself, and let them watch me shudder, faint, and piss. Or might as well. I hated every minute of every effort of every bit of what I was doing, when I wasn't writing poems in the log.

4 / Christmas Drummers

I have to back up in that year several months and tell about the first Christmas I did not go home to Dream of Pines. The radiator on my T-bird had rusted out, I could drive it for twenty minutes before steam came out of the hood, but this wasn't the only reason I didn't go home to see my brothers, my sister, my nephews and my nieces. It pained me not to be there. I thought about the mistletoe way up in the oak trees around the house; I could smell the spice of the pine needles. My sister had a new infant boy I'd never seen. To the truth, they all cared about me dearly and I'd failed in med school so quickly, I just couldn't face them. My failures had all been vague before, but now I had one, an expensive one, as definite as a wrecked Oldsmobile. At the time, I was so low, I can only look back and congratulate myself on one thing: I was not carrying the pistol around with me any more. Even though I wore the sinister reptilian coat.

Gad, what to do? All was aimless. I went down to Wright's, where Silas worked, and played a few records in the booths. I watched Silas, who stayed busy being himself. I admired his energy. He watched out for drab and puny girls entering the store. Instantly, he was their helper. He would make a date with them right on the floor, perhaps selling them a record as he did it. The girls with dry hair and impure complexions, the girls wearing glasses with rims upswept like steer horns. Once, I saw him put his hand on the shoulder of an especially odd girl, and came out of the booth.

"That girl was damn near a pygmy!"

"Hands off," Silas warned me. "All mine."

One afternoon a mulatto with flint-like patches under his eyes walked in and went straight to the revolving rack where the band scores were. It was Harley Butte. He had aged. His wife was with him, and his four boys. The wife was his same color. She looked pleasant, but was somewhat old before her time. The boys were of a fresher pumpkin color. They kept around the mother. Silas saw them and rushed over to draw a piano bench out for some of them to sit on. I was in the glass booth and heard nothing. I only saw Silas mouthing at them, with words of great courtesy, and saw the woman pull the baby boy up in her lap. The baby boy wanted to climb up in the showcase of the window and touch the drum set, an exotic collection from Slingerland all bright with an oyster and pearl finish. I had an impulse not to come out of the glass booth and show myself to Harley. I don't understand why I just watched him as long as I did. All I know is, it seemed proper and cozy in the booth, hearing nothing, and it took almost a revolutionary effort for me to open the door and give him my hand.

"Where's your band?" I said.

"And what the hell're *you* doing here?" said Harley. "I been looking for you on TV. Everybody likes those Beatles. I thought you mighta got in with them."

"It's been a long time. I've been in med school."

"Who told you to do that?" He seemed angry.

"On my own. I haven't played my horn for three years."

"What'd they tell you in college?"

"I told him, Harley. He was playing good trumpet," Silas jumped in.

"I know he was playing good trumpet. He got a scholarship on playing his trumpet." He hung down his arms, disappointed, disappointed in me almost to the point of wrath. "I'll bet somebody told you music doesn't usually make money. Yeah, I've heard that enough times, them telling me."

To change the subject, I asked Harley what brought him to town. He said there was a parade on Capitol Street this afternoon. He didn't think much of the parade. It was a penny-ante affair with a Negro Santa Claus in it. In fact, he'd put his foot down, saying he could not drag the Gladiators off to *every* occasion and anybody's parade. He said it was

290

his opinion that this practice would dilute the class of his band. But the principal of Beta Camina said he was wrong. The principal told him, "Your true school spirit has been tested and you have received a negative grade." The principal said, Well then, *he'd* walk with the band this time. Harley replied he didn't care about the walking in the white suit and that business, but it was still his band. The principal told him future events would determine that. Then the principal was in his own white uniform and helmet—which he had been hiding in his closet for months—fast as a wink. He told Harley that he might redeem his school spirit by, certainly, traveling to the parade with the Gladiators, directing them as to what music, in what order, they were playing—since the principal did not quite yet comprehend all the details like that—and walking on the sidewalk with the band, primarily to spy out for the threat of that lunatic white man who had pushed the child at him the last time he was in Jackson.

"I might go on back to the army," said Harley. "You don't get cut in the back."

"Ah! *Not* the army, man," said Silas.

"I liked the army. Everybody gave such a damn. More people were honest. I think you meet a better breed of people in the army." He looked awfully tired around the eyes then. He thumbed the music on the stand dismally. Beyond him I saw his wife and kids, all of them sitting patiently except the baby. He wanted to get at those drums.

"I don't think I know your wife," I said.

"That's Miriam." He made no move to introduce us.

"You have good music here." Harley suddenly pulled out a band piece called "Charlemagne." Lower on the page was the composer's name: *H. J. Butte.* "This is yours truly." I examined the score. It was a march, full of runs. In the margins were directives; I should say imperatives, with exclamation points, and inside the cover was a short, exhorting essay on how this piece must be played. The publisher was a New York firm.

"I can't think right off of any band that could *cut* this," I said.

"My band can cut it," said Harley.

He said goodbye. The family arose and followed him. "Get little Harley, John Philip," the wife said. The older boy took the baby's hand and led him out the door.

291

After they left, a tubby clerk came up and straightened the music on the revolving stand.

"Were you having a family reunion with that nigger?" he said.

"How well is 'Charlemagne' moving?" Silas asked. "That nigger *wrote* 'Charlemagne.' "

"Well, nobody is buying it. One band director was interested in it. But he said it was too difficult. And I no more believe that nigger wrote it than I believe the moon is the North Wind's cookie."

When the parade began, Silas and I went out and found a place next to a lamp post. There was only a thin crowd. A bum leaned against the post itself, taking stock of the two leading floats. Behind them, where we couldn't see, a band was playing "Silent Night" in march time. The bum turned around. He was tickled pink.

"Nigras!" he said. He was smoking the hell out of a roll-your-own and his eyes were wide as clocks.

"God damn!" shouted Silas. He'd just caught the wind off the bum. I'd been holding my breath.

"I might use tobacco, but I would not take the name of the Lord my God in vain," said the bum.

"Move out," said Silas. The bum drifted away, protesting. "Look at the creeps and yokels gawking at the parade. They all think it's so very amusing. Look at those goddam Central High hoodlums giggling," Silas demanded.

"Wait. Just wait a bit." I heard, or felt, the shudder of a certain drum corps putting into action a hundred yards away. "Wait for the big green band."

"Who is that?" he asked me. "That's *him,* that's who it is! And that girl." I looked, and right across the street, on the corner, was Catherine. She had seen me and was waving timidly now. Uncle Peter stood by her. He was squinting and lifting himself up on his toes, with the cane rammed behind him on the sidewalk. I felt disarmed without my cosmetic spectacles, but I had my beard as usual.

"Yeah, I know him. I know you, old snake. He's looking at us, Monroe. I wonder if that cockhead remembers me. I'll drop something on *your* head, buddy!" Silas shouted across the street at him. Luckily, for me, a band was close on us and the shout was unavailing; as the band passed I jerked Silas back.

"Shut up, shut up!"

292

"He better watch it. I'll crown him. I'll lay some kind of dent in that buckaroo hat for him."

The next band was Harley's. I nodded wisely.

"Gawdamighty! Tremendous!" yelled Silas.

The yokels along the street cringed back a bit and looked askance lonesomely. This thrilled Silas. He threw out his arms and greeted the band with his outstretched chest. I didn't recognize what the band was playing, at first. It was somehow, in a clashing, agonizing way, Moorish and Christian both: medieval feast music. Then I knew it was "Charlemagne"—gloomy in its brass, in minor key, harsh and radiant in its woodwinds, with a crowning tinkle of bell lyres at the top, all of it lifted up by a whirlpool of bass, trombone, and drum muscle. Then I picked out an odd sound: tambourines. I kept listening for the Sousa. It wasn't there.

"Magnificent!" shouted Silas, as we began walking. He was right. In front, on the other side, strode the principal in the white uniform and helmet. Now this man could *walk*. Was he smug and imperial.

"That Ethiopian's having fun, ain't he?" This was Harley talking to me. He was walking along too. Some ways in back of him were his wife and boys, walking too, but slower. The baby boy was toddling vigorously, with an apple in his hand. The band cut off with a grand weird chord. The drummers rolled like an engine that had cranked up underground and was going to drive off with the whole city.

"That 'Charlemagne' is really a horse. That's the best thing I ever heard on the march," I told Harley.

"I've made a hundred and five dollars on it. It's the best thing I ever heard, too. And to this date, that's how much . . . uh oh! Lookit there." We'd gotten out some twenty feet in front of the band. There were Peter, Catherine, and a skinny man with a potbelly in a white shirt, tie, plastic penholder at the pocket. A clerkish greaser, he was. They were all walking parallel with us on the other side of Capitol Street. Peter had his eye on the man in a white uniform. We were getting into a thicker crowd of Negroes on the sidewalks now. Peter touched his cane to the backs of people to get a clean view, moving them aside, thrusting his head and wide hat over the curb.

Harley got a pert, scandal-bent look on his face. "You don't reckon he'll use that stick on our principal?"

"I'd be surprised. He—" At that time, Peter reached the

293

cane out and tapped the principal on the arm. Just tapped him, just a flick of cane, so as to make the man look his way. The principal didn't notice, though. He was blowing the whistle and nodding to the drum major as he made inept directing motions with his arms, wanting the band to play. At last the drum major understood and the band was into an intimidating new march.

Silas rushed up to me, really furious, throwing his arms up and down. "Did that son of a bitch hit him? Did you see?!" I didn't see Silas run back up the sidewalk and borrow the apple from Harley's baby. Next thing I knew he was in front of us at the curb, making his way through the Negroes. We were at the intersection of Farrish Street, and there seemed to be hundreds of tall men in hepcat clothes around us.

"Don't let him do that," Harley said in my ear. He had a firm grip on my arm. The Negroes were backing away from Silas, who was walking in the gutter. When I reached him and looked across the street, of course it was Peter, his niece, and the other man, walking ahead of the band too, Peter studying the man in white. Silas threw the apple at him with everything he had, and it was rising when it got to him. The apple missed Peter but struck Catherine directly in the face and flew to pieces. A scream went up. I caught a view of her down on her knees, holding her face, just as the band came between. Silas turned toward me, hands on his hips, eyes down. We, Silas and I, passed Harley and his family on the sidewalk. Harley would not look at Silas. He was gesturing in anger to his wife. Then we passed them. I saw two policemen running down the sidewalk on the other side, toward Peter's vicinity. There was commotion over there. The last rank of the band went by and I saw the enormous hat waving back and forth, and heard, even over the band, a man screeching. Then an arm went up, pointing to the Negroes across the street from it. The potbellied thin man ran across the street in front of a float. Then came a cop waddling after him. Whoever the man in the white shirt was, he drove into a group of tall hepcats, and they gave for a second. Then the cop drew up, and suddenly jumped to one side. Somebody in the crowd had laid one on the fierce boy and he was hurtling out in the parade like somebody trying to lift off and fly by running backwards. He fell flat out under another float—snowy-looking flannel hanging

294

all over it—and the rear wheel of the float rolled over him. It was only a flat-bed trailer being towed behind a car, but there were several Negro girls in evening dresses sitting on it, and my stomach sank when I saw one side of the flat lift up and unseat a couple of the girls. The cop went back out in the street toward the, well, at least, outraged form. The big Santa Claus float rolled down and obscured my view. "You got to go back down and—" I turned to Silas. He was gone. He hadn't seen any of this. I walked back up to Wright's.

"Hero," I said to him.

"You know damn well I wasn't throwing at the girl."

"You left a lot of innocent people standing around back there."

"You wanted me to hang around and be arrested? I told you about that son of a bitch and what I saw him doing. I'm fed up with the people in this state like that walking around free. He hit the man with that cane, didn't he? Tell me, did he hit him?"

"No. He touched him with it."

"*Touched* him? Well what kind of touch was that? You want people touching you with a fucking stick?" Then he went on, reviewing me again on what he'd seen Peter doing at Oxford during the Ole Miss riots over James Meredith; the night Kennedy made his appeal to Mississippi on television, the night they set cars on fire and students attacked the Lyceum Building, where they had the FBI hemmed in; the night the tear gas flew and one student would have driven a bulldozer against the door of the Lyceum except he ran out of gas; the night a jukebox-supplier and a Canadian journalist were murdered by unknown snipers; when the local reporter said FBI men had attacked a girls' dorm with tear-gas guns, when the Mississippi Highway Patrol was indignant; when General Edwin Walker was alleged to have led a crowd of student quasi-lancers against the FBI; the night Silas missed, driving into town in the early morning of the next day, seeing something curious on an overpass of the railroad between the town and the campus. Parked his car and walked up there. He walked up to the scene of a group of busy adolescents with a grown man ordering them around. Some of them were scouting the traffic and others were moving crossties toward the rail. It was still gray and foggy. "Here's one!" one of the kids yelled. The older man clapped his hands and directed them to get the crosstie on the rail. "Be ready!" he said. It was Colonel Lepoyster, using his hat that way, sleepless, as at Cold Harbor or some other perimeter above Richmond, 1864, reduced to boys and no ammunition. Coming under the bridge was an olive truck with canvas over the trailer. The boys dropped the crosstie over the rail and the huge beam fell on the trailer. Then the other group dropped another crosstie on the windshield of the truck as it emerged. The crosstie hit end down and plunged into the cab as if into water. The truck roared across the wrong lane of the road and smacked into a telephone pole. The pole broke and fell back on the canvas, full of wires. The truck rolled over on its side. There was a cheer on the rails. A man with a star on his helmet put his head up out of the cab window. The soldiers who weren't hurt were angry, and squirmed out the back. Colonel Lepoyster told the teenagers to run, and they did, down the railroad in both directions and off into the high weeds. The man in the starred helmet had a .45 in his hand but was still dizzy.

"This is the Mississippi National Guard!" cried the man. "Who would do this to us?" He looked up at the rail embankment; his face was bloody. Peter turned to Silas with a cowed, sick face.

"I thought they were the United States Army. I didn't know they were the National Guard. Those boys are from Mississippi," he said.

Silas went down the hill to report to them who was responsible for that crosstie being dropped through the windshield. By the time he and the man with the .45 lumbered back up, Peter was gone into the weeds too.

This was the story. There was no reason Silas should know the final end of it, that it was General Creech, Fleece's stepfather, who had the bloody face and the .45. Fleece had seen the scar from the windshield glass which the general still carried, and I had not told Fleece, either, about who was leading the troops who dropped the crosstie.

I was concerned enough on my own and of my own. Did not tell them something else: that I'd been taking out Catherine roughly every two months, until this last three months, for two years. I'd seen her the first time in maybe an overlong time, out there on Capitol Street.

296

5 / Last Date

What do I say? The very same night I fell to dreaming
about her. I dreamed about her Christmas night; dreamed
one of those mesmerizers, where every sense you have is
sharp-edged and you sleepwalk toward the *déjà-vu* as if the
palm of a hand is pushing you from behind. You couldn't
tell the sex of the hand. It could be Geronimo's hand; it
could be Catherine's. I awoke with my tongue on my cold
pillow. In three weeks I was at their house, after telephoning. Peter answered the door.

"I've been buried in my books."

"You do look haggard. Come in. We saw you on Capitol
Street. I was about to make a call to you, but she wouldn't
let me." The place was dark. He led me through the den.
The glass peeped through the break of the curtains. I
walked over and drew one of them back, wanting to look
through the glass and see what one could see outside.

"We don't open those," said Peter. I sat down next to the
hearth.

"Where is she?"

He hung over me and said nothing for a moment. What I
caught of his face was something like a Santa Claus who
had been assaulted and shaved and who was angry.

"Don't stare at her nose. She had it broken playing vol-
leyball at the college." The lie clung about the room for a
while; he didn't follow it up immediately.

"You know, I really covet your freedom," he said. "You
sit there without one enemy in the world, enjoying your
youth and your beard. Soon a doctor of medicine." This lie
clung about the room with the other one. He clutched one
of the curtains, and kneaded it, looking out the split
through the glass which he'd just told me not to look out.
"You would never understand the term *lover*, would you? I
can't hope you could ever comprehend the term *lover*. No

297

time. Too fast a pace." I believe he had been making tiny, almost undetectable loin-movements against the curtain, but this may have been only his agitated way. "My wife never had even a high school degree. She had an endowed body which was timid, but she learned to speak with it. She *had* no speech until I came to her. She was not a being until I came. She learned a dialect in the language of love. Months, it took. She would moan out her own name, *Catherine!*, so happily when at last her praise and wonder thrilled up. Then she led me, *me!* into a humility, an immersion, not foreseen by one so proud as I. She "—Catherine walked into the kitchen, but he did not see her, and she receded, but only just out of sight—"saw me below her, trying to throw my failing wet bridges, my webs, up to connect with her being, having as much as burned my own bridges of the practical world. It was then she betrayed me. 'You have to eat,' she would say. The niggers might wander through the yard and see us. What a cold stare from her, at the last. What dry mechanical lifting up of her fingers on the hem of her skirt. But," he came away from the curtain, not looking at me, though, "*this* Catherine will finish college soon. Did you know that? She'll have some education to appreciate the one who takes her."

He might have had me in a spell, almost to the point where I saw his own old brown script on the letters, except I'd seen that unconscious mincing hunch against the curtains and knew Catherine was standing back in the shadows of the kitchen, hearing.

"Lock has come," he said. I lit a cigarette and shook the match. If he would look my way I would signal that she was back there. The fact is, I *never* saw the man eye to eye. "You are far and away the most appealing, with your medical school."

"That isn't necessarily paradise," I said.

"Would you tell her about Lock for me?"

"Tell her what?"

"Tell her Lock will not—"

Catherine walked right in and cut him off. Her nose did look a fraction flat. What a shame. It was a nice nose. She still looked fetching. She wore a green and yellow plaid dress. Her legs were very lovely in stockings. She had gold rings in her ears, after the pierced-ear fad with coeds. On her feet were brown patent-leather shoes with one strap

298

over the top of her foot. This was similar to the way Bet Henderson dressed, and Bet was always the precursor of style.

Peter simply walked out of the room.

I had in mind taking her to the Subway, a night club in the basement of the Robert E. Lee Hotel where you could take in your own bottle, buy mixers from the bar, and every now and then catch a good band, a soft one, so you could talk to your lover over the drinks and look around at a sort of wooden purple cloister. I'd been faithful to this girl, in my way. I'd had no other dates. We sat down and I ordered the soda for the Scotch I'd brought. She said she'd like that. When she got her glass, she sank down in the chair in that bent slouch she always had in the car. This posture robbed her of almost anything romantic. I heard her mouth make a slight sucking noise as she was drinking.

"You heard Peter tell about him and his wife," I said.

"Peter, he's so sweet to me. I knew his wife, it was my blood aunt, she got some notion where she wouldn't be normal with him in bed. He turned her out. I don't blame him. He gave her everything and she wouldn't let him go the normal way at all."

"He told you that?"

"Change the conversation to another topic."

"He told me not to notice your nose. What's wrong with it? I don't see anything."

"You get me into daylight and it shows all right. The niggers threw an apple and it broke my nose. I saw you at the parade and you waved? It happened on down the street. We got down amongst a bunch of niggers and one of 'em across the street threw a apple. Yes sir."

We drank more than a pint together of the fifth I'd brought, Catherine taking a drink more often than I did. The band tonight was fine, keeping guard over the mellowness, even when they played bop. I noticed that the trumpet man was getting away with a lot of bad notes playing through a steel mute.

"I can play a trumpet about four times better than the man in the band."

"Hotty toddy," she said. I had not expected this hostility. She went on to say she had noticed a lot of snoots in this place; she said she wouldn't have picked this place if she'd

299

known what it was. She enjoyed the Scotch, though, thank you.

I was all planned to tell her how she was wrong, how I knew the person who'd thrown the apple, when she came out with this, looking at the ceiling, rather smugly: "I've had Scotch and soda before with another person." She wanted me to inquire about this person. It was so tacky I couldn't let it pass. Also, I knew who she meant.

"You mean Gillis Lock? I saw him with you at the parade, didn't I? I thought you detested him."

"I never said that."

"You implied it." She drew even lower down, looking surly. I don't think she understood the word *implied*. "At school Lock was known as a *merde accompli,* if you know what I mean." This drove her into a rage of silence. I confess I was only pursuing this game out of the rotten delight of seeing her cringe even more than she usually did.

"He doesn't think all that much of you either, brother. He said you are a over-interlectuall playboy that thinks of yourself all the time."

"That son of a bitch never saw me that I know of."

We left.

I parked in the driveway at Peter's; the garage with its false steeple was above the nose of the car. I thought she would jump right out of the car immediately, but she didn't. She sat up in good posture and crossed her arms over her breasts. She had said nothing, but her anger had brought her out of that perpetual crouch. It would have been good if I could tell her how pleasing she was, out of that slouch, but I couldn't. I could imagine her as all sorts of pomped-up lovely women of thirty.

She was looking out the other window and I put my mouth to the back of her neck. She uttered a crooning sound and made her neck unavailable by bending back her head. I sought her cheek then, kissing as much of it as I could, and I put our lips together for a few seconds before her hands reached my chest and pushed off.

"That beard don't feel good, unh-uh! No hand stuff either. Who you think you are? You don't see me often enough to think you can do that."

So she called me to a halt. Again, I expected her to jump out of the car. But she didn't.

300

"What're you staying here for? Why don't you run on in the house to Peter? I'll bet I'm boring you, humh?"

She just sat there, stiff as a bust. "Run in the house!" I told her. All right, I did jam my hand up to her thigh, searching for the silk. She giggled.

"Are you giggling?" I asked her. I opened my hand and one finger touched a string. I had no idea what it was. Then she pushed my hand off and straightened up.

"I'm sorry," I said. "Have you had an operation, or something?"

"Don't be slimy. Them snappers out at the ninth grade that I practice-teach on, they're slimy. You haven't ever been slimy around me before. Being tricky-devious on me."

I was outraged. "That was Tampax, wasn't it? Does he buy that too? Your panties, your toenail polish, your Tampax."

"Okay, Uncle Peter did buy the panties and he gaven me the money to buy the unmentionable item I have on too. I don't feel shamed. I say I have on these things and I'm a lucky girl to say it, in case anybody was so nosy to ask me, if they wanted to pry out those kind of secrets. He give me . . . everything I am now." She looked at me cool and proud.

"So go on and get in bed with him," I said. I took the Cutty Sark bottle out of the well and brought it around to my mouth. "Get out of the car. Go on." But she stayed as I drank.

"You're a little bit slimy but you're really a silly old boy. We could've had a lot more fun."

I pretended I was drinking, swigging it neat. I never could do this. Even pretending, my eyes watered up and my throat snarled up, protesting. She asked for the bottle and I handed it away. In the corner of my eye I saw her plant it on her lips and give herself a large douse of it.

"Harry!" she cried to me. Her voice was choked and faint. "I'm on fire! Don't let me throw up!" I clapped my hand over her mouth. She twisted under it wildly, and I bore down harder with it. She quit squirming finally, opened her eyes, and nodded. I took my hand off.

"Oh, now my heart's like a electric blanket around it. I wish I could feel like this all the time. I feel so sleepy but I want to do just everything."

I moved in and put my arm on the seat behind her. "The

301

most wonderful thing in the world is the meeting of two bodies, in the night," I said. I was tight as a coot. What did I have on my mind?

"You silly old boy."

"Don't be afraid when I touch you. It is a disease to be afraid of being touched."

"If it's a free country you can still pick out the one you want to touch you, isn't it?"

"Give me your lips."

"You thought I was waiting on that? I know who I want to kiss me. You imagine you going to teach me a lot of stuff, treat me like a *virgin* that sponged up ever word you said, but if you think I'm a virgin, you're pitiful."

Now, one o'clock, she got out of the car and slammed the door. As she passed the fender, a light went on in the house. I put my head out the window. "Come here." She came back and dragged her foot around.

"I just wonder if dear old Peter honors your monthlies in any way or just humps on through with no vacations. Just watch it. I happen to know that somebody is going to get him. You wouldn't want that moment to find you . . ." Her face snapped up.

"I lie!" I cried. I crank the car and backed out, thinking never to see her again.

Driving the T-bird to Mother Rooney's, I had the sense of someone wanting to be let out of the car when I stopped for the lights. I do not invite ghosts; so far I've never needed them. But this was real. I thought I might still be imagining Catherine sitting in the seat by me. But when I parked in front of the rooms, it had not diminished and it was no afterimage of Catherine, I knew. I reached over and opened the opposite door. Of course there was only silence. Then a voice spoke in my head: "That wasn't even mean. That was petty. I'm leaving." Ah, Geronimo! I begged him to give me the definitions distinguishing *mean* from *petty*. I didn't quite know. I pronounced the name, *Ge Ron I Mo*. Two iambs, rising at the last with a sound which might be blown forever through some hole in a cliff in Arizona by the wind. A name which in itself made you want to cast off, even being landlocked, and kick off the past history that sucked you down. This wasn't petty, this Indian, Apache. I knew *that*. Oh, I knew that at the last he joined the Dutch Reformed church, grew watermelons, and peddled the bows and arrows that he made. But at the very last, he'd been kicked out of the church for gambling, he'd had six wives, and died of falling off a wagon, drunk, in his eighties. And that was *not* petty, whatever. But I was petty. All the letters of *Monroe* could be found in his name, a coincidence which would have bored him extremely, as did most language and English especially. He'd give a belch and a yawn.

I walked to my bed feeling like a tick, a something which scuttled around in the sheets, waiting on the body of a true warm man.

6 / So In July

The afternoon I quit the pharmacology school, I rode out to the Ross Barnett Reservoir, north of Jackson. I wore my lab coat. It was a windy day, so I kept the coat on. I'd called her, asked her out, and she seemed happy to hear from me in a remote, incredulous way. I wanted to say at least one more thing to her. I wanted to reclaim myself from being the tick I was that night with her. But she said her daddy and mother were up from Mobile spending the week with them and that they were out at the Reservoir every night till nine and then they were up to eleven cleaning the fish. That was all her daddy wanted to do while he was in Jackson. I asked where they fished, and she told me.

I parked just below the dam and walked down the hill to the spillway. Through my sunglasses, the water was a foggy boiling green, hissing down the dam wall, pooling in the deep basin of rocks, and rushing down in the Pearl River bed. The pool water was full of suds. Boats full of fishermen wallowed around at the foot of the dam; other people were fishing from the big rocks on the shore.

I saw her with her family. Only the old man was fishing. Her mother sat on a piece of slag a few feet from the water, watching the man. He had a cane pole and flicked it toward the dam, trying to get the cork way out. He leaned over the water. Her mother was jabbering at him and motioning with her hand. Catherine sat up the rise and in back of them on a piece of slag rock. She sat with her arms around her knees. She had on sky-blue tapered pants and a white blouse. Down here, five-thirty in the evening with the vapor from the dam blowing on you like a sea breeze, it was cool, as if you'd found a pit of chill in the smoldering heat. I made it down the rocks unnoticed and looked over her shoulder. Her bare forearm was frail, a little sunburned, and covered with chilly-bumps, and the downy hair on it was erect. This moved me. I came up right next to her. She'd been out here five afternoons straight.

"Hello," I said.

"You silly old boy," she said. She didn't turn around. But she knew who was behind her. I sat down by her. I asked her how the fishing was going. She said her daddy had caught a lot of white perch all week; that he was fishing with minnows.

"You need this coat. You can keep it," I said. I took off the lab coat and draped it on her.

"Thank you, honey," Catherine said. She'd never called me that before. She was never so easy with me. I asked her what kind of time she was having. She said, "I do love the water. I don't care about catching fish out of it like my daddy does. I like the waterfall on the dam. We eat supper out here and everything."

"It beats the heat."

The water slapped down loudly just a few yards away. You couldn't hear things the first time they were said. She pulled me up so I could speak right in her ear. I'd never known her to do anything like this. She pulled the lab coat close to her and nestled her cheek against the shoulder of it. She turned her face toward me, her hair blowing. "Harry the doctor. With that beard you look cut out to be a famous doctor on a rocket ship to Mars. With those sunglasses."

In this rocky valley where it was so shady and cool, I didn't care if it never changed. I asked her if her mother and daddy ever turned around or if they watched the cork like that all week. I asked her didn't she want to introduce me to her folks. They were just a few feet down from us. She said she didn't want to. I asked her, What if they turn

304

around? She seemed scared, and in reply she took off my coat and handed it back.

Over the noise of the falling water, I could barely hear her mother talking. But she had been harganguing the old man ever since I'd been there. He had been moving out farther into the water, holding the pole in a strained way. He wore leather shoes and the water was over his ankles. The back of his head was balding in a messy way, with gray and brown strands losing out to pale splotches of scalp. The woman stood up, and I took the hint from Catherine and moved off as if I was not with her. Her mother's cheek, the left one, was burned, I mean fire-burned, from some accident, and the other was covered with tiny freckles. Her teeth were brown, and she was clamping down on a Pall Mall—the pack was in her hand—one eye shut to the smoke. She saw me standing twelve feet or so from Catherine. I was trying to get a grip on the rock incline. I'd put my coat back on, and I was showing an innocent disregard for Catherine.

"Arrrrrrr!" the woman said as she sat down by her daughter. Then she broke wind, helplessly. Almost simultaneously, she cranked her face toward me to stare and check on my reaction. She had a hurt look. I gazed away like a statue. She drew her shoe down, scraping the rock in front of her to make a fartlike noise so if I'd heard I would understand that this is what made the noise when she sat down.

"Is he a Fish and Game man?" I heard her ask Catherine. She reached in the sateen high school athletic jacket on her and pulled out a paper. She said overloudly to Catherine, that in case I was, here was the fishing license if I was looking for it. She said that it was paid for. He wouldn't see it any other way, she said. Uncle Peter had paid for it. She hollered it out, so that if I knew the man—and I ought to know the man—I would know who bought the thing; hollering with pride. Then she began mumbling with Catherine, keeping an eye out for me. I saw Catherine's forehead nodding. Then her mother flew into a shrieking declamation, which seemed to be her natural style.

"Royce—you know what he doin'? Yo daddy doin'? He said he saw a normost basst feedin' on the toper thet water a piece out an' yo daddy is wadin' out on thet drop to catch 'im. He ain't usin' no minner. He usin' a live brim on his hook that we caught when we was catchin' all them little white perch. He sez he want to catch somethin' *big* an' this ud be a perfet vacation. I been a-tellin' him git back in off thatere dropoff. He caint swimb atall."

All this while Catherine, leaning backwards of her mother, was appealing to me with her hands and her eyes to please leave. I pretended not to understand her. I watched the old man.

He had something on the pole; he had something big, too; it was running back and out. The line was zipping around, and the pole bent like there was an automobile under the water. The man backed up, but the fish was too big to allow that. Then the man was pulled in, slipping down the grade of the pool to where his hips were underwater. He wanted the fish very much. His head bowed to the fish every time it moved. I wanted to see that creature myself.

The man lurched backward into the shallows in a decisive move. He fell backward all of a sudden, throwing the pole up in the air. His head hit a rock on the shore, and his back followed it, giving out a sundering thud you could hear over the sound of the dam. I saw that, but my eye was still on the pole. It hit the water, stood up like a limber weed, and was drawn down, waving in circles, until the butt itself went under. I waited for it to pop up, but it never did. The fishermen in the nearest boat paddled over to the spot where it disappeared. The pole did not come up again. The men in the boat looked over at us full of awed respect.

The old man lay with his feet in the water. There was blood on the rock under his neck. His wife and his daughter were over him on both sides. I walked down and knelt at his head. He was out cold, but he was breathing big and healthy.

"Hold one of his eyes open and let me look at the pupil," I said. The wife did this and I saw that the pupil was dead to light; the tadpole didn't jump. The man had a pretty face like a blind queen.

"Royce. Royce. Royce," his wife repeated. Then she asked me, "You mean you are a doctor right here on the spot?"

"The man's . . . serious," is all I could stay. I was trying to make all the few facts I knew stick together into something. It was a disgraceful position to be in. From the facts I knew, I couldn't come up with anything.

She picked up his head in her arms. Catherine clutched one of his hands. He had groaned yet, even. Catherine hadn't looked my way. I was glad of that. I didn't care for her to see me again in the lab coat. She didn't know I'd busted out of med school, of course; didn't know I was a fraud right here on the spot, had come to prove that I must be remembered as something besides the tick I was that night in the car. To be mean, to be kind, to be anything else. I hung my head. The thought came to me that I had not touched the man.

"It could be a concussion," I blurted out.

"You mean Royce he won't know my face when he come out of it?" Mrs. Wrag was breaking down. She began singing "Won't know my face!" as a refrain, and hugged Royce's head up and down.

Then Catherine looked at me sadly and jerked her head toward the incline. She wanted me out of there. "Not necessarily amnesia," I said, trying to save myself from ineptness.

Catherine shrieked, in a voice very much like her mother's, "Don't sit there *writin' a essay* about it!"

A speedboat rammed up on the rocks beside Mr. Wrag's feet. It came in almost full blast. It was red and white and greasy. A concerned man scorched by the sun stood in the bow. "Doctor Ainsworth is fishing down in the river," he shouted, pointing backwards, studying me. He and his buddy in the speedboat had scared the hell out of me. He crouched in the bow ogling Mr. Wrag shyly.

"Well, go get him, you dumb greaser!" I shouted, rising. He stumbled back in the boat, still eyeing my coat and beard as he fell. His buddy reversed the boat, and they blew down the river leaving a swath in the water like the river was jumping apart.

Mrs. Wrag had recovered a bit. "That man wudn't a nigger. He was a white man with a suntan. He wudn't a nigger." She spoke rather carefully at me.

Mr. Wrag woke up. "I'll kill you . . . you hawrble bitch. You come down there an' trip me up, didn you? I'll see you dead. You seen the fish I had, couldn you see? You come down there an' trip me up." He cut his words moistly— some of his teeth were missing—and struggled up toward his wife's face. She still cradled his head in her arms. He fell back spent, and she looked beyond me cracked open

307

with a smile of purple gums and brown teeth that barked and snapped for glee at the sky. Down the river, I saw the speedboat appear in the bend, wallowing and skipping toward us, with a third man in the middle.

"You *leave*," said Catherine to me. This was easy to do. As I walked up the incline, I heard her shrieking, like her mother. "Who *was* you? Who *was* you? What did you think you *was*?" I wasn't certain till I glimpsed back that she was shrieking at me.

In the parking place I leaned on the little new Volkswagen that Peter no doubt had bought for her. In the backseat were some overturned worm boxes. There was also a styrofoam picnic box; but in the driver's seat there was a teacher's manual with an Eskimo Pie stick marking the page to which she'd read. Getting ready for those slimy snappers in junior high. Incredibly, she'd graduated.

I looked down the hill and observed the tiny group of them. Royce was sitting up. The red and white speedboat idled and rocked out in the shallows, raising smoke like an old car. The doctor got Royce to his feet, and the four of them began creeping up the rocks. Catherine put her hand to her eyes. She saw me. She brushed her arm back and forth as if dusting me off the hill. I believe I heard her shriek again.

So in July I saw her the last time.

I still think about that—perhaps—two minutes, when I saw her arms slightly sunburned and covered with goosepimples in the cool wind of the dam; the odd, sudden affection she had for me—"Honey"—and her shoulders in the lab coat draped on her, her hands crossing outside it, her pulling me nearer so I could hear what she said over the sound of the water; my own love for her delicate vulnerability reviving instantly, damn near tears. This surprising butterfly of sentiment with both of us—never mind what followed—I remember, even after the disasters, as one of the strangest interludes of my time.

I was absorbed for days in trying to forget the afternoon, forget them all, kick them off. I knew if I thought of it too much more, it would fall around my neck like a noose and hang me.

I had a letter to write. The old man, for one more semester of money. And I had to read the one he wrote back to me, and whatever the sum of the check enclosed, I'd bleed out the whole amount in pennies, nickels, and dimes of misery. Maybe I'd take a job and read books on the job. I had a way to go, had to take it. It seemed to be the last one.

Thinking of the old man, I read the Columbia University bulletin on the wad outside the English office at Hedermansever. My idea was to return and take the English hours I needed at Hedermansever to get into graduate school. Just slip into a graduate school come January. As for Columbia, I could imagine those mean bastards up there reading *Finnegans Wake* upside-down and beating you over the head with their pipes. But the old man would be proud of me up there. So I took down the address and some others and went to see the chairman. When school started in September, I'd reread my Bobbie Burns and rediscovered my hatred for Pope and Henry James, and was ready to make the last dash toward a profession.

One day I was reading "The Leech-Gatherer," stopped, smiled, and realized I'd forgotten Catherine, Peter, and the Wrags for three weeks.

7 / The Old Boys at Mother Rooney's

This is the fall that Fleece was leading his class as a sophomore at the med school, Silas was still the leading ass on Capitol Street—at Wright's—and I was accepted in graduate school. It was 1965, the year I got married and the year of a lot else.

Silas had taken a trip to Europe during summer. One thing he had done was force himself into an art class at the Sorbonne. Some group of artists there told him that the West was finished and that they spat on all Old World art because it was elitist. Silas caught a terrible cold in Spain which enabled him to spit on every church, icon, and masterpiece in southern Europe from a range up to twenty feet. This was really Silas's cookie.

"More to the point, Europe scared the hell out of you, didn't it?" said Fleece. Silas was thoughtful.

"That's true." Silas turned red and took the stairs up to his room.

"You got him," I said.

"What's wrong with the bastard? He's so mild."

A week or so later, late at night, I saw Silas come down the stairs through my room and slip down to Fleece's room. I heard Silas waking up Fleece, heard Fleece swearing. Then the light went on down there, and I could hear the low tones. I went to sleep while the tones kept on.

The next afternoon Fleece emerged into my room. I was reading *The Ambassadors* by Henry James for a report and was just about fainting with boredom. It was Saturday and Silas was gone.

"You want to know what he said to me last night?" I dropped the book. Bobby Dove looked rather feeble and ill. He sat on the bed.

"He woke me up to confess to me that he couldn't help it, he was in love with Bet. That he'd gone to Europe so as to forget her. He also wanted me to know that she seemed to be falling in love with him. He asked me if she'd told me she had gone out with him, and I said no, I hadn't talked to her in a week and a half. This was the time he was concerned about. 'I don't want to hurt you. I think a lot of you. But she seems to be coming over my way, Bob,' he said. I asked him why he thought she was falling for him. You know what he said? 'Because I have changed. I've learned to be humble.' I told him maybe this was the first time he'd ever been *pitied* by a woman. He's so sincere looking at me; this tribulating little smile on his mouth. I told him to get out."

"Did you call her?"

"I'm not going to call her. Sometimes I don't call her or see her for weeks. Some time ago we found out this made it all sweeter. That maybe it would never wear out if we kept it like so. She knows I always have a lot to do, and always will. What she does in her own time . . . I wouldn't be mad if she let the rich jerk-off buy her a couple of suppers. Me, I've bought Brenda the X-ray technician coffee more than a few times. But, Bet knows about that silly tool, the things he is, does, like dragging those mousy little drabs up to his room to hear them squeak over him; like bringing that drunk over as a gift to Mother Rooney. And now he says he's 'learned to be humble.' I'm sure the confession that at last he knows what a dipshit he is bowled her over." He smirked and stood up, with his hands at the small of his back, refreshed by the irony of it. Let me comment on how Fleece had changed, physically, in the last couple of years. He was twenty-six, was twenty pounds heavier than he was at Hedermansever, was less nervous, and had replaced the horn-rim glasses with some steel ones, which opened up his face, his bald high forehead, so that he looked like a less-cringing genius who would know what to do if, say, a fire broke out in his room. When he was sick, he was more like a healthy man who'd been knocked down temporarily than someone at rest in his natural disposition, as of old.

"Love," said Fleece. "And then marriage. We're married, Bet and me."

"When did you get married?"

"About at the first of last summer, out at the Alamo Plaza Motel Courts, which we've been to again several times. The ceremony went like this: I woke up with my hand on her nipple. She left the bed and went to the television and then got back in bed. She replaced my palm on her nipple, and on the television came a gospel show, the Blackwood Brothers, because it was Sunday morning. These boys were singing in earnest, the bass man with his moustache, the slick skinny man singing high, the blind man with sunglasses on piano. So holy, you know; they'd never made a cent out of doing this. 'I take this man,' she said, lifting up the sheets, 'while these men look on and sing.' Then she kicked the sheets back and raised her toes to the ceiling, and I enjoyed her, while she hummed with the quartet on TV with her eyes closed. I happened to be on my knees holding onto her ankles above me. It was the condition of being in an ascending chariot. I cherished the music I heard behind me and the music under me. Everyone agreeing, everyone celebrating."

"But no actual marriage certificate and so on," I said.

"What do you want?" I felt like a hated skeptic as he left. He'd taken his glasses off. Since his back was to me, I couldn't tell. But he was weeping or emoting in some way.

The next weekend Fleece was supposed to be in Houston, Texas. He'd told me he was going to fly over and witness some heart surgery by DeBakey and Cooley. Saturday

311

afternoon late I ate some hamburgers at the Krystal. When I came back to the room, going up the stairs through his quarters, I glanced down and saw him sitting in a wooden chair in the shadows by one of the octagonal windows. He hadn't made a sound. But he was following me with his eyes—otherwise, a manikin. I went on up. I knew he was in a bad state. It was something new and horrifying. I'd never seen him atrophy himself like this. I tried to convince myself to go down there, but couldn't. I watched his room grow dark as the night came on. I clicked my reading lamp on and took a book.

At ten-thirty, Silas and a girl eased onto the steps below. As they came up, I looked over the edge of my book to get a load of her. She had tousled hair. I expected her feet to be about where her waist was, as she kept coming, kept getting taller, behind Silas, who had one of her hands, leading her politely. She held her shoes in the other hand. I put the book in front of my face immediately when I saw the girl was Bet Henderson. I sank back on the bed.

"Harry looks asleep," she said.

"That's right. He's out for good."

"Look what you can see up here!" she said as they got to Silas's room.

I stared at the ceiling, wondering what Fleece was going through downstairs. If he was awake, he'd seen them. Silas shut the door at the top of my stairs. The two of them creaked on the boards above my head. There was a lot of weight up there. In a while I heard Silas's coffee percolator sighing.

There was a movement below in the dark of Bobby Dove's room, the sliding of a drawer. Then the crash of a shoe.

He came noiselessly up the stairs, one pause for every step. He gave the appearance of someone who had been laid out by the funeral home but was up and about, taking a breather from death—in complete black suit, white shirt, and maroon tie. He had given a brush stroke to his hair. There was a red spot on his crown where perhaps the brush had been drawn. He licked his lips on his way over to my bed. The fool was carrying that long-barreled .22 with both hands.

"I wonder where one might find a bullet or two in this

312

room," he whispered. "I pulled the trigger to test this thing. There isn't anything in it." I shook my head.

"Don't try to look wise at me."

"I'm just wishing I didn't have to be in the same room—my room—with a crazed person."

"Get out," said Fleece. He flickered a cold merriment behind the glasses.

"What's the suit for?"

"I'm going to Houston. I already bought the ticket. I have a feeling Houston is my kind of town."

The light went off in Silas's room, I saw through the underchink of the door. There was a stomp on the floor overhead. Then his bed wrenched. The merriment left Fleece's eyes. He tried to hold his face together in a sneer. But his glasses fell forward to the end of his nose, his eyes watered, and his mouth came apart with an intake of air. He dropped the gun on the bed.

"I know where the good one is," he said. He eased out my dresser drawer—had the gun, and it was loaded—before I could get off the bed. I stood up but made no advance. The way he was, I didn't think I should.

"I'm not going to shoot *you*. I'm not out of my mind, roomie, old Harry, believe me. This is the one," still softly, merrily again. "You realize I never have missed with this gun?"

"Crime is *wrong*," I got out. "No right to—"

"How do I look?" He pulled his lapels forward.

Above us, the light was on again. It had only been off a couple of minutes. We heard their voices. Then there was a crash on the floor. Fleece glared straight at me as if nothing had happened.

"Don't worry about me, man. You don't think I'd really *shoot* either one of those pitiful creatures up there? Would I go to the trouble? Those are two *sad* people up there."

"I think maybe she just *hit* him," I said.

"Look me in the eye and see if you think I don't know what I'm doing."

I did, and he did look sane and familiar, the blue eyes coming to life. He looked fine.

"What I want to see is the two of them coming down from there. I'm going to be sitting on the bed, instead of you. Move the light a little, see. I want it to fall over my hand with the gun. I'm going to twirl it a few times on my

313

finger and then pitch it on the bed. I'm going to be giggling. This will show them they're not even worth shooting. *You* laugh too, now. We've heard their rendezvous, and this is what we think of it, how sad and trashy it was . . . laugh! or this isn't going to make its effect."

We had to wait thirty minutes, with absolute silence up there. Then the door opened, and Bet's hand appeared, carrying her shoes. Silas escorted her down four steps or so and they peered over at my lighted bed. I started laughing, hoping, but it was no use.

Fleece yanked the pistol up off the bed and fired it at Silas. I could see he was shooting at Silas's ass. I moved, with my own laugh still ringing in the room, and jerked the pistol out of his hand. The shot fell flat against the wall and was not much louder than a cap gun. Silas didn't know he had been hit and laughed himself, before he saw it was Fleece sitting on the bed.

They had walked several steps below the spray of blood on the wall before Silas fell backwards on the stairs and cried hoarsely, "Awwwrrrr!" Bet crouched by him.

"It wasn't me," I told them, trying to keep the fun in it.

"It was me," said Fleece. He walked over to the stairs and held to the supports like somebody looking into a cage. "Where did it get you?"

Silas gave a fatal moan.

"I was low. It just crosses over the bottom of his thigh."

"Were you aiming at his *heart?*" asked Bet. *"Bobby!"*

"What's her name?" Fleece said, not looking at her. Then he fainted, like a suit flopping off a coathanger.

"I don't blame him. He didn't know what he was doing," said Silas. "I forgive you, Bob. I understand it." He talked with his head thrust through the banister, looking down at the body of Fleece. He sort of waved at Fleece.

"We have two choices," I said. "We can take you to the hospital, which will bring about an investigation. Or we can wake up Fleece and see if he can't clean it out for you so you won't get gangrene. You see it's not even bleeding much. It looks like more of a burn."

Silas had taken off his pants and sat there holding the underside of his thigh. It is my guess he wasn't too, too unhappy to be doing this. Bet looked straight down the stairs, sitting on the step below him with her hands in her lap.

314

"Of course, we don't go to the hospital. But can we count on Bobby Dove?"

Bet's eyes enlarged and she pointed behind me to Bobby. Fleece was crawling across the floor toward my bed. He achieved the bed and picked up the pistol lying on the covers. Silas got up and Bet screeched.

"That one isn't loaded," I said.

"Don't, please don't shoot me!" cried Silas. He gimped down the stairs and dropped into Fleece's room. Fleece staggered away from us to my bathroom.

"He's going to kill himself," said Bet.

As I got to the bathroom the door whammed to. There was no lock on the inside. I called him. I heard him heaving away inside. When I opened the door I saw him holding himself up with his hands spread out on the bare pot, the top of his head just showing over the rim. "Haarrfff!"

"Where's the gun?"

He rolled over on his side, pink-faced, tears rolling. "Did you drop your glasses in the commode?" He held up the glasses. But in the commode I noticed the barrel of the pistol sticking out of the barf and water.

"Flush it," he told me.

"You know this pistol isn't going to flush."

"Flush it."

I hit the handle. The pistol didn't go down. All that happened was the barrel moved across and lay on the other side.

"Try it again."

"Be sane, damn you."

"I shot two people now. I haven't missed yet. What am I doing with *guns?*" He was crying. His tie was wet from the bowl water.

"You can throw yours in the river any day you want to."

"Throw yours in too?"

"Nope. I like mine," I said.

Bet and Silas came to the door quietly.

"This man has been shot, you remember," I said.

"What do I need, Bob? A tetanus shot? Can you get me one?"

"Turn around," said Fleece. Silas did. "You. Big useless thing. You get out of his light." He waved Bet over. "Well, look at that. Couldn't you get this girl to even wash it out for you? That would've been hunky-dory for him, in his

315

Tarzan underwear. I don't remember blowing his pants off. Course if I'd hit him in the ear, he'd probably have them off to make a tourniquet or something."

Silas went upstairs to get some more pants. Fleece picked himself up off the floor. "Yes sir, it's old Doctor Fleece. Y'all come into the right place. I know ever' truth of the human body." He shuffled like an old man. He stopped and reached back for the gun in the commode, yanked it up dripping. "And I brought this from the water baptized, 'cause I live by this now. The die is cast. What you say, podnah? It puts a fine edge on things of the future? Put a little edge on Silas, didn't it?"

"Bobby, you're so *hard!*" said Bet.

Silas and Fleece left for the med center together. Fleece had said he could purloin a tetanus shot and phenol. Bet stayed in the room with me. She took a seat in the wire drugstore chair beside my desk. Actually, she didn't seem so huge when she sat down. She was put together well. Her face was that of a child actress whose looks might soon change to ugly. She had on a short skirt. One toe had plunged out the end of her left stocking; she put the shoes on.

"I saw you carrying your shoes in your hand. You realize how pretty that looked to Fleece."

She made poo-pooing *kisses* toward me with her mouth.

"What are you, a *whore?*"

"Could I see that?" she asked me. She wanted the wet pistol I'd gotten from Fleece when he left. I was still holding it.

"My mercy!" she sighed, turning the gun around naïvely. "Pow! Why didn't Bobby use this one? It's more cute."

"He was sitting with me right here, hearing the two of you going at it on the bed up there. You knew *I* was here, anyway."

"Oh, he did not. Jerry just took off his shirt and told me he wanted me to see this thing, that he was going to stand on the bed so that the street light caught his image in silhouette on the window. He wanted me to see if this was classic, as a pose. It seemed to be classic to me, so he jumped off the bed and was so relieved and happy. He put his shirt back on, and that was all that happened."

"That wasn't queer to you?"

"Well, you can tell whose side you're on. Wasn't it a tiny bit queer when Bobby *shot* Jerry?"

"Well—"

"But I love this place, this inside of an old tower. I love you boys in it. You could've called me. I would've gone out with you. Would you have had a gun too tonight?"

"I know some other guys I could call up. You could love them too. I'd tell them to bring over some firearms; we could have the Millsaps football team pose in silhouette on the bed up there."

"What you mean?"

"I think you liked it." She made those poo-pooing kisses again.

"I didn't like it when it happened. I might like it a little now. Nobody was really hurt. I feel all drained, but it feels like I had fun. It does."

"Look," I said. I reached in the drawer and got the little automatic out. I came back and sat on the bed and knocked the safety back. "This is the really cute one."

I shot it a couple of times at the stair wall. "Now how 'bout a old kissy-kissy!" I came toward her all smoochy-mouthed. I really was interested in seeing how much gun-fire excited her.

"Harry!" She stood up.

"What? The thrill is gone, huh?"

"Yes. The thrill is gone. Stop."

"When they get back I'll take them both on. We'll bust up the lamps and make awful hooks and preens out of them and hack at each other in the dark. The winner will climb up into the light of Silas's room, and there you'll be waiting for him. Would that get the thrill back?"

"No . . ." she was pouting. "Oh, Bobby Dove! I've lost him!" She put her hands to her face and really broke down, bawling.

For a week both Silas and Fleece spent the night somewhere else. Then I got a phone call. Silas wanted to know if Fleece was there, and I told him no, and hadn't been. He said he was coming over to pick up his stuff. When he got to the house, he was a very wary man; and a very sweet man.

"Bet and I are getting married," he whispered. "Tonight

317

I'm taking her up to Yazoo to meet the folks. They're going to love her!"

"Speak out. Nobody's here, not even Mother Rooney."

"The night I hooked up with you, remember the night I had that cello and you on trumpet? I knew I was being led to a beautiful life. Thank you. Just thank you." He wanted to shake hands.

"You are in love. Are you sure you want to marry Bet after Fleece has banged it going on six years?"

"Don't . . . please." He still looked at me sweetly, humbly, though he was making a sort of curled club with his hand. I followed him up and watched him pack the footlockers. Suddenly he nudged me.

"What?"

"London. The honeymoon. Then all the rest of Europe, with Bet this time." He opened his jacket, revealing the ticket packet. I saw his wallet also.

"Silas. Could you give me some money?"

"For what?"

"For I don't have any and I'm hungry. And me telling Fleece about this ought to be worth something."

"You bet."

"More than *that*, man. I've also got to tell Mother Rooney about the disappearance of her favorite lodger."

"All right." He looked at the barbells. "You can have those too. You could use this room for a gym."

"Are you crying, Silas?" He was the biggest man I've ever seen weeping, huge freckled hands wiping at his cheeks.

"Listen, if you could write a poem right now for me, I'd pay. I'd pay a lot."

"About what?" I confess I was greedy, instantly, and already I felt cunning watching him cry.

"God, I don't know. About love, about leaving, about being shot . . . Ignore me. Here." He tossed a couple of twenties on the bed. Soon, he was gone, with my poem.

The next week Fleece moved back in. He asked me where I thought that sad bastard Silas was living now. I told him Silas had been in long enough to pick up his clothes and leave. Fleece continued straightening his room below. I hadn't actually seen him yet. He yelled up.

"What did he say?"

I was dreading this. "He paid me to write him a poem."

318

"You wrote him a poem?" still yelling. "What kind of poem?"

"It was 'Where the Bee Sucks.' "

He quit moving. Then I heard him on the stairs. He was narrowing his eyes, sneering a bit.

"Where the *bee* sucks?"

"He was in a rush. I came down here and cheated it. Changed a couple of words, maybe. The lit book was right on my desk. He liked it and ran." Fleece began an uncertain giggle. I showed him, in the book.

> Where the bee sucks, there suck I;
> In a cowslip's bell I lie;
> There I couch, when owls do cry:
> On the bat's back I do fly
> After summer merrily.
> > Merrily, merrily, shall I live now,
> > Under the blossom that hangs on the bough!

"He bought that? 'there suck I'? Why? What did this have to do with anything?"

"The man was weeping, Fleece. He wanted a poem."

Fleece sucked in as if to begin a howl.

"Wait," I said. "He and Bet are married and they are in London." It seemed the perfect time to hit him with it.

He held his breath, and then it left him unnoticeably. I thought he might be very, very slowly dilapidating, taking his glasses off, rubbing his eyes; then the tears came out bright on his cheekbones, and he didn't move his hands toward them at all. He put his glasses back on and drew his hand over his head to get the ropy, straggling hairs in place. His forehead shone bald and hot orange.

"I didn't know she'd marry him. Missus Silas?"

"She was a strange lady."

"Dear yes, she was."

"She bawled about losing you, you know." Fleece seemed to have resumed the slow, slow sagging again. He began commenting on himself.

"The important thing is that I'm alive and well. My mind is perfectly all right. I haven't lost anything. It had a lot to spare. The mind's a paradise. In five minutes. Give me five minutes, I'm going to feel like I could be a choirboy or a wino and everything between. Still. *Still!*" He seemed to be restaturing himself. "Part of me is in the grave. Part of me can't stand this. But that's how magnificent the mind is. It can be there and up here too. In a minute I will see the freedom. I will no longer be a little VD spirochete with my tongue wrapped around myself. Did you hear that?"

"I'm listening."

"No, I mean did you hear that image *little VD spirochete* with the tongue? Store that away, you lucky huncher. Have it, free! The genius is *back* in residence. Aw love it."

"You're doing well."

"I'm not going to oddball on you any more. Whatever there is left"—he pointed directly out the window—"I am here and I am *whole!* I can take it. God, I'm so happy for me. And *you* . . ." He turned directly at me as if angry. "You are my best buddy! You've stayed. Oh, let me mawk. Let an old man of twenty-six mawk on. You've kept me out of Whitfield, and Parchman. You've got the face of an Indian who knows the secret routes of the hills, and I trust you. Don't hang your head like I was trying to grab your thing! Truth!" he shouted. "It was my poem. You gave it to the wrong man, you miserable plagiarist. Where is it? My poem." He tore through the pages. " 'There I couch, when owls do cry/On the bat's back I do fly/After summer merrily . . . and there suck I!' Lord love a duck!" He dashed the book on the floor.

8 / Harlem in Havana

Now for the first time in a long time I got a piece of real happiness. The University of Arkansas, up at Fayetteville, wanted me—$1200 and fees paid for the first semester, renewable contingent on my performance. As for Columbia, Iowa, and Chapel Hill, they were all too precious for me to enter and I say fuck them. Always later, I have been glad to read in the newspaper that the football teams of those schools have been thrashed into the sod.

I was holding my letter from Arkansas, rereading it on the couch in Mother Rooney's dining room, and Fleece was there, and Mother Rooney, both congratulating me. It was mid-afternoon. Fleece went to the front window. "Who is that?" he asked me. Across the lawn, parked on the other side of Titpea and to the north of us, was a Buick. The owner of it was up on the porch of the two-story house across the street. The woman of the house was holding the screen door open and talking to him and pointing to our house.

"It's Whitfield Peter," said Fleece. "He hasn't got any cane. He's coming right over here!" This was true.

"Who?" asked Mother Rooney. She went with us to the lobby. We stood in the wooden shadows and saw Peter through the mottles of the glass doors. He pressed and pressed the doorbell. It activated the chime box behind us, which had two dead chimes and only a clink for the one working. He rapped on the door, and I saw his hat sweep down to his knee after each knock, expecting someone to open each time. He was a musketeer beating his knee with his hat, to no avail.

"Well, I must answer the door. What a polite man," said Mother Rooney. I held her with my hand on her shoulder.

"Not for him," I whispered.

He must have been on the porch ten minutes before he got back in the Buick and oozed around trying to get out of the dead-end street. We watched him from the window.

"He knows where we are, Monroe. How does he know where we are? Sweet Jesus, I've got the creeps."

"That was rude," said Mother Rooney.

"That was a rude, ugly man we know," I told her.

"How could a handsome man like that with his manners be rude and ugly?" she asked me. Her seeing him as handsome sickened me.

Only Delph, the pharmacist rooming in the other tower, and I were in that weekend. I picked up the phone Saturday morning late in the living room. It had rung fifteen or twenty times. Peter was on the other end. He was very polite. He wanted to know to whom was he speaking, and was flowery in his apology over the number of rings. I asked him who he wanted.

"Does a medical student, Harry Monroe, still live there?"

"He died."

321

"This was a young man with a beard and spectacles. He wouldn't have died. Someone has told me, the gentleman I arrived at this number by, that he was living."

"But he just died. This happens, that people die, of all ages."

"To *whom* am I speaking?"

I thought he knew, and I hung up. Having seen him at the door of the house, I had an occult suspicion that he knew every step I took.

Sunday night I finally fell asleep, with Byron's *Don Juan* held up to my chin like an old spicy blanket. I'd read half of it and was floating on the possibilities of the rest of it. Fleece shook me.

"What's this? Friday night he called my stepfather asking for *you*. How did he know to call General Creech's house? Creech gave him the number for *this* house. I was six feet away from the phone and . . . The bastard *comes* to the door, he now knows our telephone number. How? I was talking with Creech, I was beginning to like him, and the phone rings. It was *Peter*. Creech was fifteen minutes on the phone. Peter told him that, in light of the fact he was talking to a general, he himself was a colonel in the governor's corps years ago. This really disgusted the General. When he hung up, he told me that, whatever esteem I held him in, he had *won* his stripes, and not by marching in a herd of influential men past the governor's mansion, being waved to and coloneled right on the spot by the governor. We were talking, and the phone rang *again*. Creech picked it up. The same man. He wanted to know why the phone kept ringing at the number the General had given him. The General gave him the same number again, more carefully."

Fleece had had a ruined weekend.

"Now you ought to know it all," I said. "How does the cut on your stepfather's head look? He was talking to the man who put it there. Did he tell you about what happened at Oxford, the truck turning over and all that?"

"Yes."

"Peter was the one that dropped the crosstie. Silas saw him with a bunch of local kids, doing it."

"*Silas!*" Fleece spat out.

"He happened to see this. Hate him, but he was the one who told it to me, and he didn't know who your father, Creech, I mean, was. He simply happened to be there. And

322

I should tell you," and I told him so much my jaw ached, about taking Catherine out on dates, about having seen and heard Peter face to face, about inadvertently giving Peter the phone number and as much as the address of the house.

"Well, I'm relieved. I thought he was a spirit. I thought we were being closed in on by a phantom. You've had such *secrets*," he snarled. "Such secrets. But I'm glad to know there is an explanation."

Later in the night, I heard the phone in the living room ring, six times at least. I heard Mother Rooney open her door and try to make it to the phone before it quit, but she didn't, and the last ring clung around my room.

Wednesday, I found this one, a letter in the "Our Reader's Viewpoint" of the paper.

Mississippians who care:
The State Fair is here. I do not want to take away any of the excitement of it. It is October cool days the time we all like the sawdust under our feet at the Fair. The Royal American Shows here giving their temptations to the Mississippian in every facet.

There is one point is wrong, however, I want to point it out. It is the Harlem in Havana Show which is here again. Who is pretending there is anything to Havana, Cuba anymore than Castro's Communism?

It is the same thing when we let Negro mammies be the raiser of our white babies while we are at a cocktail party not knowing what is being whispered in the infant's ear.

Thus Harlem in Havana is here, girls of mulatto breed undressing themselves to the eyes and to the tune of rock and roll and other Negroid music. They are a mockery and a accusation on the white race that they have bred with a black woman. That is what the Liberal Press loves. To point out hypocrisy.

Let us boycott Harlem in Havana and close it down as a loss to Royal American. Tell them to carry it back home to the millionaire of the North that is having a "ball" seeing us pay money for an idea that deep in our hearts we hate. I myself will be enjoying the Fair, but Friday night, the night it is well known the high yellow girl stands all the way nude, I wonder if you readers knew this has been going on, some people pay two dol-

323

lars to see this? But I am one who will be looking in the face of the people who go in and come out of it. I wonder what those peoples faces are going to look like? Can they look me in the face?

Gillis Lock
Pearl, Miss.

"Like a sophomore in Whitfield Peter's Academy of Letters," I told Fleece. "Do you remember this son of a bitch? He was at Hedermansever shortly. The one who was beating my time with Catherine, you know."

"Yes, I know, but I don't know who he is. I'll tell you one thing. Peter has talked to his boy. You know he has. Is he right?"

"What?"

"Does the girl take off all her clothes?"

"Yes, she does. She was doing it years ago in the same show at Dream of Pines. My first glimpse of a real nude, in fact."

"Let's go. I need the fun."

I thought I might see Catherine with Lock, if he was standing where he said he would be. And really, I wanted to leave the house without my gun, but once on with the old reptilian coat, looking at my bare shaved face in the mirror, I was back with Geronimo again, and when I reached in the drawer for the pistol, the scarf was lying right by it, and I tied it on. I felt silly, but at home and warm too. When Fleece saw me, he said, "You got the pistol too, don't you?" I nodded.

"That's perfectly all right with me," he said.

The sand gullies behind Mother Rooney's were full of ledges under the kudzu vines, and you could feel for them and climb down as if on a ladder with every fourth rung intact, and even if you missed the place to put your foot you would land in a soft obliging mass of kudzu which would drag you to the next ledge with no harm. You just had to forget the idea that there were snakes sleeping underneath, grip on to what you could, and actually it was easy, landing, hanging on the vines and putting down foot softly as the vines broke. Fleece was above me, inching down. When I was at the bottom, I looked up and saw him forty feet up, missing every foothold and stripping off leaves and falling, all of a sudden, with the benevolent vines he held on to,

324

and smacking back first on the ground beside me. It could have been worse. I looked up the mean hundred-foot drop of the cliff. But he didn't land that easy, either, with his arms full of vines and leaves like some aeronaut who had bailed out of a flying watermelon. He lay horrified a moment, then found his glasses.

"We got in free," I consoled him.

"Lead on. I'm all right."

We talked through the shadows of the truck trailers. Walked over the flattened dusty grass, made it to the sawdust. The Fair was just an expanded version of the Royal American in Dream of Pines years ago. Now they had the Astro-this and Astro-that, and the World War Two Atrocities show was no longer around, but Stalin's Rolls Royce was, and the barkers, hating everybody, on the microphones with Yankee accents made of tin and cinders. Puerto Rican hoods stared at you like they would kill you if you passed by their skill-booth and would cheat your fanny off if you did stop. The air was cool, you could smell the Pronto Pups—wieners in batter—frying, and the sawdust by its nature gave you a soft falling and rising sense under your feet, tempting you to walk on air. I fell down.

"What was that? Get up!" said Fleece.

I brushed the sawdust off, and we walked on toward the midnight show of "Harlem in Havana." It was down at the end of the fairgrounds beside the giant ferris wheel, as usual, and the crowd got thicker and thicker. I saw they still had the freak shows, with the big flapping cartoon murals of what you might find inside. I was a little surprised. I thought the freaks wouldn't have made it this long as an attraction. I thought some law might have been passed. But then I realized that for the real freaks there can never be any laws. You cannot prevent the man who swallows snakes, you cannot deny employment to the world's tiniest cow, you can make no law either for or against the lady with hairs growing on her gums, and the same goes for the limbless soprano and the Siamese twins, who are engaged to be married, one wearing a diamond ring on its finger. You can't, any more than pass a law for or against death. Especially not when the people who pay to see them—I remember all the creeps at Hedermansever who loved the freak show and saw nothing else—come away feeling like crowned wonders in comparison.

The band on the balcony of "Harlem in Havana" was careless and shrill, playing the Beatles' "I Want To Hold Your Hand" while three girls in wraps and brassy sandal highheels shuffled in unison on the stage below, to warm up the crowd for the midnight show. The crowd below the stage was so thick I couldn't see anybody in particular. When the barker announced that tickets were now on sale, you had to move with the mass, up the steps toward the ticket counter. A quiet mob, is what Fleece and I were in. Buying my ticket, I saw a face close to the right edge of the stage. This was Lock. It was the man who had been run over by the float last Christmas. I had thought that was probably who Lock was. I searched the space around him for Catherine as I walked on the stage into the show. Lock pushed back from the stage and took me in. We were six feet apart. All I saw was his head and his hands on the edge of the stage.

"I know who *you* are!" he yelled.

"Where's your sweetheart?" I yelled back. Then Fleece pressed me from behind; people were waiting behind him.

"That was Lock. I have seen him before," he said.

We sat down next to a man and his wife, a young married couple. The wife was complaining about the seats, which were simply planks bolted to supports, sawdust underneath. It was the same long tent, maybe bigger, of the Harlem in Havana show back in Dream of Pines. The lights went down, the spotlight centered on the meeting of the curtains, and a master of ceremonies, who was white, darted out of the curtain, took the mike, and straightaway told the filthiest joke I've ever heard. "There was a girl from Seattle/Who loved to fellatio cattle" and worse. The wife next to us stood up and pulled her husband along, and they found their way out.

Then there appeared a line of yellow girls in these sort of tinsel bathing suits. They danced well and seemed to know about the extra price of the tickets. You could see their navels jump out from under the tinsel. They were so smooth as a group, it was impossible to pick out the one who aroused you the most. The band was also good, playing on a stand to the right of the stage—a big deep band of some twenty Negroes. When the girls left the stage, the spot raced to one side and planted on this man standing up, taking the solo on trumpet.

"He's good, isn't he?" asked Fleece.

For ten seconds he had been good, many high blue notes to the measure, but the same moment I recognized him as Harley Butte, in a blue satin jacket like the rest of the band, he began failing on the solo. He punched out a few very high notes, which would impress a musical amateur like Fleece, but he folded all of a sudden from even doing that. His face looked hurt as he put the horn down. I know I saw tears on his face, and he sat down, or fell back in his seat right in the middle of his ride, as if struck by something. Even Fleece knew something had gone wrong. Only the rhythm and piano were going, and the spotlight ducked off of Harley and went back to the bare black center of the curtain. It was a collapse in a show everybody had paid for to be gorgeously slick. The crowd murmured. I saw Harley get up and jump off the back of the stand in the shadows. The band picked up again. Me, I had gotten off my seat and was walking toward them, and Fleece was trailing me, calling to me. I got the blast of the band right in the face, heard the keys of the saxes clicking, saw the Negroes bearing down on the mouthpieces. When I passed the band a lone girl was on stage. She was rolling her stomach out with enough violence to throw her organ right off her and into the audience.

Harley was under the bandstand putting his horn in its case. The band grew mellower over us. They were doing a snaky Turkish number now. The only light we had was the overflow from the spot and the yellow dimness cast down from the bandstand lights. The bandstand was a unit of mobile bleachers, and you could see the shoes of the musicians.

"Harley Butte?" I whispered.

"You got an aspirin? You got to have an aspirin. I got a headache." He held his hands to his ears.

"This is Harry."

"My ass. Oh, my ass. You aren't wearing the beard any more. Do you just have an aspirin?" He jerked his thumb up toward the band. "That's a whole drugstore up there, they got anything you want. But all I want's an aspirin. I'm the only healthy one here, and I'm sick."

"It's hard to believe," I said.

"Nothing's hard to believe."

"I have two aspirins," said Fleece, reaching in his coat

327

pocket. Fleece was always having headaches. Harley took them down dry. He stood up and we walked toward the back of the stage. Back here there were a lot of trailers with wooden steps at their doors. In one of the trailers I saw a number of girls in bikinis and robes and caps with huge peacock feathers attached.

"I've got a girlfriend in that trailer. I don't believe it, but I do," said Harley.

"Monroe." Fleece nudged me. A man was coming toward us around the narrow walkway behind the backdrop; he came down the stairs like he had urgent business with me. He was white. Harley said that this was the road manager.

"Back up front, up front, boys. Is this man *pimping?* What are you pulling, Butte? Why aren't you in the band? Mother Nature. Shit."

"Get your finger out of my face," said Harley.

"This thing is going to fall apart if we don't have rules, Mr. Butte. I thought you were one of my leaders. I trusted you."

"I'm quitting."

The man looked at me angrily. "What's your business with this man? Butte, do you know where you *are?* You can't just jump off the tour. We need you. Please."

"I live near here. I got a wife and kids in this state. *Don't* touch me, Shamburger. I got an awful, awful headache." The man looked even more hatefully at me and Fleece.

"What *kind* of deal have you made here? Are you using this man's wife and children?"

"Not making anything," said Harley. "Getting away to the place I won't have any more headaches like this one. Get out of the way."

About that time a long line of girls came out of the trailer wearing those skullcaps and plumes. They mounted the steps and one by one broke out to the stage through the flap in the backdrop. The manager went over to time them. The band was popping and screaming now. Harley put his hands to his ears as we made our way around toward the exit. I carried the horncase. He was really hurting. He stopped. "Come on, aspirin," he said. Apparently he couldn't go any farther. "Come on." You had to root for the aspirin.

328

Five minutes later the girls poured out of the flap and across the sawdust to the trailer. Last of all came a mulatto woman with paint melting off her eyes. She was greasy with sweat. She had gotten a robe on but wore it negligently. It parted and showed her totally bare. Her feet were veiny and dirty. In her hand were two silvery high heels. Then she went on into the trailer, taking her time, not noticing us. Fleece uttered a wounded sound.

"Well, that was a buck's worth, about, I guess."

"Ahhh! Land of Jesus! Come on, aspirin!" Harley was getting relief from the aspirins. He still had the jowl beard and the mustache and looked like a man in a drug ecstasy now. Around the way, you could hear the people filing out.

"Let's go." He took off the coat and tossed it on the stage, leaving himself in white ruffled shirt and bow tie. The show was over and we were the last in the exit. It was weakly golden here, the lights were down, and the ropes around us were still vibrating in a lingering effect from the show. The sawdust was much-trampled and compact, in the exit.

Gillis Lock was waiting for us, and standing by him, Peter. Otherwise, the fair was dead at this end; the ferris wheel had stopped, the freak show lights were out, and far away you could hear a forlorn calliope, like a lone berserk bagpiper.

"Look at the last ones crawling out!" said Lock. "Wonder what they got Mustard doing for them. You carrying her suitcase for her too?" looking at me and past me. I turned around. Next to the canvas flap in the exit stood a girl the color of a tan egg; she had thrown a stage wrap over herself. Her wrists crossed, holding the wrap at her throat. She was cocking her head sideways, making some message to Harley. Harley gave her a short goodbye salute. This gal was a grief-causing beauty.

"You boys forget what you came after?" said Lock; he was tall, with thin hips but a soft pot out front. He favored the hairstyle of a high arch groomed to one side, which makes a person look headlong and earnest at all moments. "Or couldn't you afford her, Monroe?"

"I saw your letter. Come over here in the light, and bring the ancient cocksman over here too." I beckoned to Peter and was sick in my stomach as I did. "Bring your cowboy hat. See how you make out." Lock came right toward me. I may have backed up. Harley groaned something.

"Stop!" yelled Peter.

"Why? Why?" asked Lock.

"Because Monroe has a gun," said Fleece.

Lock stopped, looking suddenly limp, as if his spine had been jerked out of him. His arms fell to his sides useless and I believe he was just before begging me not to use a gun on him. "I have one too," said Fleece. I caught his big golden forehead out of the side of my eye. His head seemed about to burst in fire.

"I have a gun in the pocket of my car," said Lock whiningly, his lip sulking.

"Aw hell," said Harley, moving up between me and Lock. "Crying out loud! We got a meeting of a gun club here? You people—"

"Shut up, mustard-face!" said Lock. "I've seen you before too."

Peter eased up slowly, examining Harley. "The band-director nigger gentleman?" he said.

"He was at the parade amongst them niggers. I couldn't forget that beard," said Lock.

"I know, I know, I know, I know," Harley threw out his hands. "You hear now, you two. You're the one that pushed that child out at me, you're the one the police told, baby. And *you're* the one come across the street and got *hit,* didn't you? and got run over by that Christmas float? I recognize *you.* That's who recognizes who, goddam it. Every time I been in this town I had to look at one of you. I been all over the United States with this 'Harlem in Havana,' and the first time I hit the open air of this Jackson and this Mississippi, who do I see? Who's waiting there saying Shut up, Mustard, and like that."

"Shut up," said Lock. He had a certain courage.

"Don't look at Harry when you say shut up. Say, look at me. I don't need no damn gun. I am who I am and I'm tired of you. Look at me. All right." Harley hit Lock on the jaw with a tight abrupt punch. He had an absolutely clear shot because Lock would not take his eyes off me. Lock—I saw his closed eyes and his nose, knocked upright—went down tearing the sawdust. Then he just lay there, with his legs pulled up to his stomach. I began trembling. But Harley only watched him a moment. Kneading his right fist

330

with his other hand he walked right up into Peter's face and braced his legs.

"Don't hit him," said Fleece, rather calmly, in the way of advice. "He's too old, and he's crazy. Don't." At that moment Peter did seem such a cheap shot for Harley to take; he was wearing that severe bronco-cavalier hat, maybe a new one of that line, and he looked like a scowling propped-up dummy you'd throw balls at in one of the skill booths. But Harley was committed. He seemed to have just heard Fleece in the middle of his swing, and slowed it, hitting Peter with a sort of loose fist in slow motion. Peter turned his face with the blow and took a helpless step back. Then he put a hand to his cheek, like he'd been merely stung, and repostured, looking straight at me. He looked at Fleece.

"Who is *this* young man? Should I know him?" he asked me. "He seems to know *me*."

"The letters from Whitfield," said Fleece. I wouldn't have said that, myself. Peter became very strange in his face, and bore down at Fleece. His eyes were like red dark sightless caves; they seemed to *feel* toward Fleece; they lay on him lingeringly.

Lock had stood up, and now he looked at Harley, in amazement. He lifted one finger in front of his eye.

"You won't live, Mustard. Take my word. You had people with a gun on me when you did that. That was nigger, nigger, nigger, what you—"

"*You* shut up," said Peter, talking to Lock.

"I've got friends," Lock went on.

"Yes, your friends, fool, your secret agents. Shut up. If you do have a gun, Mister Monroe, I wish you'd use it now. I wish you would show him what a bullet feels like." Peter said this, but at the same time, he threw his arm over Lock's shoulders, as if he were Lock's real uncle. Lock shrugged the arm off, still glowering at Harley. "Very well. *Ask* them to shoot you," said Peter.

Gillis Lock seemed to be turning his fist back and forth and studying the occurrence of his bicep muscle through his shirt. "Have you really got a gun? You'd better have a gun," he said, snarling.

I took the gun out of my pocket. In my mind I heard an eruption of barking, yelping laughter. Geronimo. Hearing

331

it, I had to restrain myself from shooting him on the spot.
"Get out of my sight, both of you," I said.

I put the gun back, and walked toward the far gates.
Harley was right astride me. He wanted me to give him a
ride to Beta Camina. Fleece told me the two of them were
still back there, staring at us. I was feeling foul, in all the
ways you can feel. But I told Harley certainly I would give
him a ride home. Beta Camina was only sixty miles south-
west of us, so we went through the gates, around and up to
the house, and Fleece got in the well of the T-bird, and I
drove, on 80 toward Vicksburg, taking a left somewhere.
I've never felt sleepier. It was like having a hangover without ever having had any fun.

We passed weeds and a number of dirty asbestos-siding
houses close to the road; through the yellow caution lights,
with the lone policeman asleep in his car under the service
station port, the towns flyspecked and chilled in gray, the
lonely hound with heavy teats moving out of the headlight
beam, the fogbound Nehi signs, over the highway with its
tarred creases, sometimes beside watery ditches, sometimes
seeming to be on a concrete tightwire, sometimes cutting
ahead like the point of a hurtling plow, tossing houses and
trees to each side. On your right a delta mansion, on your
left a brick ranch-mode house, in the middle of brown low
fields. Then we crashed over some sunken railroad tracks.
My car, I thought, broke apart on them. It kept going, but
something had been opened in the muffler. There was a
new sound inside the car, like constant, violent hail.

Harley talked the whole while. He still couldn't get over
the fact that Peter and his friends were the first humans
he'd seen coming out of the tent. I was bewildered too. But
I said very little, I was so sleepy. Also he couldn't get over
what luck it was to meet me. In a sluggish dull gloom, I
tried to sympathize with the excitement of meeting myself.
After the railroad tracks, the perilous sounds of the car
kept me awake as he talked. Some months ago he had made
a trip to New York to see his publishing firm. They got him
an agent. In three days he was out of money and was phon-
ing his agent. Now he didn't know if he had a job at Beta
Camina or not. He'd written a letter to the army but they
had not replied. He had committed certain acts interpreta-
ble as grave marks on his professional record, such as being
absent the last two months of the school year; then there

332

was his absentation the first two months of this school year. They might hold this against him, especially the principal, but they knew his value, as he did. He wasn't going to beg for his job back. He had *invented* that job. The publishers in New York had assured him of his value as the band director of Beta Camina. He knew that when he left Beta Camina it was not that a position had been vacated. The position had moved *away*. He sometimes thought of the kids waiting for him in the band room. He wondered whether, if he could get over this period, this hump, which was not a hump really but a whole range of dismal mountains of funk, he might not like to be in that band room forever. He didn't know yet, even as we traveled toward Beta Camina. He had sent money home. Sometimes he had wanted to get in the letters he sent and be the face in the hundred-dollar bill, smiling at his wife when she opened the mail, putting a leg over the edge of the envelope, the boys rushing to him. Daddy, Daddy. He could barely compose himself enough to write a note to go along with the money. All he wanted was the time and opportunity to be great. He wanted to be far away from the principal and Beta Camina. Some day he wanted to call his wife and his children to a place which would give them a grandeur of comfort and ease. He did not want to simply come back to the house— I'm old me, tee hee—where they would curse you after the surprise had worn off. And another part of him wanted to commit suicide against everything in his mind, and simply fly, stroke away, nothing but muscles, nameless. Then again he wondered to what dire condition the principal had led the Gladiators in his absence. The poor kids.

We circled through a village of old bricks and launched onto a road freshly laid with red gravel.

"This will be fine," said Harley. He wanted to know if we wouldn't come in and take some coffee. Fleece had been asleep since Jackson. I was too groggy to get out of the car. I told him I'd just open a window here for a minute.

The last thing he wanted to know was whether I was pretty sure he wouldn't see Peter around if he happened to see me again. Could he count on maybe seeing me again without seeing Peter. Because maybe he would like to see me some time and talk about how this literary plan of mine was coming on.

"See if you find out you're a poet. We'd have a lot to talk about if you were. I might give you some stories."

"Sure."

"But they might not rhyme."

"Sure."

"Well?" and he went in the house.

9 / The Phone Pleadings

This was in December. I had a fiancée. I wasn't in the house much, and spent a good bit of my time riding up and down the highway, sometimes pulling off to read a piece out of a book. I'd made a trip to Fayetteville to get the feel of the place and locate a house.

The mountains around Fayetteville, the Boston Mountains of the Greater Ozarks, you bet, give me those, especially Highway 23, with the tops of the trees right up next to the highway, the trees themselves growing from sheer drops, the highway tilting, spiraling up and down, 15 mph or meet your maker, use second gear, watch for falling rocks; under the ledges dripping snow-water, then looping down to Fayetteville past the rock houses, past the cold river, past such signs as Rainbow Trout, Cider, See The Valley At Absolutely No Cost, and this one in front of a store: Trading Post and Son. Yes, give me the hillbillies for a change; give me a new sea level. Give me Fayetteville, too —a sort of flatland bum's dream of San Francisco, a sort of lost Bowery of Denver—five hundred miles northwest of Jackson. Give me all those miles away.

The days were really a nuisance when I got back, like an intolerably long train in front of you at a railroad crossing. Mother Rooney caught me going out of the room one night.

"The man called you several times last week, Mr. Monroe. Couldn't you clear your business with him so he

334

wouldn't have to call so much? Sometimes he calls very late at night."

"I know. But I can't clear up the business. I've tried. I told him. As far as I'm concerned, there *is* no business."

"You aren't making book, are you, child? You aren't in the numbers racket? I wouldn't want anything to damage your literary career."

"No." Fleece had bought her a television.

"And listen now. I want your marriage to be just *perfect.*" Her hands were clasped and she drew them downwards as she said this, the old blue eyes moist.

"She would love you," I said.

"Mr. Fleece said that she is a technical virgin." I looked instantly to catch her eyes—the same moist blue. "In my day we let certain things go unsaid but I realize this must be sweet for you."

"Mr. Fleece runs at the mouth, Mother Rooney. He has a lot of cute medical phrases that don't mean anything at all."

"The medical. It's so very nice to have an almost doctor in your very own house, being aged. He bought a television set for me."

"I know he did that. But in other ways he stinks."

"Television has opened up a whole new world for me. Bless his heart. Did you see it the afternoon the young man dove off the hundred-foot platform into the ring of balloons in the pool?"

"No, mam."

"Oh I could have just taken him into my bosom."

Fleece came in the front door. He looked like a surgeon who had seen several inoperable cases today and had turned cynical about them. You could see him as the red-eyed master under the lights. Of course, keeping the charts in the geriatric ward, he *had* seen those that had their eyes open but were not awake in the morning. He had begun holding Mother Rooney in a kind of reverence. He watched television with her. He told me, in case I shared the common notion that the old deserved death, it was hardly *ever* true. He had seen and heard a man recite *verbatim* five Damon Runyan stories, with beautiful gestures, and be cold dead in thirty minutes. He wanted me to understand how the supreme organ, the mind, leaped onward and had so much left when the body fell away from it like a sack.

335

Some of them saw heaven, some of them saw big lovely moments of their past, and some of them saw things like ocean liners on the hospital lawn. He told me he was glad he had his pistol, for the moment when he even had an inkling that his mind was trapped by his body. Those are the foul ones, he said. The others are so magnificent, you could understand how an attending pastor might speak of the soul. And what you see in Mother Rooney, he said, is a damned brave tooth-and-nail fight to keep her mind several lengths ahead of her body. Glorious.

"Don't leave," he said. "Let's see how your poems are coming along. We could have the old lady make us a pot of tea. She told me she would like to see you in the *act* of writing a poem."

"The man's been calling me again."

"We'll tell him you're out, as usual."

"I don't want to even hear the phone ring. You talk about old minds. What do you think is going on in his?"

"I'll answer, I'll talk. Stay home tonight."

Not long after that, the phone rang. I went to my room and, to tell the truth, I got under the bedspread and put my head under my pillow. I wondered about what Catherine was doing in the house as her uncle made the phone calls. I blanked out my sight, holding my eyes open against the sheet, looking straight at the black unreasonableness that this Peter thing should be going on this far. It had been years. Fleece touched me.

"I won't do. I'm afraid it's only you he wants. I told him I'd seen the letters, I'd stolen them. He called me a 'cruel interloper.' I told him I knew he oversaw the dropping of the crosstie on my father's face, then. That silenced him a minute. I told him he was disturbing an old lady over here. Then he asked me to appeal to you. I told him I wouldn't. He said then he had no other recourse but to come to this house, and look you up. I told him not to do that. I was scared, Monroe. I told him if he came over here I would, one of us, might shoot him. I told him this whole house was a hair-trigger. At the last, he wanted me to tell you this: this concerned Catherine. He said he would call at eleven, and hung up."

"Was he crazy?"

"I'm afraid not."

"What would you say about his mind?"

"The words come out a little strangled, but they come out perfectly clear."

"He wants me to come over and see Catherine, doesn't he? I picked up the phone once, he knew who he was talking to by my breath, damn him, and he asked me to please come talk to her."

"He didn't say that. Say. You didn't knock up young Catherine, did you?"

"I told you the truth. The Tampax string."

"Maybe he just wants to kill you with that shotgun he mentioned in the letter. And maybe Gillis Lock is there too. Gillis has a pistol in the pocket of his car." Fleece chuckled, wiping his glasses with his tie. "One day when things get really slow, I mean when we are bored to tears, we could go over there and have the end-all shoot-out with them. That's somehow pleasant to have in back of one's mind. Because I know I would be exquisite with my pistol."

Mother Rooney made a pot of tea for us. I brought my poems down and we talked them over under the unforgiving light of the dining room. Fleece and I sat at the end of the long table. My typed poems lay on the papers like little clusters of charred fishbones. Mother Rooney left the television to come in and watch us from the couch.

"Here's another one," said Fleece. "You think you can make music breed with language and you end up sounding like Edgar Allan Poe playing the tuba."

I stood up and wrote in some amending words; Mother Rooney rose with me and gave out encouraging mists as I wrote. "Now it's a good poem," said Fleece. "Let's go on to the next." He read a few lines and raised his head. "This is deep, you get on down there. Nightmares. Let me tell you one I've had *three* times. I'm with four other men in a motel room. We kick Bet Henderson around. Then we agree to rape her."

"Goodness!" said Mother Rooney, leaving the room. Fleece watched her, holding his tongue.

"We all sleep. She gets up and murders the other four, who are tall fellows. She chokes one, she drives a hatpin into another one, she smothers one with a pillow, she beheads one with a cleaver. I hear their screams but just lie there. She has an opaque brassiere on. Lipstick is smeared all over her face. She comes toward me, not to hurt me, but to tell me how tired she is, she wants a kiss. I pick up a

337

long knife and drive it in her breasts. I look down and see her hand holding mine, lightly, like on the first date. She speaks to me. She says she is giving me a choice of waking up or staying close to her with this hand in the dream."

Fleece seemed to be appealing to me for some answer. He held the sheet with my poem about the crab to his chest. He smiled and nodded toward the kitchen. A piece of skirt was showing behind the door frame. She must've been huddled against the refrigerator.

"See you. Come on out, Mother Rooney." She swept out, holding her hands, timid on being discovered, but wanting to say something.

"Dear boys," she said. "Could I ask you if this writing about nightmares is what is *poetry?* I thought poetry was about man's noblest aspirations." She sat on the couch.

"Monroe has a poem in which a crab chewing peppermint gum is the hero."

She settled into the couch. "Yes child, read it. I won't say anything. I would just like to know how that one ends."

The phone rang at eleven. Mother Rooney was bedded down. You could hear her bedside clock. Fleece took my manuscript on to his room. It was just me and the phone. I told him it was Harriman Monroe speaking.

"Catherine is not here. I never see her. She's at the school or she's with Lock. She doesn't come in at night, and often several nights in a row. Lock has wanted your address. She knows your address. She carries these cards in her purse, the Ku Klux Klan and The Americans For The Preservation Of The White Race."

"You taught her that kind of shit."

"Not these organizations. I have said things I regret saying in Lock's presence. He is the one who will take it out to foolishness. There is Catherine's nose. It remains damaged so that she snores when she sleeps."

"Are you saying Lock is after me? Make sense."

"He is a different order. You remember in nineteen sixty-four, the summer the Northern boys were killed near Philadelphia, the Civil Rights killing—"

"Lock was in on that?"

"No. He says he has friends who knew something about it. I didn't want to know what he was trying to tell me. There was the bombing of the real estate office here in Jackson. The same. His friends."

338

"Everything you would want in a son-in-law."

"He is not. You cared enough about her to see her at the Reservoir last summer. If you could be here one evening when she gets back from teaching. Not as her paramour, but as—"

"What? I don't trust you. I'm not coming over. Don't *think* of me. *You* do something about her."

I hung up. I walked to Bobby Dove's room.

"No peace has been made?" asked Fleece.

"Stay armed," I told him.

Later, as I was packing all my bachelor things and moving out, I called Fleece up and gave him the remainder of the .22 shells in the box. He took the automatic pistol which he had been so deadly with, and I took his long revolver, which had never been shot.

10 / Ring Around Prissy

At Hedermansever, in the Chaucer class, was a good fellow named Tommy Neicase. We liked each other and generally drank coffee in the grill after class. Once a month or so Tommy would visit his father in Pascagoula. His father and mother were divorced, and his father owned a beach home walled with polished wood such as you might find in the steerhouse of an expensive boat. His father always had him a girl waiting when he came home. The man had a job which allowed him to loiter hundreds of hours beside the desks of Pascagoula's secretaries, who were mostly girls just out of high school. The old man had a sort of soft brassy manner, the action in Pascagoula was slow for the girls, so Tommy's father didn't have much trouble bringing even morally decent girls over to the house to meet Tommy. Tommy would get out of the car after the drive down from Hedermansever, and his father would put an iced drink in his hand and lead him out to the patio. Sitting on the chaise longue would be a girl he'd never seen before. She'd know

339

what he was studying at college and be petting Tommy's
dog like it was an old friend.

The last time he'd gone to Pascagoula, the old man had
put a drink in his hand but didn't take him right out to the
patio. He was worried, and took Tommy in the front of the
house. He said something like "Well you see here, this little
girl finished high school in two years, and she looks fourteen. I was just making talk with her over at Ingall's Shipyard, no idea she might, but I invited her, out of habit, and
that was this afternoon and I didn't have you a girl. She *accepted* and she's out there drinking ginger ale waiting for
you. I'm sorry. She's too young. But be nice to her."

When Tommy first saw her, she was sitting with one calf
over a knee, petting his dog. She was what his father had
said. She was a dago seeming about fourteen years old, very
slight, and more than cute. He understood how his old man
could've made the mistake. Her name was Prissy Lombardo. She fondled her ginger ale as if it was a very serious
drink. She asked for a cigarette, and Tom's father couldn't
get away quickly enough to avoid giving her one, though he
did it with hesitation. The old man saw Tommy gazing at
her. He saw Tom mixing a drink for two in the kitchen.
"She makes me feel like a pimp, an awful one. Don't you,
as you are my son, start anything with her."

At ten, Tommy drove her home. He found out she was
almost seventeen. She lived in a rundown green-boarded
house, mainly sand in the lawn; the driveway was made of
oyster shells. She reached over and caught his cheeks and
kissed him, longly. "Please call me up tomorrow, won't
you?" she said.

He intended to, but his old man caught him looking
through the phone book. If Tom saw her again, he wouldn't
feel right about it. Mr. Neicase paid Tommy's tuition and
gave him enough extra money to make Tom feel obliged to
him. This was the first and only time Mr. Neicase had tried
to put any controls on him, and he respected it. He did hate
to see her go to waste, though.

I went down to Pascagoula an early weekend in October
with Tom. Really a generous and splendid man, Tom, and
so was his father. The house looked out to a hundred yards
of gray sand and waves, coming in weakly like mopwater
—the Gulf of Mexico, broken up by islands some miles
out, smelling high of the marine dead. Breathing on the pa-

tio, that tepid breeze which filled your nose with salt and shrimp—I loved it. The house was like a ship broken apart here on the beach. We ate under a chandelier, the wallpaper was green and silver, and the light was always low. In Pascagoula, the town, there were cracked seawalls, gulls, avenues with palm-trees in the medians, and strange weather formations you could see out in the gulf; when you went downtown you saw a lot of dark men and women rattling to each other, and the shrimp-wind was pouring in all the time.

I called up Prissy before we settled nicely in the house. We kept it quiet from Tommy's father, who was a god of a friend to me while I was there. Prissy answered at Ingall's, and when I told her where I was calling from, she accepted me for the night.

She kissed me so wolfishly, with such an art of the tongue, and even the glottis, that the nerves of my stomach stretched out—an unbearable tickle. Then there was a kiss in front of her house, as we were leaving Mr. Neicase's Imperial, that had to be the last one. I did not know that you could have an orgasm of the lips like this, which made you forget there was anything else you could do with a girl. When it was over, she collapsed on me, and we weaved together up the lawn to her dismal home. She had a way of leaning on the door, a way of being small and brown with her jumbled black hair; her eyes were dull and smoky, and she sighed out the smell of a bruised flower; the bones of her wrists, her knees, and her ankles had a childlike sharpness about them. I pitied her.

"This was so fine. Please don't forget me. Please call me tomorrow," she said.

The next night we were on the porch, kissing, the hell with the world, when Mr. Lombardo opened the door on us. He was a short man, happy, muscular in a stringy way, and poor. He was barefooted.

"Come on in, you kids. You can kiss on the setee. There's some Jax in the icebox. College pistol. I know about you, Harry-o. Going to *graduate* school, you son of a gun." When Prissy had gone back in the house, he said, "Yall just try not to wake Mamma. And don't you pull her panties off in this house. College pistol."

I knew there was a trace of Eastern accent in Mr. Lombardo's speech. We sat on the lumpy, colorless couch, and

341

Prissy explained to me that he had been moved down here in 1946 from a shipyard near Baltimore to work at Ingall's. They had had her, Mr. and Mrs. Lombardo, two years after they got here—she was their only child—and Mr. Lombardo had been cured naturally of a disease that had to do with paint inhalation, and he thought Pascagoula was divine. He changed from Catholic to Episcopal. Prissy was lovely on that old couch, telling me this. Sometimes I would fall over and lick her neck.

I suggested we cut classes this week. Tom agreed. His father had procured him a lass out of a business college in Gulfport who called herself a "swinger."

Prissy and I saw all the places up and down the beach from Pascagoula to Biloxi, Gulfport, Pass Christian, and across the bridge to Bay St. Louis. We saw Jayne Mansfield at Gus Stevens. All the way, and quite a mass, Jayne. Prissy was cowed by her. I brought her to me, my hand around her dainty ribcage. Maybe I loved her first that night. She could do no wrong. She lay down in the sand of Biloxi beach next to me, in perhaps her best dress. She had hardly any bosoms at all, but she wore silver shoes, and she crossed her legs under her dress and dangled one of the shoes on her toes. The moon was between her heel and her shoe, and I saw the ridges of sand, with the tide out, and I suppose that did it.

"Listen. We have to get married and quit this fooling around." She began sobbing. She couldn't answer me except in high whimpers. She couldn't find her voice.

We were on the couch together, late, three more nights. I hadn't seen Prissy's mother. She fled to the back of the house when I came in. I could hear her bare feet thudding. The newspaper, where she left it, would be falling apart. But the old man continued to sport around as love's chorus.

We were kissing once, and I thought I heard a smacking, smooching sound that we weren't making. I pulled the door beside the couch open. There stood Mr. Lombardo in the hall. He was pursing his lips for another kiss, only he wasn't kissing anything, just making the sounds. He gave a final leer, then disappeared into the back.

Another time, I had closed the front door and was headed for my car. I was sure the parents of the house were long asleep. It was about four in the morning.

"SSSSt! SSSSST!" came a voice behind me. His head was out the front door. "What?" I asked.

"Good stuff? Good poon?" asked the man. Then he closed the door.

I saw her once again. I didn't know when the wedding would be, but I knew it would be soon. She suggested a date.

For five days, Tommy's father had been pushing ten-dollar bills on me constantly. He would put them in my wallet when I slept, if I wouldn't take them outright. I looked once when I was out with Prissy, and, counting the little I'd brought with me, there was a hundred and ninety dollars. It was a weird boon and a new vantage, having money accumulate right on your hip. I felt lucky and began trusting in my luck. Tommy and I went out on a pier to do some fishing, and I just threw out my hook and lay back on the wet planks, closed my eyes, and felt I was in a charmed boat, hearing the water lap under us. I asked Tommy what the swinger was like.

"I don't know. Nice legs. Laughs when you put your hands on her," said Tom, who was a shy citizen if the truth were known.

"Pretty like Prissy?"

"Nobody's pretty like Prissy. You live in a tree, Monroe. And she's got some growth left to do too."

"I'd thought of that."

Tommy's old man finally knew who I was seeing. It was all right. I think he felt exculpated, knowing I wanted to marry her. "I saw her the other day. She's grown some, I think," he told me. He shoved me a hundred dollars, right over the breakfast table. Mr. Neicase looked like a playboy whose eyebrows were graying, and I think these gestures meant a lot to him.

I left Mother Rooney's on December 20th and entered Dream of Pines again. Pulling out of Jackson had been exhilarating. My parents had known I was getting married for a month. My mother was excited, thinking nothing which came from her home Mississippi could be bad. In her youth she had made some trips to the seashore near Biloxi. She adored the coastal region and trusted it completely.

The old man and I smoke hundreds of cigarettes together. Nothing really gets said. He wants to go out to the club and play golf. He loves to walk and he hits a pretty good ball. I

343

walk around with him. I understand the beauty of a nine-iron shot, the smooth chop under the ball, seeing it rise and fall just over the bunker, plant on the green, and jump lazily on the slant toward the pin. We see Swell Melton, an old buddy of his, at a tee.

"This is my youngest son, Harry. Harry is getting married next week."

"Well I'll be." The big roasted fingers coming after you in handshake.

I drove to Pascagoula three days before the wedding, having had Christmas with the folks. It was the same, just a little cooler. Prissy flew out in her yard and was on my lips. I had an engagement ring for her, which wasn't much, but her mother was out in the yard too, looking at my T-bird. Her mother finally sneaked up and brushed my cheek, then rushed back in the house, then came out and stood on the porch, dark-eyed and skinny, and said, "Say! . . ." as if she had an idea. Then she went in again. I learned later that she was happy. Prissy was very much the babyishly tender thing that night. I hardly touched her. Once she called me "Darling," but it came forced, like from reading a magazine article on love, she knew that at high peaks of emotion she must say it. She said it quickly.

It was then, afterwards in the motel—Mr. Neicase's house was closed; he was in Los Angeles—I began to feel a bad edge inside, like a large tick I could feel settling his claws into my heart; the heart, my heart, such a big, helpless organ, still beating along, but knowing the tick was there and had dug in. I developed a gaze, a numbed way of staring, say, at the edge of the motel rug, which made me deaf and stupid. And blind, in a way, because I saw nothing except the tiny geometry I was staring at.

The wedding brought a planeload of relatives from Louisiana, Texas, Atlanta, Ohio, and Virginia. These people treated me wonderfully, and I had the feeling of deep roots set down into the country. Hugging me, winking at me, smoothing me, the uncles and aunts and three cousins I hadn't seen since I started to college. We all met at the Edgewater Beach hotel. My sister was chic and stunning, with her husband the handsomest expert at gynecology in the South. My brother was rich and friendly, had traveled hundreds of miles to see my wedding. Good old Robert smoked his pipe and kept his arm across my shoulders, like

344

a warm happy branch with leaves of goodwill. He knew I needed support. I'll never recover from the family loyalty they showed me the day before the wedding. Robert's wife patting me on the back. Go get her, your bride. My mother wore a purple coat which evoked a royal aura around her I had never before seen. The old man himself was sharp as a dandy, liking his family all around him.

At the church, Lombardo brings Prissy down the aisle. Everybody in the church wears a dark suit. Yet Lombardo's suit is light tan, of a summer weave, and he wears a screwy blue tie with a Kiwanis Club clasp across it. His shoes are white; his coat is open, and his initial is on the belt buckle. Looking about, he buttons his coat while he comes down the aisle with Prissy.

Prissy looked like a pubescent Arab in her gown. The church grew quiet. My nieces were studying her and whispering to one another in the pews.

We got married. The man of the cloth, I believe, cut the service a little. It seems to me we were man and wife with blinding speed. Fleece stood Best Man. The girl who served as Prissy's bridesmaid was named Cedar Polio, or something near that, a bucktoothed daughter of Sicily who sucked in and out with joy. In the reception line, she would grab Fleece and shriek when someone she knew came by. Several boys came by who shook hands with Prissy familiarly, looking me over all the while. They gathered under the limb of a huge oak tree draped with Spanish moss and looked me over again. They wore suits but still looked like punks.

We were on the lawn behind Mr. Lombardo's supervisor's house. The Lombardos furnished for the reception very well. On the table there was everything from the usual flaky wedding morsels to a case of Jack Daniels Black. Lombardo tended the bar himself. Every now and then he would come out from behind the table and hug someone he knew, and they would bark together. It was hard to believe this happiness had anything to do with me. I walked over to the bar table when I saw Mr. Neicase working toward it with his plate in his hand. The party wasn't mixing. My father was talking to some of my relatives, out near the big oak and withdrawn from the others. He was looking iron-haired and significant in his black suit. I wanted to see Mr. Neicase. Lombardo put his arm over Mr. Neicase's shoulders.

Lombardo was tight. He hung jovially onto Mr. Neicase, seeing me come up to greet him.

"What was you daddy's name?" Lombardo asked me.

"Ode Elann."

"Both two?" he said, releasing Mr. Neicase and raising his hand, like people who are drunk do for balance. I nodded. He began shouting at my father and hooking his arm, inviting him over. My father was with his sister, many yards away.

"Hey Old Elaine! Old Elaine! Commere!"

"Daddy?" I called. He had heard Lombardo already. He looked at me distrustfully before meandering our way. The relatives were peering at us.

"Old Elaine, you know what this is?" said Lombardo, holding out his hand, as if the wrong answer would be: your hand. "It's my damn *hand*. Give me five." He took the old man's hand and put his other arm around my shoulder. "This is your last son but let me tell you, that is my first and last daughter. I didn't have a bunch like you to spare but you lookit her, that, see that, here she comes if that ain't my darling." Prissy walked to us, lifting her gown. "Want tell you somethin' else. This is my friend." He pointed to Mr. Neicase. "He is your son's friend and I didn't know if you met. He brought these two fine young people together. This is my friend Lance Neicase. He needs friends because he is divorced."

The old man looked negatively at Mr. Neicase, who blinked and turned completely around toward the bar, avoiding scrutiny. The old man said, "The bride is lovely." I knew he would have to take account of that. He smiled at her devotedly a couple of seconds. She looked a little older than his grandchildren. He didn't know how to look at her. I didn't either. The old man gave Lombardo a negligent scan, as if he would never be troubled to learn *his* first name. I wasn't sure of it myself until we got the checks from him in Fayetteville. He had a hard and vigorous signature: *Ted Lombardo.*

We were through Biloxi and on the way to New Orleans for the honeymoon, my wallet was packed with wedding gift money; we were pulling a U-Haul-It trailer full of presents, and Prissy and I were rump to rump on the seat. She had an ungainly large corsage pinned on her and a tweedy nuptial-eve outfit. Her head fell over on me. She was sobbing. I pulled off in a curbed outlet of the highway and asked her what was wrong. She wouldn't tell me. I got out and looked at the car. Some of her friends had written on the sides and the trunk in white shoe polish. "She Got Him Today He'll Get Her Tonight" and "Hot Springs Tonight!" and "Watch Mississippi Grow." And in a small neat script: "Hunch Without Fear." I suspected Fleece of that one, but no telling. I took out my handkerchief and wiped off and smeared what I could, except for the neat scriptive I thought Fleece had put on. That was all right with me; I wouldn't be ashamed to ride into New Orleans with that on my car.

"What's the matter?"

"Y'all hated my daddy," she said.

"No."

"You did."

"I think he's a hell of a guy."

"He was drunk and you were hateful toward him. I want you to turn this car around. He was scared of your daddy. I want to see you shake hands with him." She broke down again. I backed up with the trailer again. This was tedious, trying to back up a trailer.

We got to the Lombardo house just when they were getting out of the old boxy Plymouth in the driveway. The reception must've just broken up. I got out of our car and advanced toward them. Mrs. Lombardo saw me and ran in the house like a shot. Mr. Lombardo was far gone. I don't think he recognized me for a minute. He challenged me, in fact, and fell down on the back of his car.

"Who datch?"

"It's Harry. I want to thank you for this lovely bride. I want to shake your hand." He knew me then, and looked out at Prissy in the car and waved to her.

"Pretty good?" he said.

"We're fine," I said, not catching on.

"Pretty good pussy?" Then he started to weep. I let go of his hand and went back to the car.

We were at the Jung Hotel in New Orleans. The tick was on my heart and I had said nothing for hours. I knew something big and wrong would move against me shortly. I told her not to stand in view of the clerk when I registered for us. I almost jumped on the bellhop who was stealing glances at her. We got in the room, at last alone, around

347

suppertime. I wanted to have love before we went out to eat.

"I don't believe I want children this early," she told me. She sat on the bed with her tweed dress and corsage in a pile around her waist. Her breasts hung out dead white like small balls with red points on them. So we went to Moran's and I had my cigarette lit by a Cajun waiter who seemed to be lamenting over how gauche the entire world was.

When we got back, she said, "I don't think I'm going to like this." She had come out of the bathroom. While she was in there, almost an hour, I was in that deaf and dumb gaze watching these circus horses on the television. But when I saw her I took to my feet. She was naked. She had her hands at her hips. What my eyes went to was the rich brown hair around her violently overmatured and split grape.

"Great God," I said.

"Wait!" said my wife. She had her hand on the pillow. "Kiss my toe, hard! Oh that tickles too much. Kiss my mouth. Yum yum. So do you like how I kiss? I almost wore out my mouth kissing you. My lips were sore. I was sore all over thinking about getting somebody like you. And now I've got you. Ow! Oww!"

11 / Dull Sobbing Drafts

In the big dirt-creased white house in the winter light of Fayetteville, she was the same brittle and young thing I had married. It was as if I'd assaulted a child who did not call the police but followed me with wild concern everywhere I went.

In the grocery store, she didn't look old enough to be filling up the cart with such calculation. She looked like the eldest urchin in a crowd in Rome, buttoned up in cunning little adult-like clothes. I would walk a piece away from her and see the men pass by her with looks of shamed lust. The

348

poor bastards. I knew exactly what it was like, and forgave them completely. Prissy was so cute, the dream of a dago high school, and here she was choosing a roll of toilet paper, the expensive and scented kind that you imagined they hurled over a blossoming orchard of peaches and apples to get the smell all through the tissue. This was when we still had a lot of wedding-gift money.

She wanted clothes. She established accounts at every clothing shop in town. We bought furniture, and a Zenith television. I wanted a good stereo. She bought everything in the way of fashion that Fayetteville could bring down from the East. The T-bird must be rebuilt, must have new mufflers so it wouldn't sound like a redneck car. The twenty-dollar bills went over the counters and a dime and three dirty pennies came back. What we had the first month was a spending riot. My check for teaching the freshman class at the university was $216. You see the big gifts come at you at the wedding and you get the notion they'll always be coming, and all the while the credit manager at Montgomery Ward is honing his pen for the first nasty note and the magistrate is drilling the police in procedures for the collecting of bad checks.

While you listen to Otis Redding on the stereo and dip the Johnny Walker and throw a couple of parties, in honor of what a fine heedless son of a gun you are.

She wanted me to take her out for something literary, so she could understand a little bit of what I was doing. Wyatt Fred, a poet almost seven feet tall, was giving a reading in the basement of the Episcopal Student Center. We sat in the folding steel chairs. There were about twelve in the audience, everybody so much his own man that he sat lonesome and away from everybody else. Prissy and I were the only two sitting together. Two professors of mine were there; the rest of them were people with thick glasses and distressed hair. Wyatt came on and read like a wizard. The poems were quite good, and we clapped after each one, sounding like fish flapping to death in a concrete garage.

I noticed Leslie Bill Harrow was there. I wondered why. Leslie Bill taught me. He was a novelist who hated poets, every one of them. He liked to invite visiting modern poets to his house of yellow pine beams and jalousied glass on the mountain. He liked to get them drunk and expose them as specious droolers, in full view of several people who wor-

349

shiped the poet and worshiped poetry as an aloof science. First time I met him, in fact, he sent me a note asking to see my poems, and when I went to his office to pick them up, he said that he had lost them; then he admitted that he had thrown them away.

Also sitting there was Dr. Lariat. He had a mild, groomed appearance, fifty years old, a bachelor, wearing a tame plaid jacket and a tie whipping askew casually. His hair was salted and thick, and he was a stiff, almost pretty sort of man. I admired him, first, for simply being a bachelor. He had the cleanliness of the life of pure mind about him. How had he made it, how had he read all the great venereal works of all literatures, as he had, without breaking down? Why didn't he need the comfort, the warm constant flannel, of a wife? He'd taken his degrees at Columbia, before the war. He was a miserable teacher in a peculiar way; he *controlled* the misery of his classes. Lariat would stare out the window during a class for unbelievably long periods, sometimes up to fifteen minutes. Everyone knew he was supposed to be a cultural giant. He did the reviews for a Kansas City paper, and in 1950 he drew wide attention for an article describing all fiction since Henry James as "smelly." Otherwise, he had not done so much, but he had done it right. He had published four articles on Jane Austen, Samuel Richardson, Jonathan Swift, and Bernard Shaw in the right literary quarterlies. I understood that he had once had a big student following. The students thought he was pausing after they said something because he considered any and every idea provocative and seminal. They thought he was a beatnik. Then, around 1959, they found out that those long pauses were swoons of utter contempt for any human voice except his own. His heart was not present in the room at all. You did not know where his heart was, but you had the feeling that if you ever went to that place, you would be laughed at.

The Arkansas sunlight seemed to hurt him. When sunlight and the student herd mixed, you would see Lariat, distraught-looking, toiling along the borders of the hall. When the students came out of his class, *they* looked distraught. There was fear in his classes. Some feared he would, say, *strike*, after those long pauses. Everyone was worn out waiting for the bell. After the pause, he would say something like: "Henry James did *not* write about anything so

350

heinous as real life." When you spoke to him, he was polite, but he seemed to be on the verge of running away to a shadowed, violet scene of warmer conversation with one of the Muses.

His hometown, I found out, was Dream of Pines, Louisiana.

Wyatt Fred read some very strong local-color things about butchery and coitus, car wrecks, and abortions. I looked at Lariat. The thinnest, but yes, smile. He merely put his hands together when the rest applauded. Perhaps he had attended to give modern literature still another chance.

Prissy touched at me all during the reading. When it was over, she hadn't understood one iota of Wyatt's poetry, I don't think, but she was moved by the fact that Wyatt had read with such conviction. I hustled her out to the car. These were my teachers and I didn't care for her to give voice around them.

Going home, we drove down that long fall of School Street to the eight-room house sitting next to Highway 71.

It was about a month later, the night after the big March snow, I was coming home drunk from Roger's Recreation, and found myself on the top of School Street and could barely hold myself back from sliding on the ice all the way down to my house. I had two envelopes with letters from the police about two big bad checks and I'd just written another bad one to Roger—who never prosecuted me, bless him, and took my word—and I threw those envelopes on the ice, saw them take off down the hill on the ice, out of sight, lovely. I had also found this tin cup lying in the middle of a tire rut on Dickson Street, and I was carrying it, for what or to where, but I had an idea which gripped me. I would lay hand on myself and produce an audience of my own sperms in the cup, which would be a sort of amphitheatre, and lecture to them, and also pull out of my coat my new poem, and by God I would read the last drop of juice out of it, and in the cup by God there would be little ears that would hear it, and I put my ear over it; they were applauding already. But, unbuttoning my coat, I slipped and fell on the ice and took a dire lick on the back. I knew this was not a simple injury. I should be taken to a home for the hurt. The sleet was biting my face to pieces. In the air over me I saw a beam. A car with clinking chains stopped just in back of my head. Then a cop looked down

351

at me out of a nylon and fur jacket. I told him to give me a shove, I could make it on down the hill. He told me I was drunk and told me not to tell him what to do. He said: "Lie out of the road." I told him I was a student, a teacher, and poet in my spare time. I asked where my cup was. He held over me with the look of a dog pissing. Then he yelled to the other cop at the wheel. I got up, not hurt so bad as I'd feared. But I told him I was hurt very profoundly. The car drew up and they told me to get in. The inside of the car was hot and there was a grate between me and the two of them on the front seat. I was plotting my escape, how to yank the pistol from whose leg, because I could not see the disgrace of a cell. It passed my mind that they might not know I'd written the bad checks but were going to book me on a charge of attempted masturbation, plus lying in the road. I could not drag my name into this. Then the driver asked me where I lived, I told him, and they let me out at my front door.

Next to our house was old man Walker's house with the "Worms" sign nailed on the tree hard by our driveway. Walker was retired from the mortuary stone trade and sold fish bat in milk cartons. The worm bins were in his basement. Our houses were crammed so closely together that we almost had to be friends, or move. I liked the old creep, anyway. He was near eighty and looked like a dwarf who had started as normal but had been ridden into old age by some terrible concern astride his neck. One stunning cold night in February, his face passed by close to the window of my study room. I was shivering anyway, wearing my overcoat because there was no heater in this room, and he scared the devil out of me. It was about three in the morning. He had had his teeth bared, like some gargoyle who had fallen off my roof and hit the ground alive and vicious. I went out through the living room, on out the back porch and intercepted him, coming around the rear of my house, and asked him what he thought he was doing. The cold really swatted me. Walker wore only a flannel shirt over another shirt, the flannel shirt misbuttoned.

"What are you doing up?" he asked me suspiciously.

"I was reading and writing. You scared me. You could get shot."

"Well you know how it is when you don't get on with the

352

wife. You take the walk. To get rid of it. You can't go to sleep like you are. It would give you a stroke."

His wife was his age, and was yellow like the face of an old cheap clock.

"Every night it comes up something different you wouldn't expect. She come in tonight got hair curlers in her hair and in that bathrobe I don't like."

"You couldn't let that pass?"

"I lit a cigarette and she commenced shouting 'bout it would break my health. She went inside the kitchen and come out with the hammer. I got an arm hold on her. You know."

"What?"

"She said she was dying. You know women how they'll mourn on you. I let go. And she hits me in the throat with the hammer and goes to calling for help."

"Damn!"

"It ain't not occurred to me about divorce. It goes on and on. I just saw your light. It didn't look like you was doing nothing. You said you was reading and writing. You planning to *make* something?"

"You *love* your wife, Mr. Walker?" it occurred to me to say.

"It goes and comes. You know."

He was out in the yard several nights later. This time he put his face against my study window and held the outer sill, examining me forlornly. I jumped out of my seat when I saw him. The expression did not change on the old man's face. He looked at me with ghastly concern. One of his eyebrows was crusted with blood, I saw, as his facial heat defrosted the pane and his breathing made the glass clear. He prolonged his dead-eye scrutiny of me, and then drew off as if sucked away. I was furious. I went to the bathroom and threw up a small amount of something thin and bitter, from the bottom of my stomach. When I was settled down I picked up the phone and dialed his number. Prissy came down the stairs with a blanket around her and saw me with the phone.

"Who are you calling this *late?*"

"Go on back to bed." She ignored me and sat down on the bottom step with her bare feet crossed and the blanket over her head. The phone at Walker's was ringing, six, sev-

353

en times, no answer. When someone finally picked it up I'd lost my anger and set the phone down.

"I have a right to find out who you're calling so late, don't I?" said Prissy. "If you look at me with hate every time I want to do something you don't like, how do you expect me to look on you with love every time you do something I don't like?"

The ghastly face of Walker recurred to my mind. An old raw pirate's voice, Cockney, gathered in my throat, and I drew up in a crabbed, one-legged way, the old pirate in heat, looking at her as if blind in one eye but bright in the other, one overcompensating healthy boiling right eye. "My dearrrrriee dream!" I roiled out. Prissy hunched back, up a step, with her heels.

The house was frigid. There were two small space heaters downstairs and one upstairs in the bedroom, with a broken grate, letting a vapor of gas off so we had to keep the window cracked for safety. I threw off my overcoat and clawed at my snap, tearing off my shirt as the pants fell and heaving out my chest as if to disclose a beastly tattoo. "I takes my pleasure in the cold!" I swore. Prissy stood and ran upwards. I heard the blanket whizzing on the steps and the shutting of the door. There was no lock on the door. I hurled away my last shred and took the stairs naked. I was bitten by such cold that I had to take a crouching, even more sinister posture, thinking that if I ran up, the breeze would kill me. "Awrrr! Coming up the stairs to mingle with my dearie!" I proclaimed. "That maybe we could find a bit of warmth between us." At the top of the stairs I was waddling in a dishonorable position not even worthy of an old pirate. I could form no more words. The cold had me like a crab of the Arctic who had only a nerve-life, and sought heat and light. I butted in the door, holding my knees, shutting the door with a side action, quickly, to keep the beloved warmth in. I was below the end of the bed. The room was dark; a weak flaring orange came from the heater.

"Where are you?" asked Prissy. "What can this mean to you? This is not entertaining."

I waddled along the side of the bed, dedicated to this squatted position now. The numb gaze and the deafness were with me. I waddled up even with her form on the bed. My head came just over the level of the mattress. I laid it down beside her hand. She shrieked.

354

"I used to think you were well bred!"

"Wrong," said I. "Take me or leave me—" tumbling like a crab from some height into the bed. I lay there stunned a while; then I could relax my hooked hands and straighten my legs.

"Harry, I don't like this. Why must love take these forms?" she mourned. She shared the guilt with me. The heater was beating orange shadows up at the end of the bed. The wallpaper was fern green with crocus prints; we slept in the old half-finished attic our landlord once lived in. Leaks in the roof made brown stains on the wallpaper at the corners, and in spots the paper had fallen away. Over us was the tin roof, the best roof I've ever lived under. You hear the rain and the sleet just over your head and take in the weather very personally, take it into sleep with you. There were two dangling light sockets upstairs, but no electrical outlets. The house had the musk of forty years of human baggage. We had a huge bathtub with scrolled feet. Prissy had made the curtains in my study out of burlap, and it smelled like a feed store. Across the street was the R&S, a twenty-four-hour grill for greasers, truckers, and hungover college boys. To our left was Walker, to our right a house the size of ours cut up into four apartments which rotated with different collections of the outright poor, loud sluts of the beautician's college, and people like lonely barbers. The trucks put the air brakes on at the stoplight all night, coasting in to the R&S Grill. In our block, to the west, stood two high grain elevators which belonged to the Farmer's Cooperative. The train wasn't far off. I don't know what was going on, but the neighborhood stunk like someone was dropping live chickens into a cauldron. And just beyond the boarding house to our left was a house-shop: "Nantiques." A woman named Nan sold antiques, you see. This is when the money was suddenly all gone, and I'd spend hours in front of the television, trying to get stunned.

My TV broke at a terrible moment. I was watching the horror movie by myself; Prissy was asleep overhead. In the finest wino tradition, I'd bought myself a 99¢ bottle up at Mac's Liquor with our last dollar. We had food, I mean, and the first of the month wasn't long away. But here I was left with the last warm slug of the bottle and a dark room. I was rocked by the silence and the fact of my marriage, with

only me, this Prissy upstairs, and the black quiet; too stupe-
fied to think of anything else. I had a notion suddenly that I
must marry her with my mind tonight. The die had been
cast, we were alone in the house together, so we must make
it together with locked minds somehow. I took the stairs. I
did not want to be lustful, but I had the sensation of rising
on a rolling cluster of hooks, my hands drew in like claws,
and I had to fight against being a creature of pure nerves
all over. The mind, the mind, I kept saying. This time she
had the light on and was sitting on the bed, looking at me
hard away.

"Harry? Did you get drunk, Harry? Are you *happy*, honey?"

I wanted to speak but I gave out a disconsolate mating
sound.

"Now *dar*ling," she said. "You're too handsome to sound
like that. What are your hands doing? I have never liked
that stuff. I want you to whisper . . ."

"Help *me*. *Help* me!" I moaned, looking at my hands,
sinking to the posture of a crab, my mind drowning. Her
voice always drowned my mind in one way or another. I
tried to rise. Her *heartfeltness,* I couldn't stand it.

"I want you to whisper and to kiss. You know how to do
that."

"I can't. I feel stupid and silly. To prime you and start
you up like a motor. I feel like I'm reading directions to
something."

"But love isn't any of that. Love is . . . romance. I've
learned that, darling. Love is becoming softly intoxicated.
Love is two hearts beating together. Love is sacred."

"That sounds like a *list*, Prissy. Where did you get that?"
I knew she read *Cosmopolitan* and maybe the labels on a
couple of perfume bottles. I had hurt her feelings. She
clouded up and cried, while she held her feet and rocked on
her fanny.

"A *list?!* It was a Poem. For *you*."

"Well it was a *nice* list, Prissy. Darling," rolling my mind
right down Valentine alley, "Love is holding hands, too."

12 / Lariat

You were not supposed to know Dr. Lariat. He talked at length to advanced graduate students outside of class, occasionally, but you were supposed to wait in the wings for a couple of years, attending his classes, and try not to break wind during the lectures, as they say. Then he might begin speaking to you in full sentences. He might tell you of his war experiences.

At one point, in the taking of Italy, there were complaints about wanton destruction by artillery of precious structures of the Middle Ages and the Renaissance. Lariat had been in Italy before. They put him in a jeep and ran him around to vantage points and let him suggest what monuments to spare. He made the rank of captain doing this. He would tell them, hating the sun, making a roof over his eyes with his hands, that behind that wall there was a fine bust done by Vigoro Oleo. The Germans found out about him, and would crowd around precious Italian artworks and blast away joyfully. Some were taken prisoner hanging flat on these artworks like leeches and calling out Lariat's name. The German radio called out his name as a noble exception to the swarm of ruffian hobos from America calling themselves an army. The jeep would also take him back to town councils and priests so that he could explain that everything was being done to spare the priceless heritage of Italy. He spoke Italian and French, and knew the essentials of German, Spanish, and Russian. Three of the languages he had learned, academically at least, while being bored at Dream of Pines high school. One night as he was walking on the street at dusk with his face in a book, some Dream of Pines person jumped out of an alley and slugged him.

"Is Oliver Sink still there?" asked Lariat.

"Our house is right next to his."

"He's the one who hit me. He was angry with me the af-

357

ternoon before because I'd got so mad with him I blessed him out in French. The naughtier words."

"Do you know my father? He would have been a little older."

Lariat stole a direct glance at me. He could really scour one, with that crisp, temporary smile boosted on his lips. "His name was Ode Elann Monroe. That lingering name. Yes. What has he done besides have you?"

"Has the mattress factory."

"He isn't literary?"

"No. Well, I think he wanted to be."

"He wanted very much to be," said Lariat. I didn't know what he thought of my father, and didn't want to follow it up. I thought Lariat might despise him.

"And Oliver Sink, he has, or had, peacocks. They used to come over in our yard."

Lariat, well, he struck his brow. His eyes were unbelieving.

"No! Peafowl! He can't have them. *I* have peafowl. Yesterday the neighbor's brats were shooting at them with an air rifle. I would have killed them if their mother hadn't come out. I tore the air rifle into a thousand parts."-

I went in Roger's Recreation Friday afternoon, as usual, to have a beer and read the Tulsa paper. Roger is a basketball player two and a half decades out of training. The trophies won by his team sit in a high clutter on a shelf over the bar; he only bets on his city-league team now. As I said before, he was a saint about holding my worthless checks until I could pay for them. His place was dominoes, pinball machines, and, mainly, snooker and pool tables going far back into the long gray and green. In there, my soul could sit down and expand.

Down past the bar I caught sight of Lariat. He was playing the tan-felted snooker table nearest the bar all by himself. On Roger's color television, the FM station was going with a Rolling Stones tune played by an orchestra of ancient studio hacks. Lariat seemed unaware of anything but his shots. He bent and shot like he had known how to shoot very well at one time. Then he came over to the end of the bar and poured out a low amount of beer into a pilsner, from the bottle of Jax. Beside the bottle there was a pack of Picayunes. Picayunes, more than Camels, are cigarettes for men who want a real smoke.

358

"Dr. Lariat?" I said.

"Oh. Get a cue."

"I've never seen you down here."

"I've never been here before. What's your first name—Ode?"

"Harry."

"Oh. Do you know the game? This is a sport I used to love in Dream of Pines, and even more in the army. The red balls count one point. You must shoot in a red ball before each number ball you wish to shoot. Shoot for position on the higher numbered balls. When all the red balls are down, you play regular rotation on the two through seven balls. A snooker is made when—"

"I know."

We shot five games and he beat me all of them. After the games he would shoot the old shark six-railer with the cueball and sometimes it would go in. We played for the price of the games—30¢—and I had to go up and write a counter check to Roger to cover the last two. And the beer. We drank the last one. Lariat kept the crisp smile on his face and said nothing. He had not taken off the coat of his suit.

Lariat had money. He flew to New York and London to see the theater. During the summer he would fly off and tour continents. Leslie Bill Harrow said he went to visit all the famous and little-known ruins of the world. No one knew what he did when he got to the ruins. He was one of the first tourists that the Soviet Union let in. He had seen the church over Tamburlaine's tomb. Some years ago he was hurt in a jeep-wreck seeking some ruin in middle Africa and came back to Fayetteville in a cast. Further about the money, he had loaned money to a few graduate students who had been at the university many years. The ones I knew he lent to were aging fellows who somehow could not get the degree and detach themselves from Fayetteville.

Hoyd sat next to me in Lariat's class. Hoyd was pockmarked and over thirty. He had let his hair grow out to the length of his shoulders and looked like a medieval tramp. He worshiped Lariat. Lariat had loaned him money. He would cringe and wrinkle his nose and lay his head on the desk, looking at me, after the boy up front asked Lariat a question. "Why is James like a cathedral?" Hoyd cut forth a strangled hoot out the side of his teeth and eyed me hysterically. Apparently he knew something about what Lariat would say. During Lariat's pause he wrung his hands and pumped his face up and down. He loved the pause. "James wanted to be buried in the grave of his own church. The church was his fiction, his own writing. Nothing else was baroque or miraculous or, well, sanitary enough," Lariat said. Hoyd squeaked with approval, looking at me for support.

The next time I saw Lariat outside of class was up at Leslie Harrow's party in April. Leslie had lawyers, psychologists, librarians, theologians, hippies, art department camp-followers, and that crowd—all about to blow apart his place on Mount Sequoyah. When I got there, the booze had been working on them for an hour and a half. Some were dancing to the stereo—guitars and nigger-hollering. Wyatt Fred, the giant poet, was swerving about the area with six hours of whiskey in him. Hoyd passed us, smoking grass in a badly rolled paper that was falling apart in sparks all over him. Leslie was a thoughtful host. He took Prissy away from me and planted her over by the hearth between two girls who were all eyeglasses and cigarettes.

I went in the kitchen. Lariat was leaning by the refrigerator. Beside him was his Wild Turkey in a black crocheted cover. The kitchen looked over a counter to the room where many were dancing now. Lariat put his hand in the ice bag and came up with a handful that he dumped in a glass. He poured a nice potion from the black crocheted bottle into it. The drink was for me. I was astounded and honored.

"Who was that you came in with?" he asked.

"That was my wife."

"Is she coon-ass?" This means Cajun in downhome Louisiana idiom. I wouldn't have thought Lariat would say that. I simply let it go by.

"She's a nice little piece. I really wonder why you're standing here with that drink with the music going on and that nice little piece out there. I'd think you wanted to dance with her."

I looked out at the dancing mob.

"One thing I never did was dance," he said.

I was feeling smug and above it. He poured me another drink. Then he left the kitchen and went out into the living room. I smiled at Hoyd and a few other people coming into

the kitchen to make drinks. Thirty minutes later, Lariat
came back. He had talked to her. We were the only ones in
the kitchen.

"Is she stupid or is she sincere?" he asked. "Either way,
she's a nice little piece."

"She's sincere," I said. I wasn't sure on that point myself.

"What age is she?"

"Eighteen," I lied.

"She is a darling. There was a blond boy telling her what
a darling she was. He was saying he'd never seen anything
like her. A student of mine. Divorced."

I left the kitchen and lunged out into the crowd. Everybody was happy and forgiving. Some fell on the floor. A
girl dancer was suddenly jerked out of my way. Prissy was
not on the hearth where Leslie had set her, and the girls
with eyeglasses were gone too. I looked behind me. Lariat
had followed me over.

"Does she tend to run away?" he asked, right next to the
stereo speaker.

"No." I was very concerned.

"Does she ever have to go to the bathroom?"

"Yes!" I declared. Again I mashed through the dancers,
seeking the bathroom door. I broke out of the crowd and
ran to the first closed door of the hall. It was locked.

"That *is* one of the bathrooms," observed Lariat. He had
come back through the dancers too.

I kicked the door football-style. Then I turned the knob.
It was locked but the door gave. I drove in. Some girl, not
Prissy, jumped into the shower curtain of the tub and fell
in, pulling up her hose.

"Who was that?" said Lariat.

"Not her."

I led off toward the back bedrooms. Hoyd and two other
men who looked like they were in a heedless fit, one of
them a painter wearing overalls, seemed to be standing in a
line outside a closed door.

"What are you doing?" I asked them.

"Waiting," said the painter.

I elbowed through them and threw open the door. "Wait.
You'll have your turn," came a voice from the shadows of
the bed. A long-haired boy or man was squatting over the
pile of coats on the bed with his pants down, alone.

"Pray to God she wasn't in there," said Lariat.

361

"No." I wanted awfully to find Prissy. "Prissy! Prissy Darling!"

Back in the living room, the mob had grown fourfold. I pushed into the flank of the dancers. Then there was a shoulder on my hand. "Who is that?" said Lariat, who was pointing across a split in the dancers, having my hand on his shoulder. He had found her. Prissy was dancing half-heartedly with a blond man. She seemed to be the color of a new penny. I loved her, never before in this full and humble way loved her. I felt I would never be so lucky as to touch her. And would she remember me if I did? "Darling!" across the thighs and shins of the dancers. When she saw me she put out her hand, the blond man evaporated away through some slit of the house. I held her tiny moist hand with both of my hands. "Prissy, you can't run away like this. I was looking all over for you, darling. I love you. Please be my wife." I was damn near sobbing, and Prissy put her wet eyelashes against my throat.

I think Dr. Lariat had left the party. His crochet-covered bottle was still on the counter, but I never saw him again that night. Myself, I stayed in love for three months.

Lariat's lectures changed a little. He talked more. He came out with anecdotes from his past. All of them were arid and pointless episodes and were introduced with no transition from the literary items at hand. Sometimes he tried out some stories he had heard from Cajun sages long ago, and tried to do the dialect, but his voice imitations were futile. They came from a man who had cherished none but his own voice, inviolate, for too many years. Hoyd laid his head on his desk and frowned at me.

"He's down. He ain't himself," Hoyd said. "Something on his nerves. Did you hear what happened to him last week? In his side yard he's got a goldfish pool with a boy, a cherub, sits up on the base in the middle of the pool. This cherub had a dick, an open dick; not much, but a dick, a minimalized Renaissance pecker. These people come by at night and knock the little thing off with a hammer. Lariat heard them in the water, but they ran off and got in a car and drove away."

"I hadn't heard."

An afternoon in May I picked up this note in my box in the English office. Lariat wrote that if I was interested in playing snooker at 20¢ a point, I would be at his house

Sunday night about seven. He'd bought a table. He wrote: "I'll be disappointed if you don't show up."

He lived in the oak-covered section of Fayetteville at the flat meadow between the mountain and the highway. There were some rich homes here. His house was constructed of molasses-brown bricks. There was not much front yard; the pool and the willow trees sat in a rectangular basin to the south side of the house. On the other end of the house was the chipped-brick driveway and the garage. One of the peafowl picked around the house toward me as I waited at the door. "Watch it, watch it," I said.

Inside, well, very nice—potted fronds and ferns, rugs from Turkey, a banana tree, a piano, lots of solitary chairs and small couches. The south end of the house was almost all glass, so you could look out on the pool and the willows.

"I heard you had some trouble. The statue," I said.

"They waded right in and did it. I take it as a symbol of the South—I don't know whom to suspect, the Baptist minister, high school punks, an angry ex-student, a drunk, or an Episcopal aunt."

The table was in the basement. It had tan felt like the one in Roger's, and was level. Lariat had fixed up a chromium reflector for the hanging light bulb. Also there was a blackboard, a child's affair with the alphabet and corresponding animals, for scoring. Here was a man who took his gaming seriously.

"First of all," I said, "I can't afford twenty cents a point. I'm used to playing for a nickel."

The crisp, passing smile came on his face.

"Let's not make it cheap. Risk is beauty. Besides—" He opened the refrigerator, which boiled out frost; the shelves were crammed solid with Löwenbrau. "Look what the house furnishes. Cue up. Lag for break."

"All right." I chalked my stick, a new, already talced one, an 18-weight; one of five he had to choose from. Lariat of course owned a jointed stick with its own case. I believed he wanted me to notice the leather case as he joined the stick. "Dr. Lariat; you have fourteen red balls. I've never seen that. Down at Roger's, you know, there are only nine. You have an extra row." Lariat shook his head.

"This is the original snooker set. This is real snooker of the old days. What are you moaning about? Look at all the points you can make."

Look at all the points *you* can make, I thought. A shark could run the score up out of sight on you with the extra red balls. I had been in a few games with real sharks. These people were fearsome, cool maniacs. They made points as if easing a knife in a woman, slowly and impassively.

Lariat broke the balls and brought the cueball back down the rail behind the two ball—a snooker right off. I tried to rail for the red balls, but my tip glanced off the top of the cueball. Four points—80¢. I had two dollars in my wallet. He beat me thirty points the first game. Lariat swore like a wounded man every time he missed a shot or failed to get exquisite position. I was talking to the balls a good bit myself. Lariat knew a few of the old tricks, but he could not exercise them consistently. It was just that I was somewhat scared and played miserably. At one o'clock he cut off the light. I was almost thirty dollars to him.

"I can't pay now," I said.

"You'll be back next week. We'll let it ride. You *will* be back next Sunday?"

Sure. He said almost nothing to me that first night. I think he was really too happy to talk.

Then Sunday, Sunday, Sunday, Sunday, Sunday, with the big rains pounding his basement windows, and then the warm grip, the extra light, of summer coming on. I made, about the second time we played, an allusion to his being a bachelor. I was tight and told him I wondered if he ever thought about the fact that the only literary figures he was interested in were celibates. I asked him if he believed in a literary procession of fornication-proof people. That those were the real writers. He sneered at me. He looked at me like he was very sorry I'd spoken. His hair had broken away from its severe, scratched-apart combing—the part almost like a wound. He peered out the window of the basement, pausing. Would he ever speak?

"I'm not a bachelor, boy. I'm a widower."

Not even Hoyd knew this. But Lariat had married, during the first season of rest after the war, a woman from Switzerland. She was blond, and older than Lariat; she was bumptious and athletic, and loved the sun. She made Lariat promise her that they would live at Key West like Ernest Hemingway for a while. On the boat back to the States, Lariat's wife and some other foreign girls found a tall creosoted beam on deck, and prepared it for a May pole. It

364

wasn't May, but the girls had missed celebrating the last May Day and wanted to re-enact it. The pole did not stay in its stand when they danced around it pulling on the ribbons. It fell on Lariat's wife and killed her. Dr. Lariat showed me the last poem he'd written, at age twenty-nine, six months after his wife's death. The poems begins

> It wasn't May
> But the fools thought they
> Could bring back prettiness and play.
> The pole,
> The artificial May Pole, told them:
> No. And fell
> On artificial Switzerland . . .

at which point in the reading, Lariat took the poem away from me. Lariat went on to Columbia to teach a year, recovering from the tragedy.

"Or under that guise," he said. "Actually I had nothing to recover from. The only thing I missed about her was her German accent, which was pleasant and almost sleep-inducing. I heard it so often over the radios during the war, calling my name, and was charmed by the accent then. So I married it when I could. But it was only the woman, walking around naked, making dinner naked; she would have shopped naked. She was trying to play a woman in D. H. Lawrence's books. Then, I didn't know what she was trying to play. I hadn't read any of Lawrence. I was happy for her that she was dead, in that way. The blow was quick, probably painless, not very bloody. It's what happens to all farm animals at the height of their beauty. She was thirty-five, losing the beauty she had when I found her—just the time for the blow. With her perpetual suntan, she was most likely due for skin cancer had she lived; an actual visible flaking away. Neither she nor I could have borne it."

I held my tongue. What would I have said, anyway?

Another night we were talking esthetics. "Death may be the mother of beauty, and sorrow and frustration are usually tied up in beauty some way. But the *pause*, the pause between impulse and action; that makes beauty more times than you're aware of. My wife never paused, never. Never reflected, never poised, never held a tentative position. She was always straight into the action, and that's the way you

365

always saw her—acting, moving, engaged in something. Her esthetic, if she had one, must've been that beauty is energy. And that's false as a wooden nickel. If you want to get a C in my class, just write about how *energetic* somebody's work is." And later. "And furthermore, if you want to talk about *honesty*. Such a premium on that word. Being absolutely *honest*, come on: the vagina is the ugliest, ungainliest natural creation in the known world. Perhaps when they land on Mars they might find something uglier. It is a nightmare. That it gives pleasure, my friend, is an outright *paradox*, a sort of serendipity out of foulness. Hell, women know this. What a laugh to read all these lyrical hypocrites shouting that this is *not* true. *Men*, most of them! Willfully blind with those wide *honest* eyes."

I felt I ought to speak up in behalf of his dead wife, but didn't know the way to do it. I was still shy of him. Should I keep calling him Dr. Lariat? His first name was Gregory. I thought that if I called him that, he might peer at the window and wait for me to clear out. The third night, when we quit, I owed him seventy dollars. This was another anguish. Of course I would be back the next Sunday. During the week I skipped two of his classes and practiced like a wildcat on the tables. Finally I got my game back. When I played the next Sunday, I stayed loose and shot for snookers. And I had luck too. One time I ran three red balls and the rest of the numbers.

Lariat spoke to me as I shot. "What is it like back home?"

I took a rest. "I'll tell you what I think of it. First of all, if you mean the real town, where you used to live, it looks like the remnants of a pretty village," thinking, trying to get it perfect for Lariat, "that was bombed with tin. They have paved over your mother's grave . . ."

"Don't try out your poetry on me. I wasn't asking for that." He was angry. Mainly over my winning, I think.

"I was trying to give you an impression. According to you, Dream of Pines today . . ."

"Shoot the ball, snooker man."

From then on I won, although slowly. I cut my debt to forty dollars; we played one night even; the next I cut it to five dollars. The next I went wild, I had a mystic stroke, and he owed *me* nine. We did not speak to each other at school any more. In his basement, he could barely keep back his rage, waiting on me as I made the balls. What could I do? I drank the expensive Löwenbraus with guilt. I said, "Aw, *too* bad!" when he missed a shot and it was my turn.

"Don't worry about me. Shoot," he said.

The worst night was the night he didn't answer the door. I opened the door myself and heard the shower going in the back. I went over to the windows. There was more light in the evenings now. You could see his pool and the boy statue, poised on one toe, his arms out, at some position between dancing and flying. At his crotch was the whiter stone where the organ had been knocked off. It seemed awfully funny to me. I know that in the back of my mind I had thought it was, at least, risible, and had been stifling my humor. Now it looked like a little baby fop who had been taken down by flak on his first attempted launch from the earth. I giggled, then couldn't stop laughing; my stomach hurt, tears flooded out of me. I must've been laughing loudly. I was broke, final exams were over; I felt hopeless and free at the same time. No telling how long Lariat was behind me. He was in his shower robe, with dripping feet, and when I turned I saw him as the dickless grown-up version of that cherub out there, and howled even more, right in the face of his stare. I did want to stop, and was embarrassed.

"*You* did it, didn't you? That was *your* hammer I found in the pool."

"No, sir. No. My God. No."

"If you didn't, you wish you had."

"Believe me—"

He turned around and walked back to dress. "I read your final," he left me with. I went on down to the basement.

While we were about midstride in the first game, he tapped my hand with the end of his cuestick as I was lining up a six ball shot. "I read your final. I'm giving you a C for the course."

"Oh come *on!*"

"You despise James. You despise Proust. The way you despised them was ignorance. You are a fool, boy."

"I wrote a good final for you. I said I couldn't stand to read sentences three times to make sense of them."

"*What* three times? Who has to read them three times? You're a fool."

367

"Don't say that again," I said. I was blushing, I know. I looked out the window away from him.

"Look at me if you want to threaten me."

"You're treating me unfairly, Gregory. Damn you. You will not give me a C. That's robbery. You know it."

"What would you do?"

"That's nasty, asking that. You know it is. I'd take the nine dollars you owe me and hate you. You know that's all I could do. I didn't know you would turn into a son of a bitch like this." I looked at the black grass pushed against the basement window, trying to crack the glass with its full growth now: grass at its black-green peak. If Lariat gave me a C, I was through. They would take the assistantship away from me. I had made another C, or rather Leslie Bill Harrow had *given* me a C in his class. "I liked you. I went to all your classes except a few, didn't I? I was in your fan club."

"Are you begging?" said Lariat.

"No. Go to hell." I threw my stick away and started up the stairs.

Lariat called to me. "Come back. How about a B?"

"I need a straight A."

"All right. Shoot. Your shot on the six ball."

As we played on, with me 'winning twenty, fifty, sixty dollars, feeling like a gentleman for not pressing for what he owed me—a damned odd feeling for one who was ruined and broke—the basement became an attractive, fluid situation for me. Lariat spoke to me as I made the balls, and I could speak and shoot accurately at the same time. I told him about Peter, Catherine, Fleece, Silas, Mother Rooney, Bet Henderson. Lariat kept the crisp smile up all the while. I went back in time, described Harley.

"Some of that I almost believe," said Lariat. This was on the date of my publishing my first poem in a tiny booklet sort of magazine in New Orleans. Which Lariat lauded. "Success!" he cheered. I would have brought the magazine over with me, but I suspected he very urgently wanted never to have to read it.

13 / 620 MPH to Jackson

She had been sick in the mornings. Some days she was sick all the way through the afternoons. We got a $250 check from Mr. Lombardo during this period. He wrote it out in a whipping festive script. Prissy had mentioned in the letter that she might be pregnant. Lombardo thought even the idea of it was worth money.

Most of it went to buy off the creditors. We had fifty dollars left. I looked around and finally got a job at the Ralston Purina plant up at Springdale. I started at four-thirty in the afternoon and worked till about three at night. This was a plant where they processed roasts and gravy plates. They killed several thousand turkeys a day. The birds' feet were hung in the conveyor chain. They were stunned with an electrical shock. Then, a lone man with a bunch of sharp knives who had been at it twenty years cut their throats. The fluttering corpses were run through an alley of ovens which singed off their feathers. They came around to an aluminum trough where other people gutted them and cut off their heads. The trough ran a stream of water which took the gravel that the turkeys had swallowed to a depressed box. The corpses were taken on through hot water sprayers and seen to by other people. The guts and extras were the business of my crew. We came in when the others knocked off. We had steam hoses, shovels, squeegees, steel wool, and mops. The uniform was boots and yellow rubberoid aprons. The place was as big as ten gymnasiums. Canals ran everywhere and were loaded with a sluggish ooze of crops, heads, and bowels when we got there. A USDA man wandered around, and the idea was, you should be able to eat off the floor of the canals when you left. This is the sort of work that is supposed to make you a man of some past, you know; make you rugged and plucky. What a bunch of moonshit. First day on the job, the foreman on this shift

369

took me and some other new blood around the areas. "One thing you got to get over," he said. Then he jumped down into a canal thigh-high in the gut muck, holding his hands up and winking with a tough smile. Some of the regulars, who were Okies and crazy sergeants and people who wore hats with earflaps in the summer, and like that, had really vile assignments. Like the man in the pipe to the dogfood plant next door, who was a sort of human plumber's friend. As far as I know, there is no worse work in America. $1.65 an hour. And the smell, oh my. You faded away to seek the restroom and get a nose full of the deodorant bar in the toilet. And there would be another guy in there, eating a sandwich. Outside again. Somebody has to do this, somebody has to do this, I told myself. This is probably quite true, and I was comforted, really, by living with a truth. An absolute.

When I got home, it was sublime. Maybe any home would have been sublime, but I was so tired and Prissy was as sweet as sleep. I can never get out of my memory the pleasure of falling asleep as she talked, cooed to me with her head on my pillow. My daddy, daddy, daddy's home. And mommy, mommy, mommy's here too. And so is baby, baby, baby, but he can't see us and we can't see him; Prissy herself, as she cooed, I felt her thin shoulder and saw her in her rare beauty, Prissy herself—the mommy and baby both, in one body. I never knew what I had until she was pregnant.

I was sleeping late, Saturday morning, the last of June. Prissy told me Fleece was on the phone from Jackson.

"How are you?" asked Fleece.

"Waking." I could tell he was rushed.

"Do you know anything? Catherine and Lock. I suppose you would've called *me*. It wasn't in the newspapers or on the TV up there?"

"My TV's broken. What?"

"Both of them are dead. The police killed them in Beta Camina. They were trying to plant a bomb on your friend Harley's front porch. They tried it once before but the bomb didn't go off. The newspapers are full of it. Lock shot a policeman right in the heart. The bullet was still lodged in his heart when they flew him to Houston. Lock had a submachine gun. Are you on the phone?"

"Yes. Go ahead."

"Well, the police were hidden around Harley's house. They saw Lock in the driveway with the bomb in a shoebox and yelled for him to stop. He ran back to his car and got a submachine gun and let go at them. When he got in the car the police riddled it and he drove into a ditch a block away. Lock ran in back of a house and two of them got him with shotguns. Catherine was dead in the car. You hear me?"

No use faking it. I don't know what I said. "They are *dead. Dead.* They can't be, but they are. I can't stand to have known so much about them. But, listen, we know about them. I threw up when I read it."

"What do you mean? Are you going to the funeral?" I asked him.

"The funeral was yesterday. Of course I didn't go. The leading mourner of the funeral is here. This is why I'm calling. He parked his car across the street late yesterday afternoon. Maybe he came right from the funeral. He stayed there all night. He got out of the car this morning and walked over to our sidewalk. His face is torn like he'd been gouging his face all night. He has his big hat kneaded to a pulp. He just stood out there and breathed at the house. Then he went back to his car, and when he opened the door I saw a shotgun lying on the seat. He sat down on the seat with his feet in the road, hanging his head, but he also has a pistol with him now."

"Call the cops," I urged him.

"I can't. I would have to stand for too much. This neighborhood is deserted. Two houses don't even have anybody living in them any more. The woman across the street has gone to Florida. Titpea is a ghost town. Delph and the other boarder have gone. Mother Rooney and I are the only two around. I'm scared, Monroe. I've got the pistol loaded but I don't want to use it. But I'm afraid if he comes in here with a pistol I'll kill him. Mother Rooney, I've got her practically a prisoner. I can't let her out of the house, can't let her call the police."

"*Use* the phone, damn it. Call Silas."

"He isn't in town. He and Bet are separated and I've had a date with Bet."

"Call your daddy."

"I'm calling *you*. Thirty minutes ago he came over and stood right in front of the *porch* here with that pistol in his

371

hand calling for *you*, Harry. You never told him you were leaving town, did you?"

"Would you have?"

"I want you to get on a plane and fly down here. I need you. Please."

"I'm broke."

"You lousy goddam liar! You aren't either broke. You told me you had a wad enough to live on for a year at that lousy goddam wedding *I* had to drive down for, and bought a new suit! You *better* be here. . . ." I didn't reply. "All right. I'm sick of hanging around watching him out the window. He's out there to stay, I know that. I'm going out the front door with my damn never-miss pistol . . ."

"I'll try to fly down." Then he hung up.

I drove over to Lariat's house. I knew he was packing up to travel to Yucatan. He was in. I asked him if I could have the snooker money he owed me, or at least the price of a plane ticket to Jackson. I didn't know exactly what that would be. The last plane I'd been on was that one to New York back in high school. And what I needed was a jet.

"Are you in trouble? Has somebody died?"

"Yes. Catherine. That girl I . . . Whitfield Peter's niece. The police shot her trying to—" and I told him the essentials.

"You're simply pressing me for money, aren't you?" Then the crisp smile fell down. He scoured me. How was I supposed to look so as to convince him? We got in Lariat's Mercury after I called the airport. They had a plane leaving in an hour for Fort Smith. At Fort Smith I could catch a Braniff jet that went to Jackson with one stop at Little Rock. Lariat cashed a large check at the Palace drugstore, and we rushed back to his house; I had forty-five minutes. Lariat gave me a hundred. But as I was getting in my car, my eyes lit on Dr. Lariat's back—the collar above his brown suit, especially, and the combed and parted gray hair. He had, I don't know, the appearance of what? My only possible companion in trouble at the time.

"Gregory," I said. "I would like very much for you to come with me. I need a wise man to go with me."

"Oh Lord. Do I look that old? I guess I do. *Go* with you, on the *plane?* And get shot?"

"No, no. I'll get the cab to let us off at the fairgrounds.

We'll go up the back way. Then we'll simply use the telephone."

"What the hell would I do?"

"Just be there. You would lend dignity."

"Christ Jesus. Am I that old? Wait a minute." He went back to his bedroom. I heard the coat hangers raking around. He was gone five minutes.

"Let's go," he said.

"What's that?" I was stunned. Lariat was wearing a snap-brim cap, a green sweatshirt with the sleeves cut off, and Big Mac blue jeans—the baggy, manual-labor sort. I'd never even seen him with his tie off, not even at snooker.

"We're going to Mississippi, aren't we?"

"Yeah. But we're not going to a dog-kicking contest, damn it." His arms were so pale. He was completely ruined by this outfit. "Listen. You have to put the suit back on. I liked the suit." He slung the cap off and cursed going back to his room. But he returned in the suit and tie, looking impatient; locked the front door; sat in the T-bird.

"Thank you," I said.

He stood just inside the door of my house with his eyes fastened to Prissy, his smile rising and falling as I explained to her that my friend Fleece had a mental problem which I must see to. I gave her thirty dollars, Lariat coming up to make change for the twenty-dollar bill.

On the plane down to Fort Smith we sat silently. The Braniff jet was already docked at Fort Smith, and we had to hurry aboard. It had been such a race to this jet, my mind had been doing little at all. But when I sat down in it, my mind caught up with my eyes, and I was sure I was sealed up in a cartoon farce which was bound to explode with me inside it. The inside of the plane seemed to have been arranged by an interior-decorator wild about pastels and the Astro-Mod motif and I had an idea that the same man had designed the plane itself. There was a row of two seats across on one side and a row of three seats across on the other side. A fool would know that this arrangement, though novel and Mod, would make the plane dip sorely to one side, especially with a lot of people sitting in the three-seat side. Another concern was that there was almost nobody *in* the plane except Lariat and me. The two stewardesses were two just-too-beautiful blondes, in high leather boots figured like the crazy pastel seats. The wings of the

373

plane were black and stubby; the body was gold; the tail was even another color. That we were in the air at all seemed a paradox of high cartoon fun. I had grown sick thinking of this veering craft when the pilot opened the address speaker and gave us his one message: "Ladies and Gentleman, we are twenty thousand feet in the air and we are making six hundred and twenty land miles per hour." He had the voice of a Texas disc jockey, a real hot-rodding yokel.

"What's wrong with you?" asked Lariat.

I made my way to the restroom. It was a nicer place, duller, steadier. If I could stay in here, I could trust that I would not fly apart in a wreck of hot pinks, greens, and oranges, holding the boots of those blondes. I would not hail out with this thing like a roman candle. I saw myself in the mirror. *You!* I thought, shocked. Always *you!* You tick. The plane sat down in the air after making a rise. It sounded like every gear on board had fouled up. What did it matter?

I began seeing in my mind Mr. Wrag at the reservoir. He fell backward and hit his head on the rocks of the shoreline. He did it again and again. Then I saw Mr. and Mrs. Wrag. Mr. Wrag slumping between Mrs. Wrag and the doctor, walking up the slope toward me, toward the Volkswagen with fishbait in the back seat. Then Catherine, walking beside them in her sports outfit. Seeing me and waving to shoo me away, again and again. The chilly breeze from the water mounting and falling. Doing it again and again. Now I began seeing the sunburned little forearm of Catherine, covered with goosebumps. The putting of the lab coat over her shoulders. "You silly old boy." I saw it over and over. I began heaving and sobbing. Someone wanted in the restroom. I went back to my seat. When I sat down I saw her all dolled-up for the last date, her foot in the shoe with one strap across it. I saw her singing in a minor role of the musicals. "She's dead, dead."

"Did you love the girl?" said Lariat.

"For a few weeks."

When I looked at Lariat, he was staring out the window. He was slightly red-eyed himself. "Look at the sun in those clouds," he said. "Oh God, if there is a God. That's what my wife used to say. 'Oh God, if there is a God!' "

In Jackson it was twilight. The cabbie took us to the fair-

374

ground gates. They were locked. We climbed over. We walked through the field to the kudzu vine cliff in back of Mother Rooney's.

"You can't climb that," said Lariat.

We made it foot by foot on the ridges. At last we obtained the back yard. For me it was no easy thing, with the raincoat I had. After we got our breath, I eased around the side of the house and yes there was Peter's Buick parked directly across the street from Mother Rooney's sidewalk. I told Lariat. I knocked quietly at the back door. The house was alight in both towers but dark in Mother Rooney's quarters. Nobody came. I saw a candle, held by someone, cross the archway to the dining room. We were on the tiny back porch behind the kitchen. We kept waiting at the door. I looked for the candle to reappear, but it didn't. Fleece was telling the truth about the neighborhood. All the big houses on Titpea were closed up. No light came from them. Only the streetlights, making a fuzzy ribbon of illumination around the roof and edges of Mother Rooney's house, and the yellowish light coming out of the window shades of the tower. Then I went back to the porch and knocked again. I knew I had seen a feeble light going around in the downstairs area. The porch was pitch dark.

"Kick the door in," said Lariat. "Let's take a chance. Wait. I'll kick it in." I took hold of the gun in my raincoat.

Just then we heard somebody trying to turn the lock. This door had only a small pane of glass at head level. You could see into the kitchen through the glass, but there was nobody to be seen. The doorknob was turning, and the door swung out.

Fleece was hanging on the inner knob. He fell out on the porch. I couldn't see much but I knew it was Fleece. Something hard hit the floor alongside him.

"Get it," he said. I bent down to him. He whispered again. "Get it." He was hoarse. Lariat picked up the thing he was talking about, which was the Italian pistol. Now I could see his face. He was without his glasses, which meant that he was blind and that the moment was grave. He looked terribly pale.

"He killed Mother Rooney. I had my finger on my pistol when he came in the front door but I couldn't pull it. Damn me. Couldn't."

"Are you hurt?"

375

"Twice. He shot me in the leg and in my back. I *had* my pistol."

"Is that him with the candle?"

"Shhhhh! Not loud. Yes. He just went back to your room."

I picked up Fleece's arms and dragged him out, down the steps, to the back yard. Lariat came along with his feet.

"He shot her in the forehead. She's lying by the telephone nook in the hall. First he shot me in the leg. Then he saw her with the telephone in her hand and shot her. I had turned away but I heard her being shot and I went over to her. He shot me again in the back while I was holding her. I passed out . . . when I came to I was lying on her face. . . . Who is that?" he asked.

"Dr. Lariat."

"A doctor?"

"Professor of Literature."

"Aw Jesus. Why did you bring *him?*"

Lariat did seem awfully useless at the moment. I took out the long cowboy pistol I'd brought down with me in my raincoat and gave it to him. Fleece's big unshot pistol. I told Lariat all he had to do was pull the trigger.

"That's right!" said Fleece. "Kill him. He's looking for you, Harry. When I came to, he was talking to me. All afternoon he wants to know where you are. He sat on the floor and talked to me in this *squeaky* little voice. I asked him to call the hospital for me. He never even heard me. He looked at Mother Rooney. He kept squeaking for the night to come, please come the night, he said. Her corpse was driving him crazy."

"The gun you gave me isn't loaded," said Lariat. Fleece lifted up one hand and gave Lariat several wet cartridges out of his palm.

"Well, is this one loaded?" I asked him.

"Oh yes. I had plenty of ammunition. I just couldn't pull the trigger."

"Peter doesn't have the shotgun, does he?" I asked Fleece.

"Just a pistol. A black pistol. I hope it was only a twenty-two. I don't hurt all that much."

"I'll get the ambulance here." I knew I was the one. I ducked up to the porch and crawled in the house itself. I was hit by a cold wind at the kitchen door, but this was only my nerves spraying out all over me. I waddled across the kitchen floor to the cornice. I peeped around it to the hall. All was black, and smelled musty. I crept on to the telephone nook. I heard nothing and saw nothing, so I stood up and tiptoed two huge steps and put my hands on the phone. The receiver was not on the cradle. I picked up the wire and tried to lift it. It wouldn't give. Mother Rooney had it in her hand. I reached down and felt the plastic and jerked the receiver out of her grip. I dialed the operator and whispered to her. The ambulance people said they would be over.

I suppose I was in a daze, looking down at the form of Mother Rooney. "Now get him," said a voice, loud. "Don't let him get you. Don't lose your life to the man." I knew the old corpse who was speaking to me. I knew I had left him behind in this house. His ghost, or whatever, rose and gasped from a corner of the living room: Geronimo. I heard the real noise then. I saw the glow of the candle filling out the room. Peter walked into the room holding a candle on a plate in one hand and a pistol in the other. "Help me, Indian!" I shouted. Peter careened toward me. I unloaded on him, right in his face. It seemed to me stray sparks and cinders jumped out of my wrist at him.

He bucked to the floor. The plate and candle flew away; the plate shattered. He bellowed and writhed. When the gun was empty I threw it at him. My legs went useless and I fell down hard; I knelt there for a minute in the dark. Then I yelled for Fleece and Lariat to come in. They were already on the porch. Came the sound of a clearing of a throat, and a faint inquiry.

"Who got who?" said Lariat. But they kept coming. One of them hit the light. Fleece walked in bent over, Lariat helping him. Peter lay out in the middle with his hands flung out. He was bleeding from the neck, and the blood was pooling. His face looked at the floor. His hair was a shredded waxy yellow. I looked down the length of his body—a pinkish-tan suit, brown shoes—for other marks of blood. There weren't any.

"You got it! You got it! You see! *Here* Harry was! You found him," Fleece screamed at Peter. There was blood all over his left pants leg. He sat down on the couch. Peter raised his face.

"Kill me," he said. He pushed up with his arms and

377

stood. The wound, the only one, was on the back of his neck. The blood ran down the back of his shirt and flooded out in his coat. The stain just behind his neck burst out sopping and purple. I was still kneeling. His blood began to drip on the floor.

"Kill me!" he bellowed at Lariat, who held the big cowboy pistol negligently. "I *knew* there were others here! I knew!"

"Get his gun off the floor," said Fleece.

When I leaned out to catch up the gun, Peter wheeled around and saw me. He kept his arm cocked behind his head with a hand on his wound. He staggered away, examining me. His face was a horror: a mask of bruises all yellow and purple like hematomas. His eyesockets seemed to have been mauled and crushed. His lips were folded inwards. He had lost his false teeth. He began that curious squeaking voice, the voice of a cartoon rodent. "I *knew*. You were not a ghost. You were real. I knew you were in this, knew, knew you knew . . ."

"Shut up!" squalled Fleece. "I've been hearing that goddam squeaking all afternoon. *Look* at you! You had that wonderful University of Massachusetts education, you had good health, you had money. Look what you did with it! Look at *her!* Look at you in the mirror! You look like a shrunken dick!"

Fleece passed out. I thought he was dead. Lariat and I took off his shirt. There was a tiny red hole just above his right hip. Three inches away, down near his hip socket, the bullet itself could be seen under the skin. The bullet was black as coal. The skin above it was brown and puffy.

"Don't shake him. What's down there?" asked Lariat.

"The liver. I don't know."

"Did you get to the phone? You, sit down," Lariat said to Peter. "Why don't you get a blanket for the old woman?"

I went back to Mother Rooney's bedroom and pulled off her bedspread. Mother Rooney was not unsightly, dead. There was the hole in her forehead. But she had had time to compose herself. I noticed she had patent leather dollies on, no longer the wrestling shoes.

We sat there, waiting. Peter sat on the floor and held his neck, squeaking, sometimes rocking. Fleece breathed deeply. His pants and hands were bloody, but he was not bleed-

378

ing any more. The other bullet was in his calf. I caught only one word in the rest of Peter's squeaking: "Never."

When Fleece revived again he shouted at Peter to shut up.

The police came in with the ambulance squad. They looked around the room at Peter, me, and Fleece. Lariat's suit was dirty from the climb up the cliff, and he was still holding the long pistol. I had taken mine out in the back yard and thrown it over the cliff. The police ganged around Lariat, snatched the gun away, and two of them hoisted him under the armpits to carry him off.

"Not him. *Him*," Fleece said, pointing at Peter.

"This one's hurt. What's wrong with him?" asked one officer about Peter. I saw Peter was incapable of answering.

"He tried to kill himself after he saw what he'd done," I said.

"Shot himself across the back of his neck?"

"He's crazy. He knew how to kill her but he didn't know how to kill himself. Or didn't try hard enough."

An older officer, who apparently knew Peter, supported the opinion that Peter was crazy. They collected around him and dragged him out violently. Then the older officer got our names.

We had to stay in town a week. We visited Fleece at the hospital, and I talked to two men at the coroner's. Then another one at the police station. My story was one-sided. All I confessed to was bringing the loaded gun to Jackson in possible defense of Fleece. I lied concerning every issue where it was possible Fleece or I might be seen in a bad light. I defended myself as a passive citizen into whose hand fate had thrown a gun and a plea for decency in a cul-de-sac of terror. I was exonerated to the extent that my name never even got in the papers. I made them understand that I had just come from Mother Rooney's funeral.

Lariat and I attended the struggling little ceremony. We saw the coffin into the Catholic graveyard. We shook hands with two widows. The old cross-eyed priest recognized me and took my hand. "Ah, yes." She had taken time to will the house to the Robert Dove Fleece boy, the very boy who was shot defending her. Did I know that? "She had a rich long life," I told the priest. "And a painless death." I looked at Lariat. "This is a man who came to help too."

379

"Why haven't you left?" I asked Lariat. All the while he had been extremely quiet and mild. "Why don't you *say* something, then?"

"You were the one who thought you brought a wise man down here with you. Not me."

I apologized to him constantly about putting him through this. He just shook his head, and finally he told me to shut up, looking bemused and a bit haggard. I got the feeling he was lost in the longest Lariat pause ever.

The last day we saw Fleece at the hospital. The bullet had missed his liver by a half a hair, and he had been priding himself on simply being *alive* for five days.

"You know who was here this morning? Bet. You know who was here just before you came in? The D.A. We are going to be clean as a pin, Monroe. Peter is in Whitfield; he's still squeaking; sometimes he breaks out with something they can understand. Catherine, he talks about. The first Catherine. We came as close—" He lifted up the pincers of his thumb and forefinger, showing the tiny gap between them. "But look how clean that little gap is. Came as close as that bullet to my liver. By damn! You want to see where that mother went in?" He lifted his smock and peeled down the tape and gauze to show the little swollen red point. Lariat moved away. He was urping. Lariat was throwing up. He tried to make a clean blow of it into the room lavatory, but the wave came too fast. It dashed off the side of the enamel and drenched all the area by the window.

"Do say!" said Fleece.

"I'm sorry." Lariat already had his handkerchief out. "That's been coming on me for a week."

"This man needs some beauty. He hasn't seen too much down here. Give me five minutes." I found the phone in the gift shop downstairs and called Harley in Beta Camina. I got him.

"Harley says he's got the best band he ever had. He's rehearsing them for the International Lions Convention parade in New York. Would you like it if I said let's take Fleece's car and drive down to Beta Camina? I'd like you to see them and meet him."

"A nigger marching band?" said Lariat.

When we arrived at the high school in Beta Camina the Gladiators were marching on the football field full blast.

They had newer uniforms, a heavy green tending toward black. We joined Harley on the top bleacher. He was sweating. The day was hot, high, blue and golden. He had several folded index cards in his shirt pocket. I say Harley was sweating, but he was rather peaceful. He was not directing or conducting them at all.

"That's *it*," he said. "What does anybody want? They're beyond me. I can't help them any more. They got guts and grace. Thirty of them already have scholarships in music. Six of them going to Juilliard."

"Would you listen to that?" said Lariat. "They are superb. That is the best; well, you just forget they're a marching band at all. Whose music are they playing?"

"Mine," said Harley.

We left for the car. The band had quit but was still in our ears. Lariat put a hand on my shoulder.

"That *was* it. Good, good heavens. We're in the wrong field. Music!"